KU-264-791

# don't look back

*By Scott Frost and available from Headline*

Run the Risk
Never Fear
Point of No Return
Don't Look Back

# don't look back

scott frost

**headline**

Copyright © 2009 Scott Frost

The right of Scott Frost to be identified as the Author of
the Work has been asserted by him in accordance with the
Copyright, Designs and Patents Act 1988.

First published in Great Britain in 2009
by HEADLINE PUBLISHING GROUP

1

Apart from any use permitted under UK copyright law, this publication
may only be reproduced, stored, or transmitted, in any form, or by any
means, with prior permission in writing of the publishers or, in the
case of reprographic production, in accordance with the terms of
licences issued by the Copyright Licensing Agency.

All characters in this publication are fictitious and any resemblance
to real persons, living or dead, is purely coincidental.

Cataloguing in Publication Data is available from the British Library

Hardback 978 0 7553 4647 9
Trade paperback 978 0 7553 4648 6

Typeset in Plantin by Avon DataSet Ltd,
Bidford-on-Avon, Warwickshire

Printed in the UK by CPI Mackays, Chatham, ME5 8TD

Headline's policy is to use papers that are natural, renewable and
recyclable products and made from wood grown in sustainable forests.
The logging and manufacturing processes are expected to conform
to the environmental regulations of the country of origin.

HEADLINE PUBLISHING GROUP
An Hachette UK Company
338 Euston Road
London NW1 3BH

| MORAY COUNCIL LIBRARIES & INFO.SERVICES | |
| --- | --- |
| 20 27 48 01 | |
| Askews | |
| F | |
| | |

To Sam, Sandra and John,
who helped us find home

# one

It was late February when the rains finally came. It began with a few isolated drops landing on the roofs of cars with a sound so unfamiliar as to cause drivers to look out their windows toward the sky in wonder. The drops became a drizzle, turning the freeways into a single chain reaction wreck that stretched from the coast to the Inland Empire. And then the drizzle turned to a downpour that seemed intent on punishing the dry landscape and its inhabitants for the hubris which had prompted them to change a desert into a garden. It had been one hundred and eighty-six days since the last rain fell. It had been exactly half that since a resident of Pasadena had fallen violently to another's hand.

I've heard it said that weather has an effect on violence – that in the heat or rain crime rates will go up or down. But to believe that a life was taken because it rained or the wind blew you would also have to believe the opposite – that because the rain didn't fall, or the wind dropped, a trigger wasn't pulled, and a knife wasn't used, and if you believe that you may as well give up on faith altogether and turn in your badge.

There were two storms that blew in that night. The second one began with a phone call shortly after midnight when the telephone rang. I was awake sitting in the living room staring at a rerun of a show that wasn't even good the first time it aired. Since the events in the desert near Trona, sleep was something I put off as long as

1

possible, for what came with it wasn't rest, but more often than not the images and sounds of what happened the night I had become a victim, and lost touch with being a cop.

At the urging of my daughter, who believed that if I felt better physically the rest of me would follow, I had taken up running. She was right about the first part. My muscles were toned. I had lost weight, I ate less, I drank less, but instead of reconnecting with that other part of me I found myself residing wholly in the physical half, and not asking much of the other.

It had been months since I had walked inside the yellow tape of a crime scene to take part in an investigation. I stayed in my office. I took runs at lunch. I delegated. I avoided looking into another victim's eyes because I feared they would see in mine that I could offer little in the way of solace.

I sat there listening to the rain hitting the roof, hoping the phone would stop after a couple of rings, but by the fourth I knew it wasn't a wrong number, and that what was waiting on the other end was an address where a body was growing cold as a result of violence.

I hesitated just long enough to give the phone another chance at being a wrong number, then reached for it as the next ring began.

'Delillo.'

There was a pause on the other end and for a moment I thought I had been wrong about the call; then I heard the voice.

'Lieutenant . . .' He paused again before finishing what he had to say. 'I'm sorry to call.'

'I am still a cop,' I said. 'Despite all evidence to the contrary.'

'You don't have to tell me that,' he said.

It was my old partner Dave Traver and from the tone of his voice I knew what was waiting for me. There are certain crimes even a seasoned detective isn't immune to.

'There's something you have to see.'

'Where are you?' I asked.

'Rose Bowl, A gate, south side of the stadium.'

I hesitated for a moment, but I knew there was no delegating this and started moving toward my clothes draped over the back of the chair.

'Have you called Harrison?'

'He's on his way.'

'I'll be there in twenty minutes,' I said and hung up.

I didn't want to know anything else and Traver had spent enough time with me to understand that. Walking into a crime scene with the bias of another cop's or a witness's point of view was the last thing I wanted. Dave, the father of twins, had already told me all I needed to know with just the tone of his voice. The feeling of dread spreading through my stomach and a pulse already a beat or two faster was testament to that.

I deliberately dressed as slowly as I could to keep myself from falling into a pattern of rushing even the smallest detail when I stepped inside the yellow tape at the crime scene.

Outside, the landscape appeared even starker than normal in the cold rain. I stood for a moment at the edge of the garage with my hand stretched out, cupping the water in my palm. The few new houses that now sat where the previous ones had burned in the fires seemed to barely cling to the ground as the water rushed down the hillsides in streams.

There were no sounds other than the rain. No traffic, no distant car radios or televisions. No voices raised in argument or laughter drifting out of an open kitchen window. Even the strange sing-song of coyotes had vanished as they had taken shelter from the storm.

I got in the Volvo and started down the winding streets out of the hills and tried not to imagine that somewhere inside a ninety-thousand-seat stadium was a body.

# two

Dropping down off Prospect I pulled to a stop at Rosemont and sat for a moment. The heavy rain had eased up and a thin ribbon of fog clung to the concrete channel where water coming down from the San Gabriels crossed the arroyo. The pale walls of the stadium rising nearly a hundred feet glowed in the darkness. A jogger in bright reflective clothing working the circuit around the stadium stole a quick glance in my direction as she passed, weighing any possible threat. I watched her run into the darkness, resisting the urge to get out of the car and run and keep running without looking back, but instead I drove on.

Ahead I could see half a dozen black and whites and two unmarked squads parked outside the entrance at the south end. Traver, big Dave, two hundred and forty pounds, most of it heart, was waiting by the stadium gate holding an umbrella as I pulled to a stop. A Hispanic man who looked to be in his late forties wearing a hooded rain jacket stood several feet away leaning on the side of a squad car. Traver walked over as I stepped out into the damp air. There was none of his usual attempt at humor for having gotten me out in the middle of the night. He knew that the assault I had suffered in the desert had taken something from me that I had yet to get back. You don't get held down, stripped naked and violated and come out the other end seeing the world as the same place it was before it happened. It wasn't confidence I lacked, or a sense of security; I think what had been taken from me had more in common with faith, and was just as elusive. Traver unfurled another umbrella and handed it to me.

'You OK?' he asked.

I looked around at the squad cars. 'You mean have I regained my belief in our system of justice? And that all evildoers will face a reckoning?'

Dave smiled. 'No. I just wondered if you needed some coffee.'

Despite my best effort not to, I smiled back.

'Double latte with an extra shot,' I said, then looked over to the tunnel leading into the stadium.

'Every entrance has been secured; there's no one inside. Harrison's waiting by the field,' Dave said.

I glanced over to the man leaning against the squad car. 'He found it?'

Traver nodded. 'Name's Flores, assistant grounds keeper. There had been an exhibition soccer game at seven; the crowd was out by eight-thirty. Says that when the stadium was secured after maintenance workers finished cleaning the stands about ten, it wasn't there. He also says he didn't touch anything when he realized what it was.'

'Any apparent break-in?'

'Not that he's noticed.'

'We'll need to talk to every one of his workers whether they were here or not.'

Traver nodded. I walked over to the grounds keeper.

'Can you turn some of the stadium lights on?'

'City doesn't want them on after eleven.'

'Turn on just enough so we can see inside.'

He nodded.

'How many people can access the stadium once it's locked down?' I asked.

'Me and the head grounds keeper, and we both have assistants who have keys. Other staff may have them too, but I don't know names.'

'How many of them were here tonight?'

'Just my assistant.'

'Is he here?'

'No, he went home.'

'We'll need all their names,' I said.

'I've got the list all ready,' Traver said.

I motioned to one of the officers and the grounds keeper went off with him.

'How many people attended the game?' I asked Traver.

'Only a few hundred. It was a charity event, former TV stars playing soccer. They called an end to it after an hour because of the rain.'

Scattered on the ground were a few green flyers advertising the event. I reached down and picked one up.

'Save the abalone?'

'I think they must have been small stars,' said Traver.

We started into the dark tunnel toward the field. Dave held back half a step so as not to obstruct my view of what was coming. The air in the tunnel tasted as if it held some memory of the thousands of people who had passed through it since the stadium was built – Big Ten rooters from nineteen thirties and forties Minnesota and Ohio smoking cigars and drinking beer.

As we approached the far end the light began to spill into the tunnel from the field.

Inside, the bowl appeared several times brighter than on the outside. We had entered at the south end of the playing field. The green expanse of the grass gently rose toward the center of the stadium and then fell away toward the far end. The silence inside a venue that could hold ninety-one thousand people felt unnatural, and just a little unnerving when accompanied by a body.

Wisps of steam rose from the damp grass. At the edge of the track surrounding the field Harrison was kneeling and staring out toward the middle.

We walked over and Dylan Harrison slowly rose to his feet but didn't make eye contact with me. One of the only things that had kept my heart beating since Trona was that every time I took in his perfect blue eyes and powerful build I was able to forget myself, if only for the few moments we would spend together.

If Dave was aware that Harrison and I had become lovers he hadn't let on. But we had been careful about our relation-ship, or at least as careful as sex allows. Not just because I was his supervisor, but because he knew that it was still difficult for me to believe that I was worthy of love after the assault. Being ten years older than him didn't help much either if I thought about it. But he was a patient lover, more than my battered middle-aged psyche deserved. I turned my attention toward the playing field.

'In soccer they call it a pitch,' Harrison said.

Traver directed my gaze with a nod of his head. 'It's right on what would be the fifty yard line during a football game.'

In the center of the field lay a darkly colored object. A set of footprints going out and then back was visible the on wet grass a few feet from where we stood.

'Those are mine,' Traver said. 'The grounds keeper walked in from the other side and ran straight back the way he came when he saw what it was.'

'Did you see any other prints?'

'Not that would do any good. The middle of the field is full of them from the match.'

'Walk the perimeter anyway. Maybe something will stand out.'

Traver took a heavy breath and started off along the edge of the grass looking for another set of prints.

'Why here?' Harrison said.

The flapping of a pigeon's wings echoed from one of the dark tunnels leading to the field. I looked up at the empty stadium circling us.

'The seats,' I said.

'He wanted an audience.'

I nodded. 'Sunday there will be that many people in here.'

'The Papal Mass.'

'I imagine he stood out there as if a hundred thousand people were looking at what he did. Maybe even the Pope.'

'I'd say he wants attention,' said Harrison.

'He just got it,' I said.

We stepped onto the grass and followed Traver's trail out toward the center until it vanished into the footprints from the game. Several yards from the middle of the field we stopped. A blue sleeping bag wrapped in clear plastic lay in the grass. No impression of the contents was apparent from the way the bag was filled. The end had been cinched tight leaving a small opening that gave the only hint of what was inside – a ponytail of long blond hair, a small red ribbon tied in a perfect bow around it.

'A girl,' Harrison said.

I looked across the field at Traver slowly walking along the track. Each step the father of twins took looked more pained than the last. I knew right now he probably wanted to call home and make sure his babies were safe and sound, just as I wanted to call my daughter Lacy to be certain she was all right. It wasn't a rational thought, but rationality went out the door with our offspring's first breath in this world. Being a cop only made that worse. I had never known a detective worth a damn who didn't see a faint reflection of his or her child in each new victim. If I could I would send him on vacation right this instant, but wanting something and being able to do it rarely came together on the job.

Harrison circled the bag, examining the grass.

'Unless he picked up some blades of grass on his shoes when he walked out and saves them for us, I don't see anything here that is going to help us.'

The rain was little more than a drizzle now. I set the umbrella down and slipped on a pair of gloves, stepped in next to the bag, kneeled down and gently placed my hand on top of it; trying to determine how the victim lay inside. My fingers seemed to find the bend of the elbow of a small arm and I resisted the urge to pull away as quickly as possible.

'I should never leave the house,' I said to myself, not realizing I had said it loud enough to hear.

Harrison kneeled down, looked over the bag and then found my eyes with his for a moment.

'And I should never have become a homicide detective.'

'That was my fault,' I said.

Harrison forced a smile. 'You're not forgiven.'

I looked away for a moment toward Traver circling the other end of the field, the beam of his flashlight pointed toward his feet. In the darkness just above the grass I noticed the fleeting movements of bats hunting in the damp air.

'I think she's on her back, arms crossed in front.' I said, looking back down at the bag. I moved my hand along the outside, stopping at what felt like the line of her shoulder.

'Something's not right here. Feel,' I said.

Harrison slipped on gloves and rested his hand on the bag next to mine.

'It's cold.'

I reached over to the head of the bag where it had been cinched shut. I hadn't noticed it in the darkness before but steam appeared to be coming out of the inside.

'What's the temp tonight?' I asked.

'Low fifties.'

'That's cold air coming out.'

I opened the end of the bag just enough to slip my hand inside past her soft hair, and then gently touched the top of her head. My fingers began to sting as if they were burning and I pulled them away. Neither of us said a word for a moment.

'She's frozen,' I said.

'That explains the sleeping bag,' Harrison said. 'He wanted the body in this state when it was found.'

I stared at the bag for a moment, trying not to let my thoughts get too far ahead of events.

'Why?'

'Freezing is a form of preservation,' Harrison said. 'But what was he preserving?'

We both realized the answer before he had finished asking the question.

'He's preserving his work.'

Harrison started to reach toward the bag again but stopped.

'There's something here I'm not seeing,' he said.

I looked over the bag but I didn't see what it was. Harrison put out his hand and touched the red ribbon. A few crystals of frost fell onto his fingers and instantly melted.

'It's this.'

'What about it?'

'I need to see her face.'

He reached for the opening of the bag and I touched the back of his hand.

'We need to keep her as cold as we can. Any warming could destroy what the freezing preserved.'

Harrison shook his head. 'This can't wait.'

'You sure?'

He nodded.

I parted the plastic and then quickly loosened the drawstring just enough to expose her face. Her skin had the color of fine bone china and was covered in a thin layer of tiny frost crystals. Her features were untouched, perfect except that they lacked any hint of life.

'She looks to be about seventeen,' I said.

Harrison stared at her for another moment, then closed the bag up tight and looked around at the thousands of empty seats surrounding us.

'If I'm right, she was nineteen,' he said. 'Or was when she disappeared.'

'You know who this is?'

He nodded. 'I think so. Her name was Keri Bishop. It was three years ago. I was a detective then, and I interviewed her parents before the FBI took it over as a kidnapping. They eventually concluded she just dropped out to get away from something in her personal life.'

He closed his eyes for a moment. I looked around at the thousands of seats circling us.

'I want every row, every seat, searched.'

Harrison nodded. Across the field Traver finished walking the perimeter and raised his hands indicating he had not found anything.

'He's been waiting three years for this night,' I said.

'You think that means something, don't you?'

A bank of stadium lights came on, turning what had been night into an unnatural twilight. There were dozens of details I could be considering about what lay ahead, but I couldn't hold on to any of them. Only one thing seemed to matter at that moment, and I couldn't shake it any more than the sense that somewhere in one of those thousands of empty seats rising up around us a single pair of eyes was watching. I looked over to Harrison.

'I think it means there're going to be others,' I said softly.

# three

It was nearing three a.m. when the girl was transported in a refrigerated van to the morgue. Frozen, there was probably little the body would tell us about when she died, but there was everything to learn about what her killer wanted us to know, and until we understood that she would remain trapped in ice.

Harrison and I watched the van drive away and then sat in my Volvo listening to the rain as it began to fall again. A dozen more officers had arrived and were walking the rows of the stadium checking every seat.

'What time will the ME meet us?' I asked.

Harrison didn't respond, his eyes locked on some internal place in the past, I imagined.

'Dylan,' I said.

He looked at me and I could see the struggle going on behind his eyes.

'I should have been a better cop for this girl. I didn't believe she was a runaway, but I still let the FBI take it and I walked away.'

'That's the job,' I said. 'You didn't have a choice. I would have done the same thing.'

'Then what good are we?'

'It's the next victim we're here to help, not the ones that are already gone.'

'This was the next one. When I turned my back on her she was still alive.'

'She could have been abducted after she disappeared.'

Harrison looked at me. 'You don't believe that any more than I do.'

I shook my head. 'No. But that doesn't change anything. Everything I've seen inside that stadium tonight tells me this girl was not saveable. Not by me, you, or anyone.'

'But I was still the one who took the call.' Harrison leaned back in the seat and closed his eyes for a moment.

'You want to get some sleep?' I asked.

He shook his head.

'What time will we meet the ME?'

'Eight. They're setting up a refrigerated truck to work in.'

I studied him for a moment. 'You want to step away from this one?'

Harrison turned to me. 'No.'

'Good. Tell me about the family.'

Harrison watched the distorted movement of several officers through the streams of water coursing down the windshield as if they were showing him the way back to the past.

'Their name's Bishop. Father's a lawyer.'

'That sounds familiar.'

'Jackson Bishop. He had a number of high-profile civil lawsuits.'

'I remember this. There was talk of his running for state office.'

'There was. That all ended when his daughter disappeared.'

'And there was never a connection made between his political ambitions and her disappearance?'

'The FBI found nothing that supported the theory.'

'What about the family?'

'Her mother taught grade school. A happy marriage by all

accounts. They lived in a good neighborhood, went to church, had house and car payments, lived within their means, spent their lives doing good deeds. They were the family everyone wants to be . . . they were perfect.'

'And the girl?'

'She was beginning her sophomore year at SC. A good student, no drug use, popular.'

'Boyfriend?'

Harrison shook his head. 'She dated, but there wasn't one guy that stood out from the rest.'

'What were the circumstances of her disappearance?'

'It was a Friday night. She had been to a party with some friends from school. They dropped her back home around eleven and drove away after they watched her go inside.'

'She was still living at home?'

'Yeah. She was going to move out after the fall term, as I remember.'

'Her parents confirm the story about her disappearance?'

'They heard her come in, but didn't see her. When they got up in the morning she wasn't there. Her bed appeared to have been slept in. No sign of a break-in, or a struggle. She just vanished.'

'Anything missing from her room?'

'Her bag with a wallet. The clothes she was wearing.'

'Nothing else?'

Harrison shook his head again. 'Not that her parents could identify. It was as if she got dressed and walked away from her life.'

'She didn't get very far.'

A uniformed officer came up to the car and I rolled the window down.

'They found something, Lieutenant.'

We got out of the car and started down the dark tunnel toward

17

the green expanse of the field. At the entrance we stopped and waited for Traver, who was walking back along the track carrying a plastic evidence bag in his hand.

'It was halfway up in the stands on the fifty yard line in a sandwich bag.' Dave's hair was soaking wet from the rain. He wiped the water from his face and then handed me the evidence bag. 'Officer thought it was trash until he looked closer at it. Some kind of a drawing or something.'

I opened the evidence bag and removed the sandwich bag containing the drawing. Harrison shined a Mag-lite on the piece of paper.

'Anything else about where it was found?' I asked.

'It was left on the only open seat in that entire section,' Traver said.

The image was of a group of dark figures huddled over the supine body of a young woman with her breasts exposed, her arms crossed over her midsection. Shafts of light appeared to be streaming out of her body. One of the standing figures appeared to wear the tall hat of a cardinal; a few wore robes, their faces verging on the grotesque. A single woman was seated at the feet of the supine girl covering her eyes with her hand.

'It looks like a copy of a print of some kind,' I said.

'I think it's an engraving,' Harrison said.

'It looks old,' said Traver.

Just below the image were some words printed in script. I couldn't make them out so I held it out to Harrison.

'It's Spanish . . . *Murió la Verdad*,' he said and shook his head.

'The truth has died,' I said.

Harrison looked at me for a moment. 'If it's possible I think this just got worse.'

'What truth?' Traver asked.

'His version of it,' I said.

18

'That could be anything.'

'Not to him.'

I looked at the picture for another moment, then stepped out of the tunnel into the cool rain. It tasted almost sweet and as different from the substance that emerged from the kitchen taps as a sip of wine would be. Harrison and Traver stepped out next to me.

'Why did he wait for the rain to do this?'

'There's no shortage of symbolism. A storm, a flood, a cleansing, take your pick.' I looked over at Harrison. 'Whichever it is, I suspect there isn't anything this man does that doesn't have a reason.'

Out over the dark shapes of the San Gabriels a flash of lightning lit their jagged outline for an instant. A faint rumble of thunder seemed to roll down the slopes a moment later and spread out across the valley like a hand opening up.

'I want to know everything there is to know about the drawing and I want to talk to everyone who was at that party the night she disappeared. Let's also look at any missing person reports that might appear similar.' I looked out into the stadium. Officers were still moving methodically through the rows of seats looking for anything else left behind. 'Let's see how many tickets can be traced with credit cards. If they were assigned seats, focus on the area near where the drawing was found. Maybe someone will remember something.'

'You think he was inside for the game?'

I looked around at the empty seats and nodded. 'He waited three years for this moment. He was here. He would have been savoring the anticipation. He sat up in those seats imagining what was going to happen down to the smallest detail. How the first person finding the body would run from it like a frightened child, how we would approach it cautiously, slowly circling it looking for evidence, our reaction when we realized she was frozen, and then how we would look up to his seat knowing he was in control, and that there was probably nothing we could do to stop him from killing again.'

I looked at Harrison for a moment, then turned and walked out of the stadium.

# four

The dawn came with a dull gray light that seemed reluctant to open onto a day such as this. Through a steady rain Harrison and I drove toward downtown LA and the coroner's office on Mission.

One of the refrigerated trucks that the city keeps on hand for the day the big one rattles the basin was parked next to the annex where they store bodies awaiting their final trip to either a funeral home and family or a forgotten unmarked grave.

We stopped and stepped out of the car. The hum of the truck's refrigeration unit blocked out the sound of the traffic from the freeways just off to the east. The crime scene technician handling the case stepped out of the main building and started walking over to us wearing a puffy down coat that looked more suitable for a ski trip to Aspen. I recognized her as the same examiner who had conducted the autopsy on the half-brother I had never known I had until I saw his face on the coroner's table. Although she had been faced with both a victim and a next of kin unlike any she had encountered before, Chow's professionalism had helped me prove that he died as a result of murder, not the suicide the LAPD had insisted it was. She reached us and extended her hand.

'Lieutenant, Margaret Chow, if you've forgotten.'

I shook her hand and reintroduced Harrison to her.

'Her parents will be here in a couple of hours to make a positive

21

ID. That should be enough time to remove her from the bag. Since we wanted to transport her here as quickly as possible the CSI report from the scene was pretty sketchy. Anything I should know before we begin?'

I nodded. 'She disappeared three years ago. Anything we can learn about when she died might help.'

'Depending on how she was frozen that could be difficult. How important is it to know?'

'It may help us understand how long he keeps them alive.'

She looked at me for a moment. 'Them?'

'I think she's just the first.'

'I know a forensic anthropologist at UCLA who might be able to assist, but I can't make any promises. At best it won't be very accurate.'

We stopped at the rear doors of the truck.

'We set some lights up inside so there's not a lot of room. I've got some extra blankets in there to keep you warm.'

Chow climbed up onto the bumper, lifted the steel latch of the door and swung it open. The blast of cold air streaming out hit me in the face with the sting of needles. Chow handed us each an insulated blanket and we stepped into the truck and closed the door.

There was none of the smell of death that always accompanies stepping into a morgue for an autopsy. The truck had the stale odor of a freezer that had not held any food for a very long time. Work lights lit the interior in a bright white light. The plastic-wrapped sleeping bag containing the girl lay on a stainless steel table in the center of the truck.

'It looks smaller in the light,' said Harrison.

Chow gave us each a pair of latex gloves and then picked up the alternative light source and flipped off the work lights.

'This plastic would be a good medium for prints,' she said and began to move up and down the length of the bag with the black light. She covered the side facing up and shook her head.

'A few smudges; not even a partial. Do you see anything?' she asked, continuing to move the light up and down the length of the plastic.

I shook my head.

'Let's flip her over.'

We eased our hands underneath and rolled the bag over. Some streaks of mud from the field and a few blades of grass clung to the plastic. Chow went up and down the length of the bag and again shook her head.

'Either the plastic just came off a roll for the first time or it was cleaned very carefully. We may have better luck with her skin. The freezing should have preserved any oil that came in contact with it.' She turned the work light back on. 'How old was she when she disappeared?'

'Nineteen,' I said.

'How much did she weigh?'

I looked over to Harrison.

'About a hundred and ten,' he said.

'How much would you guess she weighs now?' said Chow.

Harrison slid his hand back under the bag and tested the weight. 'Not much more than that, if any.'

Chow nodded. 'We'll get a precise weight when we do the autopsy. Let's roll her back over.'

We rolled the bag and then Chow picked up a scalpel and slit the pieces of duct tape securing the plastic. The plastic was stiff from the cold as it was unfurled from the bag. Chow stared at the bag for a moment then again switched off the work lights and went over the fabric and the underside of the duct tape on the plastic with the black light. The results were the same – nothing. She switched the work lights back on.

'I'm going to open the bag,' she said, and with a pair of surgical scissors she began at the small opening at the top and worked her way down to the end. 'Help me fold it open and lay it out flat.'

We each took a section of the fabric and on her nod lifted the bag and laid it out flat. None of us said a word as we stared in silence at the figure stretched out before us. Her skin was covered in tiny crystals of frost and translucent like a light bulb. The dark lines of frozen veins were visible under the surface. One misplaced touch and she looked as if she would shatter into a thousand pieces. She wore what appeared to be a long peasant-style dress. Her feet were bare, and the dress had been pulled down to expose her shoulders and small breasts. Her arms were crossed over her waist, her head turned slightly to the right.

'Lord,' whispered Harrison.

'She's posed exactly like the print,' I said.

'What print?' Chow asked.

I removed the evidence bag containing the picture from the pocket of my coat and held it out to her. 'This was found up in the stands of the stadium.'

Chow studied it, holding it up to the light. 'Before I was pre-med, I was an art history major. I might be wrong, but I think this is a Goya.'

'The Spanish artist?'

She nodded. 'Those words must be the title.'

'The truth has died,' I said.

Chow looked at me ominously, handed back the print and returned to the body. She looked carefully over the clothes, switching back and forth between light sources as she searched for anything that appeared out of place or unusual.

'I'm going to cut the dress free.'

She slowly worked down the side of the dress, cutting through

24

the folds of frozen material. When she reached the bottom the dress lifted away from the body like the cover of a book. She began to examine the girl's head with a magnifying glass, looking for any fibers or hairs that didn't appear to belong. She then moved carefully across the scalp, parting the hair as she looked for any wounds.

From the head she moved to the neck, the torso and the legs, and then repeated the entire process using the alternative light. When she had finished she shook her head.

'There's nothing visible. No breaks in the skin that I can see, no bruising or hemorrhaging. Let's turn her over.'

I had seen dozens if not hundreds of bodies. The usual results of violence inflicted upon a victim are a constant reminder that just a short time before he or she had been breathing and laughing and dreaming of all the things that connect us as humans. This was different. The thin layer of frost that covered her removed her just far enough from what had been a beautiful young girl for the remains to take on an unreal quality. The rigid limbs locked in their awkward pose were those of a storefront mannequin. She was perfectly preserved, but that perfection was little more than a shadow of what had been.

Chow examined her back from head to toe and then stepped away.

'There appears to be no physical trauma that I can see, but maybe the freezing is masking something. As to whether she was sexually assaulted, we won't know that until we can move her limbs. I'll take some tissue samples and send them to UCLA to see if they can determine how long she's been frozen. Hopefully we'll find out more when we thaw her.'

There was a knock on the door of the truck and Chow opened it, exchanged a few words with the assistant and closed it again.

'The parents have arrived. They're waiting inside.'

I glanced at my watch. We had been in the truck for a little over an hour but it had seemed more like a few minutes.

'Were they told anything about her condition?' I asked.

Chow shook her head. 'It's not protocol to give any details on the phone.'

'We'll go talk to them first,' I said.

Chow took a sheet from a shelf under the table. 'I'll get her ready for the ID.'

I looked over to the girl one last time.

'She's like a time capsule,' Chow said softly.

'And just as silent,' I said.

'Let's hope there's some information hidden inside.'

We removed the blankets from around our shoulders, set them on the floor next to the door, then left. It felt warm outside in comparison. The rain had washed the dirt of the city from the air. I took a deep breath to get rid of the taste of the stale air from the truck, but it seemed to cling to the inside of my mouth.

Harrison was staring over at the main building where Keri Bishop's parents were waiting.

'I can do this alone if you prefer?' I said.

Harrison shook his head and then looked out toward the dark hills of Elysian Park across the river.

'Twenty years ago a climber in the Alps found the body of a man who had been frozen in a glacier. When they did a scan of his body a triangular shape was seen deep in his shoulder. He had been shot with an arrow – it had pierced an artery and he had been left to die where he would be slowly consumed by the ice and vanish for five thousand years . . . he was murdered.' Harrison turned and looked at me. 'Something tells me we're not going to find that kind of secret inside this girl.'

★

26

The interior of the medical examiner's offices looked more like that of an accounting firm than a place where death is literally taken apart piece by piece. Maybe the lack of any distinguishing characteristics was intentional on the part of the people who built it; the cynical view would be that a building as unremarkable as this was just the natural result of government at its best.

The Bishops were sitting in a windowless reception area adorned with photographs from LA's past that I supposed were meant to remind grieving family members of happier times. The bright yellow wall paint had faded and now had all the warmth of the sun on a smoggy day. When we stepped into the room they both stood up.

The Jackson Bishop I remembered from the past was a dashing figure fighting the good fight for the little people and looked like he had stepped out of the pages of *GQ*. The man in front of us bore little resemblance to that figure. He looked to be near sixty though at most he was ten years younger than that. His hair was heavily streaked with gray and his once slender build was now carrying an extra forty pounds.

I had no recollection of his wife Emily, but if there was any strength left in this couple it appeared to be hers. She stepped forward as we approached, taking her husband's arm and bringing him with her. Her eyes held a fierceness that was trying desperately to mask the pain inside her.

'Are you the police?' she asked.

'Yes,' I said and then introduced Harrison and myself.

'No one will tell us anything except that our daughter is dead,' she said, and then her eyes stopped on Harrison. 'I know you.'

Harrison nodded. 'I worked the case before the FBI took over.'

'Are you sure the girl you found is Keri?' asked Jackson.

Harrison nodded. 'I think so.'

'You think or you know?' Jackson said.

'It's been three years. Maybe you're wrong,' Mrs Bishop said.

Harrison started to answer but lost the words.

'I wish I could say we were, but I'm afraid it doesn't appear so. I'm sorry,' I said.

'I want to see my daughter,' she demanded.

'There're some things you should know first.'

Mrs Bishop's hand closed tightly around her husband's.

'What happened to our girl?' Jackson asked.

'Her body is frozen.'

They seemed to look right past me as if the words were so far beyond their understanding that they held no meaning.

'I can't tell you how she died yet,' I said. 'But we are treating it as a homicide.'

'Take us to her,' whispered Mrs Bishop.

Margaret Chow was waiting outside the truck when we walked the Bishops to where their daughter's body lay frozen with all her secrets. She explained what they would see and that the body was evidence of a crime, and must not be touched, then opened the back of the truck and took them inside. I followed them in while Harrison waited out on the pavement.

Chow had covered the body with the sheet. The blankets were not offered to them so as not to encourage them to linger any longer than necessary for a positive ID. They would have time to grieve later, but this was not the place.

I waited at the foot of the table while the Bishops stepped up along the right side. Chow stepped around to the left of the table and then reached over and pulled the sheet down, uncovering the face.

Jackson Bishop exhaled heavily as if he had been struck in the stomach. Emily Bishop covered her mouth and her eyes filled with tears. Chow gave them a moment, then asked the unimaginable.

'Is this your daughter Keri?'

28

Mrs Bishop reached her right hand out as if to touch her daughter's face, stopped a few inches short and then nodded.

'Yes, that's our daughter,' she said, her voice breaking.

They stared in silence for a moment before Chow reached for the sheet.

'I have to touch her,' said Mrs Bishop. She looked at Chow, the fierceness returning to her eyes. 'I'm going to touch her forehead.'

Chow took hold of the sheet, began to pull it back up, then hesitated.

'All right.'

Mrs Bishop stretched out her hand and gently placed it on her daughter's forehead. In an instant I could see the strength in her eyes vanish, replaced by astonishment and then the understanding that her daughter was gone. She withdrew her hand to her chest and Chow pulled the sheet back up to cover Keri's face.

Jackson Bishop turned and walked out of the truck without saying a word. His wife stood staring at the covered body of her daughter for another moment, then stepped to the door and stopped. She began to say something but her voice broke, and then she gathered herself.

'Why is she frozen?'

'We don't know yet.'

She looked at her husband walking slowly away from the truck, then back at me.

'There must be something you can tell me.'

'This isn't really the time. We can talk about it later.'

She shook her head. 'My daughter is gone, and I want to know why. Please, if there's something you know, tell me.'

I reached into my pocket and removed the print.

'Have you ever seen this before?'

She looked at it for a moment before her eyes began to register

29

what the image contained. 'God,' she said softly. She stared at it for a moment, then shook her head. 'I've never seen this . . . what is it?'

'We found it near your daughter's body.'

'I don't understand.'

'Whoever did this wanted us to find it.'

Mrs Bishop tried to draw a breath, but barely managed.

'And the writing on it, what does it say?'

'It's Spanish, means "the truth has died".'

She covered her mouth to suppress a gasp, then turned and looked again at her husband walking through the rain.

'Does that mean anything to you?'

She shook her head. Whatever inner strength she had gathered had wilted away.

'I'll need to come out to the house and look through her things and her room. The smallest detail that was missed before might help us.'

She nodded. 'I have to go now,' she said without looking back at me, then climbed down the steps of the truck and rushed after her husband.

I stood in the open door and watched the Bishops slowly walk to their car, then turned back to Chow.

'When will you get started?' I asked.

'It will take some time. I want to bring her temperature up slowly so we don't damage anything. Toxicology will take another few days. I'll call you as soon as I find anything or have a cause of death.' She turned and looked down at the body. 'How long before you think there's another victim?'

I shook my head. 'For all I know, they could be dead already.'

I stepped out of the truck and joined Harrison in the light rain. He was watching the Bishops' car as it slowly turned onto Mission.

'Did the print mean anything to her?' he asked.

Through the rain-streaked window of the car Mrs Bishop's expression of pain looked like a distorted theatrical mask.

'She said it didn't.'

Dylan looked at me. 'But you're not so sure.'

I shook my head. 'There was something about her reaction to the words on the print.'

'Could she be hiding something?'

'Have you ever really met a perfect family?'

Harrison shook his head.

'What comes to mind when you hear the words "the truth has died"?'

'That could be a long list.'

I looked down at the figures in the print which appeared to be monks and possibly a cardinal. 'But what's near the top of that list?'

'You've got something in mind?'

'Look at the figures surrounding the body. Men in robes, symbols of the ultimate truth.'

'God's.'

I nodded. 'The man who did this has lost faith, and is full of rage.'

Harrison shook his head. 'But what happened to that girl doesn't look like rage.'

'No, but what if it wasn't with her?'

'Who, then?'

'How extensively did you go into Jackson Bishop's law practice?'

'There wasn't time to do much more than scratch the surface.' Dylan looked at me for a moment. 'He punishes Bishop for some wrong by killing his daughter.'

'It's possible.'

31

'But what wrong?'

'Let's find out everything we can about Jackson Bishop's practice before his daughter disappeared.'

My phone rang and I picked up. It was Traver.

'One of the grounds staff didn't show up for work this morning. You want me to check it out?'

'You have an address?'

'Glassell Park, an apartment on Eagle Rock Boulevard. Three thousand block.'

'We'll take it, we're not that far. You have a name?'

'Goya.'

My heart skipped a beat.

'First name's Francisco,' I said.

'Yeah. How'd you know that?'

'Talk to the grounds keeper, find out what you can about him and send an unmarked squad to meet us at the address.'

'Is there something I should know about?' Traver said.

I looked down at the print in my hand. 'Art history.'

# five

The apartment building was one of three identical U-shaped two-story stucco structures that faced the rail yards to the west and the concrete channel of the river beyond that. The entrances to the apartments were on the outside of the buildings; there were no interior hallways. This was gang territory; most of the buildings in the neighborhood carried the tags of the local homeboys who ruled these streets and controlled the flow of drugs.

The apartment we were looking for was in the third building at the end of the block. We parked in front of the second one, away from the sightlines of the last building, and stepped out. The odor of diesel from a train that had just passed mingled with the sickly-sweet smell from a doughnut shop another block and a half down Eagle Rock. The other squad had not arrived.

'We've been noticed,' Harrison said, nodding toward a Hispanic teenager in baggy jeans and sweatshirt standing across the street in front of an empty warehouse.

I glanced back at the windows of the apartment buildings and saw movement in at least half a dozen. The ring of cell phones began spreading across the complex with news of our presence.

'We can't wait for the other squad,' I said, and started moving.

We reached the last building and quickly scanned the apartment numbers.

'Second floor, back side,' Harrison said.

A young mother with a Mayan face holding an infant in her arms stepped out of an apartment as we reached the top of the stairs and quickly retreated back inside when she saw us draw our weapons.

We reached the far corner of the building and stopped to peer around at the line of apartment doors. Spanish-language television drifted out from several of the apartments.

'Should be the last one,' Harrison said.

My hand tightened around the handle of the Glock and I moved forward. Each apartment had one large window that looked out onto the balcony, but not a single one was open, as if pulling a curtain would protect the inhabitants from the violence that ruled the neighborhood outside their walls.

Harrison and I stopped at the corner of the window of the last apartment. Like all the rest it had a curtain blocking the view to the inside and the sliding glass was latched shut.

'He had to have known we would find him,' Harrison whispered.

I leaned out from the wall and looked at the door. It was shut.

'The question is did he wait for us,' I said.

Harrison moved past the window and took up position on the far side of the door. I leaned in close to the window and listened for any sound coming from inside. There was nothing.

I stepped past the window to the door and nodded to Harrison. In one quick motion he kicked the door just below the handle and it flung open into the apartment. I swung around and swept the room with the Glock. The room was dark, but appeared to be empty.

'Police,' I yelled.

There was no response. I took a half-step inside and stopped to let my eyes adjust to the light. There was a small kitchen to my right and the living room to the left. A single door at the other end of the latter appeared to be closed. The air was stale, the odor of human sweat and something else lingering.

'This room's been lived in, but there's no furniture,' Harrison said.

'Do you recognize that smell?'

He shook his head. 'Chemical of some kind.'

I pointed toward the door at the far end. A faint line of light was visible at the floor.

'There's light in the other room,' I said.

'Open the door slowly and step out,' I yelled, but there was no response. Harrison motioned toward the ceiling in the center of the room. I could just make out the shape of a light fixture.

'Is there a switch on the wall behind me?' I said, keeping my weapon trained on the closed door.

Harrison reached behind me and nodded.

'Try it.'

Dylan flipped it but the light failed to come on.

'Open the curtain.'

He moved over to the window and pulled the curtain open, sending light spilling across the room. I started to take a step forward.

'Stop,' Harrison said.

I froze in place.

'On the floor in front of you.'

In the darkness I had missed it: a single piece of paper.

I kneeled down and my heart began to beat out of control.

'It's another print,' I said. 'The style looks similar to the other one.'

A male figure was lying either dead or unconscious on the ground as a large winged demon or bat-like figure landed on his chest and began to tear at his clothes. In the air above them other creatures were circling, waiting for their turn.

'There's a title, like the other one,' I said.

Harrison stepped over and read the words. '*Las Resultas.*'

I stood up and looked toward the door.

'The consequences,' I whispered.

'He's already taken another victim,' Harrison said.

I rushed to the door, flung it open and raised my weapon into the room. Harrison was right behind me. A small television sitting in the middle of the empty room was the light source. A game show was on. I took a step and then stopped. The far wall of the room had been used as a canvas for painting. The image stretched nearly from floor to ceiling. A large grotesque figure with mad eyes and long hair was about to bite into a small half-eaten naked figure he held in his hands.

'Jesus,' Harrison whispered.

The air in the room was heavy with the odor of turpentine and oil paint. Harrison stepped over and cleared the bathroom, then came back.

'The paint isn't dry yet,' I said. 'He was probably working on it in the last day or two.'

'It's probably a Goya like the prints.'

'That would make sense.'

I stepped in close and looked at the wild swirls of paint, then moved back to take in the entire picture. We both stood in silence for a moment, unable to find any words.

'Do you think this is a literal depiction or allegorical?' said Harrison.

I shook my head. 'The result is the same either way – madness.' I turned to Dylan. 'I think you've just become an art history major. We figure out why the man who's doing this identifies with an eighteenth-century painter, we might just be a step ahead of him.'

'A step may not be enough.'

I looked back at the painting. 'I don't want anyone else coming in here. Seal the apartment.'

He nodded. 'I'll get crime scene on the way.'

'When the other squad arrives have them canvass the building's residents to see if they've seen anything.'

I went to the door, then looked back. On the television a heavy-set black woman was holding her hands up to her face with her fingers crossed as a tall blond model spread out her graceful arms toward a drawn curtain.

'You think she knows something we don't?' Harrison said.

I took one more look at the painting then stopped into the empty living room where the print lay in the middle of the floor.

'Maybe which one of LA's twelve million residents is missing?'

# six

Six hours after we first stepped into the apartment Chief Chavez slowly walked around the table in the conference room at headquarters looking down at the dozen or more prints Harrison had spread out across the table's surface.

The chief was sixty now, his once jet-black hair contained more gray than black, and he was twenty pounds overweight from his love of tamales or at least eating them with his grandchildren. If he wasn't the father I had never had, he was as close to it as I would ever have in this life. My being head of homicide was a direct result not only of learning to see crime through his eyes but, more important, of his unwavering belief in my abilities. I owed him everything and would do anything for him, a fact he was aware of even as he tried to re-ignite my interest in work.

'Crime scene found nothing,' I said. 'No prints, no hair fibers, no double helix chains of DNA left behind in the painting's surface or the bathroom sink or shower or toilet. None of the residents of the building claimed to remember ever seeing the man who rented apartment 201 other than a little boy who said he saw a ghost walk out the door one night.'

'A ghost?' Chavez said.

I nodded. 'Half the residents in the building are probably illegals, and the rest, if they've got any sense, are afraid of the gangs. No one's going to talk to us.'

'What about the property management company?'

'The apartment was rented three months ago. Six months' rent paid in advance, all in cash. Apparently they waive the usual identification requirements when cash is held in front of their noses.'

'What about the Rose Bowl? They must have some record of him.'

'That depends on how you define record.'

Chavez shook his head. 'What does that mean?'

'He was hired three weeks ago to fill in part time. Worked a total of six days. The ID on his application is a fake. The DMV numbers don't turn up in any database. And neither the grounds keeper nor any of the other workers can positively match the photograph on the license they have on record to the man they worked with. And the descriptions are equally worthless. Depending on whom we talked to he's either dark or light skinned, just over six feet or just under. One remembered him as barely speaking English, probably from Oaxaca. Another believed he spoke perfect unbroken English and was from Florida.'

'How do you account for that?'

'He worked mostly alone,' said Harrison. 'Kept interaction to a minimum. As best as we can figure, every day that he did work he subtly altered his appearance just enough to create confusion without being too noticeable.'

'All that to place the body in the stadium?'

'It would seem he also intended us to find the apartment.'

'Why?'

'This isn't just random. He's more than likely had three years to plan for it. He's making some kind of a statement.'

Chavez stopped at the far end of the table and picked up the reproduction of the print we had found in the apartment.

'"The consequences." You think this means he's taken someone else.'

I nodded. 'If there's another explanation, I don't have it yet.'

Chavez turned to the wall where we had pinned a copy of the painting in the apartment. 'And what the hell is this?'

I looked to Harrison.

'It's titled *Saturn Devouring his Son*,' Harrison said.

'As in the god Saturn?'

'Yeah. Francisco Goya painted it sometime between 1820 and '23.'

Chavez shook his head in wonder. 'I'm more of a dogs playing poker kind of a guy when it comes to art. Why would a man paint something like this?'

'It's right out of the ancient myths,' Harrison said. 'Saturn killed his son to keep him from taking power.'

'By cannibalism . . . very mythic.'

'In mythology, Saturn is the god of fertility and agriculture. He taught the world how to farm and is associated with the wisdom of the earth itself.'

'This is wisdom?' Chavez said.

'Wisdom's the bright side. The dark side is a god that represents the tyrannical parent strictly upholding the letter of the law. Astrologically Saturn is supposed to intensify feelings of isolation and sadness. A place referred to as the pit of darkness.'

'So why did a killer take on the persona of a nineteenth-century painter?'

'Goya saw his art as a way to rail against the injustice and power of those who rule,' I said.

'Like these prints,' Chavez said.

'That may be part of it.'

I picked up one of the copies on the table and handed it to Chavez. It contained the image of a man being held down, his legs spread wide as another man prepared to cleave him in two with a sword.

41

'Is this what we have to look forward to?' Chavez asked.

'From the prints left behind at the stadium and the apartment it appears this man believes he's punishing his victims for some injustice or wrong.'

'What does that have to do with a nineteen-year-old girl?'

'We're looking into Bishop's law practice to see if there may be a connection to a specific case. Maybe this man lost a child and blames Bishop.'

'What kind of law does Bishop practice?'

'Civil. He made his name with some high-profile class action suits,' Harrison said.

'It's also possible Keri was just a stand-in for the wrongs society or even God had dealt him.'

'God?'

'Given the print he left behind in the stadium it seems possible.'

Chavez shook his head. 'You lost me.'

I handed him a copy of the engraving we found at the stadium.

'Figures of the Church.'

I nodded. 'This is where there may be a connection. Bishop was the lead attorney in a suit against the Catholic archdiocese.'

'Priests abusing children?'

'Yeah. The only problem with the theory is that the case was settled out of court for a huge award.'

'You said that might be part of it. What's the other part?' Chavez asked.

'Goya was a tortured soul,' Harrison said. 'Viral encephalitis or lead poisoning left him deaf. The last years of his life he rarely stepped out of his house, and he painted the walls with what were called his black paintings and the prints we've found. Some people thought he had gone mad.'

'Being a social critic and being a killer is hardly the same thing.'

42

'Goya was quoted as saying "the sleep of reason produces monsters".'

I walked over to the copy of the Saturn. 'Maybe it's the madness our man connects to.'

Chavez opened the manila file containing the crime scene photographs of Keri Bishop cocooned in the sleeping bag. He stared in silence for a moment, then closed it back up.

'You want to bring the FBI in on this?'

I glanced at Harrison and shook my head.  .

'If she was abducted we may not be able to avoid it,' Chavez said.

'They walked away from the kidnapping theory three years ago,' said Harrison.

'And if this is a serial killer?'

'Right now all we have is a frozen body,' I said. 'Until we have a definite cause of death, contacting an outside agency would be premature.'

Chavez nodded. The door opened and Traver stepped in.

'The prints were done on a home ink jet printer, probably downloaded from the same sites on the Internet where we found these. The paint used in the apartment is inexpensive acrylic, can be gotten at any art supply or hobby store or online. There's nothing there we can use.'

'So where does that leave things?' asked Chavez.

I looked over to the folder containing the photographs of the dead girl. 'He's obviously a trained painter. We're making calls to the various college art departments to see if they had a student obsessed with Goya. And we're looking into every missing persons report that may fit into this loose profile.'

'And if nothing does?'

'Then we wait for the next body,' I said.

43

# seven

By nightfall the storm had stalled off the coast, spinning like a child's pinwheel. In the Hollywood Hills a torrent of mud swept down a hillside through an actor's house, impaling his downslope neighbor's BMW with the Emmy he won for an episode of *Law and Order*. In the Valley a pizza delivery guy hydroplaned into a bus stop at an intersection killing three workers returning home from a tortilla factory.

At eight o'clock I stepped out onto the steps on Garfield and lit a cigarette. What we had learned during the rest of the day had gotten us no closer than we were at the beginning. Of the existing missing persons reports none raised any red flags. Margaret Chow was still twelve hours away from being able to begin a complete autopsy.

'I don't remember you smoking.'

I turned to Harrison, who had stepped out behind me.

'I'm not,' I said, looking at the glow of the ember. 'I'm just holding it. It reminds me of my youth.'

'I just got off the phone with professors in art departments at UCLA, Parsons, the Design Center, and SC. Apparently odd obsessive behavior is practically the norm at an art school. If we were looking for a straitlaced boring individual we might have more luck. They're looking into it but I wouldn't hold my breath.'

'So we're nowhere, or we're right where he wants us.' I glanced at Dylan, who was looking out into the night.

'I wonder which is worse?' he said softly.

Another sheet of rain blew down the street, sending spiraling patterns of rain toward the plaza.

'You all right?' said Harrison.

I shook my head. 'Ninety-three days without a murder and then this. How do you explain that? A drive-by, a domestic, a robbery gone bad, that I would understand, but how do you make sense of this?'

Harrison shook his head. I looked into his eyes. The sense that he had somehow failed Keri was still just under the surface.

'You would say making sense of it isn't our job,' he said.

I brought the cigarette up to my lips and came as close to taking a puff as I had in a very long time. 'Maybe the smart cops are the ones who make it a game. Sometimes you win, sometimes you lose, but when you're done you go home and forget about it.'

'You know many cops like that?'

I shook my head. 'Not one that was worth a damn.'

I tossed the cigarette onto the wet stone of the steps and looked into Harrison's eyes.

'How long has it been since we've made love?'

'In hours or days?'

I knew the answer, nearly down to the second. We had only been together half a dozen times in six months, so the moments were emblazoned in my memory: every touch, move of a leg, and shudder that ran through both our bodies. Dylan wasn't holding anything back – I was the one doing that. Harrison was ten years younger than me; at some level inside I think I was afraid to want too much. Not because I didn't trust him – it was the happiness that made me nervous; it was still too new a sensation to me. I leaned in and kissed him lightly on the lips then looked back toward the street as a gust of wind shook us. He looked at me and I could see the surprise in his eyes.

'Something's worrying you, isn't it?'

'Is a kiss in public that surprising?' I asked.

'Yeah, but that's not why I asked.'

'What he is planning, however this is going to play out, we're part of it,' I said. 'He's taking us by the hand right into that pit of darkness with him.'

Harrison nodded.

'I want a few hours not to think about this,' I said.

Harrison smiled. 'I'll meet you at your house.'

He turned and went inside and I stepped out from under the cover of the entrance into the rain and started down the steps toward my car in the lot.

'Lieutenant,' said a voice behind me.

I stopped and turned. A uniformed watch commander was rushing down the stairs toward me.

'You wanted to know about any missing persons reports that seemed unusual?'

I nodded. The doors to headquarters opened again and Harrison stepped back out.

'I think you'd better look at this,' said the watch commander as he handed me a report.

I read it while the rain began to spread across its surface.

'A reporter. What kind?'

'Television.'

I looked more closely at the name. Trevor Wells.

'The morning show,' I said.

'Yeah.'

'How long has he been missing?'

'This morning. We wouldn't even look into it for another twelve hours, but since you asked I thought you would want to see it.'

Harrison reached us at the bottom of the stairs and I handed him the report.

'There was something unusual other than his being a reporter on TV?'

The watch commander nodded. 'When he didn't show at the station someone called his home and got an odd message.'

'How odd?'

'The recording said he would be away for a while . . . "paying the consequences".'

I glanced over to Harrison.

'That mean anything to you, Lieutenant?'

I looked down at the report.

'This the address?' I asked.

'Yeah, above the arroyo. You want us to send a squad to check it out?'

Harrison and I were already running toward my car.

# eight

It took twenty minutes to wind our way up the narrow canyon roads of the hills overlooking the arroyo. For blocks surrounding Wells' address the power had been lost in the storm, plunging the homes into darkness. There was little traffic. The wind had littered the pavement with palm fronds and pine needles. We moved slowly along checking house numbers painted on the curbs.

'Should be the second one on the left,' Harrison said.

I pulled to a stop and turned off my headlights. In a few of the surrounding homes the flickering light of candles was visible in the windows but the front of Wells' house was obscured by a thick row of banana trees bending in the wind so we could see nothing.

We stepped out and Harrison checked the address again to be sure, then nodded. I followed a fieldstone path up to the edge of the banana trees, and as my eyes adjusted to the darkness the shape of the front of the house became visible. A slatted wood entry way protruded over the front door. From where I stood there appeared to be no windows at all.

'If our assumptions are correct, our standing here is part of our suspect's plan,' I said. 'He would be expecting this.'

Harrison turned to me, wiped rain from his face and removed his Beretta from his belt. 'That's reassuring.'

I slipped my Glock out of its holster and moved forward

through the banana trees to the front door. A soggy copy of the *LA Times* had slipped out of its plastic bag and was scattered across the entrance. Harrison nodded toward a motion detector on the ground and small surveillance camera above the door pointing down at us.

'If someone came through this way, Wells would have had a good look at them,' Harrison said. He shined his light on the door jamb. It appeared clean and unforced.

'If they did, he either hadn't locked it or he let them in. We'll need to check the system to see if it recorded anything.'

Harrison nodded and I reached out, testing the door. The handle turned and I gently pushed it open.

'What's that smell?' Harrison said.

I breathed it in.

'Fuel of some kind,' I said.

I swung around into the entrance, raising my weapon. The doorway opened directly into a large living room. The back side of the house appeared to be mostly windows looking out over Pasadena – the dark shapes of blocks that had lost power were visible amongst the flickering city lights.

I took several steps and then stopped. The air was heavy with fumes. The surface of the floor appeared to shimmer in the faint light coming through the windows.

'I'm standing in gasoline,' I whispered.

'Don't take another step,' said Harrison.

'The whole room is covered in it,' I said softly.

'Back out,' whispered Harrison.

The house was shaped like a staple pulled open, wings extending on either side of the living room. I began to step back and then stopped. Something made a sound in the darkness beyond the living room.

'Retrace your steps as precisely as you can,' Harrison said.

'There's something here.'

I heard the sound again from the wing to the right of where I stood. I raised my weapon.

'Using that would be a bad idea,' said Harrison. 'There're enough fumes in here for this place to go up like a candle.'

I flipped the safety on. 'It makes me feel better to hold it.'

Another sound came out of the darkness.

'Something's alive,' I whispered and started forward.

'Your cell phone,' Harrison said.

I reached the entrance to the far wing and stopped. 'What about it?'

'You expecting any calls?'

'I'm a mother. I'm always expecting a call.' I realized why he was mentioning it. 'Would that be enough to set off the gas?'

Harrison nodded. 'It's possible.'

I looked across the room. My steps had set ripples spreading over the surface of the gasoline.

'Do you have any other good news I should be aware of?'

'The power,' he said.

'What about it?'

'If it comes back on, circuits, lights, security systems all come back on.'

I looked at him. I had learned long ago not to question Harrison's judgment on things that blow up.

'Bang,' I said.

Harrison nodded.

'You check the other wing, I'll do this one,' I said and started down the hallway.

The sound I had heard before was not repeated. There was a single door on the right and then the hallway opened into another large open space bathed in darkness. I stepped to the door and pushed it open – it was a small empty bathroom.

The faint whimper came again from the darkness ahead. Out of instinct I raised my Glock and stepped forward. I was standing at the edge of the kitchen; the faint shapes of stainless steel cooking pots were visible hanging over the center island. The sound had come from the room beyond.

'This is the police,' I said.

There was another rattle. I moved past the center island. The gasoline had begun to soak through my shoes and I could feel it inching up the length of my socks.

'Step forward toward my voice,' I said.

A shudder seemed to come from the darkness. I took a step and then another. There was a shape ahead, but I couldn't make it out.

'Mr Wells,' I said.

I reached into my jacket pocket, removed a small flashlight and raised it toward the dull shape.

'Mr Wells, we're here to help you.'

It occurred to me that by turning on the flashlight I might send the house up in a ball of flame.

'Now step toward me where I can see you,' I said.

There was no movement, no sound. I began to press my thumb on the switch of the flashlight, hesitated, and then turned the light on. The beam cut a hole in the darkness and I froze at what it exposed. My hand holding the Glock began to shake and I lowered it to my side.

'Harrison,' I yelled.

The sound of his footsteps splashing in the gas came down the hallway then stopped a few feet behind me. For a moment he was silent, and then he whispered, 'The consequences.'

I shook my head. 'Is that what you call this?'

'The man who did this does,' Harrison said.

I holstered my Glock and stepped toward the body. It was sitting up in a heavy Mission-style chair several feet in front of a large flat screen TV. The legs, chest and one arm were bound to the chair by duct tape.

'Is that Wells?' Harrison asked.

I shook my head. 'I don't know.'

'His eyes are gone,' Harrison said.

The blood around the sockets had dried dark, looking like two holes dug in the earth. The front of his shirt and pants was soaked in blood as were his mouth and chin. I stepped closer to the body.

'Some of his teeth are broken. I think his tongue is gone too,' I said.

We turned and looked at each other.

'A reporter has his eyes and tongue cut out. Do you think that qualifies as a mythic death?'

A breeze blew through a small opening in a window in the back of the room, rattling the blinds.

'That the sound you heard?' Harrison asked.

I nodded.

'Look at his arm that isn't taped to the chair,' I said. 'His hand's taped around something.'

Harrison stepped over to the other side of the body and looked at the TV a few feet away.

'It's a remote for the television.'

'Why?' I said.

Harrison started to say something, then stopped and moved over to the TV. He stared at it for a moment in silence.

'Because of this.'

A cable plugged into the back of the set ran down to the floor. The plug on the end of the cable had been removed and the insulating cover cut away. The exposed wires lay in the fuel.

'Jesus,' Harrison said softly.

I looked down at the hand taped around the remote. 'His index finger had been positioned over the power button.'

'He was alive,' Harrison said.

I nodded. 'He was given the choice to put an end to his torture by turning on the TV.' I looked over to Harrison. 'Death by television.'

'The power went out, and he couldn't,' Harrison said. 'He slowly bled to death, or choked on his own blood.'

We both stood in silence for a moment, neither wanting to fully accept what we were looking at.

'I'll go open doors and windows and get some air in here,' Harrison said.

I turned my light back on the body and began to nod in agreement when I saw something.

'Wait,' I said.

I walked over and kneeled down in front of Wells – or what we assumed was Wells.

'What is it?' Harrison asked.

I shined the light onto the hand holding the remote. 'I thought I saw his chest rise with a breath.'

'What?'

I shook my head and shined the light on his face, or what was left of it. Without eyes it was like looking at a partially finished model, or a disfigured doll. There was no movement anywhere. I couldn't detect any rise or fall of his chest. I reached out to check for a pulse in his neck to be sure. I placed my fingers under the line of his jaw. Nothing seemed to press against my fingers.

'I don't—'

I felt a faint sensation under his skin.

'There's something,' I said. 'It was weak, but it was there.' I kept my fingers pressed against his neck but didn't feel anything else.

'Are you sure?'

I pressed my hands against his skin, waiting for another surge of blood, but there was nothing.

'No. My hands are cold, I'm not sure what I'm feeling.' I leaned in to see if I could detect any breath leave his body.

'I don't hear anything—'

Wells' head jerked violently up and I fell backwards into Harrison's arms. We both stood in silence for a moment, coming to terms with the knowledge that the man we were looking at was alive, and trying not to think of the unimaginable horror he had been through.

'He's in shock. That would account for the weak pulse.'

'I'll call a paramedic,' Harrison said.

'Hurry.'

Harrison rushed over to the sliding door, pulled it open and began dialing as he stepped outside. I moved back over to Wells and began to examine the tape binding him to the chair.

'Mr Wells, we're going to get you to a doctor. You'll be all right.' They were maybe the most absurd words I had ever spoken, but I repeated them anyway. If he heard them, there was no reaction. I began pulling at the tape holding his arm to the chair, but it was useless. He was bound by layer after layer.

'We need a knife for this tape,' I yelled to Harrison.

He stepped back to the door. 'We have a problem.' He was looking out over Pasadena spread out below us. 'The power's coming back.'

I rushed over to join him at the door. One by one large blocks of darkness were coming back to life, the light moving in our direction.

'We have to get him out of here,' I said.

We ran back to Wells and took hold of the chair to drag him out of the house. It wouldn't move.

'Pull!' I yelled.

We tried again, but it wouldn't budge. Harrison kneeled down and ran his hands around the chair's legs.

'It's screwed to the floor.'

'I'll get a knife from the kitchen. We'll cut him loose.'

Harrison shook his head. 'There isn't time.'

'To hell with time. We're not walking away from him.'

I started toward the kitchen, but Harrison grabbed me by the collar.

'No!' I shouted.

I heard the hum of power returning to the house. I turned to look at Wells and Harrison lifted me up and we were moving toward the open sliding door and the rain falling outside.

A light began to flicker in the room.

'Dylan!' I yelled.

I heard the hum of appliances coming back on and then a single light flickered to life as we crossed the threshold and tumbled onto the wet grass. I got up to my knees and started to turn back to the house, but Dylan grabbed me and pulled me back down. A few more lights flickered again and then came on. Harrison dragged me toward him, using his body to shield me from the house. A second passed, and then another, and nothing happened.

'Wait another second,' Harrison said.

Through the glass doors of the living room a ceiling light was gently swinging back and forth in the wind. We both stared at it for a moment, not quite believing that the house was still there.

'The open front door must have ventilated it enough,' Harrison said.

'Did you get the paramedics?' I asked.

'They're on their way. Fire department too.'

We both stood up and looked at the horrible figure bound to the chair.

'We need to cut him loose,' I said.

I took a step and saw Wells' free arm rise from his lap and point the remote toward the TV.

'Oh, God,' said Harrison.

I started to run and then a spark a few feet from Wells sent tendrils of fire spreading across the floor like a hand stretching out. The flames began to wrap around his legs, and then he vanished in a flash of light.

The heat hit my face and I was lifted off my feet and moving through the air. I tried to yell for Dylan, but the breath was sucked from my lungs and then the light of the explosion went dark and all I could hear was the beating of my heart.

# nine

My face was warm as if I had been sunburned. The smell of gas and singed hair filled my nostrils. It was near three a.m. when the last fire engine left the scene. The blaze had gutted the interior of the house, leaving behind a shell of walls and a roof.

The coroner had removed Wells' charred remains, frozen by flame to remain eternally in the position in which he had been bound. His hand and the remote taped to it had melted into a matrix of plastic and burned tissue so neither was distinguishable from the other – the perfect modern man, as I heard one of the arson investigators remark.

Crime scene techs were still sifting through the remains of the house like archeologists probing a dig, but had so far come up empty. I walked back into it trying to reassemble the fragments of memory of what had happened before the fire in case I had missed some detail.

Water, a black layer of ash floating on its surface, now covered the floor. Where the fire department had cut holes in the roof to ventilate the flames rain poured through in steady streams. I retraced the path I had taken when we first entered, walking down the hallway, through the kitchen and into the room where Wells died.

The charred chair still sat where he was burned to death. The TV that had been the source of the blaze had melted into a shape

Dali might have imagined. The tingling of the cooling timbers of the house added to the surreal quality of what I was looking at.

'Are you thinking we missed something?'

I turned and Harrison was standing behind me at the edge of the kitchen. A small bandage covered a cut over his left eye where he had been hit by flying glass. The skin of his face was red like mine from the heat blast. His clothes were permeated with fine particles of soot.

I nodded. 'Aren't you?'

He shook his head. 'No. I know what I forgot. I should have unplugged the TV.'

I looked at the remains of the chair, which now resembled burned bone rather than a piece of classic furniture design.

'Some things aren't imaginable until they happen,' I said and then looked at Dylan. 'He would probably have died even without the fire. And if he had survived, he might not have been able to live with the memories of what had happened to him here.'

'No, we get to do that.'

Harrison walked over next to me and looked down at the chair. The faint fabric pattern of the pants Wells had been wearing had been burned into the wood.

'What does a reporter have to do with a lawyer's daughter?' he said.

I looked around the room. 'If the answer was here, it's gone now. We'll talk to the Bishops.'

Harrison stepped around me and kneeled down, looking at the view Wells would have had if he hadn't been blinded.

'Just before he disappeared in the flames he was moving his mouth, trying to say something,' he said.

I shook my head. 'I didn't see that. I was looking at his hand holding the remote.'

'I've been playing it over in my head trying to figure out what I saw. If he made a sound I didn't hear it, but I'm almost certain he mouthed two words.'

'Could you make them out?'

Dylan looked up at me. 'I think he was saying "forgive me", or "forgive us".'

'A prayer?'

Dylan stood and walked over to the remains of the TV. 'Or an apology.'

'For what?'

We looked at each other, both knowing that the answer to that question might save the next life. I glanced around the room once more and then we walked out of the house to my car.

If either of us spoke a single word on the way to my house I don't recall them. I parked in the driveway and we walked through the rain to the front door.

'This isn't headquarters,' Harrison said, and reached out to wipe the raindrops from my face.

We walked through the house shedding our clothes until we were in the shower standing under a stream of warm water. Dylan washed the smell of fuel from my hair and then in turn my arms, hands, legs, feet, back and breasts. There were small cuts on his chest from debris from the explosion. A few tiny pieces of imbedded glass came out as my fingers gently cleaned each wound.

Dylan lifted me onto him and we sank to the floor of the tub. His skin tasted of fuel, his hair of ash, and the faster we moved our bodies together, the harder we held, the more intensely we looked into each other's eyes, trying to forget the image of Wells, the stronger the memory of what had happened became.

The water finally turned cold but we didn't turn it off as we continued to try to put the past hours behind us.

'Don't stop,' were the only words we uttered and we said it simultaneously.

But it didn't help. The more we tried to forget, the farther we slipped away from the moment. When our shivering from the cold became uncontrollable we both finally gave in to exhaustion and slipped apart.

'You want me to go?' Dylan whispered as he tried to catch his breath.

I shook my head. We walked into the bedroom and fell asleep trying to pretend we were like any other couple curled around each other, each of us knowing we weren't. We had been brought together by violence. It was always there and there was no escaping it. We sought refuge in each other the way others might visit a shrink or sink into alcohol.

Sleep offered no relief from the horror we had witnessed. Twice Dylan bolted upright into the darkness as he reached out trying to catch Wells' hand before he could end his life. My nightmares were silent and the same every time I sank back into sleep. An empty eyeless face was around every corner I turned, behind every door I opened.

After each dream we would cling to each other tighter than before but all that could finally end the nightmares was the dull gray light of dawn and the ringing of the phone.

'Delillo,' I answered, the sound of rain on the roof heralding in a new round of showers.

It was Traver.

'Channel 11 was emailed a video this morning with Wells on it,' he said.

'Have they turned it over?'

'Not yet. The city attorney's office is in negotiations with them as we speak. They're claiming there are first amendment issues at stake.'

'What's on it?'

Dylan sat up and leaned in to listen.

'I think we're about to find out. Turn on your TV.'

I grabbed the remote on the nightstand and tuned the set to Channel 11. A news anchor sat at his desk with a still image of Wells from the recording blue-screened next to him.

'What you are about to see is a recording we received this morning of our colleague Trevor Wells from Channel 5 taken in the hours before he tragically died in a fire at his home. While we are cooperating with law enforcement on this terrible event, we are also doing everything in our power to bring you the news, and protect your right to hear and see it, in an honest and trusted way.'

The image cut to a shot of Wells from the chest up. His arms were tight to his chest so I guessed he had already been bound to the chair. His face was dotted with perspiration as he looked into the camera. He hesitated as if reluctant to speak.

'Look at his eyes,' I said. 'He's reading what Goya wants him to say.'

'And it's frightening him.'

Wells took a shaky breath and then began.

'I am the first, the second will soon follow. I had a voice and I did not speak the truth. And I had sight, but I did not see . . . my death will be by my own hand . . . television is going to kill me.'

The film froze and then cut back to the anchor staring grimly at the picture of Wells.

# ten

There was no longer any possibility that the investigation would remain solely the responsibility of Pasadena PD once the tape aired. Whether the case was now defined as a kidnapping or a murder was irrelevant. It had been on television, and like everything the medium touches, everything was changed. The FBI would be a part of it now. All that remained to be seen was how much or little control I would retain.

The station delivered a copy of the Wells recording to headquarters by mid-morning. Chief Chavez, myself, and Harrison watched it with an FBI agent by the name of Utley from the Behavioral Analysis Unit in the conference room. Any hope that there had been more to it than we had seen on the broadcast faded with the first viewing.

After screening it for the fourth time I hit the pause button on the control and the room fell silent for a moment, all of us staring at the frozen image of a frightened Wells on the screen.

'I'm the first, the second will soon follow,' Chavez finally said, going back over what Wells had read on the video. 'I guess that means there are going to be more.'

I nodded. 'He chose the words carefully.'

'What about the girl? Wouldn't she have been the first?'

'Goya must see her death as a separate act, although why I don't know,' I said.

'Is there a connection between them?'

'The closest thing we've come to is that before Wells became the morning anchor he covered the abuse case against the Catholic archdiocese that Bishop filed. He asked questions at a press conference. As far as the news director knows they've never met or talked other than that one time,' said Harrison.

'We're looking through his papers and notebooks and tapes that were in his house, but most of the stuff was destroyed by the fire,' I said.

'We're also tracking everything both Keri and her father did before her disappearance for a connection but so far nothing stands out,' Harrison added.

'Does Wells have kids who may have been in school with Keri Bishop?'

'No, he was single.'

'The connection may only be in Goya's head, but finding it might be our only chance to stop him unless he makes a mistake and we get lucky,' I said.

'Has he made any mistakes yet?'

'No.'

'Where did he email the video from?' Chavez asked.

'Wells' own computer, about one in afternoon,' I said. 'It was opened this morning about five when the anchor arrived at the station.'

Chavez stared at the image on the screen for a moment then shook his head.

'I had sight, but I did not see, a voice and I did not speak the truth,' Chavez said. 'Other than the obvious, someone want to tell me what the hell that means?'

'He was a reporter,' I said. 'In Goya's estimation Wells failed to do his job, so he punished him by taking away the tools of his trade.'

'And television is going to kill me . . . is that Goya trying to be funny?' Chavez asked.

'Ironic maybe,' I said.

'TV as a weapon.'

'It's been called worse.'

Chavez turned to the FBI agent. Utley was a tall thin figure with black hair and sharply drawn features that gave him a crow-like appearance.

'The FBI have anything to add?'

'We're putting an alert out over the VICAP system, but I wouldn't expect anything useful. So far as we can tell there appears to be no connection to any of the known serial killers presently operating in the country. Goya's new, and he's unlike any of the others.'

'Is that good or bad news?'

'It's good if all you add up is a body count.'

'Meaning?'

'He's not killing for sexual gratification, or for the twisted power trip, so I wouldn't expect him to be prolific.'

'How do you define prolific?'

'Ted Bundy killed somewhere between twenty-nine and a hundred women before he was caught.'

Chavez took a breath. 'And the bad news?'

'Like Wells, Goya's targets are going to be chosen for their complicity in the specific or societal wrong he feels he suffered.'

'And that means what?'

'Someone like Bundy goes after random targets who are easily vulnerable. Goya's victims are going to be public people of responsibility who have a position within the power structure of society.'

'Can you be more specific?' Chavez asked.

Utley shook his head. 'Once we determine the wrong he

suffered we'll have a better idea who he intends to punish. The girl's death whether linked to Wells or not may have been an act of impulse. That he preserved her in such perfect condition may indicate a certain remorse about her death. Keeping her frozen may have been a way to keep her alive to him.'

'He had no feeling like that toward Wells,' Chavez said.

Utley shook his head again. 'Or with the ones to come.'

Chavez walked over to the copies of the etchings tacked to the wall and looked them up and down.

'Can these help identify the next victim?' Chavez said.

'Possibly,' I said. 'Many of the power structures that the painter Goya railed against haven't changed much in three hundred years.'

'The Church, politicians.'

I nodded.

'But that's not who he killed,' Chavez said.

'No, but it doesn't take much of a leap to add TV to a list of society's perceived evils.'

The door opened and Traver stepped in.

'The coroner,' he said, motioning to the phone.

I hit the lit up line and picked up.

'Ms Chow. You have something for me,' I said.

'There's been significant tissue damage from the freezing.'

'Does that mean anything?'

'It means she was kept in something with temperatures and humidity similar to a household freezer.'

'Can you determine how long ago she died?'

'Given the damage to the skin, it appears she's been dead for some time, a year at minimum, most likely closer to the three years she's been missing. The chances of narrowing it down any more than that are remote at best, however.'

'Do you have a cause of death?'

'It's not definitive yet. She may have died as a result of freezing, but there's another possible explanation.'

'Which is?'

'It's not what I expected,' Chow said. 'We found some objects inside her.'

A chill ran up the back of my neck. 'Objects? What kind of objects?'

There was a pause on the other end of the phone. 'I think it would be better to show you than try to explain.'

# eleven

Margaret Chow was waiting for us in her office when Harrison and I arrived. She ushered us out and began leading us to the lab.

'We brought her body just up to the point of thawing and are keeping it there until we're satisfied we've found everything. It should slow the deterioration if we want to do further tests.'

'Tell me about the objects?' I said.

'We did an X-ray while she was still frozen and found them then.'

'Where were they?'

'All but one were found in her stomach. From the markings on the inside of her throat it was clear she had ingested them while she was alive, though she could have been unconscious and they were forced down, thus causing the abrasions.'

'You said all but one?' I asked.

We reached the forensic lab, where a box of latex gloves sat next to the door.

'You'll need to put these on.'

We each donned gloves and entered the room.

'The other object was found in her throat. Whether it was put there before or after death is uncertain. If it became lodged there while she was alive it may have caused hypoxia.'

'You mean she choked to death?'

'It's possible. The blockage of the airway was significant, but the object could have been inserted after her death, so we're not certain. Freezing and hypoxia can present in similar ways. The time and the damaged tissue add to the complications. Toxicology may clear things up, but we won't have those results for another twenty-four hours.'

We stopped at one of stations and stepped in.

'What kind of objects are they?'

Chow slipped an X-ray out of an envelope and stuck it on a light board. A jumble of shapes was visible in the stomach but none was discernible from the others. The one lodged in her throat was little more than a dark mass.

'We thought they might have been organic at first, maybe bone or partially digested food that was frozen.' She walked over to another table, retrieved a towel-covered tray and brought it back to us. 'We were wrong.'

She pulled back the towel. Harrison and I stared at the objects for a moment in silence. I reached out and picked one up. They were made of plastic, about the size of a fifty-cent piece.

'Letters,' Harrison said.

'From a child's game,' Chow added.

The piece I held in my hand was a dark blue letter S. 'He's left us a message.'

Chow nodded. 'We haven't gotten anywhere with it. Are either of you any good at Scrabble?'

'Which one was found in her throat?' I asked.

'The yellow E,' Chow said.

I stared at the letters for a moment, trying to place them in an order that made sense.

'We could make individual words, but nothing using all the letters,' Chow said. 'Everything put together is just nonsense.'

Harrison leaned over the table and stared at the pieces.

'Do you see something?' I asked.

Harrison's eyes moved back and forth across the letters as he played something out silently in his head.

'Dylan?'

He nodded. 'It isn't English, that's why you're having trouble.' He began rearranging the letters. 'It's Latin.'

'*Ego sum soluta*,' I said, reading the words.

'Of course,' said Chow.

I shook my head. 'I went to public school. You'll have to translate,' I said.

'I am free,' Harrison said.

I looked down at the words, playing them over in my head.

'Free from what?' Chow said. 'That could mean almost anything.'

'Or something very specific.' I picked up the E and held it for a moment. 'Had she been sexually assaulted?'

'She wasn't a virgin, but I didn't find any evidence that she had engaged in intercourse either voluntarily or against her will just prior to her death.'

'How about after death?' I asked.

Chow shook her head. 'All I can tell you is that there was no semen present.'

'Who's doing Wells' autopsy?' I asked.

'I'm doing it this afternoon,' Chow said, realizing immediately why I had asked. 'The deaths are connected?'

I nodded. 'Could anything have survived the heat of the fire inside Wells?'

'You mean more letters?'

'Yes.'

She thought for a moment. 'I've only looked at the body once. The burning on the extremities was severe, down to the bone over much of their length, but the torso was substantially intact. It's possible the stomach contents remained undamaged. It's also possible that the stomach survived intact, but the fluids began to boil and destroyed everything inside.'

I held up the letter I was holding. 'Could that melt these?'

Chow looked at the letters for a moment and shook her head. 'I don't know.'

'If there's another message inside him, we need to know it as soon as possible.'

'I'll move the autopsy up.'

# twelve

We left the coroner's office and drove across town to the Bishop residence a few blocks south of the 134 on the west side of the arroyo. A long sweeping yard of grass led up to the front steps. A bed of roses in full bloom extended from the steps all the way around the right corner. Mrs Bishop met us at the door and walked us into the spacious living room, which had floor to ceiling glass that looked out toward the arroyo below. A dark ribbon of rushing water filled the concrete channel. The occasional thud of a large boulder being swept along in the current echoed up the slope to where we stood.

The living room looked as if it could grace the pages of *Architectural Digest* except for the heavy layer of dust that covered every single thing in the room. All the trappings of lives being lived there were present, but it was as if the house itself had died.

'Do you have news of my daughter's death?' Mrs Bishop asked.

'We would like to also talk to your husband.'

The words seemed to strike her like a small stone hitting the side of her face.

'So would I,' she said, offering no explanation.

'There are some questions we need to ask you both.'

'Would you like to see her room?' she asked as if I had not spoken.

She turned and walked down a hallway to a door halfway to the end. A small handwritten note was taped to the door. Both the paper and the ink had begun to yellow. *Please knock*, it read.

Mrs Bishop took hold of the handle with one hand and began to raise her other one to knock. She then became conscious of what she was doing and opened the door and showed us in.

There was no dust in this room. I imagined they had kept it exactly as it had been in case their daughter returned. The room of a dead girl appeared to be the only place where life was still holding on in this house.

Harrison and I glanced around the room but made no move to examine anything.

'I'm sorry. This isn't why you're here, is it?' Mrs Bishop said.

I shook my head.

'What is it you want to ask?'

'If your husband is here we would like to ask you both.'

She looked out the door of the bedroom. 'He's in his study.'

She walked out of the room and led us to a closed door at the other end of the house, where she hesitated for a moment and then knocked.

'Jackson?'

There was no response from inside the room.

'Jackson, the police have some questions to ask us. Open the door.'

I heard the creak of a chair and then the bolt on the door slid open. Mrs Bishop pushed the door wide but hesitated to step inside.

'Jackson?' she said again.

Her husband was standing in front of the window looking out at the rushing water at the bottom of the arroyo. The air drifting out from the office was stale with the odor of alcohol. Loose papers littered the floor and the large desk in front of the window. I stepped past Mrs Bishop into the room.

'Mr Bishop, I need your help. I have a few questions.'

He took a shallow breath and his shoulders sagged ever so slightly.

'Do you have a cause of death?' he said, barely above a whisper.

'Nothing definitive. I can tell you there was no evidence of trauma indicating violence.'

'Define violence,' he said softly.

He slowly turned around. He hadn't shaved; his eyes were bloodshot. He hadn't changed clothes since we saw him the day before at the coroner's office. His bearing gave the impression that he was put together like a jigsaw puzzle – one wrong touch and the pieces would all come apart.

'Had she been assaulted?'

'Doesn't appear so.'

'What is it you want to ask, Lieutenant?'

I glanced over at Mrs Bishop and she nodded as if to say it was all right to continue.

'Does the reporter Trevor Wells mean anything to either of you?'

'The TV reporter who died in the fire?' Mrs Bishop asked.

'Yes,' I said.

Mrs Bishop shook her head. 'No, nothing.'

'I may have talked to him once or twice when I was practicing law,' Mr Bishop said as if talking about a previous life.

'How about your daughter, do you remember her ever mentioning his name?'

'No,' Mrs Bishop said. 'Why are you asking this?'

'It wasn't an accidental fire,' I said. 'He was murdered.'

Jackson Bishop's eyes appeared to come alive for a fleeting moment. 'You're saying this is connected in some way to our daughter?'

I nodded. 'We believe it's the same man. So far the only

connection we have found is that Wells covered your case against the archdiocese.'

'That was years ago,' Bishop said.

'Three,' I said.

The life in Bishop's eyes drifted away again. 'The year Keri left,' he said as if she had departed for a trip rather than being abducted. He looked at me for a moment then turned and walked over to the sliding door, opened it, and stepped out into the rain.

Mrs Bishop went to the door and attempted to persuade her husband back inside but he just continued to look into the distance as the rain began to soak his clothes. She finally stepped back in.

'I'm sorry,' she said, and then bent down and began picking up papers from the floor. 'He's hasn't been himself . . .' She let the rest of the thought go and then looked at the papers in her hands and placed them on the desk. 'Is there anything else you wanted to ask?'

'Your daughter had an interest in art?' I said.

Surprise registered in her eyes and then she nodded. 'She took a night school class at the Art Center, before she disappeared, but she never said much about it. I thought she had enough with her classes at USC, but she really wanted to do it.'

'What was she studying at college?'

'She wanted to be a journalist.' She glanced out at her husband. 'Jackson wanted her to become a lawyer, practice with him.'

'Did you save any of her work from the art class?'

'Is this important?'

'It's possible.'

She nodded and led us back through the house to her daughter's room. From under the bed she retrieved several large portfolios that held loose drawings and an eleven-by-fourteen bound sketchbook.

'I don't remember seeing this when Keri first disappeared,' Harrison said, referring to the bound book.

Mrs Bishop handed it to me. 'She had left it at the center. It wasn't returned to us until months later.'

I began to page through the drawings. The first half of the book was mostly studies of bottles and jars, flowers and other everyday objects. The second half contained life studies; hands, feet, legs and eyes.

'She had a very graceful touch with the pencil,' I said.

I turned another page and stopped on a drawing of a shirtless young man in profile from the waist up. On the bottom of the page the letter M had been written.

'Does this mean anything to you?' I asked.

Mrs Bishop shook her head. 'I assumed it was just a model.'

On the following page a loose drawing had been inserted into the book. It was another life drawing of a naked girl sitting on a cloth-covered box, her back to the viewer, her slim legs spread out on either side of the box. Beyond her a set of drapes opened to what appeared to be a bed. On the bottom of the page was written *forever m.*

'Could I see that?' asked Mrs Bishop.

She studied the drawing for a moment and then held her hand up to her mouth.

'That's Keri,' she whispered.

'Are you sure?'

She nodded, her eyes filling with tears. 'I know my daughter.'

'Did she ever mention anyone whose name began with the letter M?'

She shook her head. 'No.'

'Did you know your daughter was no longer a virgin?' I asked.

The look in her eyes was all the answer I needed.

'Are you certain?' Mrs Bishop asked.

I nodded. 'I'm sorry.'

'She never talked about anyone.'

She looked back at the drawing and her hands began to shake.

'My beautiful girl,' she said softly.

I reached out and gently took the drawing from her hands.

'I would like to keep these for a while,' I said. 'I'll make sure you'll get them back.'

She nodded. 'If you think it will help.'

I slipped the drawing back into the book and she turned away wiping tears from her eyes.

'We'll find our way out,' I said.

Once back in the car Harrison opened the sketchbook to the drawing of the male figure and compared it with the loose figure study of the Bishops' daughter.

'M could stand for nearly anything . . . model . . . could be a way of signing her own drawings . . . m stands for me.'

Harrison shook his head. 'These drawings were done by two different people.'

'You're sure?'

He nodded. 'Look at the way the individual lines end. Keri's drawing of the male figure is precise; each pencil stroke stops abruptly. Each line in the drawing of her bleeds into the paper.'

'Secret lovers,' I said.

Harrison nodded and continued to stare at the drawing of Keri.

'But that's not what you're thinking about,' I said.

Dylan shook his head.

'What is it?' I asked

'I've seen this before,' he said.

'Are you sure?'

'I think so. The hair color is different, but the rest of it is the same.'

'Where did you see it?'

80

'Researching the images we found at the stadium and the apartment.'

'It's a copy of a Goya,' I said.

Harrison nodded. I slipped the Volvo into gear and swung back north toward the hills west of the Rose Bowl, and the Art Center.

# thirteen

The director of the Office of Student Life was waiting in her office when we arrived on the hillside campus. Harrison had told her on the phone that we were looking for a student or former student but had offered few details about why. Her name was Hanes and she had the air of a protective mother to the student body.

She stared at the drawing Keri had done three years before and shook her head. 'You do understand that the privacy of our student body is of great importance to us, and is in fact protected by law.'

'We've no interest in anyone's records beyond a name and an address. I can get a court order if it would make it easier for you, but time is critical.'

She took a deep breath for effect and then looked at the drawing again. 'You have nothing more than this?'

'The name may begin with M.'

'Last or first?'

'I'm hoping you can tell me,' I said.

'You don't have to enroll in the program to take a night course, though a number of our students do, so even if we could identify him we may not have any records.'

She looked at the drawing again and shook her head, then called into an adjoining office. A woman in her late twenties stepped in. She wore striped pants that looked like a nightmare from the 1970s come alive. Her pale skin reminded me of a crack addict who hadn't seen the sun in months. She had short dark hair and her nose had been pierced with multiple silver rings.

'This is Amber, the assistant director of Student Life. She knows nearly every student who steps on this campus.'

Amber's eyes gave me the once-over.

'Homeland Security's finest?' she asked.

'No, just Pasadena's,' I said.

'They're trying to find someone who may have been a student here,' Hanes said.

'Is this person wanted for something?'

I shook my head. 'We just need to talk to him.'

'And you don't have a name.'

'His name might begin with M,' Hanes said.

I held the drawing out to her. As she looked at it she stole several quick glances back at Harrison and me as if trying to read our reaction to her.

'When was it you think he was here?' she asked.

'Three years ago,' Harrison said.

She shook her head. 'I don't think I can help you.'

'Take one more look,' I asked.

She did, though her eyes never focused on the drawing.

'That could be almost anyone,' she said. 'I meet hundreds of students every year. Ms and Hs and Zs and Ds.'

'He may have taken a night class.'

She shook her head again as she looked at the drawing. 'Sorry, I wish I could help you, but three years was a long time ago. Bring a better drawing next time.'

Ten minutes after we left the administration building Amber walked out and made a beeline for her car. As she opened the door we stepped up behind her. I was sure she hadn't told us exactly the truth.

'Why did you lie to us?' I said.

She spun around in surprise, then backed away, pressing herself against her car door.

'I didn't lie.'

I shook my head. 'Now you just did it again.'

'Look, my job is to protect the student body. Helping them to get into trouble is not part of my job description. I'm late, I have to go.'

'Where?'

'Lunch.'

'This is a homicide investigation. Lunch can wait.'

She looked at me for a moment. 'Homicide . . . you think he killed someone?'

'That's what we're trying to find out.'

'Well, I didn't lie. Like I said, it could be almost anyone.'

'Did you date him?' Harrison asked.

She looked at him and shook her head. 'Hello . . . I'm a lesbian.'

'A girl he was in a night class with was murdered,' I said. 'We think she posed for a drawing.'

She let out a short gasp as if she had been slapped on the back.

'Did you model for him?' I asked.

Her eyes belied any hope that she could continue to avoid answering. She took a breath and then shook her head.

'I would prefer that the college administration did not know about my modeling for students. They might get the wrong idea, and I like my job.'

'There's no reason they have to know.'

She hesitated. 'I'm not even sure he's the same guy in the drawing. I've modeled for a lot of people.'

85

'But that drawing only reminded you of one of them, didn't it?'

She nodded. 'Maybe. I'm not sure, that's why I didn't want to say anything.'

'Did his name start with M?'

She nodded. 'He called himself Miguel, but I don't think that was his real name. I think part of his thing was getting over being white.'

A raindrop hit the corner of her eye, sending a dark line of mascara down her cheek.

'Why don't we talk out of the rain?' I said.

We walked her over to my car and put her in the back seat, then got in the front.

'Do you remember his last name?'

'No. Like I said, I don't think I ever knew his real name.'

I opened the sketchbook and showed her the nude drawing of Keri. 'Does that look familiar?'

She stared at it for a moment, surprise registering in her eyes. 'Jesus. Yeah, it's just like mine only my hair is short . . . he said mine was a one of a kind.'

'Tell me about him.'

'He was a few years older than most of the students, maybe twenty-three or four. Spoke fluent Spanish. I got the impression that he had money.'

'Why do you say that?'

'It was a really big studio space and he paid me twice the going rate to model. I don't remember much else. You don't really talk a lot when sitting naked in front of someone.'

'Is he still a student here?' Harrison asked.

She shook her head. 'No, he only took a few classes. I think he despised most of the other students.'

'Why?'

'He wanted to be a real painter. Most of the kids here want to design the next dream car or become a movie director.'

'How many times did you model for him?'

'Once.'

'When?'

'About three years ago.'

'And you haven't seen him again?'

'No.'

'Would the school have records on him, an ID picture?' Harrison asked.

She shook her head. 'No ID for a night student. I tried to look him up before I did the job, but I couldn't find the name he registered under.'

'But you still did the job.'

She shrugged. 'I needed the money.'

'Where did you model for him?'

'He had a studio downtown on Santa Fe overlooking the river. I think it was near Seventh; I don't recall the address.'

'Would you recognize it if you saw it?'

Amber thought about it for a moment then nodded. 'I think so.'

'You said you didn't know much about him, but you still remember him three years later. Why?' I asked.

'He had some odd ideas.'

'About what?'

'I think he was into suffering.'

'For his art?' Harrison asked.

She shook her head. 'For everything.'

# fourteen

The warehouse district had once occupied a few square blocks to the east of Little Tokyo but as real estate prices climbed, artists seeking cheap rent had moved farther south into skid row until the mortgage collapse halted the spread of condos and BMWs.

I rode with Amber and Harrison followed in my car. As we turned onto Santa Fe, Amber began scanning each building, trying to coax memory back to life. We made a pass south along the length of Santa Fe, then turned back north and retraced our route. A block south of 6th Street at Jesse she pulled to the side and stopped. A windowless bar occupied the corner to the west. A Mexican wearing a white cowboy hat and boots with silver tips stood in the doorway looking out at the rain. A large pile of pink cotton candy sat on the sidewalk out front of the bar, slowly dissolving.

'I was wrong, it wasn't on Santa Fe,' Amber said, motioning down the side street toward the river. 'It's there.'

A tall row of brick buildings lined the block.

'Jesse Street.' I said.

She nodded. 'The building with the faded paint along the top. He was on the fourth floor.'

The faded lettering read STINSON PAINT.

'You remember a number?'

She stared toward the building, her lips silently moving in

conversation with herself. 'Four twenty-seven.'

'You're sure?'

She thought for a moment and then nodded. I thanked her and opened the door of the car.

'Lieutenant,' she said, her eyes focusing on me and then toward the building. 'I was thinking about the drawing, and the other girl. Was she the one who was killed?'

I nodded. She tried to find the rest of the words but couldn't manage to say them.

'You have nothing to worry about,' I said.

'How do you know?'

I held out one of my cards.

'He may have nothing to do with her death,' I said. 'They could be unrelated.'

'But you don't believe that?' she asked.

'It's my job to look at all the possibilities.'

From the look in her eyes I doubted that my words offered much in the way of solace.

'I sat in that same pose for him,' she said.

'And then you went home,' I said.

'Why her and not me?'

I shook my head. 'All that matters is that it wasn't.'

'Not to the other girl,' she said.

'If you remember anything else, you give me a call,' I said.

She took the card and then I stepped out and watched her drive away. From the open door of the bar I could hear mariachi music drift out. The moist air held the faint sweet scent of the cotton candy dissolving on the sidewalk.

Harrison pulled up beside me in my Volvo and I slipped inside.

'Middle of the block, Stinson Paint building.'

Harrison pulled around the corner onto Jesse and stopped across the street from the building. 'You want to get a warrant?'

I glanced at my watch. It was already nearly four. 'Get it started and then we'll go knock on the door.'

Harrison took out his phone and began dialing. I stepped out and walked across the street into the entrance of the building. Worn gray and white checked tiles covered the floor of the lobby. The air smelled of cigarettes and a cleanser. A hallway led to stairs at the far end of the building. On the far wall of the lobby was an ancient Otis elevator and the building's directory.

I stepped over and checked the numbers for the fourth floor. Four twenty-seven had no listing. The gears of the elevator engaged and it began to descend to the lobby. The doors opened and a Hasidic Jew with a long gray beard and a dark fedora stepped out. He looked out into the falling rain and buttoned his long coat up to the neck and then looked at me.

'Are you looking for diamonds?' he asked.

'No.'

He stared at me for a moment then slightly bowed his head and exited the building as Harrison walked through the doors.

'A squad can have a warrant here in twenty minutes if we need it.'

I pulled the doors to the elevator open and we stepped inside and hit the fourth floor. As the elevator began to creak into movement my phone rang.

'Lieutenant, it's Margaret Chow.'

'Did you find anything?'

'You were right, there was another message inside Wells. It wasn't letters this time, it was written out and put in a small plastic vial.'

'Was it in Latin?'

'Yes. We're a little uncertain of its meaning, though.'

'What is it?'

'*Crimen Sollicitationis.*'

'Could you say that again?'

'*Crimen Sollictationis*. Roughly translated it means—'

'I know what it means. Was there anything else?'

'His eyes and his tongue were also in his stomach. Everything else was pretty well burned.'

'Thank you.'

I hung up as the elevator stopped on the fourth floor. We slid the door open and stepped out into the dimly lit hallway. Harrison checked the numbers on the closest doors then motioned toward the darkness at the far end.

'It will be there. Out of the way, nice and quiet. Like the apartment in Eagle Rock.'

'Wells had been forced to swallow his eyes and tongue,' I said.

Harrison looked over to me. 'There was another message?'

'Yes,' I said. '*Crimen Sollicitationis.*'

'Crime of soliciting?'

I nodded.

'Prostitution?'

I shook my head. 'You weren't raised a Catholic, were you?'

'No.'

'*Crimen Sollicitationis* refers to inappropriate contact between a member of the clergy and a penitent while in the confessional. It was also the title of a document, a directive of canon law issued in 1962 by the Vatican to be held secretly by every bishop in every diocese around the world. It came to light a few years ago in the Boston archdiocese scandal.'

'What was its purpose?'

'It directed all individuals with knowledge of the investigation of misconduct by members of the clergy to absolute secrecy. Anyone involved within the Church, investigators, judges, any witnesses, the accused, even the victims, were to be sworn to an oath of secrecy. It even directed the destruction of documents that failed to prove absolute guilt on the part of any priest.'

'Not beyond a reasonable doubt?'

'No. And failure to follow the directive could result in excommunication.'

'What happens in the Church stays in the Church.'

'That was the idea.'

'So is this about a secret kept, or broken?'

I shook my head and looked down the hallway. 'Maybe the answer's down there.'

We made our way to the end of the hallway. There were no sounds audible, no TVs, no voices, no music. Nothing seemed to be alive behind any of the other dozen or so doors we passed. Not even the sounds of the street penetrated the brick walls of the building. On the last door on the floor an envelope with *Police* written on it had been taped to the metal frame. We slipped our guns out and took positions on either side of the door.

'This could be either good or bad,' Harrison said.

'Do you really think so?'

He shook his head.

'Neither do I,' I said.

I pulled the envelope loose from the tape and opened it up. Inside was a handwritten note that I carefully slid out holding it by the edges. There were two lines of elaborate script.

' "The evil that men do lives after them," ' I read.

I looked over at Harrison.

'That's Shakespeare,' he said. 'But he didn't use the rest of the quote.'

'Do you remember it?'

He thought for a moment. ' "The good is oft interred with their bones." '

I looked back at the note.

'There's more,' I said. ' "Cowards die many times before their death; the valiant never taste of death but once." More Shakespeare?' I slipped the note back into the envelope.

Harrison nodded. 'Julius Caesar.'

I reattached the envelope to the tape holding it on the door.

'I don't think we'll wait for the search warrant,' I said.

Harrison reached out and tested the handle.

'It's unlocked,' he said.

I nodded and he pushed the door open and we hugged the frame, staring into the darkened interior. There wasn't a sound inside. The odor of ink and graphite filled the air.

'Police,' I shouted. There was no response.

I swung around and moved my Glock back and forth across the darkness. I could see nothing.

'Try your light,' I said.

Harrison took out his Mag-lite and shined it into the loft. The narrow beam cut a small window into the darkness. Dust swirled in the light as he moved it across the space. The loft appeared to be divided by a single wall with an opening covered by a piece of heavy plastic sheet hung like a curtain.

'This room's clear,' said Harrison.

I stepped inside and reached around the door looking for a light switch but couldn't find one.

'Look.'

Dylan held the light on a large drawing four feet high tacked to the wall to the left of the door. It was a highly detailed image of two hands bound together with wire at the wrists. The wire appeared to cut into the skin. There were words written below the image.

'He's titled it the way Goya did,' I said. *This is how it begins*, it read.

'There're others,' said Harrison, moving the light across the room.

One by one the flashlight illuminated drawings tacked to the walls. Each one was different from the one before it, each depicting a detail of the anatomy undergoing some kind of abuse or torture. One was a bare back covered in bruises titled *A bad day*. Another one showed ankles bound with thick rope with the words *The origins of faith*. The last one was the back of a neck with bruising in the shape of fingers.

'*A guiding hand*,' Harrison said, reading the title. 'Could these be Keri?'

'Chow didn't find any evidence of abuse.'

I walked over and looked at the drawing of the bruised back.

'I don't think this is a girl,' I said.

'So are they pictures from the past victims, or of what's to come?' Harrison said.

I shook my head and stepped over to the drawing of the bound wrists.

'Maybe this is something else. Look at the hands, the skin. Those are a child's hands,' I said.

Harrison stepped over to the other drawings and examined them. 'They're all of children's bodies.'

'And nothing about what he's done so far suggests he's going after children.'

I shined my light across the first drawing again.

'*This is how it begins*,' I said.

'Madness?' Harrison said.

I looked over to him. 'Maybe these are all of the same child.'

'You mean Goya?'

'This could be his past.'

'It could also be something he did,' Harrison said.

I nodded. 'Either way he wanted us to find these so we would understand. The question is, what are we understanding?'

'The evil men do lives after them,' Harrison said. 'Which men? It still leaves the question, why kill a television reporter?'

'Maybe Wells knew of the abuse and failed to report it accurately.'

'That makes sense if Goya is the child in these drawing. But what if he's the perpetrator, or accused as one, but was innocent?'

We stared at the drawings for a moment in silence.

'Do you see anything in this room that suggests innocence of any kind?' I said.

Harrison shook his head.

'Was Wells Catholic?' I said.

'I don't know.'

'I want to know the name of every priest and victim connected with the lawsuit Bishop filed.'

'Since a settlement was reached in the case, those records may be sealed.'

I stepped over and looked at the drawing of the bruised back. 'More secrets.'

Harrison moved over to the opening into the other half of the loft, pulled back the hanging sheet of plastic and stepped through. I took out my own small Mag-lite and shined it on the drawing of the hands. The details were lifelike in their accuracy. It reminded me of studies I had seen of Michelangelo's work.

'I think you'd better look at this,' Harrison called out.

Through the plastic I could see his silhouette and the beam of light cutting through the darkness. I walked over, stepped through and stopped next to Dylan. Against the far wall under a set of windows covered with pieces of cardboard was a large chest freezer. The faint hum of its motor was audible.

'The rest of the room is clear,' Harrison said.

There was a mattress on the floor to the left. On the other side of the room was a small kitchen with a sink and a counter. Next to the kitchen was an open door to a bathroom containing toilet and shower. We holstered our weapons and stared in silence at the freezer across the room.

'I am free,' I said, quoting the letters found inside Keri.

'Maybe there's more than just her.'

'Let's get some light in here.'

Harrison pulled some of the cardboard free from the windows. Outside, the screech of a bus pulling to a stop was the only sound. I stepped over to the freezer and hesitated, a part of me not really wanting to know what was inside.

'Open it,' I said.

Harrison removed a handkerchief from his back pocket and laid it over the handle as he lifted the lid. The cold air rose up along with the stale odor of refrigeration and we shined our lights into the interior.

'Nothing,' Harrison said.

I stared into the empty box of the freezer. 'Not quite.' I shined my light at the left end of the box.

'Dents,' Harrison said.

I reached down and ran my fingers over the small depressions.

'Heel marks,' I said.

We looked at it for another moment then closed the lid.

'Cause of death, freezing,' Harrison said.

I stepped over to the window and looked out toward the concrete banks of the river. 'He knew we were going to find the apartment in Eagle Rock and he knew we would eventually find this. I wouldn't be surprised if he is watching us right now. If you were him, what would you expect us to do next?'

'Get a look at the lease, canvass the building, put surveillance on it.'

'None of which will probably help us.'

Harrison nodded in agreement.

'Let's do something different.'

'You have an idea.'

'Surprise him.' I looked back toward the other room of the loft. 'Make him the most famous artist in LA. Put those drawings on the ten o'clock news. Maybe someone will see something in them they recognize.'

'I'll get a photographer over here.'

My phone rang and I picked up. It was Traver.

'I got a look at the original brief that Bishop's law firm did on the case against the archdiocese. One of the alleged cases of abuse was in Pasadena in '90. No charges were ever filed.'

'Are the victims' names listed?'

'Only reference is to a male minor.'

'Is the investigating officer named?'

'A Detective Chavez.'

'Chief Chavez?'

'Yeah,' Traver said. 'A report was filed, but no copy of it exists in records.'

'Why is that?'

'I don't know. I asked him, but he won't talk to me. He'll talk to you.'

# fifteen

I met Chavez at a small bar as darkness fell over Pasadena. He was sitting in a booth in the back away from the suit-clad business crowd reliving the day's conquests. There were two empty glasses sitting in front him along with the one he cradled in the tips of his fingers. I could smell the bourbon. In the twenty years I had known him I had never seen him drink anything stronger than a beer. He was also a man of faith who attended Mass twice a week.

'You want a drink?' he asked.

I shook my head. 'No.'

'What do you know so far?'

'Eighteen years ago you investigated a case of possible abuse by a priest in Pasadena. A report was filed and that report vanished. You want to tell me why?'

Chavez shook his head. I placed a photograph of Goya's drawing of the bound hands on the table and slid it across to him.

'Wells had been forced to swallow another message before he was tortured. It read *Crimen Sollicitationis*,' I said.

The words clearly surprised Chavez.

'You know what that is?' he said.

I nodded. 'My mother still holds out hope that I'll return to the Church. She sends me a monthly subscription to the *Catholic Reporter*.'

Chavez picked up the picture. His eyes held on the image for a moment as if he was replaying some piece of memory in his mind.

'We found it today in Goya's studio; there're half a dozen more of a similar nature. It's titled *This is how it begins*.'

'Were you able to ID him?'

I shook my head. 'He rents spaces low in demand and pays with cash, months in advance.'

'What about other people in the building?'

'Nothing that would help. Half of the building is empty.'

Chavez set the photograph down and leaned back.

'Tell me about 1990,' I said.

Chavez took a slow deep breath as if preparing himself for a blow. 'If you know what *Crimen Sollicitationis* is, then you know I can't talk about it.'

'*Crimen Sollicitationis* is no longer canon law.'

'Call me old-fashioned, but you can't take back an oath to God.'

'It wasn't to God, it was to the Church.'

'As a Catholic, you know there's no difference.'

'I'm not talking to a Catholic, I'm talking to a cop. What happened to that report?

Chavez hesitated.

'Tell me who suppressed it.'

He didn't answer.

'Albert, talk to me.'

'What makes you think there's a connection to Goya?'

'The look in your eyes.'

Chavez shook his head. 'The priest in question was removed from any duties where he would have had contact with children. He would be much too old now to be responsible for the things Goya is doing.'

'I'm not looking for a priest,' I said. 'I think Goya was a victim of one. Unless I'm very wrong, this drawing and the other in the loft are self-portraits.'

Chavez looked at the photograph again and then closed his eyes.

'We've tried to get copies of the suit Bishop's firm filed, but it was part of the settlement agreement that the records would be sealed. If Goya was one of the children abused by that priest, you and that missing report are the only things that may lead me to Goya.'

Chavez shook his head again.

'Do you know how many victims there were in this archdiocese, how many priests were involved?' he said.

'Yes, I looked it up. Over five hundred victims, possibly as many as a hundred and twenty-two priests involved.'

'The case I investigated wasn't part of any lawsuit.'

'How do you know that?'

'Because it never went beyond me,' Chavez said. 'No one wanted it to be made public at the time.'

'What do you mean, no one?'

'I mean just what I said.'

'In the department?'

Chavez nodded. 'And out.'

The meaning of what he had just told me began to spread through my gut like a virus. I didn't want to hear what he was about to say, I didn't want to know that he had been a part of it, but there was no turning back at this point.

'Pressure was brought down on you?' I asked.

He smiled grimly, then took another sip of his drink. 'Not even the boys' parents wanted it to get outside the church.'

'Did anyone ask the boys what they wanted?'

He closed his eyes and shook his head. Everything I believed about being a cop was because of this man, and he was about to burn it all down.

'It was you who buried it.'

He sat in silence for a moment. 'It's dangerous to look back, but after enough time and practice almost anything can be justified . . . almost.'

'I'm not doing this to hurt you,' I said.

'It's long overdue.' Albert looked at me, his soft brown eyes moist with emotion. 'Did I ever tell you who was the youngest detective to ever make captain in the department?'

I shook my head. 'I don't want to know this,' I said.

'You have to.'

I looked into his eyes. 'You.'

Chavez nodded. 'I did as I was told and acted like a good Catholic, instead of a good cop. And now I'm chief of the department.'

I sat for a moment in silence, trying to find a way out of what I had just learned, but there was no looking away from it.

'Did you do it because you thought it was the right thing, or because you thought it would help your career?'

Albert picked up his drink and looked into the smoky liquid as if he was staring directly into his past.

'The results are the same either way, so it doesn't really matter, does it?'

'It does to me,' I said.

He took a breath. 'I knew what I was doing.'

'So my career has been part of your mea culpa?'

He looked at me. 'Something good had to come out of it.'

I reached over, slipped his drink from his hands and took a sip from it. Neither of us said a word. It was as if the very ground we had been standing on for all these years had shifted.

'What do you want me to do?' Albert asked finally.

'Goya's going to kill again, and I think it's going to happen soon,' I said. 'I need to know what you know.'

He shook his head. 'It's not that simple.'

'It is, actually.'

Chavez looked into my eyes as if he had heard more than I had said.

'When my mother and I were being abused by my father,' I said, 'she went to her priest and told him in confession what was happening. He told her that if she was a good wife, it would stop, but if she left him, she would be committing a sin.'

Chavez looked down at his hands.

'A good wife,' I said softly.

Chavez glanced one last time at the photograph and then handed it back to me and nodded.

'How many children had been abused that you knew of?' I asked.

'There was only one official complaint that I investigated. The victim named two other boys.'

'Do you have a copy of the report?'

He shook his head. 'It and all my notes were destroyed.'

'Do you remember names?'

He sat silently for a moment. 'Just the one I investigated . . . Donald Bonner. It was because of him I knew there were at least two other victims.'

'How old were they?'

'Early teens.'

'Did you interview them?'

He shook his head. 'According to the church their identities were kept from me at the request of the parents.'

'Would this Donald know the names of the others?'

'He took his own life several months after I interviewed him.'

'How did he die?'

'He hanged himself from a tree.' Chavez picked up the empty highball glass and stared at his distorted reflection.

'What was the priest's name?'

Chavez hesitated and then nodded.

'Father Patrick,' he said, as if relieving himself of an old burden.

'Did you interview him?'

Chavez nodded again. 'Once. He claimed he was innocent.' The chief glanced at me and then looked down the length of the bar.

'You believed him?' I said.

'As a cop, or a Catholic?' Chavez leaned in and looked down at his hands. 'Truth and faith are strange bedfellows. He was guilty of something, I have no doubt about that, but at some level he was also telling me the truth. What that meant, I never had to discover.'

'Which church was it?'

'St Gabriel's.'

'What happened to him?'

'He became the chaplin at a small Catholic hospital in San Bernardino. Every few years they would move him again. Giving him duties that didn't require him to work with children.'

'According to the church?'

Chavez thought for a moment and nodded.

'Are you sure Donald's death was a suicide?'

He looked at me in surprise. 'I wasn't the investigating officer. I saw the report; nothing seemed wrong with it. Why?'

'In the original set of prints that Goya did in 1812, one of them was of a man who had been hanged from a tree.'

Chavez tried to work the logic out in his head but couldn't. 'Why kill one of the other victims?'

'I don't know.'

'That would make him only fifteen or sixteen when he committed his first murder.'

I picked up the photograph of the drawing. 'He had a lot of early training in violence. Would it do any good to go to the church for the identities of the other boys?'

Chavez shook his head. 'Even if the records still existed. They've had centuries of practice at keeping secrets.'

'Do you think Father Patrick would talk?'

'He talks to you, he incriminates himself.'

'He might also save his own life.'

Chavez considered it. 'I could try contacting him.'

'I think it would be better if it came from me,' I said.

Chavez looked at me and nodded.

'Do you know where he is now?'

'He's semi-retired. He'll assist with sacraments during Mass, but nothing more than that.'

'Where?'

'A small church in the high desert, St Anne's. He lives in the rectory there.'

'Is there anything else you can tell me that might help?'

Chavez stared straight ahead without looking at me and nodded. 'Wells knew of the case.'

I looked at him for a moment, not sure I had just heard the words correctly, or not wanting to believe them.

'You knew this and you didn't tell me?'

'I'm telling you now. I had to be certain there was a connection.'

'How much more of a connection than his body did you need?'

Chavez looked away from me and seemed to struggle to catch his breath. 'This was before he was an anchor. He was young and ambitious.'

'How much did he know?'

'Whispers, rumors of secrets. Whatever he had, he knew he was on to something big.'

'Did he know names?'

'If he did, he didn't share that with me.'

'Did you tell him anything?'

'No.'

'Where did he go then?'

'The archdiocese. I don't know who he talked to.'

'Did he file a story?'

He looked at me and shook his head.

'What happened?'

'I think he was bought off by the archdiocese, or someone with equally deep pockets. He killed the story, just like I did.'

'Until Bishop's lawsuit?'

Chavez nodded. 'It was public knowledge then. Even so, he never mentioned the allegations involving St Gabriel's.'

I got up from the table and started to walk out.

'That drawing,' Chavez said.

I sat back down and handed him the photograph. Chavez took it from me and stared at it.

'What about it?' I asked.

'The way the wrists are bound. The rope.'

'What about it?'

'It's cotton. Like the rope a Franciscan uses on his robes.' He handed it back to me then closed his fist tightly around his glass.

'It was one of the things Donald said had happened to him.'

At the other end of the bar Harrison motioned to me with a nod and then stepped outside. I slipped the photograph back in my pocket and stood up.

'I can't promise you that I'll keep this secret. It could become awkward for you,' I said.

Chavez looked up at me.

'Good,' he said softly.

'I'm sorry, Albert,' I said.

He shook his head. 'You have nothing to be sorry for, Alex. Everything you've ever done as a cop has made me very proud.'

I turned and walked quickly down the length of the bar past a dozen different conversations, each becoming lost in the other, all becoming the same low whisper. I pushed through the door and stepped outside. The rain had turned to a heavy mist. The brake lights of cars stopped in traffic on Colorado reflected in the mist, giving the pavement a red glow. I couldn't get the fresh air into me fast enough, as if it would help purge what I had just learned.

Harrison stepped out of the unmarked squad and walked over. He started to say something, then stopped. 'Are you OK?'

I shook my head and looked up into the mist, letting it fall on my face.

'Don't look back,' I whispered.

'What?'

'A Donald Bonner committed suicide several years ago. I need to see the report.'

'I'll have it pulled.'

I looked back at the door to the bar as it opened and two businessmen walked out.

'What happened?' he asked.

'The man who made my career just handed me the hammer to tear his own down with,' I said.

'Am I supposed to understand that?'

I shook my head. 'Not yet . . . Have you something for me?'

'A citizen called in a complaint about graffiti. A black and white was sent out and they called us.'

'It's not graffiti.'

Dylan shook his head. 'The FBI agent Utley is going to meet us there.'

107

'Goya?' I said.

Harrison nodded. 'That's my guess.'

'What is it?'

'I think it's a picture of his next victim.'

# sixteen

We drove east on Orange and then north toward the mountains, the mist seeming to get heavier with each block that we passed. We pulled off at Sierra Madre Boulevard into the nearly empty parking lot. Harrison stopped the squad and stared at the building.

'A church,' he said.

I shook my head.

'Not just a church,' I said. 'St Gabriel's.'

Harrison turned to me. 'That means something to you?'

I nodded. 'Yes, I think so.'

He waited for me to say more, but I stayed silent.

'I could ask how you know, but I won't,' Dylan said.

'Thank you.'

'Doesn't mean I'm happy about it.'

'That makes two of us,' I said, and looked back at the church's outline in the dull wet darkness.

It was one of those buildings built in the fifties that attempted to bring the Church out of its Gothic past by giving it a modern face. All it really resulted in was bad architecture.

'The painting's apparently on the east side of the chapel.'

A gray Ford carrying Agent Utley pulled up next to us and we all got out.

'You have something for me?' I asked Utley.

He looked up into the sky and pulled his collar tightly around his neck. 'Maybe. Whether it's useful depends what's on this wall.'

'It's been painted below the stained-glass window behind the altar,' Harrison said.

We followed a paved walkway around the far corner and Harrison took out his Mag-lite and pointed it toward the back wall of the church. It was a painting of a blindfolded figure bound to a pole. His wrists were tied in front of him, but his hands were gone. Blood streamed from a wound in his neck. We stared in silence.

'It's a priest,' Harrison said.

'There're words underneath it,' Utley said. '*Silentium Dei?*'

'More Latin,' I said.

'God's silence,' Harrison said.

Utley took a step closer to the painting, staring intently at it.

'Why this church?' he asked.

'I have reason to believe this is where Goya was abused by a priest.'

Both of them turned to me.

'How do you know that?' Utley asked.

'I'm not able to tell you that just yet.'

'If you know that, then you must have an ID?'

I shook my head. 'We wouldn't be standing here if I did.'

Utley looked at me for a moment. 'Nothing like an open exchange of information.'

'That's the best I can do at the moment,' I said. 'We need to inform the archdiocese about this.'

'We can't protect every priest in the city,' said Harrison.

'You don't have to,' Utley said.

'Why?' I asked.

Utley stared for a moment at the painting. 'I think this priest is already dead.'

We both looked at him.

'How do you know?' I said.

'An open exchange of information, it works wonders.' Utley looked at the painting for another moment, then turned back to us.

'I've been going through the serial killer data base. VICAP turned up nothing on similar slayings within the last few years, so I expanded the scope of the inquiry.'

'How?'

'Geographically.'

'How far?'

'Interpol came up empty.' He looked at the painting again and then reached into his jacket and removed an envelope. 'This came from the Mexican federal police a few hours ago.'

He handed me the envelope and I opened it. Inside were two snapshot-size photographs. I slipped them out.

'A crime scene,' I said.

He nodded. 'His name was Father Monroe.'

I stared at the pictures for a moment, and then turned and looked back at the painting on the wall.

'They're the same man,' I said.

Utley nodded. 'It happened three years ago.'

'Do you have a date?'

'December.'

'Where in Mexico?'

'Baja.'

'When did Keri disappear?' I asked.

'A couple of months before that. October,' Harrison said.

'He was a priest in the LA archdiocese. The Mexican police attributed the murders to drug traffickers. He was strangled and stabbed, and his hands were cut off.'

I glanced at the pictures. 'Calling these stab wounds is an understatement.'

Utley nodded. 'I think the Mexican authorities' conclusion may prove to be premature.'

'Were his hands recovered?' Harrison asked.

'No.'

'What was he doing in Mexico?' I asked.

'According to a statement by the archdiocese he was supposed to be on a fishing trip, though there is no record of him ever stepping onto a boat.'

'What parish was he assigned to?'

'He wasn't. Monroe worked within the archdiocese.'

'Doing what?'

'The Church has been vague at best with details. But along with being ordained he also had a law degree. The closest I could come to an actual description of duties is that he handled both legal and business affairs.'

'Son of a bitch,' I whispered to myself.

'That means something to you?' Utley asked.

'It's possible. Did his duties include working with cases of suspected abuse?'

'You mean did he participate in covering it up?'

I nodded. Utley turned and looked back at the painting.

'I haven't been able to confirm his duties with the Church, but it would seem a logical conclusion that someone with his expertise would participate in some capacity. But that's the thing with conspiracies, isn't it? If we had the answers, there wouldn't be one.'

'Was there any message left with the body that could connect the killing to either Wells or Keri Bishop?'

'Not in so many words.'

I looked over to the painting on the wall. 'So how did you know his murder was connected?'

He removed another envelope from his pocket and took out a third photograph. 'This was found in the priest's mouth.'

I looked at the picture, then handed it to Harrison.

'A saint's medal,' he said. 'Could have been his own.'

I shook my head. 'I don't think so.'

'Why?'

'That's St Paul.'

'And that means what?'

'For Catholics he's the patron saint of truth.'

'That's the connection,' said Utley.

'The truth is dead,' Harrison said.

I looked over to the church again.

'You said a citizen had called this in,' I said. 'They leave a name?'

'No,' Harrison said.

I looked around at the surrounding landscape. In the heavy mist visibility was little more than several hundred feet.

'You can't see this wall from any of the streets or houses. And no one is going for a walk tonight. What was the area code of the phone that called it in?'

'Eight one eight.'

'This is six two six.'

'It could be a cell?'

'I want a location on where that call originated.'

I looked at the wall that held the painting. Tucked at the south corner was a door.

'Goya called us,' I said.

Harrison nodded. 'Makes sense.'

'But he didn't bring us here to only see this.'

'What then?' Utley asked.

I looked at the painting and shook my head. 'He could have painted this anywhere. He chose this church for a reason.'

'You said it was the one where he may have been abused,' Utley said.

I stared at the door. What appeared to be a shadow wasn't one at all. I slipped my gun out of my holster.

'The door is open,' I said. 'He wants us to go inside.'

'Doing what he wants doesn't sound like a very good idea,' Utley said.

'You have another one?' I asked.

He shook his head and we started moving. The door was an emergency exit. Through the open crack I could see the faint glow from the red exit sign reflecting off the opposite wall. Harrison pulled the door open the rest of the way and I stepped inside, raising my weapon.

'Hallway,' I whispered and moved forward.

The corridor appeared to run all the way to the front of the church. At the far end of the corridor a curtain was drawn across what I presumed was an opening on the right-hand side. Before that there were two doors. I went up to the first and listened for a sound on the other side, then turned the handle and pushed it open. I waited for a response and when none came I stepped in. The faint outline of a white-robed figure stood at the other side of the room.

I raised my Glock.

'Police,' I said. 'Turn around.'

The figure didn't move. As Harrison came in behind me with his weapon raised I lowered mine.

'Turn on the light,' I said.

He switched on the light and lowered his gun also.

'Robes,' he said.

'It's the sacristy.'

A set of vestments draped over a hanger gave the appearance of a person standing on the other side of the room. I stepped back out into the hallway. Utley was standing at the second door.

'Restroom's clear,' he said softly.

We went past him to the curtain and stopped.

'I haven't been inside a church in twenty years,' I whispered to Harrison.

He half smiled.

'Good luck.'

I pulled the curtain back and we stepped through into the main chapel.

'The nave,' I whispered.

In the darkness I could make out the lines of pews stretching toward the far side of the chapel. A row of candles burning in front of a small shrine to the left of the pulpit gave off just enough illumination to see. There wasn't a sound anywhere, nor any movement.

'He wants us to find something here. Where would you put it?'

Harrison shook his head. 'Don't ask me. My parents were Unitarians.'

Utley stepped up behind us.

'You're the profiler. Where would Goya leave something?' I asked.

He looked toward the other end of the church. A large crucifix was suspended in the air behind the sanctuary. Candle-light flickered across the pale figure of Christ hanging from the cross.

'The altar,' Utley said.

I nodded. 'You go down the sides, I'll go up the middle.'

I walked over to the center aisle where a font sat on a pedestal. Out of some distant ingrained memory I found myself reaching forward, but the moment I touched the liquid I quickly pulled my hand away, staring at the dark fluid clinging to the tips of my fingers.

'This isn't holy water. The font's filled with blood,' I said.

Both Harrison and Utley stopped where they stood. I wiped the blood off and looked over to Harrison.

'Another victim?' he asked.

'Only the blood of Christ can cleanse us of sin, which we all have,' I said. 'How would Goya interpret that?'

'It could be his own,' Utley said.

'Equating his life to Christ's.'

Utley nodded. 'He sees his work as a form of sacrifice.'

I rushed up the aisle glancing down each pew until I reached the last one. Slowly I stepped up past the rail that separated the congregation from the sanctuary. There was nothing on the pulpit, nothing on the lectern to the right.

Harrison walked past me and searched around the altar.

'There's nothing here,' he said.

Utley stepped over to the candlelit shrine. 'There's nothing here either.' He shook his head and looked around. 'He must have transported the blood from somewhere else.'

'We're missing something,' Harrison said.

'Did you reach to the bottom of the font?' Utley asked. 'There could be something in it.'

I shook my head.

'I have some rubber gloves in my squad.' He started back down the aisle.

'Wait,' I said.

Utley stopped. In the darkness I hadn't noticed the three doors on the north side of the chapel.

'There,' I said. 'If he left something else, it would be there.'

'The confessionals,' Harrison said.

I nodded and started forward, my hand tightening around the handle of the Glock. I stopped a few feet short as Harrison and Utley stepped up next to me.

'Which one?' Harrison said.

116

'The penitents sit on either side, the priest in the middle,' I said. 'Goya isn't trying to unburden his own sins, he's punishing others for theirs.'

'The middle one,' said Utley.

'That would be my guess.'

I stepped forward, raised my weapon, then reached out and swung the door open. In the darkness I could just make out the shape of the bench where the priest would sit.

'Check the others,' I said, and Harrison and Utley moved to open the doors.

I stepped in, and felt fingers brush the side of my face. I swung around and another hand touched the back of my neck. I jumped back out the open door.

'I need your light,' I said.

Harrison came out and pointed the light into the center box. Two severed hands suspended by a string swung gently back and forth inside. Utley stepped out and stared in silence.

'There's no blood on the floor,' Harrison said.

I took the flashlight from Harrison and looked closely at the hands. 'The wrists wounds appear to have been cauterized.'

'The priest's hands?' Utley said.

I examined the fingers. 'They're still cold. He kept them frozen.'

'Perhaps Goya's abuse began right here,' Utley said. 'What better place for a secret to begin?'

'Or maybe this was where it was absolved,' I said. 'With the movement of a hand to the points of a cross?'

I stepped back out of the confessional and looked around the chapel.

'What is he doing?' Utley said. 'If Father Monroe knew of the abuse and concealed it, I understand why he was killed. But that doesn't explain what happened to Wells and Keri Bishop.'

'Wells knew of the abuse when it first happened,' I said. 'But he never reported it. He may have been paid off.'

Utley looked at me. 'What else do you know?'

'There may have been a fourth victim.'

'Who?'

'There were three victims of abuse in this church. The one who went to the police was named Bonner, and was found hanged several months later. At the time it was called a suicide. My guess is Goya killed him.'

'I think it's time for you share with us what you know,' Utley said.

I looked at Dylan and he nodded in agreement.

'The rope he was hanged with was identical to the one depicted in Goya's drawings.'

'There's got to be more of a connection than that.'

'Outside, Goya paints God's silence. He puts *Crimen Sollicitationis* inside Wells. I think some way or another all his victims took part in concealing the truth about what happened here. Bonner was the one whose deal with St Gabriel's started the silence.'

'That doesn't explain the girl's death,' Utley said.

'Or it does and we just don't understand it yet,' I said.

'If you're right, then that puts anyone involved with what happened in this church at risk,' Utley said. 'That could go all the way to the head of the archdiocese.'

A chill went through me.

'It may go farther than that,' I said. 'I think we have only four days to find him.'

Harrison and Utley both realized what I was talking about.

'The Papal visit,' Utley said.

I nodded. 'He's celebrating Mass at the Rose Bowl.'

'That's why Goya took the job there,' Harrison said.

'It's a possibility,' I said. 'And even if he isn't after the Pope, the entire hierarchy of the archdiocese will be present.'

'He would have his pick,' Harrison said.

'Who's handling security?' asked Utley.

'The Papal Guard and the secret service handle his immediate protection. Pasadena PD is coordinating the security of the facility, and other agencies are contributing personnel.'

I picked up my phone and dialed Chavez. After four rings I got his recording. I left a message for him to call me immediately and hung up.

'Chief Chavez?' Harrison said.

'Get dispatch to find him, and when they do, put a squad on him. I want him protected.'

Harrison looked at me for a moment. 'That's how you knew about this church and the other victim.'

I nodded.

'How did Chavez know?' Utley asked.

I looked over to Dylan.

'We're way past trying to protect someone,' he said.

I took a breath and nodded. 'Chavez was the investigating officer in the first case here.' I looked at them both for a moment. 'He was pressured to bury the report.'

'Did he?' Harrison asked.

'Yes.'

'Who pressured him?' said Utley.

'The department, the city, St Gabriel's. All their hands were dirty apparently. According to Chavez even the parents wanted the accusations to be kept secret.'

'Do you have names of those involved with silencing the report?' Utley asked.

'Other than those who are already dead? No. Chavez didn't even know the names of the other victims. They were kept from him by the church.'

'And you think Goya may be one of those victims?'

I nodded. 'It's one answer that seems to make sense.'

'What happened to the accused priest?'

'He was moved around to different parishes, given duties that didn't include contact with children.'

'According to the church,' Utley said.

'Yes.'

'Is he alive?'

'Chavez thought so.'

'If what you're saying holds, we only have four days to figure out who Goya is.'

'Get forensics here. I want a type on the blood in the font, and see if the prints on the hands match the dead priest's DMV records.'

I turned and started to walk away.

'Where are you going?' Harrison asked.

I stopped next to the font. In the dim light I could just make out my reflection in the dark pool of blood.

'To find a priest.'

# seventeen

The drive across the Valley and up to the high desert took a little over an hour. When I reached the top of the pass the clouds and mist that blanketed the basin gave way to clear skies and a nearly full moon. The lights of Palmdale and Lancaster spread out across the flat plain, stretching toward the dry lakebeds of Edwards Air Force Base and the extinct volcanoes of the empty desert to the north.

St Anne the Divine was a Spanish-style church built back in the fifties east of town to tend to the needs of the growing military presence and the expected subdivisions to come. A school had been planned to follow, but when it was discovered that the small ridge of irregular granite the church had been sited beside was the San Andreas Fault, the school was built miles to the north along with most of the subdivisions.

What surrounded St Anne's now were small bungalows inhabited by Mexican immigrants, dirt roads, and the occasional horse walking the fence line of one-acre ranchettes.

It was nearing ten when I pulled to a stop outside the chapel. The church dwarfed the small houses that lined the rest of the street. Like the old missions, it had a bell tower. The large boulders that marked the entrance to the parking lot were painted white and reflected the moonlight.

There were no lights on inside the chapel. In the windows of the rectory in back of the church I could see the cool glow of a television reflecting through the glass. I got out of the Volvo and started toward the rectory. The air was sweet with sage from the desert. A television satellite dish was mounted on the roof. The sound of Mexican music drifted from a car radio somewhere in the darkness.

I followed the stone path toward the rectory past two tall willow trees. There were two names on sliding plaques next to the front door, MONSIGNOR TAVARES and FATHER PATRICK. There was no bell so I knocked and the heavy wooden door swung open into the room.

'Monsignor Tavares,' I called out.

There was no response. I took a step in. The scent of cigarettes recently smoked hung in the air. I was standing in a simply furnished living apartment. Several crucifixes adorned the walls, and there was a small shrine with a statue of a saint in it. I recognized the figure and felt my pulse quicken.

'St Paul,' I whispered.

The picture on the television had been frozen, the remote left on the floor in front of the set. A newscaster sat at his desk, one of Goya's drawings we had found filling the blue screen over his shoulder.

'Father Patrick,' I called.

Again there was no response. I stepped through the living room into a small kitchen. A cup of coffee had been left on the table. I walked over and placed my fingers against the side of the cup – it was still warm. The back door leading outside was halfway open.

I went across and opened it. The desert stretched away into the distance. The sound of a jet taking off from Andrews rumbled out of the darkness like thunder and then fell silent. I walked around the rectory and followed the path through the willows to the entrance of the church. The heavy wooden door was open and I stepped inside.

At the far end of the chapel a dozen or more candles burned next to the altar, their light reflecting off the whitewashed walls. A figure in long white vestments was kneeling in front of the candles, his back turned to me, head lowered in prayer.

I stepped up to the font at the back of the aisle and glanced at its contents – water.

'Father Patrick,' I said.

The figure didn't move. I started to reach for my gun but as my fingers touched the cool plastic of the handle I stopped myself. I stepped past the font and walked up the center aisle through the rows of pews.

'I'm a police—' I began to say.

'I know who you are,' the figure said.

I reached the first row and stopped.

'Then you also know why I'm here,' I said.

'Yes, I know. I will not help you.'

I started to take another step. 'Father—'

'Come no closer. I have a weapon.'

I stopped.

'I didn't come here to arrest you,' I said. 'I won't come any closer.'

I reached down and slipped my gun out of the holster.

'What is your name?' the priest asked.

'Delillo . . . Lieutenant,' I said.

'Are you a Catholic, Lieutenant?'

I hesitated; I hadn't been asked a direct question like that by a priest for many years.

'I was.'

'You lost faith.'

'Yes, I suppose I did,' I answered.

'In the Church, or God?'

'I'm not sure.'

He nodded. 'I have been tested in much the same way. Those are the times we live in, aren't they? You know the Church has renamed the act of confession? Now you reconcile with God, you don't confess your sins. It's not the same thing. They've cheapened the act. Would you like me to hear your confession? It's all I've been allowed to do for many years.'

'I think I would rather hear yours, Father,' I said.

He turned as if he was going to look back at me, but stopped.

'You abused three boys while at St Gabriel's,' I said.

He shook his head. 'No.'

'I've talked to the officer who investigated it.'

'That's not the way it was.'

'One of those boys is killing those involved with covering it up. Four people are dead, and there are going to be others if I don't stop him.'

'Please go,' he said.

'You know who Goya is. I need his name.'

'I will not help you.'

'Why?'

'You would not understand.'

'One of those he killed was burned alive. Goya tortured him.'

Patrick began to shake his head.

'He cut out his eyes, cut off his tongue.'

He lifted his hand.

'Stop.'

'The boy who accused you was hanged from a tree.'

'No,' he whispered.

'Tell me what happened.'

He lowered his head and took a deep breath. 'There was a relationship. He was sixteen, he loved me and I loved him.'

'You were his priest.'

He nodded. 'I was weak.'

'You're being kind to yourself, Father.'

'Yes. When he discovered there were others I loved, he accused me of abuse.'

'How many others?'

He shook his head. 'I don't remember.'

'That's not love. Love you would remember.'

'I never hurt anyone.'

'Goya was one of them?'

'Not as you are thinking. I couldn't. I wouldn't.'

'You tied him up.'

'I never touched him.'

'Did you see the drawings? I can show you more pictures if you need to refresh your memory. Those are not pictures of love.'

'No.'

'Did you do that to him?'

He shook his head. 'I did not.'

'Then who did?'

'No one,' he whispered.

'Someone did.'

'It's not as you think.'

'Then clarify it for me.'

He started to answer but hesitated.

'Who?' I yelled.

'Donald. It was Donald. The pictures are not of Goya, as you call him.'

'Donald Bonner? The boy you had the relationship with?'

Patrick nodded. I ran it through my head, trying to understand what he was saying.

'Goya did that to him? He tortured him?' I asked.

'Yes,' Patrick said and then buried his face in his hands and began to weep.

'You knew that Goya murdered him, and you did nothing?'

'I could not.'

'Why?'

He took a deep, heavy breath.

'You learned of it in confession?' I said.

'The seal of the confessional is absolute. Breaking that law results in immediate excommunication.'

'A rope was put around his neck and he was hanged from a tree. Can you picture that, Father?'

'I didn't learn of it in confession.'

'Then why didn't you speak up?'

'He believed he was doing God's work and protecting me.'

I tried to make sense of his words running the images of the last few days like a horror show in my head.

'Protecting you? From what?'

'Lies.'

'*Crimen Sollicitationis*,' I said softly. 'That's it, isn't it? He's not murdering those who have kept a secret, he's killing those who broke the one that threatens you.'

He looked toward the altar.

'The Church changed that law,' I said.

Patrick shook his head. 'Public relations cannot change God's law. When a law is broken, there will be punishment.'

'Murder is against God's law.'

'He is not a murderer.'

'What do you call him?'

'How well do you know your Catholic history?' Patrick said.

'I went to Sunday school.'

'There have always been those in the Church who have done

what must happen to defend the faith and cleanse the Church of those who would destroy it.'

'Cleanse?' I could feel the hair on the back of my neck stand up. 'What are you are talking about?'

'History is not made without sacrifice. The Church like all great societies must protect itself. There are no names, no faces, but they have always been here, doing what has to be done.'

'This isn't the Middle Ages, Father.'

'God's law is absolute.'

'Why are you protecting him?'

'Goya as you call him did not kill those others,' Patrick said. 'He couldn't do such things.'

'How do you know?'

'Because I've been his teacher.'

'Of what?'

'Truth.'

I slid a foot forward as silently as I could and took a step. 'Truth? The truth has been twisted.'

'Truth is often difficult to understand.'

'Do you want to know what your truth looks like, Father – a young women frozen to death inside a locked freezer. A reporter burned to death after having his tongue and eyes cut out,' I said.

'God's judgment,' he said.

I took another step. 'Who is he?'

His head turned.

'Don't come any closer.'

I stopped where I stood, a dozen paces from him. 'Give me a name.'

'All flesh is weak, Lieutenant.'

'That doesn't answer the question,' I said.

'I suspect you will understand someday, Lieutenant . . . if you live long enough.'

'Who are the other boys? If you want to save their lives, give me their names.'

'I cannot.'

'He's murdering people. Is that what you call God's work?'

'I am but a servant. I will pray for them.'

'That's not enough.'

'It is all I can give.'

He looked up toward the crucifix behind the altar and then lowered his head.

'We thank God for the great gift of our son and ask him to restore our child to health if such be his holy will. This favor we beg of you through your love for all children and your mother. Amen.'

'You're going to have to come with me, Father,' I said.

'Your law has no meaning in this church.'

'It won't be in this church where you'll be judged.'

'God's judgment is the only one I recognize.'

'That will come later,' I said. 'I have reason to believe he's going to try to kill the Pope.'

He looked at me with a mix of surprise and confusion in his eyes. 'He would not harm the Holy Father.'

'How do you know?'

He began to shake his head. 'No. You're wrong.'

'He's no longer your pupil. You must help me stop him.'

He began to tremble. 'I can't.'

'You need help, Father. I can get that for you.'

'There is only one thing I can do that may help you, Lieutenant,' he whispered and raised his hand to cross himself.

'Father Patrick,' I said.

His arm dropped to his side and a knife fell from his hand onto the floor.

'Father—' I began, but the hem of the white vestments covering his legs was turning red from the blood streaming out of his body.

He shuddered for a moment, then his shoulders sagged and he fell backward off the steps where he kneeled.

I rushed over and reached out to put pressure on the wound, but the volume of blood was beyond my ability to stop it. He had cleanly cut his carotid artery with the knife as he made the sign of the cross. His eyes locked on mine and I took his hand.

'Can you understand me?' I asked.

He blinked his eyes as if to say yes.

'Who is he?'

He didn't react.

'Tell me a name. It's not too late to stop this.'

Patrick mouthed a word, but I couldn't understand.

'Try again,' I said.

He tried to say several words, but the air escaping out of the open wound in his neck made it difficult to produce a sound. I covered the glistening opening of his windpipe with my hand to stop the flow of air.

'*Filius meus*,' he said whispered.

His hand tightened around mine and then began to relax. The blood pumping from his neck decreased with each beat of the heart. His breathing began to rapidly increase and then slowed just as quickly.

'It was men I lost faith in, not God,' I said. 'I'm sorry, I don't have any prayers to say for you.'

His eyes stayed on mine for a moment, then he looked past me toward the altar and they sank into the dull glaze of death. I placed his hand on his chest then stepped back from the spreading pool of blood around his body. My hands were covered in it. I realized I was trembling, and my heart was racing. I stepped back to a row of pews, sat down and waited for the rush of adrenalin to pass. I had investigated hundreds of murders where an empty shell of a body is a puzzle waiting to be solved, but this was different. Actual death holds none of the fascination of its aftermath. A heart no matter how flawed had just stopped beating, and every time I've witnessed it I've walked away diminished.

I called LA county sheriffs to inform them of a suicide then walked back to the rectory, washed the blood from my hands in the kitchen sink and then stepped into the smaller bedroom.

There was a single bed, a dresser with half a dozen drawers and a closet. I went through the closet first. It held two sets of the dark clothes of a priest and the rest were casual clothes and a sport coat. I went through all the pockets, not sure what I was looking for, but found nothing.

A thin dark leather wallet was laid on top of the dresser. There were no credit cards, no driver's license, only his identifica-tion from the archdiocese. In the cash flap there were twenty-two dollars in bills and a small worn black and white photograph of a young pregnant women with dark hair and olive skin, staring at something just to the left of the camera lens, as if she were looking at someone or something standing next to the photographer. The beads of a rosary dangled from her hands. Behind her, the spire of a church steeple rose into the sky. On the back of the photograph a name had been written in faded pencil.

*Mary.*

As I opened the first drawer of the dresser I heard footsteps stop at the door behind me.

'What is the meaning of this intrusion?'

I turned around. A Hispanic man in his early forties wearing a bowling shirt stood in the doorway.

'You must be Monsignor Tavares,' I said.

He nodded and I showed him my badge and identified myself.

'You still haven't explained yourself, Lieutenant,' he said.

I told him that Father Patrick had taken his own life in the chapel. He raised his hand to his lips and then crossed himself.

'I must go to him,' he said and began to turn.

I stopped him as the lights of a sheriff's squad pulling into the parking lot shined through the window.

'Did Father Patrick ever mention the name Goya to you?'

It took him a moment to rearrange his thoughts. 'The painter?'

I nodded.

'He was one of his favorites. He gave me a copy of one of his drawings a few weeks ago. I have it in my bedroom.'

'Could I see it?'

'Is this necessary now?'

'Yes.'

He stepped out the room and opened the door to his own room across the hallway. On the far wall next to a window was a small drawing in a frame. It showed a priest in long robes, balancing on a sagging tightrope suspended over a jeering crowd.

'You said he gave this to you a few weeks ago.'

'Yes. I think he saw it as a reflection of his own life. He called it the precariousness of faith. Though I don't believe that was the actual title.'

'He was angry with the Church and the way he had been treated?' I asked.

'The modern Church held little appeal for him. He believed that we should return to the principles of the first Vatican council.'

'Papal infallibility. And by extension priests'.'

Tavares shook his head. 'Those days have been gone for a very long time.'

I looked at him for a moment. 'But there are still secrets.'

He looked at me with an air of suspicion. 'What brought you here, Lieutenant?'

I looked at the picture of the balancing priest. 'Loss of faith, I suppose.'

'Are you a Catholic?'

'I was once, a long time ago. Did Father Patrick ever discuss the charges that were made against him?'

He looked at me for a moment. 'If he ever had, it would have been in a context that I would be unable to discuss.'

'I'm investigating a murder, and trying to stop another one. That's why I came, Father.'

'Murder?'

I took out the photograph I had found in Father Patrick's wallet and showed it to him.

'Does this picture mean anything to you?'

Father Tavares looked at it and shook his head. 'It looks old. I've never seen it before.'

'Does he have family?'

'I know of no living next of kin. Perhaps it is his mother.'

'Perhaps.'

He took a deep breath and shook his head.

'It is a sin to take one's life,' he said. 'A terrible sin.' He turned and began to leave.

'Do you know if Father Patrick ever talked or met with a Father Monroe from the archdiocese?'

He looked at me in surprise. 'The one who was murdered in Mexico?'

I nodded.

'Yes, I believe they shared an interest in fishing. They traveled to Baja several times together.'

'You're certain of that?'

He nodded. 'Father Patrick brought back fish for a Lenten celebration once. Some of the ladies from the congregation made stew with limes and cilantro. It reminded many in the congregation of home.'

'Was he with him on the trip when Father Monroe was murdered?'

'He had planned on going with him, but was unable to. I suspect he blamed himself at some level for what happened, felt that it might have been different if he had been there. Father Patrick's life has been filled with many trials.'

'Do you know what Father Monroe's duties were within the archdiocese?'

Tavares hesitated, and then shook his head. 'No, I'm afraid I don't.'

'Do you know if he had ever interviewed Father Patrick about the abuse case against him?'

The priest looked at me for a moment, the muscles of his jaw tightening.

'The alleged case,' he said. 'He was never charged with anything.'

'I suppose he was stripped of his duties and moved around from parish to parish so he could devote himself to prayer.'

'I'm afraid I cannot help you beyond what I've already said.'

'Of course.'

'Now I must go to him.'

'Just one more thing,' I said.

He paused in the doorway and turned back to me.

'Can you tell me the meaning of the Latin *filius meus*?' I asked him.

He nodded. 'My son. It means my son.'

# eighteen

I gave the sheriff's deputy all the information I could, then drove out of the high desert and back into the clouds of the basin. It was nearing midnight. As I reached the west end of the Valley the mist began to sprinkle my windshield again. The dry sharp scents of the high desert were replaced by the faint smell of the ocean from the storm sitting just off the coast. Every pass of my wipers was like another wave breaking on the shore, bringing with it whatever secrets had been concealed in the deep.

In my hand I held the photograph of the young pregnant woman. Her eyes appeared to be looking just beyond the edge of the picture at something secret I didn't understand yet. As I turned off the 5 onto the 134 my phone rang and I picked up – it was Harrison.

'Did you get a match on the hands yet?'

'No match, but they didn't belong to Monroe.'

'You're sure?'

'Yes. Where are you?'

'The priest Chavez had questioned at St Gabriel's was named Patrick. I just talked to him. He used to travel with Father Monroe to fish in Baja. He was supposed to have been with him on the trip where he was killed but cancelled at the last moment.'

'You think he may have set him up?'

'I don't know. We may have been wrong about Goya – he wasn't a victim; at least not in the way we thought he was. Patrick saw himself as some kind of teacher to him.'

'Of what?'

'His own version of truth. He may have had some radical ideas about the direction of the Church.'

'Did he identify any of the other boys?'

'He could have but he didn't,' I said.

'Will he?'

'No . . . he killed himself. Whoever he's trying to protect, it was worth his life. Did you get hold of Chavez?'

There was a pause on the other end.

'Dylan, did you find him?'

'A black and white found his unmarked squad a few blocks from the bar where you met him.'

'What's the address?'

'Just off Fair Oaks on Palmetto. According to the bartender a priest came in a few minutes after we left, sat down and talked with him.'

Uneasiness began to spread through my gut. My foot pressed a little harder on the accelerator.

'That wouldn't be unusual for Chavez,' I said.

'Apparently they also walked out together.'

'St Michael's is only a few blocks away. The priest could have been from there.'

'I don't think so,' Harrison said.

A voice in my head began to repeat *no, no, no.*

'Why?' I asked.

'I thought the same thing so I called. The senior priest was at SC medical center performing last rites on a parishioner, and his assistant has been in all evening watching soccer on TV.'

'There's something else, isn't there?'

'Yeah. We traced the call reporting Goya's painting on St Gabriel's.'

'Where was it made?'

'A pay phone half a block away from the bar. I was just there. It has a clear view of the entrance.'

My hands were tightly wrapped around the steering wheel, but I could feel them begin to shake.

'He was watching us,' I said, the uneasiness in my gut now spreading like a wildfire through me.

'I don't think that was a priest,' Dylan said.

The voice in my head was now a scream.

'Did the bartender give you a description?' I asked, trying desperately to cling to being a cop.

'All he remembers noticing was that he was dressed in black and wearing a collar. I'm sorry, Alex.'

The phone slipped from my hand and my eyes began to fill with tears. I reached down, flipped on the siren and pressed my foot hard against the accelerator.

It took me a little over twenty minutes to get to Pasadena where Chavez's car was found. The street had been blocked off at both ends by black and whites. Several uniformed officers were walking the street with flashlights pointed down, searching the pavement for evidence. I pulled past one of the squads and stopped behind Harrison's car a half-block off Fair Oaks and got out into the mist. As I walked up Harrison stepped out and joined me. The chief's car was another twenty feet ahead. The right front wheel was up over the curb. The driver's side door was ajar.

'Crime scene is on the way to go over it.'

I started toward it and Harrison reached out and took my arm.

'You're not going to like what you see,' he said. 'Maybe you're not the right person to be doing this.'

I resisted the urge to run to the car and instead took a deep breath to slow down and shook my head.

'I'm exactly the right person to do this. Albert chose me.'

Dylan looked at me and nodded.

I looked around at the surrounding buildings – all businesses, all closed for the night. The nearest streetlight was another block away.

'He picked the location carefully, didn't he?' I said.

'We're checking the businesses on the street to see if a security camera may have caught something.'

We walked up to the back of the car. The rear window still had traces of condensation on the inside.

'They must have sat inside for while before they left,' Harrison said. 'I figure he followed the chief to the bar then moved his own vehicle here.'

'So they talked,' I said.

Dylan hesitated. 'More than just talked.'

I quickly stepped past him and walked up to the driver's side door. There were traces of blood on the handle and what looked to be several smudged prints on the frame.

I reached up on top of the door and pulled it open. There were bloodstains on the center console and along the edge of the seat. The radio had been ripped out; pieces of plastic and loose wires lay on the floor under where it had been mounted.

'He was hurt on his right side,' I said.

Harrison began to say something and then stopped himself as if he was reluctant to say what he was thinking about my daughter's godfather Chief Chavez.

'Understand something, Dylan. We're going to catch this son of a bitch, and the chief is going to survive.'

Harrison looked at me for a moment and then nodded.

'Now go on,' I said.

He looked back into the car and picked up where he had left off. 'If I had to guess I would say he was cut somewhere low on the arm. From the amount of blood, an artery may have been severed.'

'A way of controlling his victim,' I said.

Harrison nodded. 'Someone trying not to bleed to death becomes very cooperative.'

I stepped back and looked over the pavement for any signs of blood but in the heavy mist I couldn't see any. I tried to focus on the details of what I was seeing, but the harder I tried the faster memory began to replace the present. Every step I had taken as a cop had been under his guidance, every success partly his. If anyone else had been chief I doubted that I would be head of homicide.

'His picture is going out to every cop in LA,' Harrison said.

'Before Father Patrick killed himself he talked about cleansing the Church,' I said.

'Of what?'

'The twentieth century. Patrick was a believer in papal infallibility, and by extension his own.'

'In a system like that a priest wouldn't be punished for abusing young boys.'

'Yes. I think he saw the last hundred and fifty years of change in the Church as an abomination. Being stripped of his ability to minister would be part of that betrayal.'

'Through his teaching he twisted Goya into some kind of tool to turn the clock back to his version of the world.'

I nodded. 'It seems likely, except he also claimed Goya didn't kill the other victims.'

'He's trying to protect him.'

'Possibly, but why admit that he tortured and killed Donald Bonner and then deny the rest?'

'Maybe he didn't want to admit that he had lost control of him.'

'There was something else he talked about.'

'What?'

'History. He mentioned others who were cleansing the Church.'

'What others?'

'Nameless, faceless servants of God.'

'Oh, those others.'

I nodded. 'God knows the Church has more than enough blood on its hands through the ages, but believing that Vatican assassins are running around Los Angeles is a bit of a stretch.'

We looked at each other in silence for a moment.

'That would be the sensible way to look at it,' Harrison said.

I looked down the street. At the limit of my vision a coyote was standing in the middle of the road watching our every move.

'Short of a conspiracy I think there may be more to his wanting to protect him.'

'What do you mean?'

'As he was dying Patrick called Goya his son.'

Dylan looked at me for a moment, playing the thought out in his head.

'Spiritually, or do you think he was being literal?'

'He talked about the weakness of the flesh, claimed Goya was protecting him.'

'A son would do that. It wouldn't be the first time a priest had secretly fathered a child. But how does that fit into a pattern of abusing young boys?'

'We're assuming they were all boys. That may not be the case. Predatory personalities aren't always gender specific, at least in the beginning. He could have begun with girls. A pregnancy may have forced him to change his behavior.' I reached into my pocket and handed Harrison the photograph of the young woman. 'If there's an answer it may lie with her.'

Harrison looked at it for a moment.

'Mary. That would make Goya—'

I nodded. 'At least in Patrick's eyes.'

Harrison handed the photograph back to me. I stared at her vacant look for a moment and then my eyes shifted to the steeple in the background.

'If she was one of his parishioners, that could be his church.'

Harrison picked up on my train of thought and nodded.

'Goya is somewhere between twenty-five and thirty,' I said. 'We find out what parish Patrick was assigned to at the time and see if the steeple in this picture is a match. Someone in the congregation may recognize her.'

'And if they don't?'

'Then we check the birth records at the Catholic hospitals.'

'You could be talking thousands of people.'

I looked at the picture and shook my head. 'Maybe not, a young Hispanic woman, unmarried. We start with the hospitals closest to this church and work out from there.'

'I'll get it started,' Harrison said.

'Get as many people on it as you need.'

I looked back in the car to find another detail to bring me back to the moment. Scattered across the floor amongst the pieces of the plastic from the radio I found it. I picked up one of the beads and stared at it in the palm of my hand.

'His rosary,' I said and closed my fist around it. 'If he hadn't talked to me this might not have happened.'

'You don't know that.'

I stepped back from the car and shook my head. 'No, I do. Goya is going after those who have broken their silence, not kept it.'

'He couldn't have known what you two had talked about.'

'No, but the chief might have confided in a priest who sat down with him and bought him a drink.'

I looked down at my watch. A new day had begun.

'Let's say for argument's sake that Father Patrick wasn't as mad as a hatter and there is some shred of truth in what he told me.'

'That we're in the middle of a conspiracy that leads all the way back to Rome? Which shred are we talking about?'

I shook my head. 'The one that has Goya believing he's a part of something larger.'

'A soldier doing God's work?'

'Even if it's only in his own mind.'

'It helps to explain his motivation. He's not only defending the man who at least is his teacher and possibly his father, he's protecting the Church.'

'I'd buy that,' I said.

Harrison nodded. 'It also makes him difficult to stop.'

'Yes, it does.'

Harrison ran through the details, trying to find a way through it.

'We go to the archdiocese with this, maybe they would release the records of what had happened at Saint Gabriel's, and we might get an ID. Father Patrick's dead, he can't be harmed any longer.'

'I think the Church's time frame is longer than any single life.'

'We could get a subpoena.'

I looked back at Chavez's car. 'And when the court battle's finished, the dead will have long been buried.'

When I returned to headquarters I called my daughter at UCLA and told her about what had happened. I didn't hide any of the details from her as any other parent might in a similar situation.

Having been a kidnap victim herself once she knew a thing or two about terror and what it took to survive it. When I finished she said only one thing, her voice betraying none of the emotion I had been fighting to bottle up.

'When you find my godfather, tell him I love him.'

# nineteen

Within an hour of the morning papers hitting the street, headquarters had received over twenty calls claiming to have information on the whereabouts of Chief Chavez. Of those, three claimed to have seen the actual kidnapping, though could produce no credible details; one believed he had seen him walking into the ocean and swimming out to sea; a handful were gang-bangers claiming to have carried out the crime; and a grand total of ten believed he was being punished by God for sins both specific and unnamed. Of those, two claimed to have already made contact with him in the hereafter.

At nine we briefed representatives of the secret service, the Papal Guard and Agent Utley from the FBI on the possible threat facing the Pope. Assistant Chief Kelly and Harrison were the only representatives from Pasadena. The captain of the Guard was named Rezzitti, a man in his mid-forties dressed in a black suit that I imagined cost more than the entire wardrobe of Pasadena's detective squad.

I laid out the chain of events as best I could, beginning with the abuse that had taken place at St Gabriel's and ending with the events of the previous night. When I was finished Rezzitti picked up the Goya print found in the Rose Bowl and studied it for a moment.

'No specific threats have been made against the Holy Father,' he said, speaking with a smooth Swiss-German accent, softened from his time in Italy.

'No specific threat, but taken as a whole—'

'I believe this is a local problem. It is a great tragedy, but it has been my experience that artists make poor assassins, Lieutenant.'

'And what brought you to this understanding?' I said.

'Living in Italy,' he said.

'Four people are already dead, and one is missing.'

'Murder is not a political act. That is different.'

'I don't believe Goya is acting out of political motivation.'

'Then how would you describe it?' Rezzitti asked.

'I'd say he's acting out of a twisted form of faith.'

'Faith?'

I nodded.

'The belief in things that are by their very nature unprovable,' Rezzitti said. 'Dangerous territory for a policeman.'

'Yes, I think the Church has more experience with these matters. Like the goodness of all men of the cloth.'

Rezzitti smiled. 'Thankfully, I am just a policeman like you, and without proof, I can do nothing.' He looked over to Utley. 'Does the FBI agree with the lieutenant's conclusion of a threat?'

Utley nodded. 'An individual placing his actions in a historical context like Goya makes him very dangerous, even without a specific threat.'

'If Goya didn't have a weapon before, he does now,' Kelly said. 'That's proof enough for me.'

'That he is dangerous, yes, but to whom is the question. What caliber sidearm did your chief carry?' Rezzitti asked.

'Does,' I said, keeping it in the present. 'Nine millimeter.'

'This is not a problem. The only time he will be close enough to the Holy Father for a weapon like that to be accurate he will be inside the vehicle. A nine millimeter would not penetrate the glass.'

'Will the crowd have to pass through metal detectors?' I asked.

'This is a Mass, Lieutenant. You don't search people walking into church,' Rezzitti said.

The secret service agent shook his head.

'The number of people in attendance makes it impracticable,' he said. 'It would take ten hours to effectively screen those entering. There will be spot searches carried out at the discretion of officers, but only the people in the area directly in front of where the Pope will deliver his sermon will have to pass through detectors and most of those will be in wheelchairs. It will be a few hundred at most. The rest of the crowd will be at least a hundred feet back at the closest point, and most will be much farther.'

'And the Holy Father will be standing behind a protective screen,' Rezzitti added.

'How many priests will be in attendance?'

Rezzitti leaned forward.

'It was a priest your chief was last seen with?' he asked.

I nodded.

'Is it your belief that this Goya is a priest?'

'I don't know. I'm not ruling out any possibilities, including that he was fathered by one.'

'You have proof of this?'

'No.'

'Then it is speculation.'

'Chief Chavez's blood sprayed across the interior of his car is not speculation.'

'I mean no offense, Lieutenant, but I see a dozen threats against His Holiness every day.'

'There will be priests there from all over southern California, northern Mexico and other states. They'll number in the hundreds,' the secret service agent said.

'Will they be screened?'

Rezzitti glanced at the secret service agent then shook his head. 'When you have specific information regarding a threat from a priest, we will consider it. Until then, I will increase the detail directly around His Holiness, but there is little more I can do than that. And even if the threat was specific, I doubt the Holy Father would allow us to change his plans in any way. Faith is not always so different from politics.'

The door opened and Traver stepped in and beckoned me over.

'There's another call claiming to have information. They asked for you specifically.'

I started to shake my head. 'I don't have time for this.'

'I think you might want to take this one.'

'Why?'

'It's not about the chief, it's about Keri Bishop.'

There was a phone on a side table next to the door.

'Line two,' Traver said and went out.

I picked up the phone. 'You have information about Keri Bishop?'

'Is this Lieutenant Delillo?'

It was a male voice. He spoke in short clipped sentences as if he was walking and looking over his shoulder as he talked.

'Yes. Whom am I talking to?'

'I'm not prepared to identify myself yet.'

'What is it you claim to know?'

'Why she was killed.'

'Go on.'

'Does the name Father Monroe mean anything to you?'

'The priest killed in Mexico on the fishing trip.'

'She was killed by the same people who murdered him.'

'People?' I said. 'You want to be a little more specific?'

'It's too dangerous over the phone. You want to know what I know, you'll have to meet me alone, in a place of my choosing.'

'If you have information, it's a crime to withhold it.'

'You have no idea how much danger you're already in, do you? The same people are watching you.'

'I'm a little busy right now. If you have information, call nine one one,' I said and began to hang up.

'She was killed by the Vatican.'

I brought the phone back to my ear.

'And they're watching you now,' he said.

I looked across the table. Rezzitti glanced in my direction.

'Are you interested?' the caller asked.

Rezzitti watched me for a moment longer then casually looked away.

'Why would they do that?' I said.

'To keep their secrets,' he said.

'Can you prove this?'

'Do you think we would be talking on the phone if I could? Do you want to know what I know or not?'

'Yes, I'm interested,' I said.

'There's a pay phone halfway down the block toward the plaza. In ten minutes it will ring. Be careful. If you're not alone, you'll never hear from me again.'

The line went dead. I walked back to the conference table and took my seat across from Rezzitti, seeing his eyes occasionally glancing in my direction and turning away. The conversation continued for another minute, though I didn't take in a word of it.

'Do you have anything to add, Lieutenant?' Deputy Chief Kelly said.

I looked over to Kelly, not having heard his question.

'Do you have anything to add?' he repeated.

I shook my head. 'No.' I pushed back from the table and stood up.

'I'll have to excuse myself. There's a call I have to take.'

I began to turn to the door. Rezzitti stood up and walked around the table to me.

'I will be waiting for any new information, Lieutenant,' he said. 'We all want the same thing, true?'

I looked at him. 'Of course.'

He extended his hand and I reached out. His long fingers closed around mine. I noticed his nails had been polished, neatly clipped and filed.

'*Bene*,' he said.

I nodded in agreement and then walked out. Before I reached the stairs to head outside Harrison caught up with me.

'What was that call?'

Through the half-open door of the conference room I could see Rezzitti's hands gesturing in the air.

'Come with me.'

We walked down the stairs and out the front entrance onto Garfield.

'What is it?' Harrison asked.

I looked down toward the plaza. The phone booth the caller had mentioned was visible.

'You know the "others" that Father Patrick told me about?'

'The ones cleansing the Church?'

'Yes,' I said.

He nodded.

'Someone else apparently thinks they're real. He said the Vatican killed Father Monroe and Keri Bishop, and that we're being watched.'

Harrison glanced back at the stairs going inside. 'The Vatican?'

'Yeah.'

'Did he name names?' Harrison said and smiled.

'Not yet.'

'You don't believe in conspiracies,' he said.

'Believing in something and the truth aren't always the same thing.'

I glanced up and down the street searching each pedestrian, each driver of a car passing by, for the one that seemed out of place. If he was outside watching me I couldn't ID him.

'Did he offer any proof?'

I glanced at my watch. 'In six minutes he's going to call that phone booth down the block. I'll find out then.'

'This is not a good idea.'

'You think I should just let it ring?'

I looked at Dylan and he shook his head.

'The voice sounded frightened, not a threat,' I said.

'I would still like to get some backup set up.'

'There isn't time; you're it. You watch from here. If something goes wrong . . . then maybe we'll want to rethink the conspiracy theory.'

# twenty

The rain had finally stopped as I walked the half-block to the phone booth, though the dark gray clouds appeared to touch the tops of the surrounding buildings. A large flock of green parrots was circling the street in front of the plaza screaming out their mad calls with each pass.

I stopped twenty feet from the phone and glanced around for anything that appeared out of place. A Mexican man selling brightly colored balloons and stuffed animals was walking across the street toward me. A Japanese family stood on the plaza steps having their picture taken. I glanced back toward headquarters. Harrison was standing at the bottom of the steps looking in my direction. As I raised my wrist to check the time the phone rang.

I walked up to the phone and looked around one more time, then picked it up.

'I'm here,' I said.

The sound of tires sliding on gravel came from behind. I turned around as a small light-colored Ford sedan skidded to a stop beside me. The driver appeared to be in his late twenties or early thirties, his eyes obscured by sunglasses.

'You want to talk, get in.'

I glanced back up the street. Harrison was moving in my direction.

'That wasn't the deal,' I said.

'It is now. Are you coming?'

I looked back at Harrison, who was now running toward me.

'Yes or no,' the driver said and then glanced in his rearview mirror. 'I'm leaving.'

I looked one more time at Harrison and then reached out and opened the passenger door and got in. The man immediately stepped on the gas, checking his mirror as we drove away.

'I told you to come alone,' he said, his voice rising.

I slipped my hand down onto the handle of my Glock.

'And you didn't say anything about a ride,' I said.

We turned the corner and Harrison vanished from sight.

'This isn't a game, you just started this, I've been working it for years, you don't know anything. You don't know, you understand, you don't know.'

'That was my partner. Nothing to worry about.'

'Worry? I'm not worried, I'm fine, everyone should live like this.'

The words came out of him as if a fuse had ignited them. The back seat of the car was covered with boxes and papers bound with string. The floor was layered with crumpled coffee cups and energy bar wrappers. His face was younger than I had thought at first, mid to late twenties maybe, though under the edge of his glasses I could see stress lines at the corners of his eyes. His clothes appeared to have been slept in for more than a few nights.

'You need to slow down.'

He started to shake his head.

'Running into someone isn't going to do either of us any good,' I said.

He kept his foot on the gas as we sped around a corner, checked the mirror, then eased up and sat back into his seat.

'Where are we going?' I asked.

He looked at me for a moment. 'You're wearing a wire?'

I shook my head. 'No. You've seen too many movies.'

He took a quick left and then just after the turn he abruptly turned into a parking garage. We drove up to the first level and went to the end and stopped in the closest empty spot to the exit.

He sat for a moment, his hands gripping the steering wheel; then they began to relax and he took several breaths.

'Suppose you tell me your name.'

'John.'

'Just John?'

'For the moment, until I'm certain I can trust you.'

'The godfather of my daughter was kidnapped last night by the same man who probably killed Keri. I think we want the same thing here. And I don't have a lot of time.'

He looked at me for a moment then released his grip on the steering wheel.

'Morrison. My name's Morrison.'

'OK, John, now why are we here?'

He looked cautiously over his shoulder down the length of the parking structure. 'I'm a journalist.'

'Who for?'

'Freelance. I've been working on the same story now for four years.'

I looked around at the boxes of papers on the back seat.

'Is that what all this is?'

He nodded. 'I keep it all with me to protect it.'

'From whom?'

'Them,' he said excitedly. 'The Church, their people, it's not like they have names or carry IDs. Since Keri was kidnapped, I've been on the move, never stay in the same place more than one night.'

'You sleep in the car a lot.'

He reached up and slipped off his dark glasses. His eyes had the look of someone thirty years older than him.

'I never sleep a lot,' he said, reaching up and adjusting the mirror so he could see behind us.

'Suppose we start at the beginning,' I said.

He nodded. 'I was working on a story about abuse in the Church— are you a Catholic?'

'I was.'

He nodded. 'So was I.'

'Go on,' I said.

'I started in the usual places, trying to identify priests, there were many, dozens. Only a few were publicly ID'd, I began to track them down, but it was difficult, the Church kept moving them, and since their records can't be accessed . . . so I started looking at it in other ways.'

'Such as?'

'Money . . . you know the old saying, follow the money, that's what I did, it always leads to something bad.'

'And where did this lead?'

'Father Monroe.'

'The one murdered in Mexico.'

John nodded. 'The archdiocese settled five hundred and eight suits at the last count, over seven hundred and twenty million dollars in payments. And nearly all their secrets are intact. How does something like that happen? History. This country hadn't even been formed yet, and the Church already had centuries of practice. Think of it, a continuity of governance that dwarfs any other country on the planet. Crusades, world wars, Dark Ages, the Renaissance, you name it, every government has fallen, every monarchy has become irrelevant, but not the Church, the Church survived it all. *Templum est eternus, vir nusquam est.*'

'You speak Latin?'

'You want to understand the Church, you have to know its language.'

'And what does that mean?'

'They were spoken by one of the first Popes. "The Church is eternal, man is nothing." And now Keri is dead, and so is Trevor Wells.'

'Tell me about Father Monroe?'

'Ahh . . . that's where it got interesting.' He turned around and began riffling through a file box full of papers.

'Why don't you just give me the broad strokes,' I said.

He turned back around. 'Do you know what he did for the archdiocese?'

'I know he was a lawyer.'

'I like to think of him as the facilitator. He did what had to be done, he managed things, made it all work, one day he was a bag man delivering payoffs, another day – do you have any idea how much the archdiocese is worth in real estate alone?'

'No.'

'By conservative estimates, four billion dollars, and Monroe managed it.'

'What does this have to do with Keri Bishop?'

John turned to me and in an instant all the manic energy he had barely been able to contain vanished.

'I got her into this.'

'Into what?'

'I was trying to trace payoffs that took place at a church in Pasadena in the eighties.'

'St Gabriel's?'

He looked at me in surprise. 'You know it?'

'Yes.'

'I had information that Monroe had paid off city officials, families, the press, even . . .' he hesitated, 'even Pasadena PD.'

'I've heard the same rumors.'

'I talked to a journalism class at SC. The teacher is a friend, I was supposed to talk about the life, the real thing, not CNN, a day in the life of a journalist . . . blah blah blah, the working-class hero routine.'

'Keri was in the class.'

John nodded. 'We talked after class and I found out who her father was and asked her if she might be interested in doing some real work.'

'Getting inside information about her father's lawsuit against the archdiocese.'

'Yeah, exactly. It started simply enough, she began tracking down the unnamed victims.'

'Do you have names?' I asked.

He nodded. 'A couple, but that wasn't the big thing.'

'The big thing?'

'The reason she was killed. Money. Each time Father Monroe made a payoff, bought and sold real estate, he was taking a piece for himself.'

'How much?'

'By the time he was murdered he had stolen millions, I don't know how many. It's one thing to take the Lord's name in vain, but if you steal his money, you're in deep trouble. They killed him.'

'How did Keri find this out?'

'Her father was the one who discovered that Monroe was a thief. It was simple paperwork that any good tax accountant would find, but since none of the Church's transactions are subject to that kind of outside scrutiny it was easy to hide. That's why the suit was settled so quickly out of court. But the size of the payoff was much more than what the families of the victims received.'

'And the rest of the money went where?'

'Just before Keri disappeared she had found some account numbers in her father's papers that didn't match up to anything or any bank she could identify.'

'You're saying Monroe paid off her father?'

'That's what Keri believed, but I can't prove it.'

'And you can't prove she or Wells was killed by the Vatican either.'

'Did you never have a case where you knew who was guilty, but didn't have the proof?'

'Do you have anything that approaches proof for Father Monroe's murder?'

He sat back in his seat, his shoulders tensing up. 'I'm offering you information. If you don't want it—'

'Did Keri ever meet with Trevor Wells?' I asked.

Morrison shook his head. 'No, but I did a few weeks before she disappeared. I'm fairly certain he was paid off by either Bishop or Monroe but I don't know which, he wouldn't talk to me then. I called him again when her body was discovered, and he agreed to meet with me this time, but we never got to have that conversation.'

'How did Keri get access to her father's information?'

'He wanted her to become a lawyer, and she agreed to "intern" in the office to find out if she liked it.'

'But she was really digging up information.'

'Yeah.'

'Did her father ever discover what she was doing?'

He thought for a moment. 'I'm not sure. A few days before her abduction something happened between them, and she told me there wouldn't be any more information about the suit.'

'Does the name Goya mean anything to you?'

He shook his head.

'Did you ID any of the victims from St Gabriel's?'

'I tracked down one, but he's since vanished.'

'Did you talk to him?'

'I tried, but it didn't do any good.'

'Why?'

'This is where it gets good.'

'What do you mean?'

'The order he was a part of was a contemplative order for which some of its brothers observe what we would call a vow of silence.'

I wasn't sure I had heard him right. 'The order?'

John nodded. 'Yeah, a Trappist, he was a monk in an abbey in the high desert past Palmdale. Monroe used money to silence a man who hasn't spoken a word in years.'

'Do you have a current ID or picture?'

Morrison shook his head. 'All I found was his old high school ID from when he was eighteen.'

'From St Gabriel's?'

'Yes.'

'What's his name?'

'It was Michael Sanchez then.'

'He changed it?'

'Yeah, he took another name when he joined the order. Brother Paul.'

'Paul?'

'Yes.'

'You certain of this?'

'Absolutely. I couldn't make up this stuff. He takes a payoff from the Church, then joins a holy order and adopts the name of the patron saint of truth. It's medieval really when you think of it. The Dark Ages got nothing on us.'

'When did he leave the order?'

160

'I don't have an exact date, but it was sometime in the first few months after Keri disappeared.'

'I'd like to see that ID.'

He leaned over the back of his seat and began digging in one of the boxes and then pulled out a file. He riffled through it for a moment then pulled out a piece of paper and handed it to me. On it was a copy of a school ID from the late eighties. Sanchez had short dark hair, light olive skin. I stared at the face for a moment, trying to find a likeness to either Father Patrick or the young pregnant woman in the picture, but the connection was elusive at best.

'Did you ever track down his parents?'

John shook his head. 'If they're living I couldn't find them. I think his mother may have been from Mexico; she might have gone back there.'

'And the father?'

'I never found anything on him at all. I tried to get information through St Gabriel's, but you can imagine the answer.'

'And that was the only victim you found?'

'Keri may have found one of them, but she hadn't gotten any information from him when she vanished.'

'Did she give you a name?'

Morrison shook his head. 'I think she was being protective of him until she knew he was actually one of the victims.'

'She find him through her father?'

'Yeah.'

I sat back in the seat, looking at the photograph, trying to find a reason to believe in Morrison's story.

'If Father Monroe and Keri were both killed by someone within the Vatican, as you say, why is her father still alive?' I asked.

'He wasn't a threat because they had made him a partner; he

had been bought and paid for. To break his silence would be his ruin. Keri was the one who was a threat. Just like I am . . . and your—' He stopped himself.

'Go on,' I said.

'Was your chief the one in the Pasadena PD that Father Monroe paid off to drop the investigation into St Gabriel's?'

I folded up the copy of the ID. 'I'll need this.'

'You didn't answer the question, Lieutenant,' he said.

'I'll let you know.' I opened the car door. 'There'll be squads out looking for me. You'd better be moving on.'

'There's something else. I haven't put all the pieces together, maybe it's not possible to, but the Pope's visit to LA can't be unrelated. He could have chosen a dozen other cities, but he didn't, he's coming here, now. Why?'

'You have a theory on this?'

He nodded. 'I have a source within the Vatican who says there's a power struggle going on in Rome between traditionalists and reformers, which is nothing new, it's been going on for centuries. Publicly the Pope has shown a penchant toward the conservative, but the abuse scandal has apparently pushed him in some directions the traditionalists are not happy about.'

'Such as?'

'One, allowing the scandal to become public. In the old Church it would never have happened. And two, money. The seven hundred and twenty million the Church has paid out in this archdiocese alone is a drop in the bucket to what it could eventually cost the Church worldwide. I've heard rumors that the Holy Father will be meeting with every American cardinal here in Los Angeles, and that he's going to make changes. Very powerful people are going to lose power. They're not going to just sit back and let that happen. I don't have any specific information, but if I'm right that an assassin within the Church has already murdered

Monroe and possibly Keri, when I put that together with the other pieces, it adds up to someone else dying while the Pope is here, maybe him.'

'A coup d'état in the Church.'

'You think it hasn't happened before? Two thousand years of Christianity, it's all happened.'

I slipped the copy of the ID in my pocket and stepped out of the car.

'How do I get hold of you?' I asked.

Morrison wrote a number on a card and handed it to me. 'It's a service. Leave a message and I'll get back to you.'

'What was the name of the abbey where you found Sanchez?'

'St Timothy's.'

From the other end of the parking ramp came a squeal of tires. As I turned to look, Morrison quickly stepped on the gas and disappeared down the ramp to the exit.

For the first time in days shafts of sunlight broke through the clouds. Steam was rising off the wet pavement as Harrison pulled up in an unmarked squad and jumped out.

'Are you all right?' he asked.

I nodded. 'I'm fine.'

Harrison started to take a step toward the parking ramp.

'He's already gone,' I said.

'What did you find out?'

'I'll get to that,' I said and got into the squad.

Dylan walked back around and slid in behind the wheel.

'Tell me about the rest of the meeting,' I said.

'The secret service and papal security will let us know if they require any further assistance.'

'Don't call us, we'll call you.'

'That was the general drift. I tried to get a copy of his itinerary the day of the Mass, and they promised to have it to us before he arrives.'

'Then it's no longer our problem.'

We looked at each other for a moment, neither believing it.

'Anything new about the chief?' I asked.

'Nothing good. One of the businesses on the street had a security camera in the lobby.' He handed me a still image from the recording. 'If there was any doubt about what we found last night, it's gone now. There were three images. This was the best – in the other two they're just entering frame and then leaving it.'

It was a grainy black and white picture. Chief Chavez could be clearly seen moving across the plane of the camera. The sleeve of his right shirt was stained dark, his left hand supporting the arm across his chest. I stared at the chief's face, clearly contorted in pain. My pulse began to jump at speed. The palms of my hands grew clammy.

'This is not going to be the last image we have of him.'

'It won't be,' Dylan said.

'I don't want his daughters seeing this on TV.'

'No one will see this outside the department.'

I turned my attention to the second figure. He stood a few feet behind the chief. The white-collar tab stood out against the black suit. His face was blurred as if he had just turned from the camera to look at something to his right.

I glanced back at the chief's bloody arm.

'You were right about the wound,' I said.

'Look at the priest's left hand.'

It was blurred, as if he was raising it from his side. The dark shape of the chief's weapon was just visible in his hand.

'I've sent it over to Cal Tech to see if they can enhance it.'

I stared at the priest's face, trying to find detail where there wasn't any.

'What do your instincts tell you?' I asked.

Dylan shook his head. 'You don't want to know.'

'No,' I whispered. 'Every second he's gone, he slips farther away.'

Harrison looked up toward the parking structure. 'What did you find in there?'

'A great big white rabbit going down a hole.' I leaned back and took a breath. 'His name's John Morrison. He's a fringe journalist; paranoid doesn't begin to describe him.'

I wrote down his license plate number and handed it to Harrison.

'See if you can find out anything about him. As he sees it Father Monroe was murdered by Rome because he had stolen millions of dollars from the archdiocese.'

'Can he prove that?'

'No, but according to him, Keri's father could, so he was paid off. Morrison met Keri at class at SC. He was using her to track down information from her father's law practice. He believes she was killed because she had found proof of both Monroe's payoffs to her father and his stealing from the archdiocese. He's also come to the same conclusion that we have, only with entirely different information.'

'The Pope,' Harrison said.

I nodded. 'He's convinced there's a power struggle going on in the Vatican and that the Pope is going to be assassinated while in Los Angeles.'

'He's not aware of Goya?'

'No.'

'Did you believe him?'

'I believe he believes it. In his world the Church is something akin to the Corleone family.'

'You think it's possible that we could be looking at two separate crimes?'

'That Monroe was killed by the Vatican, and Keri and Wells by Goya?'

Harrison nodded. Until I had actually spelled it out myself I hadn't believed a thread of Morrison's story, but saying it out loud had somehow opened the door a crack for doubt to creep in.

'There is a kind of logic behind it even if it is half-baked.'

'Two killers instead of one? I'm not sure which is worse.'

'Two,' I said.

'Particularly if one of them is a professional.'

'I'm not quite ready to become a conspiracy theorist, but he may have stumbled on a few things that can help us.'

'Such as?'

'Morrison tracked down one of Father Patrick's victims at St Gabriel's.' I handed Harrison the copy of the ID.

'Michael Sanchez.'

'A school ID from St Gabriel's.'

Harrison looked at it for a moment. 'There's nothing more current?'

'Not on paper.'

'He was maybe sixteen when this was taken. A lot can happen to a face in ten or twelve years. Wouldn't St Gabriel's have information on his family?'

'According to Morrison the mother may have returned to Mexico, and he could find nothing about the father.'

'And that's as current as it gets?'

'Morrison had tracked him to an abbey in the high desert where he had taken a vow of silence.'

'He was a monk?'

'Apparently.'

'There's that word again.'

'Silence, yes. Morrison also said that just before she disappeared he believed Keri had made contact with one of the other victims. She never told him the identity, but sometime shortly after she vanished, Michael Sanchez vanished too.'

'And he never found him again?'

'No.'

Harrison held up the ID and looked at the picture.

'An abbey in the high desert, that wouldn't be far from where you found Father Patrick. You think he's dead? It could explain the hands we found at Saint Gabriel's.'

'There's another possibility.'

Harrison ran it through his head. 'The Franciscan's rope used in Goya's drawing.'

I nodded. 'Michael Sanchez and Goya are the same person.

'The name Goya used at the Art Center was Miguel. That tracks.'

'And the name he'd taken in the monastery was Paul,' I said.

Dylan turned to me. 'I think that rules out coincidence.'

'It's time we had another talk with Keri's father.'

# twenty-one

There was something different about the Bishops' house when we pulled up outside. I reached out and stopped Harrison from opening the door, then looked back toward the house.

'Tell me what you see,' I said.

'What do you mean?' Harrison asked.

I shook my head as my eyes moved across the front of the house. 'Look at the house, something's changed.'

Harrison studied the house for a moment.

'The roses,' he said.

I opened the door and started up the walkway, my pace quickening with each step. I stopped a few feet from the steps. The bed of roses that extended to the right front of the house had been destroyed, the plant's canes lying like scattered bones amongst the bright red petals of the flowers across the dark ground.

'They've been hacked to pieces,' Harrison said.

I rushed up to the front door and rang the bell. A moment later a voice came from the other side of the door.

'Who is it?'

'It's Lieutenant Delillo, Mrs Bishop.'

A security chain was removed and the door slowly opened. Mrs Bishop's hair was unkempt, and she looked exhausted.

'Is it my husband?' she asked.

'What happened here, Mrs Bishop?' I asked.

Her eyes drifted toward the destroyed rose bed, then she turned and walked back into the house. We stepped in and followed her down the hallway to her husband's office where she stopped at the door.

'I was out for dinner with a friend last night. When I returned I found the plants out front as you saw, and then this.'

She pushed open the door. The air inside the room was heavy with the scent of cigarettes and alcohol. Jackson Bishop's office had been destroyed in the same manner the roses had been. The dark wood paneling of the walls, the furniture, a painting, had all been hacked to pieces. Wood chips, torn and shredded documents, everything that had been inside the room, lay in pieces on the floor. An axe was embedded in the wall next to the window.

'I don't know where he is,' she said, then turned to me. 'Do you know?'

'No,' I said.

Harrison and I stepped into the room and looked around at the destruction. Next to the remains of the desk was a paper shredder that had been smashed to pieces. Dylan reached down and picked up a shred of paper that had Bishop's law firm's masthead on it.

'He was destroying documents,' Dylan said. 'From the amount of paper I'd say a lot of them.'

'And then things got out of hand,' I said.

'Since you came here he had rarely left the room.'

'Has he talked to anyone?'

'Not that I'm aware of. Can you tell me what's going on?'

'Do you know what papers he kept here?' I asked.

'Mostly our own, a few from the firm.'

'Cases, or business?'

She shook her head. 'I don't know.'

'Where did he keep the rest of the firm's paperwork?'

170

'A storage facility downtown.'

'Do the roses have a connection to your daughter?'

She nodded. 'How did you know that?'

'What was it?'

'Jackson planted the first one when she was born, then he would put in a new plant on each of Keri's birthdays. What is happening, Lieutenant?'

'When Keri disappeared she was helping a journalist investigate the abuse scandal against the archdiocese. Through your husband's lawsuit she may have been trying to identify the victims.'

Mrs Bishop looked somewhat bewildered as she tried to put the pieces together. 'That's why she began working in Jackson's office?'

'I think so. Keri may have found one of the victims, and he may be the one who abducted her. Did your husband ever discuss the identities of the victims with you?'

She shook her head. 'He promised the families that their children's identities would never be made public. As far as I know he kept that promise. He never talked about it with me, not even anyone working on the case with him knew their real names. In documents they were always referred to as John Does one, two and three.'

'And since it was settled out of court, their names never entered the public record.'

'That's right.'

'Does the name Michael Sanchez mean anything to you?'

She silently mouthed the name to herself. 'I don't think so.'

She reached down and picked up a small photograph frame that was now empty.

'Why would my husband have done this?' she asked.

'It's possible your daughter uncovered something else that your husband would want to cover up.'

171

'What?'

'He may have received payments that went beyond the parameters of the lawsuit.'

'Parameters?' Mrs Bishop looked at me for a moment. 'Are you saying my husband was bribed?'

'The journalist Keri was working with believed it, though I have no evidence of it, or that it's connected at all to your daughter's death,' I said. 'Do you have any reason to believe it's possible?'

She looked about the room and shook her head. 'I have long since learned that the things I thought were impossible have eclipsed what is real.'

'Keri apparently found some account numbers that she couldn't identify. Does that sound familiar?'

'You mean where he had hidden money?'

'Yes.'

'I oversaw our retirement investments. If he had other funds hidden somewhere then I didn't know about it.'

'I'll need the address of that storage facility.'

'It would be here somewhere if you can find it. You're free to look if you want to.'

'We're running out of time, Mrs Bishop. Is there anyplace you can think of where you husband might have gone?' I asked. 'A place from his past he might seek out?'

She shook her head and then looked at me. 'Are others in danger?'

I nodded.

'The police chief, is that a part of this?'

'Yes.'

She thought for a moment, then took an exhausted breath. 'I wish I could help you, but wherever the personal hell is that my husband has entered, he never shared that with me either.'

★

The few shafts of sunlight that had broken through in the morning had retreated back into the clouds by the time we stepped back outside the Bishops' house. We drove north to the Art Center and met Amber in her office. She was the only person that we knew of who could ID Goya by sight, or at least could have three years ago.

Harrison handed her the picture and she studied it for several long moments in silence.

'This is the best you have?'

I nodded. 'It will have to do. He would have been about sixteen at the time it was taken.'

She took a breath and shook her head. 'If I had to swear to it, I couldn't say this is absolutely him, but I couldn't say it isn't either. This looks like every awkward kid who ever had his picture taken.'

'You posed for him. Take a closer look,' I said.

She did and again shook her head. 'I deal with hundreds of students every year, and most of them try really hard not to look like the kid they were in high school. The guy I sat for was already ten years older than this when I met him. And that was three years ago. Sorry that's the best I can do.'

Mist had begun to fall once again outside. The air was heavy with the scent of lemon tress from the backyards of homes downslope from the Art Center.

We sat in the car as beads of moisture began to build up on the windshield. Since the storm had first struck the basin there had been some six hundred car accidents reported. The roof of a hardware store in El Monte had collapsed under the weight of the water, injuring two people. A man walking his dog next to the LA River near Griffith Park had fallen into the rushing water and been carried two miles downstream before he slipped under its muddy surface. In a burn area in the mountains to the east of

Pasadena the rain had sent a mudslide rushing down a narrow canyon where it swept through a small white ranch house burying a retired couple asleep in their bed. There were urban flood warnings for the valleys, debris flow watches for the foothills. A subway station in Hollywood was closed when the street drains became clogged with trash, turning the stairs leading down to the platform into a waterfall. At the happiest place on earth, the *Pirates of the Caribbean* ride was closed when moisture short-circuited the track, trapping a dozen Japanese tourists for two hours next to a one-eyed peg-legged sword-wielding buccaneer shouting AHOY MATEY over and over again. Paradise was under assault, and not one of LA's millions had a clue of what was yet to come.

# twenty-two

There would be no sleep now, no rest. The memories of what Goya had done to his other victims were too fresh. Imagining that Albert Chavez, my chief and my friend, was enduring some of the same torment was unthinkable. That it was in some way a result of his unwavering faith's overwhelming his loyalty to the law years before made it even crueler. I had left the Church because I had lost the ability to believe. Chavez had remained in it, because he had never lost his belief in its ability to redeem.

After my divorce and then my ex-husband's death I had told Chavez that I saw no evidence of God's hand in anything any longer. He replied, like any good cop would, that if evidence was easy to come by, what would be the value of faith?

Harrison and I drove away from the Art Center toward the high desert and the abbey tucked in a grove of wind-whipped trees in a wide valley between the Angeles National Forest and the Tehachapi mountains.

The day had slipped away too fast and we had made little progress. The light was already failing on the eastern horizon. The air had turned colder as we had driven up the pass. Where the clouds met the surrounding mountains a line of snow was visible against the dark trees. The abbey comprised a number of small buildings with clay-tiled roofs interconnected by a series

175

of stone-lined paths that converged in the center of the compound at the chapel and a bell tower.

As we stepped out of the squad a figure dressed in the dark robes of the order approached from one of the surrounding buildings. A hood covered his head from the early evening chill, though he wore only sandals on his feet.

He stopped a few feet from us, his face in shadow from the hood. I identified us and he held up a hand to indicate we should wait there, and then walked away.

'A vow of silence,' said Harrison.

The monk disappeared into one of the buildings and in a moment another monk in identical robes came out and walked toward us. His head was uncovered, revealing thick sandy-colored hair streaked with grey. He held his hands clasped in front of him as if hiding something between their palms. He looked to be in his fifties, and his grey eyes projected a calmness I had rarely seen in adults.

'You must forgive Brother Andrew. He is a novice and has just taken a vow of silence. I'm Father Unger, the abbot here. You're from the police?'

I introduced us again and he invited us inside the nearest building. It was a pottery studio and shop. Long tables were stacked with brightly glazed cups and bowls, the richness of the colors startling in comparison to their makers' dark brown robes.

'You haven't taken a vow of silence, Father?' I asked.

'Every brother here does at one time, and it is often revisited, but it does pose certain challenges for administration, as you can imagine.'

'We're looking for a man who may have spent time here. His name could have been Michael Sanchez.'

He thought for a moment. 'Is this man wanted for a crime?'

'A very serious one.'

'Leaving behind your given name is part of the discipline of what we do. It's the first step towards letting go of your past life and embracing God. Still, that name is not familiar.'

'This is the latest picture we have of him.'

I handed him the ID of Michael Sanchez. He studied it, then shook his head. 'This is but a picture of a boy?'

'He would have arrived here about three years ago. He may have taken the name Paul.'

Father Unger's eyes gave away a familiarity with the name.

'There was a Brother Paul here about that time, but I can't say that the man who was here is the same person as this boy. The Paul I knew had a beard and was of course much older.'

'Can you tell me about him?'

'Men come here for many reasons. All of them are leaving something behind. By asking little of them, we pass no judgment. The ability to embrace God's charity can only thrive in an environment that is absolute in its ability to protect those who seek this path.'

'In other words you're not going to tell me anything.'

'I can show you something,' he said, then motioned for us to follow him out the door.

We walked down the stone path to a large building and stepped inside the entryway. In the next room twenty or more men sat silently at two long tables, the only sound coming from inside was the chink of utensils. One monk in the room stole a quick glance in our direction then returned to eating, his head turned slightly away from us. I couldn't help but think that we had just been made by someone whose past would probably shock the believers sitting next to him.

'This is what I can show you,' Father Unger said in a whisper, motioning toward the wall next to the archway to the dining room.

On the wall hung a small drawing of a supine woman, surrounded by grotesque figures in robes, light streaming from her body in bright streaks.

'Brother Paul did this?' I asked.

The abbot nodded.

'It's another copy of an original Goya,' Harrison said.

'*Si resucitara*,' I said reading the title.

'Will she live again,' Harrison translated.

'Resurrection is a foundation of belief,' Unger said.

'In this case, Father, it's a foundation of something else entirely.'

'It's almost a prequel to the drawing we found in the Rose Bowl,' Harrison said. 'Do you think she was still alive when it was drawn?'

'Maybe somewhere in between life and death.' I took a step closer, looking for a detail I might have missed. 'It asks a question the next drawing answered.'

Harrison nodded.

'What next drawing?' Unger asked.

I glanced into the room of silent figures bent over their food. Is that what peace looks like, I wondered. And if it is, how could Goya have blended into to this world unnoticed?

'Did he ever talk to you about his mother?'

The abbot began to shake his head.

'Lives depend on our finding answers, Father,' I said. 'I don't have time for any more secrets.'

'Lives can be saved in ways you don't understand, Lieutenant.'

'And they can be taken in ways you can't imagine, Father. This is a homicide investigation.'

Unger began to say something, then hesitated.

'Perhaps one of them would remember something,' I said, looking into the dining room.

Unger looked into the silent room then motioned us toward the door. We stepped outside into the chill. The wind had begun to blow; clouds and the advancing darkness now obscured the mountains. I could smell moisture in the air, but none was falling yet.

'Brother Paul was here for a little over two years. Most of that time he spent in silence. He kept very much to himself. I couldn't tell you what his voice even sounded like. In practice he was extremely devout. Faith, as we all know, can consume an individual in ways that are not always healthy. There were concerns that his devoutness could become dangerous.'

'To whom?'

'Himself.'

'If he had been practicing silence, where did that concern come from?' Harrison asked.

'I passed his room late one night when the Santa Annas were blowing. His door had been blown open a crack by the wind. He was sleeping on the bare wooden floor, next to his undisturbed bed. His back bore scars that appeared to have come from flagellation. Some of them were new, still covered in dried blood.'

'Did he ever receive visitors?'

'No. Some will have family visit, but he appeared to have none.'

'Did he ever mention a Father Patrick?'

Unger looked at me in surprise. 'How did you know that?'

'In what context did he talk of him?'

'He once referred to his teacher by that name.'

'Nothing else?'

'No.'

'Is it possible for them to leave for short periods?'

'Yes, brothers are free to go away from the abbey as long as it does not interfere with their study.'

'Did he?'

'Yes. Toward the end of his stay he spent more and more time away from the abbey. It often happens that way when someone decides to re-enter the outside world.'

'Would you have a record of those dates?'

He shook his head. 'This is not a prison.'

'Did you notice any change when he returned?'

'None that I can remember.'

'What were the circumstances of his leaving for good?'

'Nothing appeared to have precipitated it. One morning he didn't appear for prayers. Someone was sent to his room, and he was gone. Sometime during the night he had simply walked away.'

'Did he leave anything behind?'

'The drawing I showed you, and an envelope containing ten thousand dollars in cash.'

'Do you have any idea where that money came from?'

'No. Now that is really all I can tell you,' Unger said.

I handed him one of my cards.

'Should anyone else here remember something, I would be grateful for a call,' I said.

'Of course. I must get back,' he said and smiled. 'Friday is bingo night.'

'One other thing, Father. Will anyone from here be attending the papal Mass?'

He nodded. 'Yes, most everyone will attend. We've rented a bus to take us.'

He began to turn away then stopped and looked back at me. 'I will pray that no one else is harmed.'

'Do it often, Father,' I said.

Unger walked back into the dining hall. A moment after the doors closed the sounds of voices began to drift out from the hall.

'Nothing like a good game of bingo,' Harrison said and then turned to me. 'So Morrison was right about him being here. The money he left behind could have been part of his settlement from the lawsuit. The irony gets better by the moment.'

'He could have killed Monroe in Mexico on one of his trips away from the abbey.'

'Unless of course Morrison is right about that too and it was someone in the Vatican who had him killed.'

'I'd prefer to keep it simple,' I said.

Harrison studied the dining hall for a moment. 'For him to have done that drawing he must have met Keri already, so he had begun the classes at the Art Center.'

I nodded in agreement. 'He must have discovered who she was, and made the decision to kill her.'

'And then walked away in the middle of the night and did it.'

My phone rang and I picked up.

'Wells' news station just received another recording. How soon can you meet me at the studio in Hollywood?' Traver asked.

'Is it of Wells?' I asked.

'No. They're going to hold it until we evaluate it. But they want to air it at eleven.'

It had just passed seven. I motioned to Harrison and began moving to the squad.

'What's on it?'

Traver took a deep breath. 'Chavez.'

# twenty-three

I t was an hour and a half back to the city and the news station. On the descent down the 14 a semi trailer carrying a load of lemons had jackknifed and burst into flames, sending citrus-scented fireballs rolling across the pavement and dark landscape like so many bright yellow missiles.

The rain had begun to fall again as we drove into the east end of Hollywood, forcing the crack junkies, street hustlers and runaway teenagers trading sex for a meal at Poppy's fried chicken to take shelter in the doorways of shuttered storefronts.

Assistant Chief Kelly had already arrived at the station, as well as two unmarked Crown Victorias with government plates that belonged to the FBI.

We were escorted down a long hallway that had been adorned with celebratory posters commemorating the 200th episode of *Extreme Dating* and into a large conference room.

A monitor had been set up at one end of the long table. On one side sat the station personnel – the news director, Lang, the station president, Wallace, and the station's counsel, who was called Levinson. On the wall behind them was a poster of Edward R. Murrow during the London Blitz, and one for *Alien Abduction 3: The Untold Story*.

Kelly sat on the other side along with Agent Utley and another agent I recognized named Hicks.

'This arrived a little over two hours ago. Only one other individual has seen this recording,' began Wallace.

'Who?' I asked.

'Wells' producer. He's been monitoring Trevor's email. It came just like the other one.'

'From where?' Hicks asked.

'Wells' personal address. We're assuming that whoever has done this took Wells' laptop and is using it.'

'How many copies have been made of it?' I asked.

'Two,' said the news director, Lang. 'This one and one other we're working with.'

'How many other computers has it been down loaded to?'

Lang began to answer but was interrupted by the station's legal counsel.

'I think we all want the same thing, Lieutenant.'

'Play it,' I said.

'The numbers on the bottom of the screen are a time code,' Lang said.

The counsel nodded to Lang and he turned on the recording. The video began in black; no image for nearly a minute, and then a sound began to become audible, but it seemed little more than white noise. And then there were several short clipped gasps.

'That's him breathing,' said Lang.

I pressed myself against the back of my chair, my hands tightening around the armrests with each desperate attempt for air that came out of the darkness. The breaths would speed up and then slow down with no apparent rhythm, as if being controlled by an outside force. I waited for the sound to change but it continued to stop and start with no apparent pattern. A minute passed, and then another and another, and then I just wanted it to end. I stared at the time code, watching the seconds ticking by, one after the other, hoping they would stop, and when they didn't

I focused on the darkness of the screen trying to see detail where there wasn't any. Another minute passed, then one more. I wanted to take my gun out and empty the clip into the television. I pressed my chair back away from the table and stood up, crossing my arms over my chest, trying keep myself from screaming in rage at being able to do nothing but stare at the damn screen and listen. Goya was in complete control. He was playing with us.

No one in the room made a sound. Seven minutes into the recording another sound became audible but not distinguishable. The breathing began to increase in speed and intensity, like someone running, or spiraling into panic. And then there was a flash of light that illuminated the nightmare for a brief instant before it plunged back into darkness. My heart began pounding against my chest. I reached out and gripped the back of the chair as if I was clinging to it for survival. I looked over to the station's counsel; his face had drained of color, a bead of sweat sliding down the corner of his temple.

A whisper came out of the darkness of the screen and I felt my knees give as if I had been struck in the stomach.

'*Posterus praeteritus est* . . . Forgive them, Father, they know not what they do . . .'

And then the recording abruptly ended, the blackness turning to static. For a moment no one made an attempt to speak, then Lang broke the silence.

'That's all of it,' he said softly.

I looked over to Harrison, who shook his head.

'Was that Chavez's voice?' Hicks asked.

I forced a deep breath into my lungs, trying to slow things down.

'Yes, that's him,' I said.

'We haven't been able to understand the first part of what he said at the end.'

'It's Latin,' Harrison said. 'The future is the past.'

'Riddles?'

I shook my head. 'Not riddles. All of Goya's messages have been very specific. That means something.'

'Outside of the obvious, is there meaning to what he said at the end, "Forgive them" and all that? Forgive who?' the station president Wallace said.

'Most meaning I find is outside the obvious,' I replied.

'Can we be sure of what it was we saw in that flash?' Wallace said. 'Even if we freeze the frame is it possible to make an ID?'

Assistant Chief Kelly looked over to me as if to ask the same question.

'I'm sure,' I said.

'It didn't appear clear to me,' Wallace said. 'It was little more than a blink of the eye.'

'It was more than that,' I said. 'Go back to the flash and pause it.'

Lang reversed the disc until the light flashed across the darkness and then paused it as the screen went dark again.

'The flash lasts about two or three frames. I'll move it forward one at a time.'

In the first frame the light could be seen spreading out like a small explosion illuminating the bottom third of the screen. The figure was visible from about the waist down. His feet were bare; a thick rope was secured around his ankles.

'He's seated,' Harrison said. 'Look at the rope.'

I nodded. 'Like the drawings.'

Lang advanced another frame. The light spread across the figure illuminating him with a ghostly white light. I stared at the screen for a moment and then looked away. His hands were in his lap, tied at the wrists. A bloodstained bandage was just apparent under the rope on his right wrist. Another rope was around his neck, securing him to the back of the chair. Duct tape covered his mouth. His face was nearly washed away by the brightness of the light, his dark eyes the only features untouched by the brilliant flash. The structure of his skull appeared almost visible under his ghostly translucent skin.

'Something's written across his chest on the white of his shirt,' Kelly said.

'*Crimen*,' said Harrison. 'It's Latin for guilt or fault. It implies that he is guilty.'

'Is that Chavez?' Lang asked.

'Advance it to the next frame,' I said.

Lang advanced it. The light in the picture was dissolving back into the darkness. His features were now highlighted by the presence of the returning shadows.

'Is that him?' Agent Hicks asked.

I nodded.

'What's he guilty of?' Lang asked. 'Whoever did this thinks Chavez did something.'

'He hasn't done anything,' I said quickly.

'Then why was he targeted?'

'Because he's a cop, that's all.'

'Would you characterize this as an act of terrorism?' Lang asked.

I stared at the face of my daughter's godfather on the screen for a moment.

'No, I'd call this an act of terror. Would you turn that off,' I said.

The screen went black.

'Albert has two daughters. You can't air this,' I said.

'This is news. With all due respect, I don't believe that is for you to decide,' said Levinson.

'This is material evidence in a federal crime,' Hicks said. 'You either agree, or I'll have forty agents here in fifteen minutes and

I'll confiscate every computer in this building. You want to argue the first amendment, I'm sure you can get a judge to look at it after the weekend and maybe then you'll have your computers back in another forty-eight hours.'

Lang looked over to the station president, who nodded, and then turned to me.

'Are you convinced that the same man who murdered Trevor Wells did this?'

'Yes,' I said.

Lang glanced at the lawyer then turned back to me. 'Trevor was my friend. I'll hold this until you say otherwise.'

'Would there be a record of who he may have interviewed in the last few weeks?'

He shook his head. 'The assignment desk would have records of any formal interviews, but they wouldn't have Trevor listed. His work is primarily behind the anchor desk.'

'Was he working on any stories?'

'Not to my knowledge.'

'How about informal conversations he'd had with people?'

'I'll check around the newsroom.'

'Would you excuse us for a moment?' I asked Lang.

He nodded and he and Wallace and Levinson stepped out of the room.

'Did anyone see anything during the flash of light that hints at a location?' I said.

They all shook their heads.

'There was something,' Harrison said.

'What?' I asked.

'Not during the flash, before.'

He reached over the table, picked up the remote, reversed the disc nearly to the beginning and then began to play it again.

'It's just darkness,' said Kelly.

'It's something else,' Harrison said.

I stared at the screen, the darkness ticking away, seeing it as a weapon that was about to fire.

'There,' Dylan said, and paused the disc.

'I didn't see anything,' said Hicks.

'It's not visual.'

I stared at the darkness for a moment, then turned to Dylan. 'Background noise.'

He nodded. 'The chief's being held in a controlled environment. I think this is coming from outside the building.'

'Outside?' Kelly said.

'A busy city street. Most older buildings have no insulation, single-pane windows. I'll turn it up and play it again.'

The time code ticked back ten seconds and then began to move forward. The sound lasted for little more than three or four seconds and then the first of Chavez's clipped breathing was audible.

'Just before the chief's breaths. Did you hear it?' Harrison said.

I nodded.

'There was something,' Hicks said.

'Two different sounds,' said Dylan. 'There's the first one, and then the second one a few moments later. I'll play it again.'

The seconds began to tick by again.

'There's the first sound,' Harrison said.

It seemed little more than a rush of air at most. Three more seconds ticked off on the counter and then the other sound became audible.

'A voice?' I said.

Harrison nodded.

'It could be,' said Utley. 'But I couldn't make out the words.'

'It's distant, but I think it's Spanish,' Harrison said. 'Now listen to the first sound again.'

I listened as intently as I could but the source of the sound eluded me.

'It just sounds like air moving, maybe wind,' Hicks said.

Dylan shook his head. 'I might be wrong, but that could be the door of a bus opening.'

He played it one more time.

'Right there,' he said. 'Compressed air . . . whoosh.'

I listened. It was little more than distant whisper, but we weren't imagining it.

'Like the door of a bus opening. There could be a bus stop outside that building,' I said.

'Why would you hold someone next to a busy bus stop?'

'Because the people waiting for their buses are worried about getting to work on time, or not getting caught by INS, not about what's going on inside a building behind them that's none of their business. You do the same thing on a residential street and you end up with snoopy neighbors wondering about what's going on behind the closed windows.

'I'll send it to Washington and get it enhanced,' Hicks said.

Kelly shook his head. 'How does this help us?'

Assistant Chief Kelly's skills as a cop had always been more political than investigative. If he had ever worked a crime scene, his instincts for it had long ago become little more than a memory.

'A door of a bus opens, someone steps out, or is about to get on, and they say something to either the driver or another passenger,' I said.

Hicks turned to me and nodded. 'It could be, if we get lucky.'

'Could be what?' Kelly asked.

'They could have been asking for directions,' I said. 'That could give us a location.'

'That's it, the sound of a goddamn bus?' Kelly said. 'Do you know how many bus stops there are in this city?'

'It's a chance,' I said.

He pushed back from the chair and stood up. 'What the chief said at the end. It's from the Bible, isn't it?'

'It's from Luke, Jesus' words from the cross,' I said.

'Are those the chief's own words, or Goya's?'

I shook my head. 'There isn't anything on that disc that Goya doesn't want there.'

'Then what's it mean?'

'I don't know.'

'How long will it take to do the sound analysis on the rest of the disc?' he asked.

'If there's something there it shouldn't take long. If we get lucky, maybe by dawn our time. If we're not . . . it will take longer,' Hicks said.

'And how much time does Chavez have?'

The room remained silent.

'One way or the other this ends with the Pope's Mass at noon on Sunday,' I said.

Kelly glanced at his watch. 'Thirty-eight hours.'


Lang was waiting for me when we stepped out of the conference room.

'Could we talk in private?'

I nodded and Harrison excused himself. I walked a short distance down a hallway and stepped into an empty editing room.

'You found something?' I asked.

Lang nodded. 'He was working on something. In the last few days he had a series of meetings that took him out of the office. One of our producers asked him if he needed a cameraman and he said no.'

'Is there any record of who it was he was talking to?'

'Just some notes written on a desk calendar.'

'I'd like to see it.'

He reached over and opened a file sitting on the table next to us. 'If this violates a source he was working, Trevor wouldn't be happy about it.'

'I'm only interested in who killed him.'

Lang nodded and removed several sheets from the calendar and handed them to me. 'Two phone numbers, and some letters.'

I recognized the first phone number as the one Morrison had given me to get hold of him. I didn't know the second. Along with the numbers were three capitalized letters. The one next to Morrison's phone number was M. The second letter, B, had no number next to it. The second number wasn't familiar. Below it was the letter K.

'Trevor often used shorthand. I think the letters represent people.'

'Did you try the numbers?' I asked.

He shook his head. I took out my phone and dialed the second number. On the second ring it was answered by a recording. 'You've reached the archdiocese of Los Angeles.'

I hung up.

'I'd like to take this with me,' I said.

He nodded. 'Did that mean anything to you?'

I shook my head. 'We'll see.'

I walked outside where Harrison was waiting at the car, and handed him the page from the desk calendar.

'Before he died Wells talked to the reporter Morrison and someone within the archdiocese. I'm guessing it wasn't about loss of faith.'

Harrison's eyes went over Wells' writing.

'If the letters stand for people it looks like he may have also talked to Jackson Bishop.'

I nodded.

'What about the last letter, K? Could be one of the victims, or someone else who took a payoff or helped to cover up the abuse,' Harrison said. He handed it back to me and I looked at it.

'It could also be his killer.'

My phone rang and I picked up. It was Traver.

'We found the church in the picture. It's in East LA.'

# twenty-four

It was nearly eleven when we stopped outside the church on the other side of the river from downtown. Boyle Heights had been founded by an Irishman, and then settled by every race that the city to the west of the river didn't want: Jews, Japanese, Mexicans, Slavs and Russians. During the war the Japanese were loaded onto buses and sent to relocation camps. The Jews moved to West LA, and the Slavs and Russians drifted away. The Mexicans stayed. What was once one of the most diverse areas in the city was now nearly all Latino.

The church was just as it was in the photograph. With its bell tower and large wooden doors, it appeared to have changed little except for an elaborate mural painted on a retaining wall of a convertible lowrider driven by Cesar Chavez with John Kennedy and Jesus sitting in the back.

A number of women were milling about outside holding candles under their brightly colored umbrellas.

'A vigil,' I said.

'Gang violence,' Harrison said.

'This looks different.'

We parked and stepped out. A taco stand down the block was doing a brisk business despite the light rain. The scent of grilled chicken, cumin and cilantro drifted on the light breeze. An unmarked sedan with government plates was parked across the street from the church. The dark forms of two figures could be seen sitting inside.

'INS,' I said.

As we approached the front of the church the group took notice of us and a chant began to rise from the gathered women as they moved toward the door to block our entry. '*Santuario, santuario . . .*'

'Sanctuary,' Harrison said.

'The church is shielding someone.'

The door opened and a priest stepped outside and saw us approaching. He held up his hand and the women fell silent. He stepped through the small crowd and approached us.

'This is a house of God. You may not enter as we have claimed the right of sanctuary,' he said.

The priest looked to be in his early thirties, his blond hair appearing nearly white against the darkness of his clerical black. I held out my ID and explained that we were here on another matter.

He glanced across the street toward the INS vehicle parked in the shadows.

'We have to be very careful. They've made several attempts at gaining entry. I'm Father Samulson.'

We introduced ourselves and he walked us into the chapel past the suspicious eyes of its candle-bearing guardians. As we stepped inside a number of young women rose to their feet. Their faces bore the traces of Indian and Mayan decent. One of the girls began to tremble visibly.

'*No estoy aquí para tí,*' Father Samulson said, assuring them that we were not here for them.

'How long has this been going on?' I asked.

'Ten days,' he said. 'The shop they were sewing in was raided. You know what they were sewing? Socks with pieces of fruit embroidered on them. And now they are being treated like terrorists.'

'We're trying to find someone, Father. She's not wanted for a crime, but it may save a life if we can find her. She may have been a parishioner here at one time.'

I showed him the photograph of the young pregnant women. He walked over to the altar and studied it by the light of the burning candles.

'I don't recognize her. But I've only been here a few years.'

'Her name may be Sanchez,' I said.

He shook his head again. 'There may be someone who would know.'

The priest called over a young women who was sitting with the illegals. He said something to her and she rushed down to the doors of the church and went out.

'Was a Father Patrick ever assigned here?' I asked.

He thought for a moment then nodded.

'I believe so, but that would have been almost thirty years ago.'

The doors opened and a heavy-set women stepped in and began walking toward us. She wore a thick string of colorful beads around her neck along with a large cross. A dark elaborate blanket shawl covered a watermelon-colored shirt.

'This is Marisala,' said the priest. 'There's little about this church that she doesn't know.'

She was in her late fifties, I guessed. Her dark brown eyes gave the impression that there was no burden they hadn't held. She looked Harrison and me over, then turned to the priest.

'Yes, Father?' she asked. Her voice carried a faint hint of the barrio that seemed as much about politics as upbringing.

'These people are from the police.'

'Yes, I know,' she said.

'They're looking for someone. You may be able to help.'

197

'And why would I do that?' she said defiantly.

'Because you could save the life of a man I care very much about,' I said.

The women looked me in the eyes for a moment, seeming to judge my ability to conceal a hidden truth. After a moment she nodded. I handed her the photograph.

'We think her name may be Sanchez. We need her help, but don't know where to find her.'

Marisala shook her head. 'No.'

'Are you sure?'

'I'm sure her name was not Sanchez.' She glanced back and forth between us, taking a kind of stock.

'She's your boss?' she asked Harrison.

He nodded. 'In every way.'

The faintest smile appeared on her lips. 'It's Perez. Her name was Maria Perez.'

'She had a son,' I said.

The woman turned to me.

'No, she had no children.'

'Are you certain? Look at that photograph. She looks pregnant.'

She didn't bother to look at it.

'I have twelve grandchildren, I know what pregnant looks like. She had no children.'

She handed me back the photograph.

'How would I find her?' I asked.

'I don't know. I think she went back to Mexico.'

'When?'

'Maybe ten years ago, I don't remember.'

I took out the ID picture of Michael Sanchez.

'Have you ever seen him before?'

She studied the picture and then gave it back to me.

'No.'

'Did you know Maria Perez well?' I asked.

She cocked her head to the side and took a short breath.

'I knew her, but not well,' she said.

'Tell me about her.'

'She came as a young women to work the strawberry fields in Oxnard. Then she found work in the garment district. Then she came here.'

'She was illegal?'

Marisala looked over toward the women who had taken shelter in the church.

'How can a human being be illegal?'

'Why did she go back to Mexico?' I asked.

'She missed her family. They were all there.'

'She was pretty, why didn't she marry? She could have become a citizen.'

She reached out and took hold of my left hand, noting the lack of a wedding ring.

'Some people are not lucky with love.'

I smiled.

'Was she here when Father Patrick was the priest?

She thought for a moment, then shrugged.

'It would have been around the same time . . . I don't remember.'

'He took his own life yesterday,' I said.

The strength in her eyes momentarily vanished, replaced by something else, though I wasn't sure what. Father Samulson crossed himself and shook his head.

'Why?' he asked.

I held up the picture of Maria Perez.

'I think it had to do with her,' I said, and looked back at Marisala.

'Did you know him well?' I asked.

She shook her head.

'He was not here long.'

We walked back outside and got in the squad but didn't drive away. The group of women standing at the entrance to the church had begun to thin with the advancing time. Those that remained had put up an awning and were sitting in lawn chairs with blankets to see out the long chilly night.

'She didn't tell us the truth, or at least didn't tell us everything,' Harrison said.

'If she knew that Patrick had fathered a child it could have just been embarrassment at acknowledging that in front of her priest.'

'She doesn't strike me as someone who embarrasses easily,' Harrison said.

'Did you see her eyes when I told her about Patrick's death?'

Dylan shook his head.

'What was her reaction?'

I thought for a moment, trying to understand it.

'Satisfaction.'

I looked back toward the entrance to the church as Marisala stepped out and looked around. She said something to the group of women, then fixed her eyes on us and began walking in our direction.

'I guess this rules out having to follow her,' Harrison said.

Marisala walked up to the squad and I rolled down the window.

'Would you like to get out of the rain?' I asked.

She shook her head.

'Rain washes away all our sins.'

'Does that include lying inside a church?' I asked.

'God understands.'

'I would like to also,' I said.

'Are you Catholic, Lieutenant?' she asked.

'I was once,' I said.

'Were you a good Catholic? Did you always tell your priest the truth?'

I smiled and shook my head. 'That depended on which truth.'

'Yes,' she said.

'In this case the truth involves a murder – more than one. Lying about it is a crime.'

'So is rape. But you can't accuse a priest of rape, can you? Not then.'

'Father Patrick raped Maria Perez?'

She nodded. 'More than once. She couldn't go to the police for fear of being deported. She couldn't go to anyone in the congregation. And she couldn't go home because of the shame.'

'She told you though, didn't she?' I said.

Her eyes fixed on mine.

'What kind of a policeman are you?' she asked.

'A desperate one,' I said.

'She didn't tell me until she was pregnant, when she didn't know what to do. I knew a doctor who was willing to help, but she couldn't do that. It was a sin to her.'

'What happened?'

'Patrick took her away somewhere, a convent maybe, I never knew. One day she was just gone. Shortly after that Patrick was moved to another church. I never saw him again.'

'Did you see her again?'

Marisala nodded. 'Several times many years later. She said she had a son and was looking for him. He would have been a teenager by then. The last time she came she went to the archdiocese, but they refused to help her.'

'When was this?'

'About three years ago.'

'Did she ever find him?'

'I don't know. Maria wasn't well in the head. She had become convinced that her son was a result of a virgin birth, not a rape. She was not unlike the young girls inside. She wasn't educated; she wanted nothing more than a chance for a better life. I'm third generation Angelino. I speak their language, but I can't even imagine where they find the kind of courage to come to this country and do what they have to do to survive.'

She looked up into the sky and let the gentle rain fall across her face before she looked back at me.

'That man took it away from her.'

'Yes,' I said. 'Did she ever say anything about the years after Patrick took her away?'

'All she talked about was finding her son.'

'Did she call him by a name?'

'I think it was Miguel.'

'But she never said anything about where she might have lived during those years?'

'No.'

'Do you have any idea where she may be now?'

'She talked about going back to Mexico. In her mind it had become a paradise for her. I don't know if she ever did go.'

'And you haven't seen her again?'

She shook her head. 'Is it her son that you are looking for?'

'It is.'

'Did he kill someone?'

'Very likely more than one.'

'Then I will pray that she never found him and is at least spared that pain.' She started to turn away and then stopped. 'I will say four Hail Marys for lying in church, and I will thank God for Patrick's death.'

She turned and walked back to the small group of women gathered around the flickering light of the candles.

202

'You think Patrick could have been leading a double life, being an abusive father and a priest at the same time?' Harrison asked.

I nodded. 'It begins to make sense.'

'And when the boy was old enough to run away, Patrick abandons Maria and she goes quietly insane.'

'According to Marisala, Maria Perez last came looking for him about three years ago,' I said.

'The same time as his first murder. You think there could be a connection?'

'Maybe her finding him helped push him over the edge.'

'I'll run their names through the system, see if they come up,' Harrison said.

The women outside the church began to sing a song softly in Spanish.

'A child out of rape. Goya's world did not begin very well,' I said.

'The painting in the first apartment we found begins to make even more sense.'

'Saturn Devouring his Son?'

Harrison nodded.

'Goya must have seen it as autobiographical,' I said.

'One he already knew the ending to.'

Down the street, smoke from the taco stand began drifting across the pavement, which was glistening in the darkness from the rain.

'What Goya had Chavez say, the future is the past, what's that mean to you?' I asked.

Harrison thought about it. 'Is he talking about the recent past or the distant?'

'Everything he wants us to know he has either shown us or told us. The painting of the father devouring his son, the drawings of abuse. He wants us to feel what he feels.'

'You think we've missed something?'

'We must have.'

'That still doesn't point us to where.'

'So we go through it all.'

'Where do we start?'

'What was the message on the door of his studio? Cowards die many times before their death; the valiant never taste of death but once.'

'The downfall of the hero in a Shakespearean tragedy.'

'His studio,' I said.

Harrison looked at me and then turned on the ignition.

# twenty-five

It was past one when we pulled to a stop across from the side of the building where we had found Goya's drawings and the freezer that had entombed Keri Bishop.

Harrison turned off the engine and the lights. My eyes began to adjust to the darkness. In a doorway across the street, a homeless person had converted a large cardboard box into a shelter. I looked back at the Stinson building. Halfway up the brick façade were the windows of the studio.

'When did crime scene finish with it?' I asked.

'They were there for about eight hours after we left. That's over twenty-four hours ago.'

I opened the door, stepped out and looked up toward the fourth floor.

'It would be the two windows at the end, wouldn't it?' I said.

Harrison nodded.

'Look at the bottom of the window on the right. Something's different.'

Dylan stared at it for a moment. 'It's open. Crime scene could have left it like that.'

'And if they didn't?'

We rushed across the street and around to the front entrance of the building. I pushed on the door and it swung open.

'Someone's working late,' Harrison said.

A fluorescent light at the far end of the lobby flickered on and off, illuminating the space with a dim blue glow. The stairway leading up was as black as a cave. I tried a light switch at the first step with no result. From the darkness above a door opened and closed with click.

'Was there a rear stairway?' I said.

Harrison nodded.

'Lock the elevator, then go up the back. I'll meet you at the studio.'

Harrison turned and headed down the hallway. I turned on my small Mag-lite and moved up to the first landing, stopping next to the fire door leading into the hallway. I switched off the light and slowly opened the door. Nothing moved. There wasn't a sound.

The faint odor of cigarette smoke hung in the air of the landing. My hand drifted down to the handle of my Glock as I closed the door and shined my light up the stairs.

From somewhere above I heard the sound of a footfall and then silence. I hesitated, waiting for more movement above, and when it didn't come I started up to the next landing and stopped at the door. The smell of cigarette smoke was stronger, along with the heavy odor of human sweat. I took a step and then heard the creak of movement behind me.

I swung the light around and saw the door handle begin to turn. I had begun to draw my Glock when I heard the latch clear the frame and saw the blur of movement. The heavy steel door struck my shoulder and I was moving backward. The light fell from my hand, the beam cutting a pinwheel through the darkness as it spun in the air.

I hit the stairs with my back, the air rushed out of my lungs and I gasped for breath. I tried to pick myself up, but it was as if the weight of the air was holding me down.

The Mag-lite rolled to a stop against the wall and I saw the dark silhouette of a figure move toward me. I touched the Glock but I couldn't close my hand around it as I gasped for breath. I tried to say police, but couldn't manage a sound.

The figure stepped up next to me. He stood silently for a moment then kneeled down. His clothes seemed to cover him in layer upon layer as if he was wearing them like a second skin. His face was dark from soot and dirt, hiding all his features except his light blue eyes, which almost shone in the darkness.

'Are you her?' he whispered, in a halting voice with an accent that seemed to be a creation of madness. He leaned in and cocked his head. 'Are you the one?'

'One?' I managed to whisper.

'You're her, aren't you? He said you would come.'

The air began to haltingly return to my lungs.

'Who said?' I asked.

'God almighty himself.' He stared at me for a moment, then reached down and took hold of my left hand and pressed open my palm. 'This is for you.'

He placed something in my hand and stood up. The door on the next landing opened and the figure standing over me rushed away down the stairs, making a kind of strange sing-song noise as he vanished.

'Alex?' Harrison called out from above.

I took another breath, the heavy odor of the homeless man filling my mouth.

'I'm here,' I managed to say and then heard Harrison coming down.

The beam of his light found me and he jumped the last few steps and helped me sit up.

'Are you all right?'

My shoulder ached where the door had hit me but nothing else seemed damaged. I took a slow deep breath and slowly stood up with Dylan's help.

'I'm all right,' I said.

'What's that's smell?'

'A messenger from God.'

'I heard a door slam so I came this way.'

'That was the sound of it hitting me.'

'What happened?'

'I surprised a homeless man bearing gifts from God.'

'Gifts?'

I raised my left hand and looked at the object the homeless man had placed in it. My heart began pounding against my chest and I struggled to take another breath. I looked up the stairs to the fourth floor, towards Goya's studio.

'He's been here.'

'What is it?' Harrison asked.

I held out my palm for him and he shined the light on it.

'It's the crucifix from Chavez's rosary,' I said.

Dylan retrieved my light and we rushed up the stairs to the fourth floor door and pushed it open. A single ceiling light halfway down the hallway was on. At the far end of the hallway I could see the crime-scene tape blocking off the studio door. We hesitated for a moment, listening for a sound or movement, and then started down each side of the corridor.

At the tape we stopped and Harrison shined his light on the door.

'It's been opened,' he said.

The evidence seal had been cleanly cut. We drew our weapons and ducked under the tape to get to the door. I glanced at Dylan and he nodded, then I reached out and took hold of the handle.

'Ready,' he said and I flung the door open and we raised our weapons.

The beams of our lights cut through the darkness of the front room. The drawings had all been removed from the scene. The black smudges of fingerprint dust were spread all over the interior.

I shined my light on the sheet of plastic separating the two spaces in the loft.

'He's been and gone,' I said.

I stepped inside the room and lowered my gun. Harrison walked over to the sheet of plastic, lifted it and pointed his light into the second space. I walked through the first room looking for the smallest of differences, but nothing stood out.

'There's nothing here,' I said and stepped around the plastic into the second space.

Dylan was holding his light on the freezer at the far side of the room. Print dust smudged much of the exterior. More evidence tape had been placed on the lid to seal it closed. The freezer emitted a gentle electric hum.

'He's plugged it back in,' I said.

'That tape's been cut also,' Harrison said. 'There's something inside.'

My left hand closed around Chavez's crucifix and I rushed over to the freezer, reaching for the handle.

'Wait,' Harrison said, his hand closing around mine. 'He expected you here, and he expected you to do exactly what you're doing. Let me check it first.'

I shook my head.

'To hell with him,' I said. 'We're not what he's fighting, it's his past that he's punishing.'

I stared at the freezer and took a breath. The image of Trevor Wells staring at me with his empty eye sockets came out of the darkness of memory. My hand holding the lid of the freezer began to tremble. I tried not to picture the godfather of my child lying inside, but I couldn't escape it.

'Let me do it,' Dylan said.

I started to resist and then gave in, letting go of the handle as if it were burning hot. Dylan reached down and lifted the lid. Cold air rushed across our faces, condensing into a thick cloud as it streamed out. I began to frantically sweep the air with my hand to clear it as Harrison shined his light into the interior of the freezer. The swirling cloud of frost particles parted and we both stared into the space.

'Nothing,' I whispered. 'It's empty.'

Harrison shook his head. 'There's something here.'

A piece of paper covered in a layer of frost crystals was just visible where its edges had curled. Dylan took hold of it by the corner and lifted it up. I closed the freezer and Dylan laid it on the top.

As the warmer air of the room started to melt the remaining crystals an image began to appear.

'More Latin. *Justitia caeca est*,' Dylan said.

'You don't need to translate that,' I said. Anyone who understands even a little about the law has heard those words. 'Justice is blind.'

I stared at the writing for a moment, then turned and looked around the rest of the room.

'This doesn't feel right,' I said. 'He's left images before, not words.'

I looked back at the message and gently ran my fingers across the writing. It was raised slightly above the paper.

'He's used paint for this, not ink.' I turned and began shining my light across the walls of the space.

'What are you looking for?' Harrison asked.

'Justice is blind. He's challenging us to see something.' I stepped away from the freezer and began to search for the slightest change.

'Look in the bathroom, see if anything's different,' I said.

I moved back to the sheet of plastic separating the two spaces and stepped into the room where we had found the original drawings. The walls were lined with a soft particleboard where Goya had pinned the drawings. I walked over and began working the light across the surface.

'There's nothing in the bathroom,' Harrison said as he came through to join me.

I walked over to the wall where Goya had placed the drawing titled *This is how it begins*. Tiny particles of the composite board were scattered on the floor. I ran my fingers over the heads of the screws holding the board to the wall. The bottom screw was a turn or more from being secured all the way into the board. I tested the screw above it. It was the same.

'This board's been removed and then replaced.'

Harrison kneeled down and examined the floor under the far corner of the board. 'This looks like dried gesso.'

'Gesso?'

'It's medium you apply to surfaces to paint on.'

He took out a small pocketknife and began removing the screws. When the last one fell out we lowered the board from the wall and raised our lights. We stared in silence for a moment at the image we had uncovered. The painting was about three feet by four.

'It's not quite finished,' Harrison said.

'It's finished enough.'

He reached out and touched the edge of the painting with a finger. 'It's not even dry. He couldn't have left here more than a few hours ago.'

On the left a figure was bound to a post or a tree, his mouth open in a scream. His eyes were filled with terror as he stared at several soldiers raising their rifles to shoot him.

'A military firing squad,' I said.

Harrison nodded.

'Do you remember seeing this image in the original Goya prints?' I asked.

Dylan took a step toward the painting and examined it for a moment.

'Not as a whole.'

'What do you mean?'

'It all looks familiar, but not like this. It's as if he's taken several different images and combined them to create this one. I remember a firing squad in one, but they were shooting at a crowd, as I remember. The screaming figure I think was in another.'

'The message he wanted to leave couldn't be found in any single work, so he created this one.'

Harrison stepped back next to me.

'So what exactly is the message is the question?' he said.

I looked back to the freezer. 'He writes that justice is blind, and then creates a painting of an execution. What's that say to you?'

'The firing squad is composed of soldiers . . . in the original Goyas they represented the law and all that was corrupt about government.'

'It's a picture of us,' I said.

'Yeah. I think it's safe to assume that the figure who is about to die is innocent in his eyes.'

'Not exactly a ringing endorsement of the legal system.'

'This could be a picture of his own death,' Harrison said.

'And if it's not?'

'Then someone else is going to die.' He turned to me. 'And probably by our hands.'

# twenty-six

Dawn seemed to come reluctantly, as if the day was hesitant to shed light on the events to come. From my office window it appeared as a faint line of blood-red sky rising over the dark outline of the San Gabriels.

I opened the window and let the air wash over me. The rain had flushed it clean of particulates. Each breath was an act of turning back the clock to a time before the automobile had arrived with its promise of a suburban paradise only to shroud it in a haze of smog.

The street below came alive in small steps as light moved from east to west. A jogger getting in her early miles rounded the block. A catering truck, trailing the odor of frying bacon and chorizo, passed. Newspapers were delivered. Black BMWs of stockbrokers headed toward the seats of empire. Three miles away in the shadow of the arroyo the first of the faithful had begun to arrive at the Rose Bowl for tomorrow's Mass.

Harrison lay on the couch, his eyes closed in an attempt at rest. The door to the office opened and Traver stepped in.

'Anything from the FBI?' I asked.

He shook his head then handed me a piece of notepaper with a Tujunga address on it.

'What's this?'

'A missing person's report filed yesterday. Look at the name,' Traver said.

'Michael Sanchez,' I said.

Harrison got up from the couch and walked over to the desk.

'How was it reported?'

'By phone from a family friend.'

I quickly ran through the report. 'Says he was last seen the day before Keri's body was discovered.'

Traver nodded. 'I ran his name through DMV and the address matched the one on the missing person report.' He handed me another sheet of paper. 'That's his driver's license.'

I got up from my desk and walked over to the bulletin board where the Michael Sanchez ID from St Gabriel's was tacked.

'There would be about a fourteen-year difference,' Harrison said.

I held up the new copy next to the old one and my gaze was drawn to his dark eyes. He was clean-shaven; his features could almost be called delicate.

'It's him,' I said.

'He still looks like a boy,' Harrison said.

'Not exactly the face of a monster,' Traver added.

I looked back at the report, going through the few details.

'We took this call?' I asked.

Traver nodded.

'Tujunga's in  LA county sheriffs' jurisdiction. Why didn't it go to them?'

'The friend who called it in must live in Pasadena.'

'Was it forwarded to them?'

'Yeah.'

'Which means it will be another few days before they check it out.'

'If it's a slow day,' Harrison said.

I looked again at the picture. Harrison was right: the soft features were still those of a boy.

'What does a monster look like?' I said.

214

★

The address was on top of a small ridge overlooking a debris catch basin at the base of the foothills. It was just after seven when we pulled to a stop half a block from the house. A tactical squad was waiting at the base of the ridge. The street was like any other subdivision that popped up in the foothills during the sixties. Ranch houses; split levels, all nearly identical except for size and positioning of the attached garage and driveway.

Traver pulled to a stop behind us in another squad and then Harrison stepped on the gas and drove slowly down the street past the house. Curtains were drawn in the front windows. The lawn was neatly mowed.

'Papers,' I said.

On the walk and in a flowerbed next to the front door were half a dozen or more visible newspapers in plastic lying where they had been tossed. We finished the pass then Harrison turned the squad around and pulled to a stop in front of the house next door.

'Does something about this strike you as odd?' I said.

Harrison stared at the house for a moment. 'That Goya would live on such a normal street?'

'No, the street's perfect; there are a thousand others just like it.'

Across the street a garage door opened. A silver Audi backed out and turned to leave. The driver was Asian, already working a phone as he headed toward work.

I picked up the copy of Sanchez's license, looked at the picture and shook my head.

'What's odd is that Goya would have a friend close enough to notice he was missing. He's a fanatic; the only people he would allow close to him are ones he's using to finish his work.'

I stared at the newspapers, neatly sealed in plastic, scattered on the grass like so many random body bags.

'Oh, God,' I said, then reached down and opened the door.

'What are you doing?' Harrison said. 'Wait for tactical to go in.'

'It's too late for tactical,' I said.

'Alex,' Harrison said as I stepped out and started running toward the house.

Harrison jumped out and I could hear him rushing after me. Out of the corner of my eye I saw Traver's squad come skidding to a stop against the curb in front of the house as I reached the front walk and stopped.

My hand dropped to the Glock on my hip, but I didn't slip it from the holster. My eyes traveled over the front of the house for a moment and then I turned and looked at the homes across the street. Harrison reached me and stopped.

'We don't need to go in this way,' he said.

I shook my head and looked back at the house.

'Yes we do. Look at the windows,' I said. 'Every one of them has shades or curtains drawn, even the ones on the side of the house. It's the only house on the block like that. He's been here.'

'Let tactical go in,' Harrison said as Traver joined us.

'No. This is a crime scene. They'll make a mess of it.'

'You can't be sure of that.'

I nodded as the first strong sun we had seen in days began shining through the broken clouds.

'Look at the curtains on the big window, tell me what you see,' I said.

Traver shook his head. 'I don't see—'

'An image,' Harrison said.

I nodded. 'Something's been painted on the other side of that curtain.'

I walked up to the front landing and stopped.

'Dave, check in the garage and see if there's a car, then walk around the perimeter of the house and see what you find.'

'Am I looking for anything in particular?'

I shook my head. 'You'll know it when you see it.'

Traver disappeared around the corner.

'If this isn't Goya, then who is it?' Harrison said.

'All Morrison said was that Sanchez was one of Patrick's victims at St Gabriel's.'

I started to take a step, then stopped. 'Do you hear that?'

Harrison nodded. 'Choral music. It's coming from inside.'

I halved the distance to the front door then stopped and listened to the rise and fall of the voices.

'Latin again,' Harrison said.

'I know this. It's a requiem.'

Harrison listened for a moment and then began to translate. 'Deliver me . . . from eternal death on that fearful day when the heavens and earth are moved, when you come to judge the world with fire. I am made to tremble and I fear the judgment that will come, and the coming wrath . . . That's not exact but it gives you the general idea.'

'It's not a happy ending,' I said.

Traver stepped back around the corner. 'I think you'd better look at this.'

We walked around the corner of the house and followed the driveway down the side to the garage. A row of cypress trees and a tall fence shielded the structure from the neighboring property. There was nothing beyond it but the hill sloping down toward the catch basin.

'There's no car inside. The garage was used for something else,' Traver said.

The overhead door was closed. The entryway next to it was open. I walked over and stopped at the threshold. The air inside was heavy with an odor I couldn't identify.

'What is that?' Harrison said as he stepped up next to me.

217

I reached around and turned on the light switch, took half a step and stopped.

'That's what that odor is,' I said.

In the center of the garage floor was what appeared to be a pool of dried blood. Above it a rope dangled from one of the rafters. On the end of the rope were two leather cuffs.

I walked up to the edge of the dried pool of blood and looked closely at the rope. The end next to the leather cuffs was soaked in blood.

'Torture,' Dylan said. 'It's the same rope as in the drawings.'

I nodded. 'I think we may have found the owner of the severed hands.'

I stepped away from the pool of dried blood and went out the door to look at the house. The back windows were shuttered like all the rest. Traver was kneeling down examining something in the grass. I walked over to him.

'What is it?' I asked.

'Grooves dug in the grass. Like someone was being dragged and they were clawing with their fingers trying to stop it.'

'Keep searching for anything else out here,' I said, then went past Traver and up to the back door and pushed it open. Inside was the kitchen. Everything about the room appeared normal except that several chairs from the table had been turned over, and a cabinet door and been partially ripped off and hung by only one of its hinges. Dylan stepped up beside me and looked it over.

'He was dragged through this room,' I said. 'He tried holding on to the handle on the cabinet, and then the chairs.'

Harrison kneeled down and looked at something. 'He grabbed the door at the bottom, too. This looks like blood.'

It didn't require much imagination to hear the frantic struggle for survival that had taken place within this room. I followed the apparent direction the victim had been dragged to a door at the far end of the kitchen and stepped through into the dining room. On one side of the table plates and bowls were spread out along its entire length. In the center was a half-full bottle of wine, and next to that a loaf of bread torn into pieces.

'That looks familiar somehow,' Harrison said.

'The bread, the wine, it's about betrayal.'

'The last supper?' Harrison said.

From beyond the other end of the dining room came the sound of the choral music again. Harrison pulled his weapon and held it at his side and glanced at me.

'Humor me,' he whispered.

We walked over to the other end of the dining room, hesitated, and then Harrison swung around raising his weapon. He held it for a moment, staring into the far room, and then lowered it. I stepped around behind him and stopped. The furniture had been pushed back against the walls. Much of the floor was splattered with paint. The music was coming from a boom box sitting on the floor. A canvas had been hung across the front window. A painting covered nearly every inch of it.

'Do you recognize it?' I asked.

Harrison looked at it for a moment and then nodded.

'It's from the same group of Goyas as the others. It's called *A Collection of Dead Men*.'

I moved past Harrison to get a closer look. At first it appeared to be little more than an abstract collection of shapes, but then the shapes began to take form. It was an image of a pile of bodies, the limbs intertwined so you couldn't tell which belonged to which victim.

'In Goya's original the dead would have been victims of war,' Harrison said. 'He must see what he's doing in the same terms.'

'A holy war.'

Harrison walked up and examined the paint on the canvas.

'This has been dry for several days, maybe longer.'

I stared at it for a moment.

'Just like the blood out in the garage.'

'So where's Sanchez?' Harrison said.

I turned and looked down a hallway leading to the west side of the house. At the far end a door appeared to be cracked open, the light streaming out giving a red glow.

'Turn off that music,' I said.

Harrison walked over and switched it off as I started walking down the dark hallway. I paused at the other doors and looked into the rooms – each was empty and untouched by what had happened in other parts of the house.

At the last door I hesitated at the edge of the red light spilling out from inside the room, then went in. It was a bedroom. Nothing appeared odd about it, other than the red light bulb that had been fitted in a bedside lamp. I looked around for the smallest detail that was out of place.

Harrison came in and looked over the room.

'It looks untouched,' he said.

'Looks that way, but Goya wanted us in here for a reason.'

I stepped over to the dresser. A series of framed snapshots were lined up on it. I picked up one of him and four other people who I assumed were his two sisters and his parents.

'This looks relatively recent,' I said. 'He's got family some-where. We need to find them. If he was one of the abused boys at St Gabriel's, they might know who the others are.'

'So what's happened to him?' Harrison said.

I shook my head.

'I don't know.'

I started to turn then stopped when my eye caught something else on the dresser. It was one of those formal studio photographs of Michael Sanchez, the boyish features from his school ID still present in his face as an adult. A thin layer of dust covered the top of the dresser, except for an outline of where the frame had sat a short time before.

'Look at the outline in the dust. This picture's been moved.'

Harrison stepped over and examined it.

'An inch or two. Why would Goya do that?'

I looked back across the room in the direction the picture was pointed.

'He's getting more sophisticated in his games. He's enjoying it now. He wants us to see something.'

We both stared across the room looking for the detail Goya had wanted us to see. Harrison shook his head.

'I don't see it. The change in perspective doesn't alter the view to anything specific.'

I continued to look.

'Maybe it's not meant to. Maybe he just wants us to look more closely at something we're already seeing.'

The picture was pointed toward the bed and then a window. I walked over to the bed, kneeled down and looked underneath.

'Nothing,' I said.

I looked across the bedspread, ran my hand over the surface.

'Something's not right here,' I said. 'This should be smooth. There's something under here.'

I stood up and looked it over. It had been neatly made, hospital corners and all; it was perfect. I stepped up to the headboard.

'Help me pull it back,' I said.

Harrison walked around to the other side and we slowly pulled the bedspread off the pillows. The pillowcases were clean, with barely a crease in them.

'It hasn't been slept in,' Harrison said.

We began to pull the spread down toward the foot of the bed

but stopped after only a foot or two. We both stared for a moment at what we were seeing.

'Dirt?' Dylan said. 'He's lost me with this.'

A layer of dark soil had been spread across the surface of the sheets. I reached down and took some of the soil in my fingers.

'Dust to dust,' I said softly, and then dropped the bedspread and ran over to the window and opened the curtains.

'What is it?' Harrison said.

The window looked out over an expanse of grass toward the far corner of the backyard and a tall wooden fence trellised with bougainvilleas in full bloom. Traver was standing at the edge of the grass staring toward the fence line. I turned and ran out the bedroom, down the hallway to the kitchen and stepped outside. Traver was examining the grass.

'Something's been moved across this. Looks like it was heavy – see how the blades of grass are bent.'

Harrison came out of the house and joined us as we started across the lawn to the row of bougainvilleas next to the fence. The plants were spaced five or six feet apart at the base. The soil between the plants was covered in dried orange and red petals. I kneeled down and brushed the dried flowers aside and tested the soil. It was packed and firm. I checked the soil beneath the next plant and it was the same. Beneath the third one the air held a heavier scent than under the others and the soil gave way.

'This ground's been worked,' I said and looked at Harrison.

I began to scoop the dirt aside, and on the third handful I exposed what felt like the fine root system of the plant only it was dark and did not belong in the soil. I removed some more dirt and then stood up, my fingers tightening around the soil in my palm.

'He never left here,' I said.

I glanced at the dirt in my hand and then let it slip through my fingers. If the body in the ground was Michael Sanchez, I had exposed the back of his head and neck. He appeared to have been buried in a crouching position. His fine dark hair stood in stark contrast to the lighter thread-like roots of the bougainvilleas that spread through the dark soil surrounding him.

'From the line of his shoulders it looks like his arms might be behind his back,' Harrison said. 'If those were his hands we found in the church, why bind his arms?'

I looked at him for a moment. 'Maybe the hands belonged to someone else.'

'I'll get the ME on the way,' Traver said and walked away.

'Goya's making a point with each of his victims. He didn't do this to hide the body, so why bury him?' Harrison said.

'What words or image does the act of burying make you think of?' I said.

Harrison looked down at the strands of hair exposed in the dirt.

'There could be something buried with him. Ritual death has a long history of putting objects in the ground with victims.'

'What if he was alive when he was placed in that hole?'

Harrison thought for moment.

'If he was buried alive . . . silence.'

I nodded.

'We don't seem to be able to get away from that word.'


It took an hour of careful digging to free the body from the dirt. It was still stiff with rigor as they lifted it out; death had taken place sometime within the last seventy-two hours. The body was nude and as we had guessed it was sitting upright, knees tucked under, the arms bound behind his back. The skin on his back, neck and chest was covered with a series of long shallow wounds.

'Does this remind you of anything?' Dylan said.

I nodded. 'Ritual wounds, like the kind the abbot saw on Brother Paul in the high desert.'

I kneeled down and examined them more closely.

'These weren't the cause of death.'

The ME tilted the body back and shined a light into his open mouth.

'There's dirt present,' he said.

I glanced back up at Dylan. Michael Sanchez's fingers were curled tightly around small quantities of dirt gripped in his hands.

'From the bruising around the lips it's likely he was alive when he was put in this hole, or the dirt was forced in his mouth before he was put in,' said the ME.

I shook my head.

'He was alive. Look at his fingers – the nails are full of tightly packed dirt. He was clawing at the earth behind his back,' I said. 'Trying to dig his way out the only way he could.'

I stood up and looked back toward the house where crime scene techs had begun to work.

'The hands from the church,' Dylan said. 'We still have another victim to find.'

# twenty-seven

We went through Michael Sanchez's house room by room searching for a connection to St Gabriel's and the abuse that had taken place there, but found nothing. It was as if the past didn't exist inside those walls. There wasn't a single picture, school-book or paper. Nothing to suggest he had ever been young, or had memories that were something to cling to rather than run from. He had created a home that he thought was safe from the past until it had reached into the present and violently taken his life.

His parents lived in a sprawling ranch house within view of the tall palms that decorate Santa Anita Race track. I would have preferred to give them more than an hour to adjust to the news of their son's death, but we had no such luxury.

His father greeted us at the door dressed in an expensive suit, a small silver cross pinned on his lapel, and showed us in. If their son had spent his adult life trying to escape his past, his parents appeared to be intent on preserving at least portions of it. The entryway, the hallway leading to the bedrooms, and the living-room walls all held photographs of a young family as yet untouched by darkness.

Mr Sanchez showed us into the kitchen and we sat down at the table. I noticed a crucifix hanging on the wall behind me.

'You said this couldn't wait,' he said as he took a seat across from us.

'Other lives are in the balance. You might be able to help us, but it means answering questions that may not be easy,' I said.

'Will it help catch the man who did this to my son?'

'Yes,' I said without hesitation.

'Then I'll try to help. My wife is lying down. I don't know if she'll join us.'

I nodded.

'Your son was a victim of abuse along with two others while a student at St Gabriel's?'

Of all the questions he had probably imagined my asking this was not one of them. His face briefly drained of color, and the muscles of his jawline tensed and relaxed, then tensed again. He started to answer, then hesitated, then shook his head.

'I can't talk about that,' he said haltingly.

'I know that a settlement was paid out by the church, and your silence was part of that settlement. I also believe that both public and private individuals took money in exchange for their silence.'

He shook his head and repeated his words just above a whisper. 'I can't talk about . . .'

'It's our belief that your son's killer was somehow a part of that abuse. We also believe that he may try to kill the remaining victim or others connected to the cover-up before tomorrow.'

'My God,' he whispered.

'Three people have already been killed, possibly more. Our problem is that we don't know who the other victim was. That's how you can help us.'

He sat motionless, his eyes looking to some point in time or space that he didn't want to remember.

'I can't talk about that—'

'You have to talk about it,' came a voice from behind us.

I turned. Mrs Sanchez was standing in the doorway, her hand

gripping the edge of the door. They looked at each other in silence for moment.

'If you don't I will,' she said.

She moved from the doorway over to the table. She was a slight, frail-looking women, walking as if each step she took threatened to shatter her bones. She took a seat without looking toward her husband again.

'I'll tell you anything I can,' she said.

'Your son was a victim at St Gabriels?' I asked.

She nodded.

'Do you know if anyone had tried to contact your son recently about what had happened to him there?'

She hesitated, then Mr Sanchez started to shake his head.

'We haven't seen our son in over two years,' he answered.

I looked to Mrs Sanchez as she took a deep breath.

'That's not entirely true, is it?' I said to her.

She glanced at her husband.

'No, it isn't.'

'Had someone contacted your son about what had happened?' I asked.

She nodded.

'Someone had been calling him. I don't know who it was, but I got the impression it was a reporter,' she said.

'Why do you say that?'

'He talked about telling his story so everyone would know the truth about what happened.'

'Does the name Morrison mean anything to you?'

'No, I don't think so.'

She looked over to her husband.

'Michael wanted to talk about it very badly. The secret was eating away at him.'

'Did he talk with you about it?'

227

She again glanced at her husband.

'I think he would have, given more time.'

Mr Sanchez stared at his wife for a moment, then pushed his chair back, stood up and walked out of the room. Mrs Sanchez folded her hands on her lap and looked down at them.

'You have to understand my husband is a very traditional Catholic. This has all been very difficult for him.'

'Your son couldn't talk to him about it.'

She shook her head.

'The Church ordered silence, and in my husband's world he wouldn't and couldn't break that agreement.'

'Do you know any details about what happened?'

She took a breath.

'I know it wasn't what we were told.'

'Can you elaborate?'

She ran a memory through her head. 'There was something that wasn't right about the way it came out.'

'What do you mean?'

'The priest came forward himself, before any accusations had been made. Why would he do that?'

I shook my head.

'Why do you think?' I asked.

'I always wondered if he was protecting someone else, another priest maybe, I don't know. He took the blame, and it was over.'

I glanced at my watch; the day was slipping rapidly away.

'I don't have a great deal of time, Mrs Sanchez. As I understand it there were three victims at St Gabriel's. Donald Bonner died shortly after the initial investigation; your son is the second. Do you know who the other victim was?'

'His name was Andrew Simms. They were our neighbors. We didn't know the other family.'

'Here?'

She shook her head.

'We lived in Pasadena at the time.'

'Have you stayed in contact with them?'

'No. What took place put a strain on all the families. The silence that we had to maintain became too much – it was like having an extra person looking over our shoulder each time we talked. We finally moved away, changed churches.'

'Do you know if the Simms are still in Pasadena?'

'I don't think so.'

'Do you know if your son had any contact with Andrew Simms recently?' I asked.

She looked away and seemed to drift into memory, then let it go.

'He never mentioned it. The last time I spoke to Michael he said something about trying to visit the past, but I don't know if that was what he was talking about.'

She looked out the window toward the backyard and a row of roses.

'Could you give me a description of Andrew Simms?'

She thought for a moment then stood up.

'I think I can do better than that. Come with me.'

She led us out of the kitchen and down a hallway to a door.

'This was Michael's room.'

She opened the door and stepped in. It was an office now, the far wall covered by a large bookshelf. She walked over to it and picked up a photograph of a basketball team.

'This was their sophomore year, just before it all happened.'

She handed me the picture.

'That's Michael, second on the left, first row.'

He was looking directly at the camera, serious, not smiling. Trying to connect the youthful features to the body we had found in the shallow grave was a leap of imagination I didn't pursue.

'Andrew is the one standing directly behind him,' Mrs Sanchez said.

Of the nine young men in the picture Andrew Simms was the only one not staring stoically at the camera. There was an ever so subtle smile on his lips, the kind of smile someone who is trying to hide a secret might have. His eyes were as dark as coal.

'Is there anything you can tell me about him?' I asked.

'He had his problems even before the incidents at St Gabriel's.'

'What kind of problems?'

'Behavior issues.'

'Do you remember specifics?'

'He was prone to violence, even as a little boy. When he was in grade school a number of pets went missing in the neighborhood, and about a month later one of them was found in a shallow grave, badly mutilated.'

I glanced over to Harrison. We had not told her any of the details about how her son had died.

'It was never proved, but I always suspected it was Andrew who had done it,' she said. 'His parents never quite knew what to do with him.'

'Were Andrew and Michael friends?'

She nodded.

'When they were young. Something happened about the time they were in junior high and the friendship ended.'

'Do you know what it was?'

She shook her head.

'Michael would never tell me.'

I looked at the photograph. Andrew Simms' skin tone was slightly darker than the rest.

'Did either of his parents have any Spanish in their family history?'

She shook her head.

'Andrew was adopted.'

'Are you sure?'

'Oh, yes. I remember the Simmses had tried for a very long time before they took that step.'

'Do you remember what agency handled the adoption?'

'It was through the Church and Catholic charities.'

The sly secret smile in the photograph began to take on an ominous quality.

'What grade did he begin in at St Gabriel's?'

'First, same as Michael.'

'Do you remember when it was that Father Patrick began ministering at the church?'

The name had a jarring affect on her, almost as if a blow had struck her. She exhaled lightly then took a deep breath.

'I'm sorry. That name hasn't been spoken in this house for a very long time.'

'Do you recall when he came?' I asked again.

She nodded.

'He came to the congregation during that first year of school, as I remember. He was the assistant priest then; later the parish became his.'

'May I borrow this photograph?'

She nodded.

'Is Patrick connected to any of this?'

'Father Patrick took his own life two days ago,' I said.

She stared at me, seeming to replay the words over and over in her head until she believed them, and then closed her eyes. When she opened them they were moist with tears.

'There are some details about the payment you received from the church that I need to know,' I said.

'I'll tell you what I can.'

'How did you receive the payment?'

'The lawyer handled the negotiations.'

'Bishop?'

'Yes.'

'Was he the one who actually presented you with it?'

She shook her head.

'We were summoned to a meeting.'

'Where?'

'The old cathedral downtown. I think the idea was to impress us with the power of the Church . . . it worked.'

'Who was at the meeting?'

'The cardinal, our city councilman, several other Church officials, all dressed in their finest robes. I don't remember names, but one I think had come all the way from Rome.'

'A priest?'

She shook her head.

'No, he was something else, wore a dark suit, said nothing the entire time.'

'Was Bishop there?'

'No, we were on our own.'

'What was the name of the councilman?'

'Brown.'

Harrison glanced at me.

'The present mayor.'

She nodded.

'He gave us a talk about the good of the community and that sometimes sacrifices must be made for that community. He never even mentioned our son's name, then he left us alone with the Church officials.'

'Before the money was exchanged?'

'Yes.'

'And you were handed a check?' I asked.

'An account book from a bank. The money was already

deposited in it; our name was on it, very clean and simple. It wasn't even as if we were taking money. Just an agreement with God.'

'Was there anyone else you can remember who may have known about the agreement with the church?'

'There must have been others, but I don't know who they would have been.'

'Forgive me for asking, but was your son gay or bisexual?'

She glanced down the hallway where her husband had walked away.

'We never talked about it, but yes, I believe he was.'

I handed her a card with my number on it.

'If you can think of anything else, please call me.'

She turned and looked out the window.

'How does something like this begin, Lieutenant?'

I looked at her for a moment and shook my head.

'I don't know.'

'I've tried to understand why the things that happened to my son took place,' she said. 'I've always thought there must be an answer that would make sense of it all. For a long time I even prayed for it, but I've never found it. He was a child, a beautiful child. Why does that kind of thing happen? Why did all the people who could have stopped it do nothing, not the church, not anyone at the school, not the law, not his father or myself? We took their money and then sat silently around the dinner table each night as if nothing had ever happened. Time was all that was needed to fix it, but time doesn't really fix anything, does it? It never has. It just slips through your fingers.'

I started to turn to leave then stopped.

'Do you remember if Andrew Simms had any interest in art?' I asked.

Mrs Sanchez looked at me in surprise and nodded.

'Yes. It was something his parents were very proud of.'

'Thank you.'

She walked us back through the house in silence. Through an open door in the hallway I could see her husband seated in a chair, staring blankly at a wall.

We sat silently in the car outside the house for a moment, putting together what we had just learned, and then I looked at the basketball photo I held in my lap. Eight serious young men, and one who seemed not to belong at all with the others, his dark eyes containing more secrets than I could imagine.

'Let's run him though the system and see if we get lucky. Maybe he's been arrested. Check DMV, passport, anything you can think of. Then let's look for his parents.'

'Is this our suspect?' Harrison said.

'Look at him, a basketball player who doesn't belong on the team, pretending to be something he isn't,' I said. 'When I talked to Chavez about the investigation into St Gabriel's he said Patrick had claimed to be innocent.'

'You think it's possible his son was responsible for the abuse and Patrick took responsibility to protect him?'

I shook my head.

'I'm not sure which alternative is worse.'

I looked at the photograph.

'Either way I think we found a monster.'

# twenty-eight

It was nearing six o'clock when Assistant Chief Kelly, FBI agents Utley and Hicks and the head of the Papal Guard Rezzitti sat down at the conference table and passed three photographs to each other.

'This is our suspect,' I said. 'His name's Andrew Simms. He's thirty years of age. The first picture is of him in the St Gabriel's basketball team. The other two are his driver's license and passport, both issued a little over a year after he graduated.'

'Nothing after that?' Kelly asked.

I shook my head. 'No.'

'How much do we know about him?'

'After receiving his passport he flew to Zurich and then Rome, spending some eleven months there. Upon returning he vanished until he entered an abbey in the high desert a little over three years ago. After spending a number of months at the abbey, he abruptly left. About the same time he rented a warehouse space downtown, which we discovered two days ago. It's during this time that we believe he murdered Keri Bishop and possibly Father Monroe. He then didn't resurface until the murder of Trevor Wells.'

'What about family?' Hicks asked.

'We're trying to locate their whereabouts as we speak.'

'How is it possible for someone to fly under the radar like that?' Kelly asked.

'He's had a lot of practice. His first murder was probably Donald Bonner, one of the other abuse victims at St Gabriel's while they were both still in school.'

'So we have no idea what he looks like now?'

'We should have a computer image of what his appearance may be, but since he is apparently a chameleon when it comes to his looks, it may not be of much help. This morning we found his latest victim.'

'Who?' Kelly asked.

'The last of the victims from St Gabriel's, Michael Sanchez.'

'I must remind the lieutenant that the charges of abuse were only alleged,' Rezzitti said.

I turned to him.

'Well after allegedly forcing Michael Sanchez to eat a ritual last supper, he buried him alive. His fourth victim that we know of, possibly fifth if we include Father Monroe who died in Mexico.'

Rezzitti looked up at me but did not say anything.

'Does the FBI have any update on the recording of the chief?' Kelly asked.

Hicks looked at Utley and then towards me.

'Apparently when it was first sent to Quantico it went to the wrong email address.'

'You're joking,' Kelly said.

Hicks grimly shook his head.

'It took a while before this was realized and then communicated to us.'

'How long?' I asked.

Hicks cleared his throat.

'We were only made aware of this a short time ago. They now have the recording and are working on it.'

The room fell silent.

'These things happen—' he began to say.

'No,' I said.

Hicks looked at me and nodded.

'Do you have a new time estimate?' I asked.

'Nothing definite,' Hicks said.

Kelly stared at Hicks for a moment then looked at me.

'And you're no closer to understanding where Chavez is being held?'

'No,' I said.

'That's the best you can do?'

'The past is what's guiding Simms' actions. There's no separating what happened to him yesterday from what he's going to do tomorrow,' I said. 'If we want to find the chief alive, then we have to understand everything about what happened in Simms' life.'

'The past?' Kelly asked.

I nodded.

'Simms was born to a young Mexican illegal who was probably raped by Father Patrick.'

That caught Rezzitti's attention. Kelly tried to work it out in his head for a moment, then turned to me.

'You're saying Father Patrick abused his own son at St Gabriel's.'

'That's one possibility.'

'What's the other?' Hicks asked.

'That Simms was responsible for raping and torturing the other two boys at St Gabriel's and Father Patrick took the blame to protect his son. Or they worked in concert together, or that Simms was acting to protect his father. Which is the truth we don't know. What we do know is that Simms' actions are part of an extreme form of faith.'

'How extreme?'

'At the abbey he seemed to believe that the Church should

237

return to some form of dogma better suited to the Middle Ages. From what we have gathered those beliefs had began to take form inside him from a very early age.'

'And killing the Pope is a part of this?' Kelly asked.

'It could be.'

'And Chavez? Where's that leave him?'

'Everyone else Simms has touched he's killed except the chief. There has to be a reason: he's had years to plan this. My guess is the chief's life is somehow connected with his plans for the Pope.'

'But you have no idea what those are?' Kelly pressed.

'Not yet.'

'If Simms is in the Rose Bowl tomorrow, what do we need to be looking for?'

'We know he can pass himself off as a Hispanic or Caucasian, he speaks fluent Spanish, he could be dressed in the robes of a monastic order, he could even be dressed as a priest.'

'Will he try to get close or make an attempt from a distance?' Hicks asked.

'If there is an attempt, it will be close,' I said.

'If?' Rezzitti said. 'You're not certain there will be an attempt?'

'On the Pope? No, I can't say with certainty. That Simms is not finished, I am certain.'

'Why?'

'The act of killing is what's giving his life meaning.'

'Are there other possible targets you're aware of?' Kelly asked. I nodded.

'Anyone with knowledge of what took place at St Gabriel's. Both Mayor Brown and Cardinal Laughlin were present at a meeting where Simms' parents were paid off by the archdiocese, though the mayor had excused himself before any funds were exchanged. That makes them both potential targets.'

'What is the source of this information?' Rezzitti asked.

'I'm not at liberty to discuss that,' I said.

'Well, I would like to know,' Kelly said.

I looked at him.

'My answer would still be the same.'

Kelly stared at me for a moment, trying to contain his displeasure.

'Did you inform the mayor's office of this?'

I nodded.

'Both the mayor and the cardinal's office are aware of the threat.'

'Are you certain of this information?' Kelly asked.

'Mayor Brown denied any knowledge of what took place at St Gabriel's or that he was at any meeting where a settlement was discussed. He has, however, cancelled plans to attend the Mass and will be spending tomorrow in Lake Tahoe. Apparently something about the threat seems real to him. The cardinal's office would not discuss security issues with me, but he will be in attendance, though they too denied any knowledge of a meeting with the Simmses.'

Kelly pushed back from the table and stood up.

'When you are able to discuss this information, I would like to know it. Is there anything else?'

I shook my head.

'Then find this Simms, and find Chavez,' he said and turned and walked out.

The rest of the room emptied and I got up to leave. Rezzitti was standing at the door waiting for me.

'How certain are you that Father Patrick fathered this child?'

I studied him for a moment. There was more to the question than the spoken words.

'I doubt I will ever be able to prove it on paper, if that's what you're asking. A DNA test would be the only proof. That would require the Church's assistance in getting a sample from Father Patrick's remains.'

Rezzitti nodded.

'Father Patrick's wishes were to be cremated; I believe that has already taken place.'

'Pity,' I said and turned to leave.

'It is our belief that Father Monroe was a victim of random crime,' Rezzitti said. 'You have evidence to support this notion that it was something else?'

I stopped.

'Not at this time,' I said.

'Then that is speculation, isn't it?'

I looked at him for a moment. His physical presence reminded me of a house of mirrors at a carnival. What was real about him and what was a reflection of something else seemed impossible to separate.

'Are you here to protect the Pope or the Church?' I asked.

'The Church and the Pope are the same, are they not?' he answered.

'Do you know what Father Monroe's duties included within the archdiocese?' I asked.

He shrugged.

'I could not say.'

'Did they include the paying off of victims' families, bribing public officials, taking part in covering up the events at St Gabriel's?'

'Again I could not say,' he said, without showing any emotion.

'At the time of his murder was Father Monroe being investigated for stealing from the archdiocese?'

He stared at me in silence for a moment.

'I thought we had come here to discuss the possible threat to the Holy Father at tomorrow's Mass. Is this related?'

'I was hoping you could tell me?'

Rezzitti shook my head.

'My answer would be the same.'

'I thought it might be.'

I started to turn to leave.

'I understand you are divorced, Lieutenant.'

I stopped.

'Yes.'

'You were excommunicated.'

'Only after I ran from the Church as fast as I could,' I said.

Rezzitti smiled.

'Perhaps you are angry with the Church over this,' he said.

I looked at him and shook my head.

'No, I got over that a long time ago. I'm angry because a monster that institution helped create kidnapped my Chief and, more important, my friend.'

He nodded.

'Perhaps it would be best to leave the past alone, then, and focus on the task at hand.'

'Is that advice, or a threat?'

He shook his head as Harrison came walking down the hallway towards us.

'Neither, it's just understanding history. Find your chief, Lieutenant. Let me worry about the past; you're out of your depth.'

'Why is it you seem unconcerned with the Pope's safety?'

He looked at me for a moment.

'The Swiss Papal Guard has been in existence for over five hundred years, Lieutenant. I trust our record is better than yours.'

'You're not Italian?' I asked.

He smiled and shook his head.

'None of the Guard is. The Vatican learned long ago not to trust their existence to the emotions of their own people.'

He looked at me for a moment and then walked out, nodding to Harrison as he left.

'What was that about?' Harrison asked.

I watched Rezzitti until he disappeared around the corner.

'A history lesson,' I said. 'You have something?'

'We found an address for Simms' parents, but there's something not right about it,' Dylan said.

'How?'

'According to county records, the Simmses died three years ago in a car accident.'

'Was it investigated?'

Dylan nodded.

'It was a single car wreck. No cause was ever determined.'

'Do you have a date of death?'

'Just days before Keri Bishop disappeared.'

'Goya killed his parents?'

'It seems likely.'

'So who's living in their house?'

Dylan shook his head.

'It's still in their name.'

# twenty-nine

The Simmses had lived at the end of a narrow winding lane in the hills overlooking Encino. The lots were large and widely spaced because of the steepness of the terrain. The nearest house was more than a hundred yards around a corner, the nearest streetlight a block before that.

We stopped and got out of the squad in front of the garage. The bright lights of the San Fernando Valley spread endlessly toward the east. For the first time in days the pale presence of stars was visible through the broken clouds.

A winding series of steps led up through thick vegetation toward the house perched on the hillside above. From where we stood no lights could be seen. A heavy metal gate over six feet high with pointed spikes at the top blocked the stairs. In a city of nearly four million people the house was about as isolated as one could get.

'The Simmses look like they had been hiding from something,' Harrison said. 'Probably their son.'

I nodded.

'It wasn't enough.'

Harrison walked over to the garage and shined a light under the crack below the door.

'No car inside,' he said and walked back.

I stepped over to the gate. The buzzer on it had been removed. All that was left were the wires.

'Try the number,' I said to Harrison.

He dialed the number. From the darkness above we could hear the phone ringing. No one answered. No machine picked up. By the tenth ring the sound seemed to take on the quality of a scream.

'I'll climb up around the back and see if there's another way in,' Dylan said.

'Wait,' I said.

I looked down at the lock for any signs it had been tampered with. None was visible. I reached out and touched the gate – it swung open.

'Why have a gate like this and not keep it locked?' Dylan said.

I shook my head.

'You don't.'

Dylan reached down, slid his Beretta out and held it at his side. The steps wound their way through a hillside thick with agave plants, their pointed spikes reaching out toward each tread.

Twenty steps up Harrison stopped and kneeled down. A motion detector was hidden under one of the plants. He reached down behind it until he found what he was looking for.

'It's hard wired. If someone's inside they know we're here,' he said.

I started back up taking each step faster than the one before it until we rounded the final corner that reached the landing outside the large double front doors. Dylan joined me a second later. No lights appeared to be on; not a sound came from inside. Something had been painted on the front door but in the darkness it was difficult to make out. I slipped my light out of my pocket and turned it on.

'He's been here,' I said.

Two bright red slashes had been painted on the wood in the

shape of a cross. There had been no attempt to do it neatly. Paint dripped from the edges as if the cross had bled.

'You want to interpret the meaning of this?' I said softly.

Harrison studied it for a moment.

'In the Middle Ages red crosses were painted on doors of houses as a warning not to enter.'

'Why the red cross?'

'It meant there was plague inside.'

I slipped my Glock out and slowly walked up to the door, began to reach out toward the handle and hesitated.

'A pox upon your house,' I whispered and looked at Dylan.

'You think Goya is being metaphorical?' he asked.

I looked at the slashes of red paint; the violence with which each stroke was completed was impossible to miss.

'How do you think Trevor Wells would have answered that?'

'I think he would say Goya's a literalist.'

I nodded. Dylan reached out and touched the paint.

'It's still tacky.'

'How long do you think it's been drying?'

Dylan raised his fingers to his face and sniffed the paint residue.

'It's oil. Depending on its makeup it could be hours, could be days.'

I turned off my light and Dylan raised his weapon. I reached out, took hold of the door handle and pushed it open. I stood for a moment looking into the house. As my eyes adjusted to the deeper darkness the interior began to be visible.

'Do you see what I'm seeing?' I said.

Harrison nodded.

'Is it about what you expected?' I asked.

Dylan shook his head.

'I don't know what I expected.'

I stepped through the doorway, my hand tightening around the grip of the gun. Dylan entered behind me and moved over to my left. It was a large open space; the far wall was mostly windows that looked out onto a small yard and then the lights of the Valley. A wing continued to the right, while a set of stairs led up to the second floor to the left.

'This is different from the others,' Dylan said.

I nodded. Dylan kneeled down and picked up something from the floor. It was a shattered piece of wood.

'This was part of a chair.'

'You notice anything else?' I said.

Dylan nodded.

'There's a thick layer of dust on everything. This happened a while ago.'

'What does this look like to you?' I said.

He looked around for a moment.

'Rage.'

'That's what I would call it.'

The floor was covered with broken and shattered pieces of what had been the contents of the room. Nothing appeared to have been spared. There were wood fragments, glass, plastic, paper, books. Anything that had once been whole had been ripped to pieces or smashed.

I took a few careful steps around the debris and stopped.

'Look at the walls,' I said.

I switched on my light and shined it across the room.

'More red crosses,' Harrison said.

Every foot of every wall contained a painted cross. Some were big, some small. Hardly an inch had been left untouched.

'Hundreds of them,' Dylan said.

'If this is a picture of what's inside his head, then we know what madness looks like,' I said.

'Did this happen before or after his parents were killed?' Harrison said.

I shook my head.

'If they were alive to see it, they must have known what they were in for.'

I shined the light on the floor. There were multiple footprints in the dust leading toward the kitchen.

'He's been back,' I said.

I moved the light around. More footprints led to the stairs.

'Let's check the kitchen first.'

We quickly crossed the room and entered the kitchen. The faint odor of spoiled and dried food filled the air. Just as in the other room, food and shattered plates and glasses covered the floor. In the darkness I could hear the sound of roaches scurrying for cover as we stepped in. The walls contained more crosses. Nothing appeared to have been spared.

Dylan reached down and picked up an indistinguishable piece of food that was as dry as wood.

'Most of this has been here for a very long time. Only a little bit of it appears recent.' He stepped through into the dining room and looked around.

'It's the same here.'

I flipped a light switch, but nothing happened. The ceiling light had suffered the same fate as everything else.

'Let's check upstairs,' I said.

Dylan came back into the kitchen and started back toward the entryway. I began to follow, then stopped when I heard a faint sound. I turned and raised my flashlight.

'The refrigerator's on.'

Harrison stopped and turned. It was a large stainless side by side.

'Why is it on if all the food has been thrown out?'

247

We both stood still for a moment, as if not wanting to acknowledge what we were thinking, then I closed the distance and reached out to take hold of the freezer's handle.

The door swung open and I shined the light inside. The interior was empty, but it was not untouched. I held the light on the center shelf. Dark crimson drops were frozen to the wire. A small pool of the liquid had gathered on the bottom of the freezer, its surface covered in tiny frost crystals.

'Blood,' said Harrison.

'Someone didn't leave this house alive,' I said.

'Or whole?' Harrison said.

'The severed hands.'

I closed the freezer and started back toward the stairs, stopping at the bottom step. The darkness above appeared complete. It seemed to move as if it had mass. Unlike the rest of the house the stairs had no debris on them, but they were not untouched. What looked like pieces of thread were lying on the treads.

'Fibers of some kind,' Harrison said.

I held my light on them and shook my head.

'Not fiber. It's human hair.'

A gust of wind rattled a window up in the darkness. I stepped carefully around the hair, worked my way up to the second-floor landing and shined my light down the hallway. The ghostly imprints of where pictures had hung on the wall spread down its length. The floor below them was covered with shards of glass, broken frames and photographs ripped to pieces.

I reached down and picked one up. It was what was left of the kind of formal family portrait taken in inexpensive shopping mall studios. There were three figures, two adults and a child. The picture had been torn separating the heads from the bodies. I left it on the floor and moved the light across the other bits and pieces of family memories ripped apart: vacations, graduations and birthdays.

I stood up and shined the light toward the end of the hallway. There were two doors on the right, one on the left.

'Two bedrooms and a bathroom,' I said.

Harrison stepped forward to the first door and pushed it open.

'Bathroom,' he said and looked back at me, his face grim.

I raised the light into the room. The mirror on the medicine cabinet had been shattered.

'There's dried blood in the tub,' Dylan said.

I pointed the light toward it. The blood was cracked like the surface of a dry lakebed.

'How old do you think this is?' I asked.

Dylan kneeled down and examined it.

'Weeks at the very least.'

'Maybe even longer,' I said.

'Could be.'

I stepped back into the hallway and looked back down the stairs.

'Some of that spoiled food isn't old,' I said, and then looked back at the two remaining doors at the end of the hallway. 'Look at the walls up here. It's not like downstairs. What's been happening inside this house has been going on since his parents died, a slow-spreading virus, consuming one room after another.'

I moved down the hallway to the next door, pushed it open and shined the light inside. We both stared in silence for a moment.

'You have an explanation for this?' Harrison said.

Nothing had been destroyed in the room. It seemed as out of place as one of those preserved rooms you stumble upon while wandering through a museum, completely out of context with its immediate surroundings. I stepped inside and looked around.

'Try the light switch.'

Dylan flipped it and the ceiling light came on. We both stared in silence for a moment at what surrounded us.

'What does this look like to you?' I said.

Harrison shook his head.

'If downstairs is madness, then this is its dark cousin.'

There was no furniture in the room other than a bare mattress. Along the walls were half a dozen cardboard boxes. Dylan walked over to them.

'Clothes.'

'He was living here,' I said.

The walls had been painted black and they were covered by line after line of writing. Every inch of the room had been used.

'He's turned it into a blackboard.'

I looked at Dylan.

'Like at Catholic school.'

Harrison stepped up closer to examine the writing.

'More Latin,' he said.

'A lot more. There're thousands of words here.'

I stepped to the center of the room. The floor was littered with dozens of spent felt-tips.

'This would have taken months to write,' I said.

'What do you think it is?' Harrison asked. 'A manifesto?'

'What was it he wrote on the note at the studio? "Cowards die many times before their death; the valiant never taste of death but once." '

I looked around at the thousands of words.

'You don't think like that without leaving something behind.'

'A biography.'

'I suspect there's little he left out. We want to know what he's going to do, it's probably written right here.'

'Translating this entire text could take days at best, and that's if we could find the proper order to it.'

250

I glanced at my watch. We had less than thirteen hours until the Mass began in the Rose Bowl.

'We don't have days.'

I looked around. The lines of writing appeared orderly in their own way.

'If you were to begin writing in a room like this, where would you begin?'

'That would depend on the level of madness.'

I shook my head.

'He wants us to read it. He wouldn't hide it.'

'Unless the end hasn't been written.'

'It's here. He knows exactly how he wants it all to end.'

Dylan began reading a random portion of the writing. He ran his fingers along the line as he read it again and then moved several lines away and repeated the process. He read a third passage and then looked around the room in amazement.

'What is it?'

'Unless my Latin is suspect, he refers to himself over and over again as Goya.'

'It's written in the third person?'

Dylan nodded.

'He's acting as his own biographer,' I said.

'Which could mean that when he's killing, he's watching it as an observer.'

'See if you can make sense of any of it. I'll check the last room.'

I stepped back into the hallway and turned toward the last room. With each step the glass on the floor cracked under my feet. The faded rectangles on the walls where the pictures had hung felt like ghosts staring out from the past. No faces, no voices, but there.

I reached the door and stopped. Another word in Latin I had seen before had been carved into the wood. I tested the handle but it wouldn't move. Large nails had been driven through the corners of the door into the frame.

'Dylan,' I called out.

He stepped out of the room, came down the hallway and looked at the carving in the door.

'Silence.'

I nodded.

'You find anything that made sense?' I asked.

'Sense?'

Dylan shook his head.

'Is eramprognatius a bastard filius of dues.'

'My schoolgirl Latin hasn't come back that much.'

'More good news. He calls himself the bastard son of God.'

'It gets better. The door's been nailed shut,' I said.

'To keep someone out, or to keep them in?'

Dylan reached out and touched one of the nails. They weren't the kind of nails one found in a hardware store.

'They're more spikes than nails,' he said.

'They remind you of anything?'

'In what sense?'

'Biblical.'

Dylan thought it through.

'Like used in a crucifixion.'

He ran his fingers around the rest of the frame.

'There're other holes here. It's been opened and nailed shut several times.'

I slipped my gun out.

'Open it.'

Dylan reared back and kicked the door just under the handle. The wood of the frame cracked but didn't break. A second kick and the door swung open. I shined the light into what had been the master bedroom. The interior had been transformed. Pieces of plywood had been nailed over the windows. All the furniture had been removed except for a mattress that was placed against the far wall and covered by a large white sheet.

'He's turned this into a cell,' I said.

I took several steps and stopped. The walls were streaked with more painted crosses. There was another word painted on the ceiling. I held the light on it.

'*Profiteor*?' I said, not knowing the translation.

'Confess,' Dylan said.

I turned the light on one of the crosses on the wall.

'That's not paint,' I said. 'This is blood.'

'There's something under the sheet,' Harrison said.

We walked over and took positions on either side of the mattress. A heavy steel ring had been screwed into the floor at its head. I took a breath, not really wanting to pull the sheet back, then looked at Dylan and nodded.

He reached out, took hold of the sheet and lifted it back. The edges of the mattress were stained with blood and sweat. The rest of it was covered with drawings of faces, close up and highly detailed. Nine in all, or at least nine pieces of paper. Two appeared to be unfinished and unidentifiable.

'Do you recognize them?' Harrison asked.

I nodded.

'Most of them,' I said. 'I can guess who the others are.'

I kneeled down and took a closer look.

'Keri Bishop, Donald Bonner, Trevor Wells, Michael Sanchez. The two older faces must be his parents.'

'That would be my guess,' Dylan said.

I looked at the last finished drawing and lost the breath in my lungs.

'Chief Chavez,' Harrison said.

My voice faltered and then I managed a whisper.

'A perfect likeness.'

The expressions on all the drawings were similar but not exactly the same. The subjects were staring straight out at the viewer, their mouths grimacing ever so slightly as if they were in pain.

'They were alive when these were drawn,' I said.

'Or are meant to look alive.'

I shook my head.

'It would be part of Goya's ritual, making his victims sit for a portrait, all the while knowing what was to come for them.'

'That's a grim picture.'

I shined the light onto the unfinished drawings.

'What do you make of that?'

'He has two more victims planned,' said Harrison.

I stared at the spare lines on the paper that gave a shape to a face but held no details. 'That would be my guess.'

I moved the light back to the other drawings. 'We're missing something.'

Dylan looked over the drawings again and shook his head. 'What are you seeing?'

'It's what I'm not seeing.'

Harrison looked again, his eyes moving back and forth across the images.

'There's no drawing of Father Monroe,' I said.

'He could be one of the unfinished drawings? Or he couldn't do one because he murdered him in Mexico?'

'It's possible.'

'But you don't believe it?'

'No.'

'It could also be that Monroe was killed just as the Mexican police report shows: drug violence.'

I shook my head. 'Monroe's relationship with Father Patrick

and his possible part in the investigation into the abuse makes that all but impossible.'

'There is another possibility,' Harrison said.

'Morrison's conspiracy theory.'

'He was killed by the Vatican.'

We both let that sink in.

'That's a different picture altogether,' Dylan said.

'I'm not saying I believe this, but what if they're connected?' I said.

'How?'

'We know that Patrick had many of the same extreme beliefs about the Church that Simms showed while at the abbey.'

'Patrick did say he was his teacher.'

'Exactly, but what if it goes beyond that?'

'I'm not sure I want to hear this,' Harrison said.

'Shortly after Simms murdered Donald Bonner he left the country and went to Rome via Zurich. If Morrison is correct about extreme sects within the Church, perhaps Patrick had connections to them and sent his son to them.'

'To be trained?'

I nodded.

'As what, an assassin?'

'He had already proved his skills.'

We looked at each other, neither of us wanting to step into that world.

'The rational view is that Goya's killings are an act of personal madness,' Harrison said.

'He could also have just lost control of them because he lost the ability to separate the personal from the job.'

'It's still a leap.'

I nodded.

'There's more.'

'I was afraid you'd say that.'

'Why travel through Zurich?' I asked.

'The simple answer is cheap flights.'

'Morrison's answer would be that it's the home of the Swiss Guard whose job is to protect the Pope.'

'And they're part of it?'

'Or a faction within it are part of it.'

We looked at each other in silence for a moment.

'If any of this is even half true, then I think we've officially gone down the rabbit hole,' Dylan said.

'Which still leaves us with two unfinished drawings, and two more victims,' I said, shining the light back on the unfinished drawings. 'Who are they?'

'If he is intending to kill the Pope, that fills in one of the faces.'

'Which leaves one more individual who represents a threat to him.'

'Or the people who trained him if you want to jump into that boat.'

'Only one person works either way.'

'Morrison,' Harrison said.

We looked at each other for a moment.

'Not that we believe any of this,' Dylan said.

'Of course not.'

I took out my notepad, flipped through it until I found the phone number Morrison had given me and dialed it. Before the second ring it was picked up.

'I've left you messages. Why haven't you returned them?' Morrison said.

His voice carried with it an edge I hadn't noticed before – that extra jolt of adrenalin that comes with fear.

'I've been out of the office.'

There was silence on the other end.

'Are you all right?' I asked.

'Are you having me followed?'

'No.'

'Who is then?'

'Are you sure about this?'

'It's my job to notice things like that.'

'Where are you?' I asked.

'Is your phone secure?'

I hadn't had any doubts until he asked. And now it felt like I was holding a grenade in my hand that was about to go off.

'I have no reason to think it isn't,' I said, half lying.

'I might,' Morrison said.

'What were the messages you left?' I asked.

He hesitated.

'You called me,' I said.

'I think I found something that can prove Monroe was killed by the Vatican.'

'What is it?'

In the background I heard the sound of a car horn and then silence.

'Morrison,' I said.

'Do you know who's following me, Lieutenant?'

'You're in danger. Tell me where you are and I'll have a squad there in ten minutes and they'll pick you up.'

'No, no other cops. I'll meet you.'

He started to say something else then stopped.

'Why should I believe you?' he asked.

'Because I believe you,' I said.

There was no response.

'I can help,' I said.

'The southeast corner of the Rose Bowl parking area. People are gathering there already – go there.'

'How will I find you?'

'I'll find you,' he said and hung up.

I turned the phone off and slipped it in my pocket.

'Where are you going?' Harrison asked.

I shook my head in wonder. 'Down that rabbit hole. Morrison says he found evidence the Vatican murdered Monroe. He's scared; he wasn't before but he is now. You keep working on what's written in the other room. I'll see if I can get someone here to help you.'

'There isn't time, Alex.'

'And we're out of options.'

I turned the light back on the drawing of Chief Chavez.

'He's alive still,' I said.

Harrison wanted to agree, but couldn't manage to say it.

'Alex . . . How do we know that moment hasn't come and gone?'

I looked down at the drawing again. 'The belief in things not supported by fact . . . faith.'

# thirty

I couldn't remember how many days it had been since we found Keri's body in the center of the field. That first touch of frozen skin now seemed as remote as my memory of sleep. By the time I reached Pasadena the passenger seat was littered with three drained cans of caffeine drinks, an empty grande cup of coffee and several opened packets of NoDoz that I had gone through like a handful of skittles.

The sensation produced by the three together along with the adrenalin that I'd been riding since Chavez disappeared seemed to be a combination of the bed spins and the aftermath of giving birth – just the thing for someone carrying a loaded weapon on her side.

When I crossed the bridge over the arroyo and looked down toward the Rose Bowl I wasn't prepared for what I saw. The headlights of thousands of vehicles streaming toward the stadium lit up the winding streets. The plan had been to not allow crowds to gather until the following morning in order to have a better chance of spotting Goya. Something had changed that.

It was nearing midnight when I exited at Orange and turned toward the arroyo. A line of unmoving cars clogged the street. Attempts were being made at traffic control but when faced with being turned away the faithful just parked their cars and buses. The sidewalk was full of pilgrims walking toward salvation.

I hit the flashers on the squad, cycled the siren and made my way around the traffic to the first police barricade. I recognized the cop as one of ours and stopped. On the gas tank of his cycle I could see Simms' passport photo.

'Lieutenant,' he said.

'What happened here?' I asked.

'It's like trying to stop a river,' he said. 'We turned people away at first but they just began parking their cars and walking so someone decided it would be better to simply let them begin to gather at the stadium.' He shook his head. 'If you're going down there you won't get through this way. Best go back down to Arroyo and head north.'

I swung the squad around and wound my way down to the bottom of the arroyo. With the flashers going I drove up the empty oncoming lane of traffic toward where Morrison had asked me to meet him. The parking lots were already filling with thousands of cars and buses. I worked my way through the traffic to the corner of Arroyo and Rosemont, got out, and stared at what was unfolding in front me.

What had been empty parking lots a few hours before were now a combination of street festival, revival meeting and tailgate party. The odor of grilled meat and charcoal and the sweet scent of cotton candy filled the air. Vendors walked through the crowds selling anything and everything commemorating the Pope's visit. There were baseball caps with crosses on them, plates showing pictures of the Holy Father with his arms raised like Charlton Heston spreading the Red Sea, buttons and scarves and T-shirts with the image of Jesus in every imaginable pose.

I began walking through the crowds toward the stadium. I passed a family who had the dark Indian features of Mayans sitting on a brightly colored blanket reading Bible passages. A small Spanish man wearing only a rag around his waist had been tied to a large wooden cross and was being carried through the parking lot. As he passed people began to throw coins at his feet and then they kneeled and lowered their heads.

A black street preacher dressed in a red suit was standing on the hood of a car exhorting the small crowd around him to agree that the end of days was coming down and he knew the way to salvation. Hymns were being sung and prayers repeated in more languages than I could identify, mingling into one single Esperanto-like murmur that rose into the darkness.

I reached the southeast corner of the stadium and looked around. A figure moving to my left through the crowd turned and looked in my direction. I started to call his name but he turned away and vanished back into the steady stream of bodies.

'Morrison,' I said to myself, though I wasn't sure.

I had taken a step to follow when a loud *pop pop pop* erupted from behind me. I swung, my hand slipping to my Glock, to see a young Hispanic boy light the fuse on another string of firecrackers and toss them onto the pavement, where they erupted in a quick series of flashes.

I looked back to where I had seen the figure and scanned the crowd, but if it had been Morrison, he was gone. In the distance the sound of a siren began to break over the noise of the celebrations going on around me.

My phone rang and I reached for it.

'Morrison?' I said.

The line went dead. I looked slowly around, searching through the crowd to see if I was being watched.

A scream came from somewhere, and then laughter. Someone yelled, 'Jesus saves.' Twenty yards away people were beginning to gather around something. I pushed my way through until I reached the commotion. A young girl was on her knees, hands held out to her side as if keeping balance. She was speaking rapidly in tongues, the stream of words flying out of her mouth sounding more animal than human.

My phone rang again and I picked up.

'I'm here,' I said.

He didn't respond.

'Morrison?'

'Did you do this?' he said, his voice cracking with emotion.

'Do what?'

'Why?'

'Where are you?'

He didn't respond.

'Morrison?' I said.

'Oh, God,' he whispered.

The line went dead again. I quickly dialed his number. It rang three times and then went silent as if the phone had simply ceased to exist. The siren I had heard was moving in the distance, growing closer. It wasn't one of our squads; I knew that sound. This was a fire engine.

'Look,' came a shout.

'Lord,' said another voice.

Jesus came rollerblading past wearing tie-dye robes. In the sky toward the north of the stadium, a glow began to rise. Sparks and embers were streaming into the darkness.

'He's coming,' someone yelled as the siren drew closer.

I started walking toward the glow and then broke into a run, trying to work my way through the crowd. I reached Rosemont and stepped into the street where I could see. A block north a vehicle was on fire, flames shooting out of the open windows with the intensity of a furnace. Silhouettes were moving around the blaze. One was hopelessly spraying a small extinguisher.

A scream came from the darkness across the road from the burning car. I dialed Morrison's phone again, and again got nothing as the lights of the approaching fire engine began reflecting off the pavement. I pushed past a group of people and began running toward the flames.

When I reached the car a large circle of people was standing and staring at the swirling flames. The driver's side door was open. Ash and bits of burning paper were floating out of the interior and rising into the darkness until they burned themselves out. Burning rubber and plastic was dripping from the window frames onto the pavement.

In the flames I could make out the silver letters FORD on the trunk. In the back seat I could just make out the burning outlines of boxes.

'Beautiful,' someone behind me said.

'Did you see him?' said a woman's voice.

I turned.

'Did you see,' she repeated.

I pushed through the crowd, looking for the speaker.

'Did anyone see,' she said again, her voice rising in pitch. 'Look.'

I stepped past several more bystanders staring mesmerized into the flames. A young thin woman with long blond hair had her back to the fire, staring out toward the darkness of the golf course north of the stadium.

'See who?' I said.

She began shaking her head but didn't turn around. Her shoulders were trembling. I stepped around. She was holding her arms across her chest. Her eyes were filled with tears.

'Who did you see?' I asked.

She tried to speak but couldn't form the words. I grabbed her by the shoulders.

'Tell me what you saw,' I said.

She stared past me into the darkness and then the words came rushing out of her.

'Him . . . the driver, the driver,' she said. 'Somebody do something.'

I turned and looked toward the golf course. In the darkness I could see a small orange flame. It was moving away, stopping and starting like a broken toy falling, getting back up and moving away toward the darkness.

'The driver,' the woman whispered.

I shook her until she made eye contact with me.

'Tell the firemen when they arrive,' I said. 'Do you understand?'

A tear slipped from her eye and she nodded. I started running toward the darkness of the golf course, keeping my eye on the small glow of flame running down the empty fairway. The white sand of the sand traps seemed to glow as he passed them.

I worked my way around a small fence and then ran onto the grass. He had crossed a green near the dark clubhouse. Bits and pieces of glowing ash still smoldered along the line of faint footprints in the damp grass leading toward the darkness.

*Run*, ran through my head as I crossed the green into the longer grass of the fairway. The glow of flames seemed to nearly vanish and then appeared again. A hundred yards, another fifty. I wasn't getting any closer. My lungs began to ache as I gasped for breath. A piece of burning shirt lay on the grass, then a shoe, one side burned away. The figure moved in and out of view as it passed some trees. More burning cloth, pants this time, or a sock.

'Run,' I said, trying force my legs to respond. My heart was beating audibly against my chest. My legs began to slow.

'No,' slipped out. *Run, faster, faster.*

A scream echoed from the center of the arroyo and the burning figure stopped, seemed to rise up, and then vanished. I stared across the distance thinking I had missed something. He didn't reappear. My legs gave out and I slipped to my knees and gasped for breath, my heart pounding in my ears.

I pulled myself back up, my legs wobbling under me, then took a step and then another and began to run toward where I had seen the small stick figure of flame vanish. As I moved closer a layer of ground fog hovering a few feet above the dark grass became visible. The white noise from the crowds to the south of the stadium faded away. I stopped at the edge of another dew-covered green – more footprints, a piece of burned cloth. Another sound began to rise and I ran across the green and stopped on the edge of the fog bank.

Water was rushing, torrents of it. I followed the footprints to the edge of the flood control channel. Against the pale concrete walls a dark ribbon of water pulsed like a vein through the center of the arroyo.

The prints moved in a confused fashion back and forth as if looking for something and then turned north. I followed them a hundred feet, passing beyond some brush, and stopped. The prints led to a footbridge suspended twenty feet over the water.

I followed the prints to where they vanished halfway across. A piece of burned fabric had caught on a splinter of wood. In the dew on the railing was a faint outline where a hand last touched this world. I stared into the dark water and watched it disappear around the corner of the stadium past the thousands of the faithful unaware of what was slipping by them in the darkness. The heavy thud of boulders and other debris bouncing against the concrete echoed like shots rising up into the night.

If the burning man I had followed had been Morrison, in a few hours his last journey would end in a plume of chocolate-colored runoff drifting out into the green waters of Santa Monica Bay. Maybe a surfer walking to a break would find his broken body on the tide line in the morning, or perhaps a rip current would reach out like a hand and pull him even farther into the darkness.

★

I walked back, retracing my steps, hoping I would find something he had dropped on his run that I had missed, but the ground produced no evidence. The fire department had extinguished the flames by the time I returned. The faithful walking toward the Rose Bowl no longer stopped to look. The young woman who had seen the burning figure running away was sitting on the curb staring at the wreck. I walked over to her and kneeled down in front of her. She looked at me blankly for a moment and then recognition flashed in her eyes.

'Is he all right?' she asked, her voice shaking slightly.

I shook my head.

'I'm a policeman, I need you to tell me what you saw.'

She hesitated.

'Is he dead?'

I nodded and she covered her mouth with her hand.

'What did you see?' I asked.

She bit her lower lip. 'I was walking by and noticed the man in the car looking for something in the back seat, he was speaking to himself or maybe he was on a phone. He seemed kind of frantic. He got out and was walking around to the passenger door and opened it and it just burst into flames. His sleeve caught fire, but he patted it out, then he tried to get something out of the car and the fire just seemed to reach out and start wrapping around him.'

'Did he take anything from the car?'

'I don't think so. When the fire started on him it was like he was trying to brush it away, but it just got bigger, and then he ran off.'

'Did you notice anyone else near the car?'

She shook her head. 'No one else seemed to notice until he was gone.'

I wrote down her name and number, then walked over toward the vehicle.

The smell of burned plastic and rubber and gasoline rose with the faint white smoke that drifted from the charred wreck. The car now sat low on its axles, the rubber of the tires having melted. As the metal began to cool it pinged and popped like a dying campfire.

I showed my ID to one of the firemen and walked up to the open passenger side door. The inside had burned nearly completely. The seats were little more than springs; whatever hadn't been made of steel had turned to ash.

'It burned hot enough to melt the glass,' a voice said from behind.

I turned to see the fire captain standing behind me.

'Is that unusual?' I asked.

He nodded. 'For an average car fire, a little.'

I looked into the back seats; nothing remained of the stacks and boxes of paper that Morrison carried. Under the passenger seat was a small metal lock box, charred black.

'The inside was full of papers and documents, boxes of them,' I said.

'You know this car?' he asked.

I nodded. 'If an accelerant was used, there should be traces of it, shouldn't there?'

'If it was chemical in nature, most will leave residue behind.'

'You'll need to seal off the area and call arson to preserve the scene. This is a homicide,' I said.

He looked at me in surprise and then back in the car.

'Did I miss something?'

'The body's drifting downstream in the arroyo,' I said. 'LA fire will have to be notified. Swift water rescue will need to be looking for it.'

The captain looked across the dark expanse of the golf course.

'He ran burning from the car,' I said. I looked back inside at the small metal box. 'I need to know if anything inside that survived.'

The captain looked at the box for a moment then slipped on his heavy gloves and retrieved it from underneath the seat.

'You want me to pop the lock?' he asked and I nodded.

He retrieved some tools from the truck, then broke the seal and shined his light into the box.

'Is this what you were expecting?' he asked.

I kneeled down.

'Saints,' I said.

The box was filled with perhaps half a dozen little statues. The heat of the fire had cracked them, but they appeared more or less intact. I stared at them for a moment, then turned to the captain and shook my head.

'No, this wasn't what I was expecting.'

I reached out and touched one. It was still warm from the fire, but not too hot to handle.

'He was trying to retrieve this box when he caught fire,' I said. They were little more than curios from a souvenir store.

'Not the kind of thing you want to die for,' said the captain.

'In my experience, that's a very short list.'

I picked one up and it fell apart in my hand. I picked up another and noticed that something appeared to be inside its hollow core. I gently broke it apart and a tightly wrapped piece of paper fell into my palm. I carefully unrolled it and looked at it. It was a small piece of worn notepaper; the masthead for the Bishop law firm was on the top. Below, Jackson Bishop appeared to have written a note to himself.

*Remind Monroe of Charity Arms.*

I flipped it over; there was nothing on the back.

'That mean something to you?' the captain asked.

Its full meaning eluded me, though the fact that Morrison had deemed it important enough to hide meant it was somehow at the very least related to Bishop's payoff from Monroe.

I stood up and looked back toward the crowd gathering south of the stadium, and my phone rang.

'It means we're running out of time.'

# thirty-one

I laid the remaining statues of saints out on the conference table of headquarters and opened them one by one. Three were empty; the remaining two each held a slip of paper that contained a set of numbers, none in an order that made obvious sense to me.

The door opened and Traver stepped in.

'We went through every listing in LA County. There's nothing under Charity Arms. You want me to widen the search?'

I thought about it for a moment and then nodded. 'Keep looking.'

Dave looked down at the slips of paper.

'Numbers? Those mean anything to you?' he asked.

'Morrison said that Keri had discovered some account numbers in her father's papers. They could be that.'

Dave leaned in and looked them both over, then picked up the second one.

'You see something?' I asked.

He looked at it for another moment, running it through his head. 'I don't know about the first one, but I think this could be a phone number.'

There were fifteen numbers in the sequence.

'It would have to be an overseas number,' I said.

Traver nodded.

'Before the twins were born, my wife wanted to go to Italy. I think that's where this is.'

'It would be about noon there now.'

I picked up the phone and punched in the number. It took a moment to connect and then it rang. On the fourth ring it was answered.

'*Congregazione per le Cause dei Santi*,' said a female voice.

The words seemed familiar, something I had heard in Catholic school.

'Is this Vatican City?' I asked.

'*Si.*'

I placed the phone back in its cradle.

'What is it?' Traver asked.

I ran it through my head, trying to retrieve the memory. 'It's a Vatican number. If I remember the translation it's the Congregation for the Causes of Saints.'

'Which is?'

'It's the body in the Church that's responsible for investigating the canonization of individuals.'

'They decide who gets sainthood?'

I nodded.

'What the hell does that have to do with anything?' Dave asked.

I shook my head. 'I don't know.' I picked up the other piece of paper with numbers on it. 'Call Utley at the FBI and see if they can help us with this.'

'What do I tell him we're looking for?'

'Numbered offshore or overseas accounts where banking laws make it easy to hide cash.'

Traver copied the number down and went out. I picked the phone back up and called Harrison.

'Have you made any progress?' I asked.

'That depends on how you define progress. I've found nothing about the chief yet. Did you meet Morrison?' Dylan asked.

'Not quite. If I'm right, he's dead. Someone set his car on fire. He was trying to retrieve something when he became engulfed in flames.'

'So you don't know what he wanted to show you?'

'No. If he had proof of the Vatican's connection to the murder of Father Monroe, it's probably gone. We found what are probably the account numbers Keri discovered in her father's papers, and a phone number in the Vatican for the council responsible for canonizing saints. What good either will do us I don't know. Neither gets us any closer to finding the chief or Goya.'

There was a pause on the other end.

'What is it?' I asked.

'You said saints?'

'Yes.'

'This is very slow going, but the early part of the text is written like Goya's version of the Bible. He refers to his mother a number of times, and in places he even calls her a saint.'

Traver stepped back in the room and nodded to me that Utley had the information.

'Saint Maria?' I asked.

'Yes. She comes over as a cross between Joan of Arc and Mary Magdalene.'

'The woman at the church said the last time she saw Maria she believed her son was the result of a virgin birth.'

'Goya calls his birth a miracle.'

'No mention of rape.'

'No.'

'Does any of this help us?' I asked.

'If I'm reading this right, when he refers to her it's in the present tense as if she's alive. But then whenever he gets specific

273

about her he says she's in the arms of charity which sounds like his version of heaven.'

'What did you say?'

'He says his mother is in the arms of charity.'

'Arms of Charity? You're sure?'

'Yes.'

'It's not heaven,' I said. 'Keep working, I'll get back to you.'

I hung up and turned to Dave. 'See if you can find a listing for Arms of Charity.'

'Reverse the order?'

I nodded. 'Bishop might have had the wrong name, or his daughter or Morrison wrote it down wrong. That's why we didn't find anything.'

We walked to Dave's desk and he Googled the name. There were over two hundred hits. The third one caught my attention.

'Try that one,' I said.

Traver opened the website.

'Arms of Charity Catholic home.'

'A nursing home.'

Dave scrolled down.

'Foothill Boulevard. It's in La Crescenta. That's maybe twenty minutes from here,' he said, but I was already heading toward the door.

# thirty-two

The moon began slipping down into the Pacific as I drove up out of Pasadena and passed into the San Gabriel valley. Foothill Boulevard stretched the length of the valley from east to west in nearly a straight line. Most of the strip malls that lined either side were built before there were enough of them to be called a strip mall.

The Arms of Charity Catholic home sat on the top of a large expanse of grass on the north side of Foothill. I pulled into the circular drive and stopped. It was a Mission-style single-story building with wings spreading out to either side of the main block.

Through the glass entryway I could see the lighted reception desk. In the center of the grass rising up from Foothill were several benches around a small flower bed. The chopped-down stumps of palm trees lined the inside of the drive. I pulled forward to the entrance, stopped and got out. Just beyond the light that spilled out from reception a single vehicle sat in the parking lot off the circular drive.

I walked over to the entrance. No one was visible inside. A sign at the door read AFTER NINE P.M. RING BUZZER. A small TV was on behind the reception desk. Across from the desk was a small alcove that contained a statue of a saint. I started to reach out to push the button and instead took hold of the door handle and gave it a push. The door swung open and I stepped in.

The air inside held the scent of cleanser and that more undefined odor of slow death. The lights on the wing that went off to the right were on. The lights down the other corridor were dark. I stepped up to the desk. A spilled cup of coffee lay on the floor behind it. I looked up and down the adjacent wings, then stepped around to the other side of the desk and reached down and touched the coffee with my fingers. It was still warm.

I stood up and looked toward the corridor to the left. The rhythmic sound of a medical device rose and fell in the darkness like breathing.

'What the hell are you doing in here?' came a voice from behind me.

I turned around. A large black woman in a pink uniform wearing a white sweater was standing there holding a mop.

'Are you the only one on duty?' I asked.

'It's nearly three in the damn morning. You're going to have to leave now,' she said.

A tinge of Texas or the midsouth was in her voice. I slipped my jacket back and showed her my badge and told her my name.

'What's the police want?' she asked.

'Why is there coffee on the floor?'

'I spilled it,' she said sarcastically.

'Is anyone else working tonight?'

She hesitated then nodded. 'There's a nurse on duty.'

'Where is she?'

'She's probably checking on a resident. I ain't seen her for a while. What the hell's going on?'

'Do you have a resident here named Maria Perez?'

She looked at me for a moment.

'Santa Maria?' she said.

'Last name Perez?'

'Yeah, that's her.'

The meaning of Bishop's note was now clear. If he knew of the existence of Maria then he probably also knew of the rape, the child, and the Church's or Patrick's part in covering up his actions. The price for his silence just got more expensive.

'Everyone is asking about Maria tonight,' the woman said.

'What do you mean everyone?'

'Some man from the Church came by. A foreign feller. Said he came all the way from Italy to talk to her.'

'Did he say why or give you his name?'

'No. I figured it had something to do with her becoming a saint.'

'A saint?'

She nodded. 'That's right. A priest wrote the Vatican and nominated her to become a saint. We all thought it was just the Alzheimer's, but I guess she must have done something when she was young.'

'A priest did this?'

'He used to visit her every week.'

'You know his name?'

She thought for a moment, then shook her head. 'Might have been an Irish name.'

'Patrick?' I asked.

She looked at me and nodded. 'That's it.'

'When was the last time he was here?'

'He comes every week, but he didn't come this week. She was upset about that. Is there a problem?'

'Did anyone else ever visit her or ask about her?'

She began to shake her head, then stopped. 'There was a lawyer once, he tried to interview her for somethin', but that was a long time ago.'

'Three years?'

'Could be. And a journalist came one time saying he was going to do an article.'

'You remember the name?'

'No.' She looked at me for a moment then over to the door. 'How did you get in here?'

'The door was open.'

'That door's supposed to be locked. I didn't open it.'

I looked down the dark corridor. 'Someone did.'

'What the hell's going on?'

'Why are the lights off down there?'

'They weren't when I went to get the mop.'

'How long were you away from the desk?'

She hesitated.

'No one will know but you and me,' I said.

'I had a sandwich in the break room. I wasn't keeping track of the time.'

'Is Maria in that wing?'

She nodded. 'Room 27 at the end on the right.'

'Is that your or the nurse's car parked in the lot?'

'What car? My daughter drops me off and the nurse takes the bus.'

I stepped around the counter and looked at her nametag. 'Augusta, is there a room you can lock yourself in?'

She looked at me in surprise. 'Why would I do that?'

'You hear something that isn't right, you call nine one one and tell them an officer needs assistance, then go to that room.'

'What if I don't hear nothin'?' she asked.

'Then go to that room and wait until I come and get you.'

She set the mop down and nodded. I started down the hallway, slipping my Glock out from the speed holster as I stepped out of the light from reception. The corridor curved around to the right like a lazy C. Most of the residents' doors were closed, their names on written on removable placards. I hugged the right wall and slowly moved around the corner. The faint sound of breathing seemed to fill the dark hallway from the open doors. A faint cry rose and then fell silent as if a nightmare had come and gone.

I stopped at an open door at the end of the curve and checked the number. Nineteen. I took a step and a hand reached out and touched my shoulder. I spun to see the faint outline of a frail old man standing in the doorway wearing a long coat.

'Are you here to take me home?' he said.

His features were barely visible in the darkness, his eyes hidden in their deep-set sockets.

'Not now,' I whispered.

'Later, then?' he asked.

'Yes.' I started to take a step.

'Like Maria.'

I turned to him. 'What about Maria?'

'I want to go home too,' he said, then turned and walked back into his room.

I looked back down the corridor into the darkness then started moving quickly. As I came around the final corner I saw a figure lying on the floor, the pink uniform appearing to almost glow in the darkness. I raised the Glock and moved up to the body. She was lying face down, her arms at her side, a blood pressure cuff on the floor next to her.

I reached out and placed my fingers on the side of her neck and felt a slow but steady pulse. She was unconscious, but alive. I rose and raised the gun toward the last door on the right. It was closed. I eased past the door in front of me and stopped in front of the last one. The nametag read Perez. I listened for a sound coming from inside the room but there was only silence. At the end of the hallway was a faint red light above an emergency exit. It appeared to be closed.

I placed my hand on the door, took a breath, pushed it open

and held the Glock on the darkness inside. The air smelled sweet, a mix of flowers and vapor rub. The room was colder than the hallway. I stepped inside, and pressed my back against the door with the gun raised. The door to the bathroom was opposite me. I reached out with my foot and pushed it open, then lowered the Glock. There was nothing in the bathroom. Her bed was empty. The one window in the room was wide open. Goya had already been and gone.

I stepped back into the corridor and called out, 'Augusta.'

'That you, Lieutenant?' she called back.

'Call the paramedics and then come down here.'

I moved back into the room. There were several large crucifixes displayed, and a drawing in a frame hung on the wall. I recognized the work as Goya's. It was a version of Mary holding the baby Jesus. I recognized Maria's face in the drawing from the small photograph that Patrick had kept. I went over to the open window and looked out. There was no sign of anyone.

'Oh, sweet Jesus,' I heard out in the corridor.

I stepped back out of the room.

'She's been knocked out. Stay with her,' I said, and ran back down to reception and looked outside. The car in the lot was still there. It sat in the shadow of a tall palm cast by the streetlight on Foothill. It was a dark Crown Victoria, a cop's car, but that didn't feel like what it was. I pushed the door open, went outside and stared at the dark interior of the vehicle, but could make nothing out.

I let the door close behind me, slipped my weapon back out and started walking down the circular drive toward the car. In the palm trees lining the drive I could hear the rustling of rodents in the dried fronds. The sugary sweet smell of a twenty-four-hour doughnut shop a block away hung in the moist night air.

I stopped thirty feet from the car, stepping into the same

shadow that shielded it. Half a dozen or more cigarette butts littered the pavement below the driver's door. I glanced at the plates. They carried diplomatic tags. As my eyes began to adjust to the darkness of the shadow the faint outline of a figure sitting behind the wheel became visible, though the tinted glass kept any details within.

My hand tightened around the handle of the Glock and I stepped forward to the driver's door. The individual inside didn't move, or react to my presence, just continued to look straight ahead. I knocked on the glass but got no response.

'Polic—' I started to say, and then stopped.

On the edge of the door a single drop of blood slid down its length and landed on the filter of a spent cigarette. I glanced quickly around at the surrounding darkness to reassure myself that there was no one there, then reached out with my free hand and opened the car door.

I held my weapon on the figure for a moment, then lowered it to my side. His head was tilted forward, his chin resting on his chest. He was wearing a dark suit and a tie. I reached in and placed my fingers on his neck to check for a pulse. His skin was still responsive to touch: he hadn't been dead for very long. His dark hair concealed a small wound just behind the lower tip of the ear. Blood had run down onto his neck and soaked into the white collar of his shirt, turning it a dark crimson. He appeared to be in his early thirties, and his shoulders and arms had the thick musculature of a soldier.

The skin under the matted hair around the wound looked dark. His left hand was sitting in his lap just inside the edge of his suit jacket. Cigarette ash covered his left thigh. I reached across him and opened his jacket. A shoulder holster held a pistol tight against the side of his chest. His right hand sat on the seat next to him holding an open cell phone.

I slipped it from his cold grasp and checked his recent calls – the numbers were all the same. I placed the phone back in his hand and then wrote down the number. From the left pocket of his suit jacket I removed a thin black leather wallet. Inside was a passport identifying him as a Swiss National.

His name was Peter Stenson. And if I was right he was a member of the Swiss Guard. Rezzitti had sent him to watch for Goya. He had either fallen asleep or was smoking a cigarette when Goya had surprised him, placing a small caliber pistol directly against his head. He had lived long enough for Goya to question him. The questions had gone on long enough for him to open his phone with his right hand as if trying to secretly make a call. His left hand had been reaching for his weapon when the bullet entered the back of his head directly into his medulla oblongata, killing him instantly.

I closed the door and made my way back to into the Arms of Charity.

'Lieutenant,' came from back down the hallway.

I retraced my steps. The nurse was sitting up against the wall, Augusta next to her with an arm over her shoulder. I kneeled down in front of her. She looked at me, her eyes struggling to stay focused.

'She's doing better,' Augusta said.

'Can you tell me what happened?' I asked.

She took a shallow breath and steadied herself, closing her eyes for a moment.

'I was doing rounds, I stepped out of a room and the lights were off. I turned and he was right behind me.'

'Did you see a face?'

She shook her head. 'Just the collar.'

'Collar? A priest?'

She nodded.

'You're sure?'

She closed her eyes and nodded.

'I don't remember anything after that,' she said.

I stepped back into the room and flipped on the light switch. In the darkness before I hadn't noticed the other drawing lying on the bed.

'Augusta, come in here,' I said.

A moment later she appeared in the doorway.

'Can you describe to me the man who came earlier from the Church to talk to Maria?'

'He must have been in his forties, light hair, color of sand.'

'You're sure?'

'Yes, I'm sure.'

'Was this drawing here before tonight?'

She looked at it and shook her head.

'I'd never seen that before,' she said, then looked around the room. 'Where's Maria?'

'She's been taken.'

'Taken,' she said, her voice raising several octaves. 'Why would—' she started to say, then stopped herself and stared at the drawing.

'Lord, that's her. That's Maria.'

'Yes,' I said. 'Who gave her the other drawing, in the frame?'

'I think that priest did.'

'Patrick?'

She nodded, her eyes glued to the drawing.

'Can you tell if anything else is missing from the room?' I asked.

'She didn't have much,' Augusta said.

'Take a look for me,' I said.

She looked around the room for a moment then stepped over to the nightstand next to the bed. 'Her rosary isn't here.'

'How about clothes?' I asked. 'Are any gone that would be recognizable?'

She walked over to the small closet next to the bathroom, opened the door and went through it. 'I don't see nothin' missing here.'

'How about the chest of drawers?'

She went through each drawer, shaking her head as she did, and then turned to me.

'Only thing that's not here is her housecoat. It's yellow like a daisy. She always wore that at night before bed.'

'Did she ever talk about a son?' I asked.

Augusta looked at me in surprise. 'How did you know about that?'

'Tell me,' I said.

'Maria talked about a child, but we never gave it much mind.'

'Why?'

'She would go on and on as if she was the next Mary and that she had given birth to the second coming of Jesus. We didn't give it no mind.'

'I want you to go call 911 and tell them that a man has been shot out in the parking lot.'

Her eyes widened. 'Shot?'

'When they arrive tell them he's in the car in the parking lot. Tell them the police were already here, and then tell them about Maria.'

'What the hell is goin' on?'

'You make the call, then come back and sit with the nurse,' I said.

She started to walk out, then hesitated and looked at the drawing once more.

'Why would someone make a picture like that?' she asked.

I walked to the bed and looked at the drawing again. Like all Goya's images the lines were finely drawn, the detail precisely rendered. Maria Perez stood amongst dozens of bodies, with flames rising up from her feet and beginning to engulf her. She was surrounded by faceless onlookers, except for one that was recognizable – the figure of the Pope, his hand raised in front of him as if conferring a blessing.

'That's just wrong,' said Augusta, shaking her head. 'Maria wouldn't harm a soul. That ain't Christian.'

She walked back to reception to call 911. I looked down at the drawing, trying to find the piece of the image that would unlock its meaning, but it eluded me. We had been going on the assumption that when Goya was finished a pope would lie dying, but that wasn't what he had drawn. This was something else.

I carefully picked up the picture and walked out to the squad. Overhead a few faint stars were visible through the glow of the city. The passing storm had left cold air in its place and my breath was visible. Across the expanse of grass I looked over each of the handful of cars that were parked on the street, unable to escape the feeling that Goya was there watching, waiting to see if I could unlock the puzzle he had created, but they were all empty.

In the distance the sound of the approaching siren broke the silence. I opened the passenger door and placed the drawing on the seat as the red lights of the ambulance began reflecting off storefront windows across Foothill. As I reached for the keys my phone rang. It was Traver.

'We found Bishop,' he said.

'Where?'

'He's checked into a motel on Colorado. His car's parked in the lot, but there's no answer. You want the uniforms to go in?'

I looked down at the drawing of the burning figure standing amongst a pile of bodies.

'No,' I said. 'Don't open that door until I'm there.'

# thirty-three

The Motor Coach Motel sat on the eastern end of Colorado where new development hadn't quite reached. It was one of those holdovers from the early sixties when traveling by car was made to feel like an adventure worthy of a log cabin: a series of eight individual units that looked as if they had been built of Lincoln Logs.

A black and white and Traver's unmarked squad were waiting in the parking lot when I pulled up and got out. The Motor Coach Motel had seen better days. Paint on the faux logs was peeling. The dried vines of dead bougainvillea hung across the roofs like webs. It had the tired feel of a place you find only when you've taken a wrong turn.

The only other vehicle in the small lot was Bishop's Lexus.

'He's in the last cabin; the rest are empty,' Dave said. 'According to the manager he checked in two days ago, but hasn't been seen since.'

'Do you have a key?' I asked.

Dave held it up.

'He didn't run very far,' he said.

'Maybe there's no getting away from what's chasing him.'

The shades on the cabin windows were pulled down, and no lights were on. I looked over to the Lexus.

'Did you check out his car?'

287

'It's locked, but looking through the windows nothing seems out of the ordinary. A leather bag on the back seat, some fast food wrappers, what looks like a cell phone on the floor in back under the driver's seat.'

'The cell phone's in the car?'

Traver nodded.

'Why would you leave your cell phone on the floor of the back seat?'

'Maybe he misplaced it.'

I took the key from Traver, walked over to the cabin and knocked on the door. 'Mr Bishop, this is Lieutenant Delillo. Open the door.'

There was no response. I knocked again with the same result and then slipped the key into the lock and turned it.

'Jackson Bishop?' I said again and then cracked open the door.

'You smell that?' asked Dave.

I nodded. 'Bourbon.'

'Stale bourbon.'

I pushed the door open and waited for a response, but none came.

'Turn on the light,' I said.

Dave reached around and flipped the switch. We looked for a moment without saying anything, then I stepped inside. A leather bag that appeared to match the one still in the car sat on top of a small dresser. The spread on the bed had wrinkles in it but hadn't been pulled down. The chair from a small writing desk in the corner was now in the middle of the room. An empty bourbon bottle lay on the floor a few feet away.

'I'd say Bishop tied one on,' Traver said.

I walked over to his bag on the dresser. It had been opened, and contained a toiletry bag, a few shirts, pants and underwear.

'Check the bathroom,' I said.

Traver walked over, pushed open the door and entered. I went to the desk chair that had been pulled out. The carpet around it was stained with liquid. I kneeled down and touched it with my fingers – it was still damp.

'If that was Bishop's bottle, he spilled more of it than he drank,' I said and stood up.

'There're some blood stains on the sink in here, and some clothes in the tub,' Dave said, coming back out.

'Check and see if the clothes are soaked with bourbon.'

Dave nodded and went back into the bathroom.

'They're still damp,' he said as he re-emerged. 'The shirt has some blood on it. His wallet and keys are in the pants. You think he got hammered and hurt himself?'

I looked around the room. 'Given what happened to his daughter, it's possible. But if he did, then where is he?'

'Went for a walk, decided not to come back, maybe he was picked up and admitted to a hospital.'

'Leaving his wallet behind?'

'Maybe he was too drunk to notice. Maybe he just wanted to disappear.'

I looked at the chair that sat in the middle of the room. It had been placed in front of the TV, but facing away.

'Why turn the chair away from the TV?' I said.

'He didn't like what was on?'

I shook my head.

'Something's not right with this.'

'You think Goya found him?'

I glanced around the room and shook my head again.

'This doesn't feel like Goya.'

'What then?'

'I don't know.'

I looked back at the chair and the bottle and then kneeled down again. On the carpet underneath the chair were tiny slivers of wood that I hadn't noticed before. I ran my fingers up and down the rails of the legs. There were scrapes in the wood.

'I don't think he was watching TV,' I said.

'What then?'

'Metal cut into this wood. I think he was handcuffed to this chair.'

'Handcuffed?'

I stood up and looked around the room.

'He wasn't alone here.'

'This place has been busted for prostitution more than a few times,' Dave said. 'Given his state of mind, maybe he wanted to be treated rough.'

'Punished for his sins?'

'Something like that. Or else he just likes kinky sex.'

'Check his wallet and see how much cash is in it.'

Dave went back into the bathroom and came out with the wallet, going through a stack of bills. 'There's over fifteen hundred dollars in here. A hooker has him handcuffed and drunk, and leaves behind that much money?'

I shook my head. 'He wasn't here with a prostitute.'

'Which leaves what?'

I looked around the room. 'If it was Goya, he would have left something behind.'

'Another drawing?'

I walked over to the dresser and opened each of the drawers. They were all empty. I turned and looked across the room, my eyes settling on the wrinkled cover on the bed.

'Pull the bedspread back.'

Dave took hold of it and pulled it down. There was nothing there.

'Check under the mattress.'

He lifted the mattress up. 'Nothing.'

'And under the bed.'

He got on his knees and took a look.

'Dust bunnies,' he said and stood up.

I walked over to the window, lifted the shade and looked out at his car.

'What does this look like to you?' I said.

Dave shrugged. 'What do you mean?'

I turned and looked back into the room. 'There're blood stains on his clothes, he was handcuffed to a chair and booze was forced into his mouth.'

'You mean if it wasn't sex?'

'Yeah.'

'An interrogation.'

'A violent one.'

'My money's on Goya,' said Traver.

I shook my head. 'No, Goya's not looking for anything. He already knows what he wants. Whoever did this wanted something from Bishop.'

'But what?'

I glanced back out the window at his Lexus.

'What's Bishop have that could warrant this?' Traver asked.

'Money.'

'Whose money?'

'If Morrison was right, Bishop had discovered that Monroe had stolen millions from the church. Monroe not only paid him off to settle the suit, he paid him hush money to keep the theft a secret.'

'So we're talking about the Church's money?' Dave looked at me and winced as if he had stepped on a nail.

'Only Monroe's secret didn't stay one. And now they want their money back.'

'The numbers you found in Morrison's car.'

'It tracks.'

'I ain't Catholic, but I think we're getting into a gray area here.'

'Not getting. We've been in it from the first step we took.'

Traver walked over to the chair, kneeled down and ran his fingers over the grooves made by the handcuffs.

'So how did they find him?'

I looked back out the window toward his car then turned and walked into the bathroom and removed Bishop's car keys from his pants and started outside with Traver right behind me.

'What am I missing?' he asked.

'How did Bishop pay for the room?'

'Cash, three days in advance.'

I hit the remote and unlocked the doors.

'Which gets back to how he was found if they didn't trace a credit card,' Dave said.

I opened the back door and picked up the phone from the floor under the driver's seat. 'Maybe with this.'

'They called him?'

I turned on the phone and opened his recent calls. There were four from the same number. 'Someone wanted to talk to him very badly.' The number seemed familiar, but I couldn't place it.

'Do you recognize this number?' I asked Dave.

'No.'

'Where's the Pope staying when he's here?' I asked.

'Our Lady of Angels cathedral downtown.'

I hit the call back button. It was answered on the second ring by a recording. 'Our Lady of Angels . . .'

I closed the phone and turned to Dave.

'Get crime scene here and see if we get any prints off anything. Then check with all the hospitals and see if anyone answering Bishop's description has been treated or admitted.'

'Does any of this help find the chief?' he asked.

I took a look back at the cabin. 'I'm going to find out,' I said, and started toward my squad.

'Where're you going?'

I turned to Dave and shook my head. 'You don't want to know.'

I slipped into the squad and called Harrison.

'Have you found anything?' I asked when he picked up.

Harrison hesitated. 'I'm done here. The FBI translator arrived, and he'll take over.'

'Did you find anything?'

'It's possible, but like I said my translation—'

'Dylan, what did you find?'

He took a breath.

'You,' he said.

I wasn't sure I had heard him right.

'Me?' I asked.

'It's confused, and my Latin is suspect.'

'What does it say?'

'I could be wrong.'

'Dylan, what is it?'

'He's written his own death into it.'

'His?'

Dylan said nothing.

'And I'm a part of it?' I asked.

'Yeah.'

'How?'

'I'm not sure of my translation.'

'What does it say?'

'It says you kill him.'

The words hit the pit of my stomach as if I had just come around a corner onto an accident.

'Where does this happen?'

'That's not clear.'

'Is there anything else? Details how I do this?'

'It says you execute him.'

'Execute. Nothing more than that, nothing about the chief or the Mass?'

'No. I only stumbled on that because of your name in the writing.'

'He knows my name?'

'Yeah.'

'He probably learned that from the chief.'

'That's my guess.'

'At least we have an ending now.'

'They're the ramblings of a madman, Alex, that's all.'

'It ain't over till it's over.'

'That's right.'

'But we're not there yet, are we?'

'No. What do you want me to do?' Harrison asked.

I looked over toward the motel and tried to shake Goya's ramblings from my mind, but the word *execute* held on as if it was being physically pressed against me.

'Alex?'

I took a deep breath and settled myself.

'How do you feel about helping me create an international incident?' I said.

There was a pause on the other end.

'Where shall I meet you?' he said.

I turned over the engine of the squad. 'Church.'

# thirty-four

Our Lady of Angels cathedral sat on the northern edge of downtown like a postmodern adobe fortress. In a town where the Disney Corporation built a temple to its history by having the seven dwarfs hold up the roof, the church made no such allusions to its past. There was no great round dome, no old world symbols, no saints. Even the one prominent cross on the exterior was created out of negative space and light, suggesting perhaps that faith, like the past, is very difficult to get your hands around.

Harrison was waiting in a squad at the corner of Temple and Hill when I pulled up and stopped. LAPD had set up roadblocks on the length of Temple that ran along the south side of the cathedral. A long row of black Suburbans and squad cars lined the outside of the building. In the darkness I could make out the movement of secret service agents placed on the roofs of the building and the parking garage.

Harrison stepped out of the squad and walked around to the passenger side of my car and got in. He looked at me for a moment.

'Are you all right?'

'I'm fine,' I said. 'The words of a madman, as you said. Nothing more.'

Dylan nodded. 'That's right.'

His eyes held on mine for a moment, then he looked over toward the cathedral.

'If we're here to arrest the Pope, I may want to reconsider my participation,' he said and smiled.

'Morrison's death wasn't an accident,' I said.

Harrison turned to me. 'Can we prove that?'

'Given the state of his car, I don't know.'

'Goya?'

'It's either that or we buy into his conspiracy theory and believe the Church killed him.'

'And the proof he said he had?'

'Gone.'

'So you don't know what he wanted to show you.'

'I know some.'

'What?'

'He found Maria Perez,' I said.

'Goya's mother?'

I nodded. 'I think he also found account numbers of the banks that Bishop was hiding the payoff money from Father Monroe in. The FBI is tracking them down. He also had on him the telephone number in the Vatican for the Congregation for the Causes of Saints.'

Harrison worked on that for a second, trying to understand what I had just said. 'Maria Perez?'

'Yeah. Either Father Patrick or Goya put Maria up to be considered for sainthood.'

'Sainthood?'

I nodded again.

'Is she dead?'

'No, her canonization is a little premature, she's in a Catholic charity nursing home.'

'Arms of Charity,' Harrison said.

'It's off Foothill. She was very popular today. I was the third person to visit her. A Church official was the first, Goya was the second.'

Harrison looked over toward the Cathedral. 'A Church official?'

'With a foreign accent, no name.'

'Rezzitti?'

'The description was a match.'

'And Goya?'

'He took her with him and killed one of Rezzitti's men who had been left behind to watch for him.'

'Does Rezzitti know?'

I shook my head. 'I doubt it. It will take LAPD some time before detectives get there and then they track him to here.'

'Why did Goya kidnap his mother?'

I handed him the drawing I had found in the nursing home. Dylan studied it for a moment.

'Santa Maria?' Harrison asked.

I nodded. 'Every good son believes at some point in their life that their mother is a saint. Goya's just taken that to a whole new level.'

'The Pope's alive in this drawing,' Harrison said.

'But a lot of people aren't.'

'Which people, is the question.'

'I don't know. If Goya's telling us what he's going to do, somehow his mother is part of what's going to happen today.'

Harrison looked over to the cathedral again. 'You think Rezzitti knows more than he's said?'

I nodded. 'A lot more.'

'Based on what?'

'Earlier today someone also found Bishop. They handcuffed him to a chair and interrogated him.'

'That doesn't sound like Goya,' Harrison said.

'Sometime before Bishop was found he received four phone calls from in there,' I said.

'The cathedral?' Dylan stared at it for a moment. 'Which brings us back to Rezzitti,' he said.

'I doubt very much it was the Holy Father who made the calls.'

'You think Rezzitti was the one who interrogated Bishop in the motel?'

'Yes.'

Harrison worked through it. 'The account numbers?'

I nodded.

'They want their money back?' Harrison said.

'That's the easiest explanation,' I said.

'Where's Bishop now?'

I looked at the tall sand-colored walls of the cathedral.

'He could be inside there for all I know.'

'What's the not-so-easy explanation?'

'That answer isn't quite so simple.'

'Morrison's conspiracy theory?' Harrison said.

'Even if only pieces of that theory are true, it could explain certain things.'

'But which pieces?'

'If it was Rezzitti who showed up at the Arms of Charity, then it's clear he's known more about Goya all along than he's let on,' I said.

'I agree, but why would he withhold information? His job's to protect the Pope.'

'Let's say Morrison was correct, that there are factions within the Church fighting a power struggle. Perhaps Monroe was a part of it, using the money he stole to finance the opposition. Take that to the extreme and Rezzitti isn't here to protect the Pope at all, and later today the Pope will die at the hands of an assassin from inside the Church. Maybe that assassin is Goya, maybe Goya was set up to be a patsy, or maybe it's just good timing from their perspective that they can take advantage of.'

'And the other version?' Harrison said.

'Monroe was a crook and Goya's exactly what we think he is, a killer, who won't stop until he's finished his work.'

'Which could still be the Pope.'

I nodded.

'And how does Rezzitti fit into that story?'

'The Pope and the Church can be harmed in more ways than physical ones. Stories of an abuse victim who turns to murder and a dead priest who stole millions from the archdiocese and then dies in suspicious circumstances aren't going to do a lot for the Church's image.'

'What are you saying?'

'In either version the best outcome from Rezzitti's perspective is silence.'

'That word again.'

I nodded. 'Which means he could be more interested in Goya's dying than our catching him.'

'That could explain his not sharing information,' Harrison said.

'What if part of that information could lead to the whereabouts of a cop involved in the original abuse cover-up?'

'The chief.'

I looked over to the cathedral. 'Father Patrick is dead, all of his victims are dead. The two reporters who knew the details are gone. The priest who arranged the payoffs is dead. Bishop has vanished. Chavez is the only one left with direct knowledge of what took place. From Rezzitti's point of view it might be in the Church's best interest if the chief never told his story.'

'So which version is the right one?' Harrison asked.

299

I looked at my watch. It was after four a.m. 'If it's the first one, then nothing we do is going to change the outcome.'

'So we assume it's the second.'

I nodded.

'What do we do?' Dylan asked.

I took out my notepad where I had written the phone number from the murdered Swiss Guard. 'The only thing we can.'

'Which is?'

'Lie.'

I took out my phone and dialed the number. Rezzitti answered on the second ring.

'Lieutenant. How did you get this number?'

'I want to talk about the Congregation for the Causes of Saints, and Maria Perez.'

There was a pause on the other end. 'Why would I be interested in discussing that at this hour?'

'Because if we don't, we'll have to discuss what took place at the Motor Coach Motel. And the witness we have.'

He didn't respond for a moment, then spoke in almost a whisper.

'The Holy Father is in morning prayers.'

'Good,' I said. 'You're going to need all the help he can get. I'm waiting outside.'

# thirty-five

Rezzitti came walking out of the cathedral dressed in a black suit and a crisp tie. Harrison and I stepped out of the squad. As he approached he slipped a hand into his jacket past the slight bulge of his weapon, removed a slim dark cigarette from a pack and lit it.

'I was under the impression we would be talking alone?'

Dylan looked at me and I nodded.

'I'll take a walk,' he said and moved. Rezzitti watched him until he was half a block away and then he turned to me.

'I trust you're not wearing a wire?'

'If I had time I would be, but I don't. Where's Bishop?' I said.

'You're aware, of course, that I and all my staff have diplomatic immunity.'

'From prosecution yes, but not from arrest, or the publicity that would come from it. And if you think I won't arrest you right here and now if you don't tell me what I want to know, you're mistaken.'

He took a casual drag on the cigarette and flicked the ash onto the pavement.

'That would be a terrible waste of time,' he said.

'Something neither of us has.'

'Indeed.'

'Where's Bishop?'

'And what would I gain from sharing that information?'

'A living Pope,' I said.

Rezzitti flicked his cigarette into the gutter, its red ash shedding embers as it flew through the air.

'That is the outcome we're all interested in, isn't it?' he said.

'I'm a homicide cop trying to find the killer of a young girl. The rest is your job.'

'Bishop was very much alive and well when we left him at the motel,' Rezzitti said. 'We had a brief conversation, nothing more.'

'You handcuffed him to a chair.'

Rezzitti open his jacket.

'As you can see, I don't carry handcuffs. If Bishop is no longer there, then I can't help you.'

'I hope you can prove that.'

'Proof is your business, Lieutenant, not mine.'

'Did he give you the account numbers?' I asked.

He looked at me and smiled.

'As I said, it was a brief conversation.'

'I will find out,' I said.

'When you do I will be eager to hear all about it.'

'Were you or any of your people near the Rose Bowl last night?'

He looked at me as if it was the first time I had said something he hadn't anticipated.

'We have people at the site with their secret service counter-parts, but as you have already noted, I was elsewhere. Why?'

'Does the name Morrison mean anything to you?'

He shook his head.

'He claimed he could prove that the Church murdered Father Monroe.'

'Have you seen this proof?'

'No.'

'As I have said, I was elsewhere.'

'Tell me about Monroe.'

'A victim of random violence according to the Mexican police.'

'He was a thief who stole millions from the Church and arranged the payoffs that silenced Bishop and the victims' families.'

'The Church is not in the business of murder, Lieutenant.'

'Just the business of silence.'

He took a deep breath.

'Tell me what you know,' I said.

'Know?' He shook his head. 'What I know is of little help.'

'Then what do you believe?'

'What I believe is that Father's Monroe's death was anything but random.'

'Goya,' I said.

'Yes. Not that I could prove it.'

'How long have you been aware of Goya?' I asked.

He paused, choosing his words carefully. 'His presence has been noted for some time.'

'Since Patrick sent him to Rome?' I said.

Rezzitti looked at me for a moment and then nodded.

'Do you know what he did there?'

'We believe he spent time with a number of conservative priests who opposed certain teachings within the Church.'

'And Patrick? What did you know about him and when did you know it?'

'He was known to us long before the abuse case.'

'You knew he raped Maria Perez?'

'That was before my time.'

'He sent her to a Catholic hospital to give birth, arranged for her son to be put up for adoption through Catholic charities; don't tell me someone within the Church didn't know the truth.'

'Tell me, Lieutenant, has every rape you've ever investigated been prosecuted?'

'You knew Goya was his son, though.'

Rezzitti hesitated. 'In retrospect it became clear to us. Patrick wanted to make Goya into his own image, and he succeeded beyond his wildest nightmare.'

'Was Patrick connected to other radical elements in the Church?'

'That would depend on how you define connected.'

'What's your definition?'

'As far as we were able to prove, it was philosophical in nature.'

'There's nothing philosophical about Goya,' I said.

'No.'

'Is there a conspiracy within the Vatican to kill the Pope?' I asked.

'The Church has existed in one form or another since the first century, Lieutenant. There are always conspiracies, divisions, power struggles. Understanding which are real and which are imagined is what creates history.'

'That's not what I asked you.'

He reached into his pocket and pulled out the pack of cigarettes, but it was empty. He stared at it for a moment, then tightened his fist around it.

'I don't know. My job is to know the answer to that question, and I don't have it. I don't know if Goya is insane and working alone on some twisted crusade to protect his father and his image of what the Church should be, or if he had assistance beyond Patrick.'

'You know Goya traveled through Zurich on his way to Rome.'

He nodded. 'That was known to us only after his appearance in Rome.'

'So you don't know if he had made any contact with anyone in Zurich.'

'No.'

'How confident are you that elements within the Swiss Guard are not involved in some way?'

Rezzitti considered his answer carefully before he spoke.

'As you can imagine, our people are very closely screened. There's no evidence to support that possibility. We are not by our design ideological in nature.'

'You could have just said you were certain.'

He glanced at the cathedral and then back to me. 'The Holy Father will be finishing prayers soon. I will have to get back.'

'Why did you visit Maria Perez last night?'

He looked at me and smiled. 'You haven't missed much, have you?'

'Why?' I repeated.

'We had surveillance on her hoping Goya would make contact. When he didn't, I went to talk with her, but it was unproductive. Her mind is quite useless.'

'And the Congregation for the Causes of Saints?'

'It was something Patrick had done. We let it go on, hoping we could keep tabs on Goya.'

'Did you know Goya had murdered Patrick's other victims?'

'We had our suspicions.'

'If you had shared that information we might not be standing here right now,' I said.

'How would that have changed anything? The police here had all the same information we did, but you never made an arrest, did you?'

'Goya killed your man at the Arms of Charity. He put a bullet into his head.'

Rezzitti looked at me, his eyes full of doubt for a moment.

'You must be mistaken.'

'His name was Stenson,' I said. 'He was trying to call you when

305

he was killed. That's how I got your number – his phone was in his hand.'

The doubt in his eyes vanished, his cool European veneer shaken.

'After Goya killed your man he kidnapped Maria from the home,' I said. 'My guess is he's going to use her in whatever he does today.'

Rezzitti shook his head as if trying to dislodge the information I had just given him from his mind.

'How do know that?' he said, his voice taking on an edge of urgency.

I reached into the squad, removed the drawing and laid it on the hood of the car. Rezzitti stared at it for a moment in silence.

'There's your saint,' I said.

Harrison came walking back and stopped twenty feet from the squad.

'If this is a picture of what's to come, we're talking about more than just the Holy Father's life,' I said. 'Does that image appear to match with anything the Pope is doing today?'

Rezzitti stared at it for a moment, but if any of it registered he didn't show it.

'Does it?' I repeated.

His eyes finally appeared to take in the details.

'This drawing is not specific. It could be anything,' he said.

'Goya was dressed as a priest when he entered Arms of Charity.'

'You're certain of this?'

I nodded. 'How many priests will be at the Rose Bowl today?'

'I don't have numbers. Many hundreds.' He took one last look at the drawing.

'I will go over the itinerary and see if I can find a connection. I must go.'

'Can you tell me anything that would help me find Chief Chavez?' I said.

Rezzitti stopped and looked back, making eye contact with me, then glanced over to Harrison as he stepped up to the back of the squad.

'Our belief is that he's already dead. I'm sorry.'

He started to walk away.

'Based on what?' I said.

Rezzitti stopped.

'Based on what?' I repeated.

'On what's happened to everyone Goya has touched . . . as we both now know.'

'If I don't find Bishop, I will come for you,' I said.

He looked at me for a moment.

'If you don't find him, it won't be because of me.'

'I'm sorry about your man.'

Rezzitti started to turn away, but then he stopped and looked back.

'Did you know him well?' I asked.

He shook his head.

'No, but I knew him.'

Rezzitti walked away toward the cathedral. I sat back on the hood of the squad as Harrison stepped up beside me.

'Anything?'

I shook my head. 'He says he doesn't know any more more about the chief than we do.'

'And Bishop?'

'They were at the motel but he says he was alive and well when they left him there.'

'Did you believe him?'

Rezzitti stopped at the entrance to the cathedral, looked back in my direction, then walked into the courtyard out of sight. My phone rang and I picked up. It was Traver.

'Did you find anything?' I asked.

'We checked every emergency room within a twenty-mile radius: nothing. No one matching Bishop's description was admitted. I also checked cab services in case he was picked up. Nothing.'

'All right,' I said and began to hang up.

'There is something that could be related,' Traver said.

'Go on.'

'I went through the nine one one logs. There was a call at eight ten from a citizen a few blocks from the motel. He reported seeing a man wearing pants but no shirt or socks running down the street. He thought the man was being chased by a vehicle, but the black and white that responded found nothing.'

I looked over toward the cathedral and the line of black security vehicles. 'Did they give a description of the car?'

'Just that it was dark, no make or model.'

I hung up and turned to Harrison.

'I'll be right back,' I said.

'Where you going?'

'To find out if I've been lied to.'

I started walking toward the line of cars and SUVs in front of the church. An LAPD officer challenged me as several secret service agents closer to the gate watched our conversation. I showed him my credentials and he directed me to the gate leading into the grounds. I repeated my conversation and showing of credentials to the secret service agents and then was let through.

Inside the walls, the courtyard gently sloped up toward a series of dark steps that led up to a pair of sculpted doors at the entrance to the cathedral. There, two members of Papal security watched me approach and then held up their hands to indicate that they wanted me to stop.

'Rezzitti,' I said.

One of them looked at my ID then spoke into a wrist mike and nodded when the answer came over his earpiece.

'This way,' he said, leading me into the nave of the church.

He walked me halfway down the side aisle, gestured for me to take a seat in the pews, then put his index finger to his lips and motioned for me to be quiet. I nodded and he walked out of the light and into the darkness.

A faint light shone on the altar at the front, but the rest of the interior was bathed in darkness; the ceiling seemed to vanish into infinity like the night sky. The sound of voices, the words indistinguishable, drifted out into the main chamber. Footsteps became audible and slipped away into silence and then I heard the soft sound of fabric brushing against the wood of the pews behind me.

I spun around and saw a figure dressed in white moving toward me down the aisle. I rose to my feet as he stopped, his face little more than a faint outline in the dark. The palms of my hands turned cold as the gold crucifix on the chain around his neck caught the light from the front altar and glistened. He walked to the pew directly behind me and motioned with his hand for me to sit back down.

I hesitated for a moment, taking in the lines of the Pope's face. He looked older than the man I had seen on television. His hair was steel gray, with streaks of white. His eyes seemed to contain the kind of weariness that I had seen in very few people, mostly cops. It wasn't a physical exhaustion. It came from the weight of awareness of the nature of the world they walked through.

'Please sit,' he said in his heavy accent.

'I need to talk to Rezzitti, Your Holiness,' I said.

He nodded.

'Humor an old man,' he said.

I sat down, trying to understand why I had been given this audience. The failed Catholic inside me was trembling. The cop was curious. Was he using the bully pulpit of his robes to shield Rezzitti from my questions? Or was there something else he wanted from me? I imagined that like any good politician he did nothing without a very good reason.

The Pope looked past me into the expanse of the cathedral.

'One of my guards has been killed?' he said softly.

'Yes,' I said.

'You discovered this?'

I nodded. He leaned back against the pew, closed his eyes and took a deep breath.

'Others are in danger,' I said.

If he heard my words they had little effect on him.

'Yourself included,' I added.

He sat in silence for a moment and then looked at me.

'How many others?'

'I don't have a number. Many, possibly,' I said. 'Some have already died.'

He nodded as if the information was not new.

'I understand this Goya is the illegitimate son of a priest?'

'Yes,' I said. 'A result of a rape.'

'A terrible sin,' he said softly.

He fell into silence; clasping his hands tightly together as if trying to squeeze out of them the information I had just given him.

'Why did you choose Los Angeles to come to?' I asked.

'I came here to heal.' He looked at me for a moment as if to read my reaction and then he briefly smiled. 'That wouldn't be a satisfactory answer by your standards, I suspect.'

I shook my head.

'A lot of damage has been done by too many priests. You should have come sooner,' I said.

He nodded. 'I have many faults.'

'Did you choose Los Angeles, or was it chosen by someone else?' I asked.

The Pope looked at me for a moment and then toward the cross at the front of the cathedral.

'You're asking if I believe it's possible that there's a conspiracy within the Church to assassinate me?'

His bluntness caught me off guard.

'Yes,' I said.

'I approved the decision,' he said and then looked back at me.

'Is that an answer?'

'It is the only one I can give you.'

'Crimes were committed in the name of the Church,' I said. 'Possibly even murder. If that's the case, I'll follow it as far as I have to.'

He nodded. 'We are as imperfect as God created us, both in and out of the Church. As a policeman you would understand that more than most.'

'Did you come to find out what I know?' I said. 'Or to tell me what you want me to know?'

He smiled.

'What would your answer be to that question?' he asked.

'Both,' I said.

'I was told you were a good policeman.'

'Do you trust the people around you?' I asked.

'One has died for me. I will pray for the rest.'

The muscles in his hands relaxed and he sat back. I had seen others carrying burdens in their lives, but what I saw in the face of this man was unlike anything I had seen before. It was more than just the weight of responsibility. What he shouldered must be as immeasurable as the faith or lack of it behind every gesture made in every waking moment of any given day.

'You were once a Catholic?' he asked.

'A long time ago,' I answered.

The pontiff looked at me and then toward the lone light at the front of the church.

'I was once a priest, a long time ago,' he said, and then stood.

'Do you miss it?' I asked him.

He looked past me into the space rising up above the altar and then shook his head.

'I miss the simplicity.'

He stepped out of the pew, turned, and began to walk away.

'You could have sent anyone to talk to me to keep me away from Rezzitti. Why did you come?'

The Pope stopped.

'Is that what I've done?' he said.

'Why am I here with you?'

His shoulders rose with a breath and then he appeared to nod.

'I wanted to know what was in your heart.'

'And whether my intent is to harm the Church?' I asked.

He turned and looked at me.

'Did you get your answer?' I asked.

He nodded.

'Perhaps you will return to the Church some day.'

'Why?' I said.

'That answer is different for everyone. But the reward is the same, to receive God's blessing.'

He started to walk away.

'Why did the Church let it happen?' I asked.

His hand rose to his chest and covered the crucifix hanging around his neck.

'They were children,' I said. 'And the Church hid in silence and did nothing.'

The Pope lowered his hand.

'Do you believe there's an answer to that question?' he asked.

'I'm a cop, Your Holiness. In my world there's usually an answer.'

He turned. 'Are they always what you hope they are?'

'No, they usually aren't.'

'Then our burdens are not so different, or our answers, are they?' He looked at me for a moment. 'Something else troubles you, Lieutenant?'

I had said nothing to give that impression, yet he asked about the one thing I had left unsaid. I nodded. He opened his hands as if asking for me to place my question in them.

'The man who we are after . . .' I hesitated.

'Go on, my daughter.'

'He's written that when he has finished his work, I will be the one who will kill him.'

No surprise registered in his eyes. 'I was wrong. Your burden is much greater. It is a sin to take a life.'

'Even in defense of yours?'

'Mine is no different from any other.'

He looked at me for a moment, and at last it fully dawned on me why he was really here. He wasn't here to protect the Church; he had come as a priest.

'You knew, didn't you? You knew what Goya had written.'

'Nothing is written but God's word. You must never forget that. God will be with you, my daughter.'

The sound of footsteps came out of the darkness and Rezzitti appeared, made brief eye contact with me and then whispered something into the Pope's ear. The pontiff nodded and Rezzitti walked over to me.

313

'You have one more question for me, Lieutenant?'

I looked at the Pope for a moment, trying to gather myself, and then I turned to Rezzitti.

'There was a report that Bishop was chased down the street by a dark vehicle. Was that you?'

Rezzitti didn't hesitate. 'No. You have my word. As I said, he was in the motel when he we arrived, and he was there when we left.'

As Rezzitti finished speaking my phone began to ring.

I reached into my pocket and removed it. It was Traver's number. The Pope looked at my hand holding the phone for a moment and then spoke.

'I will pray for you this day, Lieutenant,' he said as if he already knew what news awaited me on the other end of the call.

'Something's happened, hasn't it?' I said.

'I think you had better take that call,' Rezzitti said.

The Pope looked at me for a moment longer, then he and Rezzitti walked away into the darkness.

I looked down at my hand holding the phone and realized it was trembling, and then I answered.

'The FBI traced the recording,' Traver said.

# thirty-six

First light was rising over the basin as Harrison and I drove north on the 110 out of downtown. The FBI had come up with a location from the recording of the chief that Goya had sent to the television station. A hostage rescue team was already assembling.

'If this is right it's less than a mile from where we found the chief's car.'

Harrison nodded.

'How sure are they on this information?' I asked. He had been working the phone since we left the cathedral.

'They gave it a ninety-nine percent probability.' He glanced over to me to judge my reaction. 'That makes you uneasy?' he said.

'Ninety-nine percent?' I nodded. 'When has anything been certain with Goya?'

Dylan looked at me. 'Only that he was going to kill.'

We sped back up the Pasadena freeway along the Arroyo Seco, exited at Fair Oaks and turned north. Within another minute we had reached the parameter that had been set up closing off a square block around the address. Assistant Chief Kelly was at the command post half a block from the location. Pasadena's own tactical squad had gathered but there was little we could do as the FBI had taken control once the case became a kidnapping.

315

Agent Hicks from the FBI was in charge of the operation. It was a commercial street, small manufacturing and warehouse businesses lining both sides. In the center of the block was a bus stop; across from it was the abandoned building the FBI had targeted from the recording.

I stepped past the tactical vehicles blocking the street and looked down its length. I stared at the building, its derelict exterior becoming recognizable behind the chain-link fence that surrounded it. In the front structure was a chapel; connected to it in back was a second smaller building.

'An empty church,' I said and looked over to Harrison.

'It makes a kind of sick sense,' he said.

I tried to work through something I wasn't seeing.

'It's more than that,' I said. 'It's perfect.'

'What do you mean?'

I shook my head. 'What we found at Goya's parents' house suggested that he took the chief there, bound him, drew him.'

'Goya could have brought him here first, made the recording and then moved on.'

'Yes, he could have.'

Harrison looked at me for a moment. 'But that's not the problem, is it?'

I shook my head. 'Everything about the other deaths has involved Goya's twisted sense of humor – Wells killed by television, Keri frozen, Michael Sanchez buried alive. How does the chief fit in?'

'You lost me.'

'He's a cop. His death would reflect that.'

'How?'

'I'm not sure.'

The light of day was just beginning to illuminate the street. Outside the buildings surrounding the church I could see the black-clad figures of the FBI rescue team moving into position for an assault. I looked at Dylan for a moment then walked over to Hicks who was working the radios with the tactical team.

'Did the location come only from the recording?' I asked.

Hicks said something into the radio and then turned to me.

'No, a call came in reporting screaming. We made the connection with the recording only after that.'

'Screaming? What time?'

'Few hours ago.'

I looked down the street. There were no residences, and being Sunday morning none of the businesses were open. And the buses that ran down the street would not have been operating in the middle of the night.

'Did you get an ID on the phone call?'

He shook his head. 'Pasadena PD took the call, not us.'

'Hold the team,' I said.

'Why?'

I tried finding an answer that made sense but it eluded me. 'Something's not right.'

'You want to be more specific, because that's not enough to go on.'

Assistant Chief Kelly stepped up. 'Is there a problem?'

'The lieutenant seems to think so,' Hicks said.

Kelly looked at me. 'What is it?'

'What do you know about the call?'

'Motorist driving by on a cell.'

'Did you trace the number?'

'No.'

'This isn't right,' I said.

'The recording confirmed the location, Lieutenant.'

I looked back down the street, trying to work through the details of the last few days.

'Unless you got something and you got it now, I'm giving them the go-ahead,' Hicks said.

'I don't think the chief is here.'

'You don't know that.'

'If we found this because of that recording or the phone call it was because he wanted us to.'

'All the more reason to go in,' Hicks said.

'You didn't have a problem before,' Kelly said. 'It was your thinking that brought us here.'

'A lot has happened since then,' I said.

'If Chavez is in there and he's still alive, we can't wait any longer.'

'I'm telling you something isn't right.'

'You tell me what that is and I'll wait, otherwise let us do our job.'

Hicks looked at me, waiting, but I couldn't give him a reason. He looked over to Kelly, who nodded his approval.

'Take it,' he said into his radio.

I turned and walked back to the line of tape and looked down the street. There was a loud pop, followed by the shattering of glass.

'They're good at what they do,' Harrison said, but I didn't hear his words.

Two of the assault team slipped down the side of the building and the loud concussion of a stun grenade shook the air.

'What did you say?' I asked.

'I said they're good—'

'That's what's wrong,' I said.

'What is?'

'Goya's studio,' I said.

Dylan tried to catch up with my thinking, but didn't see it. 'What about it?'

'The painting, the words he wrote.'

'Which ones?'

I reached down and grabbed hold of the crime-scene tape and twisted it in my fist.

'*Justitia caeca est.*'

'Justice is blind,' Harrison said.

'He wrote that on the back of a painting.'

'The firing squad of soldiers.'

'The cops of Goya's time. He's playing with us, just like he did with Wells and the TV.'

Harrison looked at me for a moment then down the street toward the church.

'Son of a bitch,' he said. 'He's telling us how it ends.'

'We kill the chief ourselves.'

I looked back at Hicks.

'Pull them out,' I said.

'They're already in,' Hicks said.

'Call it off.'

'It will be over before I can do that,' Hicks said.

I looked back down the street and then tore the tape with my hands and started running toward the church. There was yelling behind me, but I didn't hear the words. I crossed the distance in a matter of seconds.

White smoke drifted out of one of the shattered windows. The front door hung loosely on the hinges where the battering ram had breached it. I stepped through the opening in the fence the assault team had made and rushed up the steps to the open door.

There was little light inside. The interior appeared to be gutted. The remains of the pews were scattered across the floor. At the far end of the main chapel the beams of the assault team's flashlights were cutting through the darkness. I stepped in, keeping my hand away from the Glock on my hip. The air was heavy with the smell of the powder used in the concussion grenades.

'Down clear,' someone yelled.

There was movement somewhere at the back and then the rush of footsteps up a set of stairs. I started across the chapel toward where the assault team had gone up into the back building but I stopped halfway. Something had been painted on the floor in what appeared to be the same red paint we had found at Goya's parents'. I took out my light and shined it on the floor as Harrison rushed through the door and stopped next to me.

'A red cross,' he said.

'A warning to stay out,' I said.

I heard the crack of a door give way somewhere in the other building and I ran across the chapel to the stairs and started up.

'Clear!' was yelled.

'Move, move, move,' followed.

I reached the top step and the floorboard snapped and my foot slipped through and I fell. Another crack as a door was knocked open.

'Clear.'

The beams of flashlights were slicing through the darkness down the hallway. I pulled my foot up through the broken slats and got to my feet, as the movement of the flashlights stopped at the end of the hallway.

'Take it!' someone yelled.

I started running down the hallway toward the assault team. There was a crack of splintering wood.

'No!' I shouted.

The doorframe gave way with the second hit.

I shouted again. 'Wait!'

The door was flung open.

'Go, go, go.'

'Stop,' I yelled.

The team moved through the door in quick succession as if they were connected at the hip. A deadly conga line.

'FBI!' was yelled.

I was almost to the door when there was another shout.

'Gun!'

'Don't!'

'Gun!' Louder.

'Put it down, put it—'

A shot reverberated out of the room.

I was screaming, 'No, no, no!' but my voice was lost in a burst of automatic gunfire and I dropped to the floor, covering my head with my hands.

The firing went on for a second and another and another and then the room fell silent except for the sound of shell casings rolling across the floor. I looked up at the sound of more voices.

'Clear left.'

'Clear right.'

'Anyone hit?'

The room fell silent again and I rose to my feet.

'Jesus,' someone said.

I rushed through the door as Harrison came up from behind me. The agents were spread out, two standing, two on one knee. Their automatic weapons were still at the ready, the beams of the flashlights connected to the weapons' stocks all trained on a figure across the room. A single agent walked forward, his weapon raised on the target.

'Clear those windows.'

Another agent walked over to the blackout drapes and pulled them down. The soft warm light of morning streamed in illuminating the room.

'Jesus,' one of them said again.

'What the hell is this?'

'Oh no,' I whispered.

I stepped past the agents as the one in front reached the figure. It was dressed in white robes that were now stained red with blood.

'He's finished,' said the agent.

I rushed forward, shaking my head.

'Someone want to explain this?' an agent said.

'A cross, a damn cross,' another one said behind me.

I walked past the forward agent to the limp figure and stopped. He had been tied to a cross that was bolted to the wall, into which a large spike had been driven through his right hand. Another had been hammered into his ankle but had not penetrated all the way through. A hand-painted Halloween-like mask covered the face.

'The damn gun's taped in his hand.' The forward agent looked over to me. 'You want to explain this? The mask mean anything to you?'

I had no words for him. A small silver pistol had been duct-taped into the right hand. My heart sank. Harrison stepped up next to me. I started to reach for the mask to remove it but my hand began to tremble.

'I'll do that,' Dylan said.

I shook my head. 'No. I'll do it.'

I reached out and took hold of the bottom of the mask, barely able to hold it in my fingers, and then slipped it over the figure's face. His lifeless eyes were half open. More duct tape covered his mouth.

'Rezzitti wasn't lying,' I said.

Harrison nodded. I looked at the body for a moment, trying to take in the detail, but I couldn't absorb it.

'The mask,' Harrison said.

I lifted it up and looked at it. It was, like Goya's other work, highly detailed, a perfect reproduction of the original.

'Is that who we're looking for?' asked the agent, staring at the body.

'No.'

I handed Harrison the mask and he studied the face.

'You recognize the image?' I said.

He looked at it for a moment longer and shook his head. I knew the face from memory. It had been ingrained in me since Catholic school.

'It's one of the disciples from the last supper painting,' I said. 'He was third to the left of Jesus.'

'Judas,' Harrison said.

I nodded.

'Someone want to tell me what the hell is going on here?' the agent said as more people came through the door of the room. 'Who the hell is he?'

'He was a victim,' I said.

The agent stared at me for a moment, the confusion clear in his eyes.

'Victim? Why didn't he lower the gun? Why the hell didn't he lower it?'

'Justice is blind,' I said.

'What?'

I stepped over to the body. Other wounds were apparent on the corpse beyond what the FBI rounds had done to him. I looked at the spike driven through his hand into the wood and the one that had partially gone through his ankle.

'He wasn't trying to shoot you.' I said. 'I doubt he was even aware there was a gun in his hand.'

The agent stood in silence for a moment, then reached up and pulled his black balaclava off, said 'Shit' and walked away.

Hicks and Kelly stepped past the assault team and came forward, stopping several feet away when they saw the figure slumped on the cross.

'Oh, no,' Kelly said.

After a moment Hicks came forward, his eyes locked on the body.

'You should have listened,' I said.

He stepped past me without a glance and up to the figure on the cross. He tried to put the pieces together in his mind, then gave up and turned to me.

'Who is that?' he asked.

I handed him the mask. He stared at the painted face with its dark hair and heavy beard.

'Judas,' I said.

He looked at me and then down at the mask. 'As in—'

'Yeah, that Judas.'

Hicks looked at the body. 'And that makes this?'

'It was Jackson Bishop,' I said.

He stared at the body then turned back to me. 'Bishop?'

Kelly turned around in disbelief.

'Where's Chavez?' he asked.

I shook my head, walked over to Bishop's body and began searching the robes he was wrapped in. There was nothing concealed within the fabric.

'You think Goya might have left another message?' Harrison said.

'Would you miss an opportunity like this if you were him?'

I began to move away, then stopped and looked back at Bishop.

'His mouth,' I whispered to myself. I looked at Harrison.

'Like Keri,' he said.

'Do you have any gloves?'

He removed a pair of latex gloves from his jacket pocket and handed them to me. I slipped them on then went up to the body.

'Is this really necessary?' Kelly said.

'We've already killed him. He won't notice,' I said. I looked over to Hicks. 'This is your crime scene. What do you want to do?'

Hicks looked at me and nodded. 'Check it.'

I stepped up next to Bishop, trying to avoid the gathering pools of blood at his feet. The scent of torn flesh and intestinal gases released by the bullets filled my nostrils and I tried not to breathe as I reached out and peeled back a corner of the duct tape over his mouth.

The adhesive clung to the heavy stubble of his unshaven face. As I pulled the tape free follicles of facial hair came with it and his jaw fell open. I took out my Mag-lite and shined it in his mouth. His teeth were covered with a thin film of blood that had been forced up his throat by the explosive power of the rounds that had pieced his lungs.

'There's something here,' I said.

I carefully reached in and managed to pinch the object between my fingers and slide it out. At first I didn't recognize it with the film of blood covering it, but as I wiped it off it became clear.

'It's a patron saint medal,' I said. I took out a Kleenex and cleaned it off. 'St John Nepomucene.'

'Do you know it?' Harrison asked.

I shook my head and then turned the medal over.

'The back's been engraved.'

I tried to read it, but the engraving was too small. I handed it to Dylan and he began to read.

Who by his invincible sacramental silence won his crown, teaches us to prefer torture and death to offending the creator with our tongue. How many times each day do we forfeit grace and strength by sins of speech.

'Someone want to explain that to me?' Kelly said.

Harrison handed the medal back to me and I looked up at Bishop's torn and tortured body.

'The patron saint of silence,' I said.

'How does this help us?' Hicks said.

'It doesn't. It just confirms what we already know.'

'Which is?'

'The only thing he's ever been interested in is silence, and when he has it, his work's done and then he will join St John Nepomucene.'

'How are we certain of that?'

'Because on the wall of his parents' house he said I'm the one who kills him.' I handed Hicks the medal, slipped off the gloves. 'I'm the chosen one.'

We went through the rest of the church and annex room by room to see if Goya had left more than the medal behind, but there was nothing. When we stepped outside the dawn had already slipped into morning. High clouds were beginning to drift back in from the Pacific.

'More rain is suppose to move in later,' Harrison said.

'Before or after the Mass?'

He shook his head. 'I'm not sure. If it's early maybe it will keep down the size of the crowd at the stadium.'

'I wouldn't count on it,' I said, and looked back at the church.

'No,' Harrison said. 'We should be getting there.'

I nodded but made no attempt to move.

'Have we missed something, Dylan? We should have found the chief by now. There's got to be a reason we haven't.'

'We'll know it when we find it.'

'That's what I'm afraid of.'

The assault team came out of the church and walked past us. Their hoods and helmets had been removed. One glance at the look in their eyes and you knew that no amount of body armor could shield them from what they were feeling at this moment. The lead agent glanced in my direction but said nothing, just filed past in silence.

'I talked to the Pope,' I said.

Dylan looked at me in surprise.

'You talked to the Pope?'

I nodded, not entirely believing it myself.

'A private audience. Part of me wanted to interrogate him, see if I could get him to confess all the crimes of silence the Church had committed. The other part of me was like a terrified girl in Catholic school afraid the Mother Superior was going to whack me with a ruler if I said the wrong thing.'

'Did he have a ruler?' Dylan asked, half smiling.

I shook my head.

'I asked him why he had come to LA.'

'What did he say?'

'He said he had come to heal.'

I looked over to the derelict church.

'I told him he was late.'

'You said that to the Pope?'

I nodded. 'I've been trying to figure out why he chose to talk to me. He didn't have to. I thought perhaps he was trying to protect Rezzitti, or wanted to know if I was the kind of cop who could be silenced.'

'You come up with an answer?'

'I think he wanted me to know that if we failed, and he's killed today, it wasn't our fault, it was his.'

Hicks and Kelly came walking out of the church. I glanced at my watch. It was nearing nine a.m. already.

'The Mass begins at noon?' I said.

Dylan nodded.

'What happens between then and now?'

Dylan shook his head. 'I'm not sure.'

I walked over to Hicks as he approached.

'What's on the pontiff's schedule between now and the Mass?'

'A series of private audiences.'

'With whom?'

'Your usual selection of LA types. Politicians. Celebrities. They've all been vetted, it's fine.'

'Are all the meetings at the cathedral?'

'No, one is at a Catholic school.'

'A school?'

'Yes, St Thomas. It was added this morning. It's not been publicized, no one knows about it outside the Church and security. The school was only told about the visit today.'

'When does he leave the cathedral?'

Hicks checked his watch. 'He should have already left.'

I glanced at Harrison and we both started moving toward the car.

# thirty-seven

St Thomas was a few miles north of downtown at the terminus of the 2 freeway. It was built in the Spanish style, whitewashed walls and red-tiled roof. Traffic squads had the blocks adjacent to the school barricaded. Short of a badge or a ten-year-old with a school uniform there was no chance of gaining access to the property.

The Pope's motorcade was less than a mile away when we pulled to a stop on Glendale and stepped out. In the playground an assembly was in progress. Teachers were trying to marshal the excited students into several orderly lines and march them back inside the school. We walked around the perimeter of the grounds to the school's entrance and showed our IDs to the sergeant in charge of the location.

'Is there a problem?' the man asked.

I shook my head. 'I'd like to look inside.'

'Secret service secured the buildings. I've got a man inside now with Vatican security going over it again. They've checked everything, and the exterior is locked down.'

'I'm sure it is, but I'd still like to look.'

A burst of sound came over the sergeant's radio. He responded to it with a clipped 'Ten-four', and considered our request.

'Is there something I need to be worried about?' he asked.

'I hope not.'

He thought it over for a moment and then nodded. 'You've got four minutes before he arrives.'

'What are the plans once he gets here?' I asked.

'He takes a quick tour of the classrooms and then there's an assembly in the gym and the school choir is going to sing for him.'

I looked over toward the building. The parish chapel was a separate structure on the other side of the school.

'Nothing in the church?'

He shook his head. 'He's going to bless it, but that will be private, no students or faculty.'

An advance motorcycle from the motorcade stopped out on the corner of Glendale and blocked the exit from the freeway. Farther south I could see the LAPD helicopter flying above the motorcade.

'If you're going to look, you'd better hurry,' the sergeant said.

Harrison and I rushed through the doors of the school and into the lobby. Teachers were marching the last of the lines of students toward the gym to our right. The sound of the students gathered there already echoed through the granite floors of hallway.

'You start in the classrooms, I'll check the gym,' I said and we moved off in opposite directions.

The floor of the gym had all but disappeared beneath rows of seated, cross-legged children. A teacher was standing in front clapping her hands, trying to get their attention.

'Silence, everyone. Boys and girls, I want complete silence!'

The voices began to soften into a murmur with the occasional laugh or shriek. I walked around the perimeter of the gym looking up and down the rows, but I saw nothing that was out of place. In the front of the gym a large chair had been set up for the Pope and beyond that the choir was settling onto a series of raised benches.

I stopped a teacher moving toward the front.

'Could you tell me where the policeman is who was here?'

She looked at me and shook her head. 'Policeman? I haven't seen any.'

A girl a few feet away jumped up from the floor and turned to face the boys behind her, yelling at the top of her lungs.

'You're dead!'

The teacher stepped past me toward the girl as the teacher at the front of the gym began to clap her hands again.

'Silence. I want silence right now, everyone.'

I walked around the rest of the room, took one last look across the rows of students, and then started down the hallway toward the classrooms. As I reached the front lobby Harrison came out of the room at the end of the hallway and met me.

'Anything?' I asked.

He shook his head. 'They're all empty. Windows and doors secure, nothing out of place.'

'Did you see the LAPD or the Swiss Guard officer?'

'No.'

'I didn't either.'

A door marked ADMINISTRATION was just off the lobby. I walked over and opened it. There was no one at the reception desk. The sound of a computer printer could be heard in one of the interior offices. I stepped past reception and down the short hallway leading to the other offices. The doors were all open except for the last one where the sound of the printer was coming from. I walked to it and opened the door. The printer was running, but the room was empty, just as the others were.

'Everyone's probably in the gym,' Harrison said.

I turned and looked back toward reception.

'So where's the cop and the Swiss Guard?'

'Walking the perimeter one more time.'

'Maybe.'

We went back out of the offices and started toward the lobby's door just as the LAPD sergeant came in.

'They're less than two minutes out,' he said. 'You finished?'

'Where's your officer?' I asked.

He looked down the hallway toward the gym. 'He's in—'

'No, he isn't, or the Vatican security,' I said.

He grabbed his radio handset and keyed the mike. 'Lambert, what's your ten-twenty?'

From the gym the choir began practicing a song.

'Lambert, what's your location?' he repeated.

'*Jesus loves me . . .*' came drifting up the corridor. Nothing came back on the radio.

'When did you last talk to him?' I asked.

'About an hour ago.'

'We checked the rest of the building, but we didn't see them.'

'They must have gone outside. Or over to the chapel.' He picked up the radio again. 'Anyone have a ten-twenty on Lambert? Or the Vatican man?'

Half a dozen negative replies came back.

'Did you see the Swiss Guard's ID?' I asked.

He looked at me, more annoyed than concerned.

'Yeah. He was a real snappy dresser.'

'Where's his vehicle?'

'I didn't see him drive up. He must have stopped on the other side of the building from where I was.'

'What was his name?'

He tried to remember, then shook his head. 'I don't remember. I saw his ID, it was fine.'

'You've seen a lot of Swiss Guard IDs over the years?' I asked.

'I know a fake ID when I see one. Is there a problem?'

'He could be here,' Harrison said.

'What? Who's here?' said the sergeant.

'How do you get to the chapel?'

He motioned to a door on the other side of the lobby and we started toward it. As I reached for the handle it opened and an LAPD officer was standing there.

'You calling me, sergeant?' he asked. 'My radio died.'

The sergeant looked over to me. 'Are we done now?' He turned to the officer. 'Go stand at the gym.'

The uniform started to walk away.

'Where's the Swiss Guard?' I asked.

The officer stopped. 'Left him in the chapel.'

'How long ago was that?'

'About an hour.'

'Get to the gym, Lambert,' the sergeant said.

Another round of singing came echoing up the corridor. '*Jesus loves me . . .*'

'Did you get his name?' I asked the officer.

'Lieutenant,' said the sergeant, wanting to put an end to it.

'Did you?' I repeated.

The patrolman looked at the sergeant, and then nodded. 'Sten something.'

'Stenson?'

'Yeah, that was it.'

'Slow the motorcade down,' I said

'Are you frickin' kidding me? You better have a good goddamn reason.'

'A Swiss Guard named Stenson was murdered last night.'

It took the sergeant a moment to fully grasp what I had just told him. Then he picked up his hand mike again.

'Hold the motorcade. I repeat, hold the motorcade until I clear the location. All units, a ten-fourteen may be present inside the perimeter.'

'Was the Pope coming into the school the same way we did?' I asked.

'No, he was coming in past the church.'

I walked over to the door, opened it and looked out at the chapel across the courtyard. 'And he goes in the church?'

The sergeant nodded.

'He was going to bless it,' he said.

'Before or after the visit in the school?'

'After. He walks in and then back to the vehicles waiting right out front.'

I stared at the church for a moment. A series of windows opened onto the center courtyard where the Pope would be walking. One of them was open.

'Make sure the kids remain in the gym. No one comes in or out of the school building,' I said to the sergeant. 'We'll check the church.'

Harrison and I ran over to the doors of the church and stopped as an LAPD helicopter came swooping in overhead and began circling the grounds.

'This was a surprise visit,' Harrison said. 'How did Goya know about this if it wasn't publicly announced?'

'Stenson could have told him before he killed him.'

We looked at each other for a moment.

'And if he didn't?' Dylan said.

'You're saying someone within the Church told him?'

'It's the only other way he could have found out.'

'Which means he's not working alone.'

'More good news.'

I pulled my Glock out, and then pushed the door open and slipped through into the interior of the chapel. A display of candles was burning at the far end, the lights were low, but I could see.

I moved my weapon left and right across the interior and then Harrison slipped in past me sweeping the pews with his Beretta. We held our ground for a moment, waiting to see if there was movement or response to our entering. Dylan looked over to me and shook his head.

'Nothing,' he said.

The interior appeared to be untouched.

'The Pope was going to bless the chapel,' I said softly.

Dylan looked at me. 'What are you thinking?'

'Holy water.' I looked over to the font at the foot of the aisle.

'St Gabriel's,' Dylan said.

We moved across the back row of pews to the font and stared at its contents. Like at St Gabriel's, the water had been replaced with blood.

'The blood of Christ,' Harrison said.

I shook my head.

'That's not Christ's blood,' I said. 'Let's check the rest of the church.'

We stepped a few feet farther into the nave. I motioned to Dylan and he moved over to the left side and began moving forwards as I did the same on the right. When we reached the front of the chapel we both stopped.

'It's clear,' Harrison said.

I turned and looked around the chapel.

'Maybe,' I said.

My eyes settled on the doors to the confessional and I raised my weapon and motioned toward it.

'Like St Gabriel's again,' Dylan said.

I nodded and started toward the confessional. Dylan moved over too and I took up a position on the left door and he on the right. I hesitated for a moment, listening for any sound coming from within; then we both reached out and pulled the doors open.

'Nothing here,' Harrison said.

My eyes settled on a white object.

'It's here,' I said.

Dylan stepped over behind me. On the kneeler in the confessional was a white letter-size envelope. I reached down, picked it up by its edges and stepped back out into the chapel. My name was written on the front.

'He left something for me,' I said, and broke the seal and opened it.

'What is it?' Harrison asked.

I reached into the envelope and slipped the contents out. It was a ticket to the papal Mass.

'An invitation,' I said.

We started for the doors and I handed Harrison the ticket. 'Find out where this seat is, then get surveillance on it.'

Harrison was already taking out his phone. As we reached the doors they swung open and in walked Rezzitti.

'You did this? You stopped the motorcade?'

'He was here,' I said.

'That's impossible.'

'Go look at the font,' I said.

Rezzitti hesitated, then walked over to the font and looked at its contents.

'He has Stenson's credentials,' I said.

Rezzitti stared at the blood for a moment.

'Did Stenson know about this stop here?' I asked.

He turned to me.

'What are you saying?'

'Goya either found out about this from Stenson, or found out another way.'

Rezzitti looked around the chapel as the meaning of what I was asking him became clear.

'Would Stenson have known about it?' I repeated.

'I'm not sure . . . it's possible.'

'Goya was here more than an hour ago. Which means he's probably already inside the Rose Bowl,' I said.

He nodded in agreement.

'Tell me about the Mass,' I said.

'What about it?'

'When I talked to the Pope he said he had come here to heal. Is he going to discuss the abuse that took place in the Church? Is that part of his sermon?'

He nodded.

'Yes. There will be both silent and spoken prayers offered.'

'Silence?'

'Yes.'

'That's when Goya will strike,' I said.

Rezzitti turned to me. 'The archdiocese announced this morning that a section of seating directly in front of the Pontiff was to be reserved for invited victims of priests.'

'You just found out about this?'

He nodded.

'The archdiocese didn't want the press to know about it,' he said.

'So they kept the information secret, even from you.'

'Old habits die hard. They also believe that what they call radicalized elements of the victims movement may try to disrupt the Holy Father.'

'Radicalized?'

'Their word, not mine.'

'How many?'

'Several hundred could be present throughout the stadium.'

'We have to get to the Rose Bowl.'

Rezzitti nodded. 'The Holy Father will make his stop in the school as planned. I'll go ahead to the Bowl.'

We walked to the doors and as I started to open them Rezzitti reached out and took hold of the handle and stopped me.

'Goya has written that you're the one who takes his life.'

I looked back at him and nodded.

'Why?' he said. 'There'll be hundreds of police at the Mass. Why did he single out you?'

'I'm not sure,' I said.

We looked at each other for a moment.

'Doesn't matter,' I said. 'I have it from a very highly placed source that nothing is written.'

# thirty-eight

We stopped on Linda Vista where we had a view of the arroyo and the Rose Bowl. In a little over an hour the Mass would begin. The stadium appeared to be nearly full yet there were still thousands of people gathered outside hoping to catch a glimpse of the Pope as he passed by.

The skies over the ocean to the west were dark, but the threat of more rain had not materialized in time to reduce the size of the crowds.

'The Popemobile takes him into the tunnel on the south side. He exits onto an elevator which takes him up to where a platform has been built several sections up from field level,' Harrison said. 'The ticket Goya left is on the west side, nearly at the top of the stadium under the press boxes. Traver's set up surveillance, but so far nothing.'

I stared at the stadium for a moment.

'We should get down there,' Dylan said.

'Why did he choose me?' I said.

Dylan looked at me. 'Does there have to be a reason?'

I nodded. 'Yeah.'

'He's created his own myth about his life on those walls in his parents' house. Chavez could have told him about you. You've been his pursuer. It's logical.'

'Logical?'

'What passes for it in his mind.'

I shook my head. 'Rezzitti was right. There're a hundred thousand people in that stadium, hundreds of cops inside and out. Everything Goya has done, from his drawings to the way he's killed, has been done with attention to every detail. Why would his death be any less so? The chance that I'm the one who stops him isn't even remotely plausible. So why me?'

'I don't know,' Dylan said. 'You think we're missing something.'

I slipped the squad in gear and headed down into the arroyo toward the stadium.

'We have to be,' I said.

Outside the stadium the impromptu festival of the night before had now been overtaken by commerce. Vendors lined the streets leading up to the stadium. Anything that could hold an image of the Pope was for sale: buttons, towels, hats, flags, shirts, plates, and umbrellas. One man dressed in a cardinal outfit was even selling white suede Pope shoes.

We passed through a police checkpoint and into A lot at the south end of the stadium, where the Pope would be entering. The lot was fenced off, only emergency vehicles allowed inside the chain-link. There were a dozen ambulances, fire engines, and enough squad cars to police a medium-size city, which the Rose Bowl had become. On a yellow tarp several paramedics were setting up a triage station.

We both looked at the rows of bandages and IV bags neatly stacked and ready for use as a roar from the crowd inside the walls shook the ground like a small earthquake.

'Sounds like a game in there,' Harrison said.

Just beyond the ambulances a row of palm trees shielded two large panel trucks that carried FBI tactical assault teams.

'A deadly game,' I said.

Rezzitti's sedan pulled up and he stepped out to join us.

'Where will you be?' he asked.

I held up the ticket. 'Where Goya wants me.'

Rezzitti looked over to the stadium.

'What would Stenson's assignment have been if he was alive?' I asked.

'Down on field level, where the victims are going to be.'

'Goya might know that,' I said.

He nodded, started to turn away, and stopped.

'Good luck, Lieutenant,' he said.

He looked at me for a moment then hurried off, and Harrison and I started toward the entrance. Traver was waiting as we entered the one tunnel that led to field level. The rest of the tunnels the crowd would be using entered on the concourse level a quarter of the way up into the stadium seating.

'There's not an empty seat in the house,' Traver said. 'Except one.'

'Still nothing?'

He shook his head and then handed us both small radios.

'One guy tried to sit in it, but he just had the wrong row. No one's hesitated by it, and as far as we can tell nothing's been placed under it, but we didn't want to look too close in case he's watching.'

'He's watching,' I said. 'Where's your surveillance?'

'There're two officers dressed as ushers within fifty feet. You want to check it out?' Dave asked.

'He left the ticket for a reason,' I said.

With each step closer to the field the roar of the crowd became louder.

'But what reason?' Traver said. 'You can get farther away from the Pope in the stadium, but not by much.'

'That seat wasn't for him, it's for me,' I said.

We reached the end of the tunnel and stepped out into the

sunlight. The green grass of the field was completely obscured by row after row of thousands of people covering its length. In the seats of the stadium the crowd had begun doing the wave and shouting 'JESUS' as they leapt to their feet and threw their arms toward the sky.

I turned and looked toward the platform where the Pope would be standing. It was adorned in the yellow and white papal colors, and had been built to give the impression that the pontiff would be standing on a balcony of the Vatican. The seats behind him all the way to the top of the stadium were filled with men in black suits.

'Priests,' I said.

'Hundreds of them,' Harrison said.

'The surveillance on all the entrances came up with nothing on Goya,' Traver said. 'Do you think maybe the security frightened him off?'

I shook my head. 'He got a body inside here with no one noticing. He's here. What about Maria Perez?'

'A Hispanic woman in her fifties, with little or no description? We stopped counting after two thousand came through the gates.'

The wave came roaring around the south end of the stadium and the clergy filling the seats behind us all joined in the chorus and threw their arms toward the sky and roared 'JESUS!'

'Where's the group of abuse victims sitting?' I asked.

Traver motioned directly below us toward the front of the field. The Pope would be looking down on them, perhaps sixty feet away give or take. Half a dozen secret service officers stood at the front of the field surveying the crowd. I glanced at my watch.

'The Pope's due to arrive in twenty minutes.'

'Last I heard they're running about ten minutes late,' Traver said.

'Get me up to the seat,' I said.

Traver led us up to the concourse and then we started toward midfield as the roar and movement of the wave continued to gain in speed and decibel level with every pass. The crowd appeared to represent nearly every color, every nationality, that had ever stepped off a boat or a plane onto the streets of LA. Some in traditional dress, others in street clothes; all of them, African, Indian, Asian, brown, white, black, yellow, and all shades in between, cheering for Jesus with each crest of the wave.

We reached midfield and stopped. A priest walked by brushing my shoulder and I spun around, reaching for my Glock as he walked several paces then looked back at me. He had white hair, was probably sixty. He smiled and nodded, then walked on.

'Last section all the way up,' Traver said. 'Two seats in from the end. The ushers on either side of the section are our people.'

'What channel are the radios on?'

'The ones I gave you are on six. Everything else inside the stadium is on four except the two officers dressed as ushers, who are also on six. You need assistance they're only fifty feet away.'

I looked up toward the seat, then turned and looked out across the sea of people in the rest of the stadium.

'He watching us, right now,' I said.

'That's safe to assume,' Harrison said.

The wave came roaring around the corner of the stadium and swept by like a gust of wind.

'I'm not sure which is more disconcerting, an empty stadium with a single body, or a full one with none.'

'None yet,' Dylan said. 'Where do you want me?'

I turned to him and made brief eye contact.

'He left one ticket for a reason,' I said. 'The more he thinks I'm on my own, the better.'

'For whom?'

'Check out the section in front of the platform with the victims

343

of abuse,' I said, and then turned to Traver. 'I want you walking through the section with the priests above the platform.'

Neither of them moved.

'Maybe we should wait here,' Harrison said.

'There're two officers up there already. I'll be fine. I'll call you when I've checked out the seat.'

Outside the stadium the first beat of the helicopters flying over the Pope's motorcade became audible.

'You'd better get going.'

Harrison looked at me for a moment then they both turned and headed off. I started up the stairs toward the top of the stadium. As the rake of the rows grew steeper I tried to work out in my head a scenario that Goya might have imagined for this day, but it eluded me. Was the Pope the target, or the victims of priests, or had I entirely missed some clue that pointed toward the outcome his tortured mind had envisioned.

'Radio check,' Harrison said in my pocket. I took out the radio.

'You worry like a grandmother,' I said.

'I was hoping you had another image in mind,' he said.

'I'll get back to you on that,' I answered and slipped the radio back in my pocket.

Above me the press and luxury skyboxes hung over the seating where I was headed. An inflatable beach ball with crosses painted on it was being bounced back and forth across the rows. People were laughing. It was the happiest church service I had ever walked in on. I passed one of our people dressed as an usher and nodded to him.

'Everything's fine, Lieutenant. Next section last row,' he said without making any eye contact with me.

I climbed up to the last section and stopped a few rows before reaching the one I was looking for. The empty seat was there, two in from the end. A young Hispanic mother wearing a sweatshirt from Disneyland sat in the one on the left, her young daughter sitting next to her. On the other side a young man in his teens and a girl occupied the two seats next to the aisle; they were holding hands, and around their necks were large crosses on silver chains. I quickly scanned the rest of the neighboring seats for anything that appeared to stand out from its surroundings, but there was nothing.

On the far side of the section I made brief eye contact with the other officer dressed as an usher and then I climbed the final steps to my row.

'Excuse me,' I said.

The young couple stood up. They were maybe in their twenties. The boy looked at me and smiled, his eyes holding that light you only see accompanying blind faith.

'God bless,' he said.

I carefully stepped past them over to the seat and stopped. Nothing about the seat appeared any different from any of the others around it. I kneeled down as if to tie my shoes and took a quick glance underneath it. Goya had left nothing for me.

I rose back up and then turned and looked around. The entire stands seemed to have a view of me. Over the top of the south end of the stadium I could see the Pope's helicopter escort drawing closer. I looked down at the papal platform. Traver was right. From this seat the Pope would be little more than a stick figure. I reached into my pocket and took out the radio.

'There isn't anything here,' I said.

Nothing came back for a moment. Then Harrison's voice came over the airwaves.

'What do you want to do?'

I took a glance at the helicopter. The sound of its rotors had begun cracking the air like shots.

'They're his rules. I'll wait,' I said. 'Are you in front of the platform yet?'

'No, the aisles are filled, it will take some time to get through.'

'Same here,' Traver said.

'Call me when you're there.'

I placed the radio back in my pocket and settled back into the seat. From somewhere within the stadium came the sound of a trumpet. The wave came curling around the rows toward me again.

'Have you found him?' said the young man next to me.

I turned to him. 'What did you say?'

The crowd around me began to cheer in anticipation.

'Have you found Jesus?'

I glanced at him and shook my head.

'I'm looking for someone else at the moment,' I said.

'He's waiting for you.'

I forced a smile.

'I'm sure he is.'

The young man shook his head.

'No, he is.'

'I know,' I said.

'Just go through the tunnel on the concourse. That's where he's waiting.'

The wave swept past us and the crowd erupted and jumped to their feet.

'What did you say?' I asked again.

'He's waiting for you, go through the tunnel. He'll find you.'

'Who will?'

'The one you're looking for.'

'How do you know?'

'He told us.'

'Where did he tell you this?'

'Outside. He gave us our tickets and these.'

His hand reached down and picked up the cross on the chain around his neck. The young woman next to him smiled and placed a hand on hers.

'You should go,' she said. 'He has a gift for you also.'

'But you're to go alone or he won't be there.'

'And there won't be a gift,' the girl said.

They both looked at me with their faith-filled eyes and smiled.

'Have you ever seen this man before?'

They shook their heads.

'I'm a policeman,' I said.

'Yes, he told us that,' the young man said. 'You're supposed to leave the radio with us.'

'Or no gift,' I said.

The girl nodded. 'He said he would be watching.'

'Have you seen him again, since you've been sitting here?'

They both shook their heads.

'When your friends come for you we'll tell them where you went,' he said.

The sound of cheering began to be audible outside the stadium as the Pope's motorcade drew closer.

'You'd better go. He said he won't wait.'

I glanced around for a moment then reached into my pocket and removed the radio.

'He said you can't talk into it. You can't tell anyone.'

'What did he look like?' I asked.

They both smiled.

'Holy,' the boy said.

'He had robes,' the girl added.

'Like a monk?' I asked.

They both nodded.

'He said he'll help you find what you want,' the girl said.

'Just like he did with you?' I said.

'Praise the Lord,' she said.

The young man held out his hand and smiled with a kind of clueless joy. I imagined his mother didn't sleep very well at night knowing he was out on his own in the world. I glanced at the radio and then pressed my thumb on the receiver button opening the mike.

'After I leave an usher is going to come over here and ask about me,' I said. 'You give him the radio and tell him everything that you told me. You tell him I went into the tunnel to meet Goya and that he is dressed as a monk and that he said I was to come alone. Do you understand?'

They both nodded and I released the button on the radio and placed it in the boy's hand.

'Hurry, or you'll miss your gift,' the girl said.

'I won't miss it,' I said then stepped into the aisle and looked down at the entrance to the tunnel on the concourse.

I glanced over to the nearest officer dressed as an usher, but whether he had heard my transmission I couldn't tell from the look on his face. He began to move toward me and I shook my head and he stopped.

I ran down to the tunnel leading into the interior and stopped. A wheelchair access sign was above the exit. A police stanchion was blocking the entry. A Rose Bowl usher was standing next to it, and I showed him my badge.

'Has anyone been through here?' I asked.

He nodded.

'How many?'

'Just two.'

'What did they look like?'

'The man was in a chair, and a nun was pushing him.'

'Which way did they go?'

He shook his head. 'I didn't notice.'

I looked down the tunnel. 'Was there anything else about them that you did notice?'

'The man was breathing through a mask.'

'What about the nun?'

'She was wearing a habit.'

'Why is this tunnel closed?'

'It's not an entrance. It's just used for concessions and for disabled access down to field level.'

'Does the elevator access anything else?'

'Yeah, the grounds crew shops are down there.'

I glanced quickly around at the surrounding seats looking for the one face that didn't fit, but it was hopeless. I stepped past the stanchion toward the dark passageway but stopped when the helicopter accompanying the motorcade came low over the stadium and began to circle.

The wave sweeping around the stadium began to falter and then died altogether and the crowd fell absolutely silent. After several moments applause rose from the far corner of the Bowl and began to spread through the crowd as anticipation of the Pope's arrival grew.

I started down the tunnel, slipping my Glock out of its holster as I entered the dark interior. Like all the tunnels in the stadium, it was narrow and dark, built to a standard when fire and safety codes had yet to be written. It had always been the nightmare scenario for Pasadena PD and Rose Bowl officials that disaster was waiting inside these narrow walls should a panic ever spread within the confines of the stadium and the crowd rushed for the exits. The estimated number of dead, either crushed or suffocated, was conservatively estimated at thirty in each tunnel. There were a total of twenty-eight entrance and exit tunnels throughout the stadium, all the same size as this. The math wasn't difficult to figure out.

I reached the end of the tunnel and stopped. Several lights illuminated the elevator fifty feet to my left. A series of empty concession stands lined the walls on the far side of the narrow concourse.

I stepped out and crossed over to the empty Frosty Freeze booth. The doors were padlocked – there was nothing there except the sweet lingering odor of sugar. I started toward the elevator and took out my cell phone and hit Harrison's number.

It rang and stopped then rang again and Harrison picked up.

'Where . . . you . . . Alex?'

'Did you get my message?' I asked.

'I'm . . .' The call cut off. The thick concrete structure of the stadium was blocking cell service.

I tried again and this time couldn't even acquire a signal. I rushed to the elevator and pressed the button. It was an old machine, oversized, and the doors had to be opened manually. Inside the shaft the cables and pulleys began to turn and I heard the elevator moving up.

My hand clenched around the Glock and I stepped several feet back and raised the weapon. From inside the stadium another sound began to rise. With each rhythmic beat it grew louder and the stadium seemed to shudder. The crowd was clapping hands and stomping their feet as if they were awaiting a rock star.

The gears of the elevator ground to a stop and a small red light over the door turned green. I held the Glock on the door, waiting for it to open, and when it didn't I stepped forward and reached out for the handle. I hesitated, listening for a sound from the other side, then I yanked the door open, swinging my weapon into the interior. It was dark; the light inside lay in pieces on the floor. It took a moment for my eyes to adjust, and then it became clear it was empty.

I stepped inside. The door closed and I was plunged into

complete darkness. The shaking of the stadium from the foot-stomping was more noticeable inside the elevator. Each shudder went through the suspending cables like blood coursing through an artery. As I reached my hand out, trying to find the button, the elevator doors locked, the wheels and pulleys began to grind and I started down.

I pressed myself against the back wall, intending to put every inch between the doors and myself once I reached the bottom. I was holding my gun out in front of me, but I couldn't see it. The descent seemed to go on beyond what I would have thought was field level and then the cables began to screech and the elevator began to slow, and then it stopped with the abruptness of a door being slammed.

I tightened my grip around the handle of the Glock, waiting for a response from the other side. In my head I counted out five and then ten seconds – nothing. I stepped forward away from the back of the elevator until I could reach the door with my free hand, took hold of the handle and slid it open.

I swung around against the corner of the door, one foot out and one foot still inside the elevator, holding my weapon out in front of me, staring into more darkness. The air inside smelled of fuel and cut grass. I stepped out of the elevator and the door slid shut with a loud bang. I ran my free hand against the wall, steadying myself.

To the left, maybe thirty or forty feet away, I could see the faint glow of a red exit sign. If I had understood what the usher had told me, through those doors was the field, which meant that to the right of where I stood was the grounds crew shop. The floor was littered with delicate shards of glass from the shattered ceiling light overhead – Goya wanted it dark.

I eased myself along the wall in that direction, moving the gun back and forth across the darkness. With each step I took, the shudder going though the stadium from the stamping of the feet grew in intensity. My free hand hit the metal links of a fence cutting across the hallway. I followed it left until my hand found the latch that opened the gate into the shop.

I carefully lifted it until it cleared and then pushed the gate open and stepped into the shop area. Light was coming through a crack in a door on the far wall. To my left I could just make out the dull shapes of lawn mowers and tractors lined up against the wall.

The smell of fuel and fertilizer chemicals filled the air, making it difficult to breathe. I was sliding my feet along the concrete, trying not lose my balance, when my foot hit something and I began to stumble. A hand closed around my ankle and I jerked free and fell backward onto the floor, holding my gun on the darkness in front of me.

'Don't move,' I said.

There was a faint gasp, a struggle for breath.

'Police,' I said.

I got on my knees clutching my gun with both hands.

'If you move, I will shoot,' I said.

Another gasp for air. I inched forward and reached my hand out along the cool concrete until I touched the fabric of a suit jacket, and then a hand closed on mine, the fingers trembling as they tried to hold on to me.

'I'm a policeman. I'll help you,' I said whispering.

He tried to form a word, but couldn't manage it. I crawled up next to him and leaned in as close as I could get. The vague outline of his features became visible.

'Delillo,' he said weakly.

'Rezzitti?'

I moved my hand over his chest and heard the whisper of air moving through a puncture in his chest wall. There was little blood, but I imagined from the sound that a lung had been damaged. I took hold of his hand and placed it on the wound.

'Keep your hand there,' I said. I reached across his chest to his shoulder holster. It was empty. 'Your gun?'

He shook his head.

'Where is he?' I whispered.

No reply.

'Where's Goya?' I said again.

Rezzitti tried to speak again but I couldn't hear the words. He reached up with his free hand and motioned for me to come closer. I leaned my head down next to his.

'Get them out,' he whispered.

'Who? Get who out?'

He seemed to drift toward unconsciousness but fought it off.

'Get who out?' I asked again.

He started to speak, then stopped, and then finally managed a word.

'*Jedermann*,' he said in German.

'*Jedermann*?' I asked, trying to remember what it meant in English.

'*Jedermann*,' Rezzitti repeated.

'Everyone?' I asked. 'Is that it? Everyone?'

He nodded.

I tried to make sense of what he was saying. 'From where?'

He tried to speak again, but his voice grew even weaker. I turned my head so as to place my ear right next to his mouth.

'Stadium,' he whispered.

My heart began to pound against my chest.

He started to say something but I couldn't make out the words. 'What has he done?' I asked. 'What's going to happen?'

Rezzitti's hand tightened around mine for a moment; then his grip began to relax and his hand slipped away. I reached up and

353

placed my hand on his neck. His pulse was still there. He had fallen into unconsciousness, but he was alive.

I crawled around him, toward the office where the light flickered through the crack in the door. A foot past him his compact Beretta revolver lay on the floor. The magazine was still in place. I slipped it in my pocket and slowly got to my feet, holding the Glock on the door ahead. I stepped back against the wall and began working my way toward it.

More glass from the ceiling lights covered the floor. With each step I took toward the door glass cracked under the soles of my shoes. I reached out to my left and guided myself along the workbench that ran the length of the wall. Empty containers of what smelled like fertilizers and fuel were spread across the top of the counter.

I followed the bench to the end a few feet from the door and began to reach toward the handle. The shudder going through the stadium from the stomping of the feet fell silent. Voices became audible from behind the door.

I looked at the light flickering through the crack at the bottom of the door. I took hold of the handle, turned it halfway, and hesitated as I listened for a reaction on the other side. Then I flung it open and raised my weapon.

A small television sat on a desk across the room in the darkness. Live coverage from inside the stadium directly above me was on the screen. A chair was placed in front of it. The room was empty; there was no one inside. I had started to turn to leave when I felt the cold touch of a hand on the back of my neck.

As I began to spin around the blow struck the side of my face and I felt myself falling backward. I hit the concrete floor and the air rushed out of my lungs and I gasped for breath.

'You've come for your gift,' said Goya.

I took a half-breath, and then another, and tried to sit up. From the light of the television I saw him spin in his dark robes from the abbey as he drove his foot into my side and I crumpled back to the floor. I tried to breathe but the air entering my lungs felt like a knife blade slicing through me.

Goya walked several feet away and picked up my Glock where it had flown from my hand. He pushed it in his pocket and then came over to me and slid the hood of his robe back off his head. In the light from the television his eyes were empty and black like two holes in space. His features were drawn, his cheekbones pressing against the skin. He bore more resemblance to a corpse than to the pictures I had seen of the boy Andrew Simms from St Gabriel's, but it was him, there was no mistaking the eyes. He reached down, lifted me up by the shirt and slammed my back against the wall, then let go.

My legs gave out and I wilted to the floor. How many seconds passed I couldn't say. When I finally gasped for air and managed to get a breath into my lungs I saw he had stepped over to the TV and was staring at the screen. On the television the Pope stepped out onto the platform and raised his hands to the crowd, then moved them through the air in the sign of the cross.

'Your name is Andrew, not Goya,' I said, barely getting enough air to form the words.

He swung quickly around. 'Andrew is dead. He was stillborn.'

'You can stop this.'

'Stop!' he yelled, and then laughed. 'God gave me life so I could do this.'

'What are you going to do?'

'You are about to see my gift, the birth of a new Church,' Goya said. 'The old one is weak and corrupt, it abides by the laws of men, not God. I will stop all of that hypocrisy. I will return it to where it belongs. It will have a new beginning.'

'Your father doesn't want this. He told me that before he died.'

'God is my father.'

I shook my head. 'Patrick was your father.'

'No. He was my teacher.'

'He raped your mother. That's how you were born.'

'No!' he yelled. 'I am chosen. Do you understand?'

'Maria Perez was your mother.'

He shook his head. 'I am not one of you.'

He walked back to me, took hold of my hair and dragged me over to the TV.

'Now you watch and you will see that it is true.'

He reached down and took my head in his hands and forced me to look at the television as the camera panned across the massive crowd. Thousands of faces, one after the other, jammed together in the stadium. My heart began to pound against my chest.

'*Jedermann*,' I whispered to myself.

He looked down at me. 'What did you say?'

'She said everyone,' came a voice from the door.

Rezzitti slumped against the doorframe and then slipped to the floor. Goya let go of my head, took my Glock out of the pocket of his robe, then walked over and placed the gun to Rezzitti's head.

'*Geh' zur Hölle*,' Rezzitti said.

'Speak English, clockmaker,' Goya said.

I slipped Rezzitti's gun out of my pocket.

'He said go to hell,' I said.

Goya looked at me and saw the gun pointing at him and began to laugh.

'Where did you put it?' Rezzitti asked.

Goya looked down at him and spat on his face.

'What did you do?' I asked.

'Chavez,' Rezzitti said.

'Chavez?' I said, not understanding.

356

'Shoot me,' Goya said.

'Where's Chavez? What have you done?' I shouted, and pulled the hammer back on Rezzitti's weapon.

'Don't,' Rezzitti pleaded.

Goya pressed the gun to the top of Rezzitti's head. 'Kill me, don't be afraid, my work is finished.' He looked at me and laughed. 'You can't stop it. You're too late.'

'What have you done to Chavez?' I said.

'He's building the new Church, just as I have written,' he said, and pressed the gun harder against Rezzitti's head.

I got to my knees.

'Don't shoot him!' Rezzitti yelled. 'We need him alive.'

Goya swung the weapon and hit Rezzitti on the side of the head. The guard captain slumped to the floor and then began trying to pull himself back up using Goya's robes.

'Kill me,' Goya yelled. 'You have no choice, you are nothing, you are only what I have written. God is waiting for me.'

'I'm not part of your story,' I said. 'Put the gun down.'

He shook his head.

'*Fiat voluntas tua, sicut in caelo et in terra.*'

He kicked Rezzitti back against the frame of the door and then placed the barrel of the Glock against the captain's forehead.

'You're not in heaven yet,' I said.

'Then I will send him.'

Goya's hand began to tighten on the handle of the Glock and I pulled the trigger. The muzzle's flash lit the room with a burst of light. The round hit him high on the shoulder, breaking bone as it traveled through him and into the wall with a thud. He tried to turn to his left as if to spin away from me and began to raise the weapon toward Rezzitti again. I pulled the trigger three more times, illuminating the room with flashes of light that gave his movements the disjointed flow of an early silent movie. The

357

second round hit him low in the chest, turning him to his side. The third round pierced his neck, filling the air behind him with a bright mist of blood. With the fourth shot his body stiffened as if he was reaching for something over his head and then he collapsed like a puppet whose strings had been cut.

I got to my feet and walked over to him, clutching the weapon with both hands. I reached down and picked up my Glock from the floor next to him and held the gun toward his face. He moved his head to the side, and then his black eyes dulled and a final whisper of air slipped out of his mouth.

I placed my Glock in the holster and turned to Rezzitti as the beam of a flashlight came cutting through the darkness of the shop. I kneeled down and he weakly lifted his head and looked at me.

'What has he done?' I asked.

He took a weak breath as Harrison came running up holding his weapon.

'Alex?'

'I'm all right,' I said. 'Goya's dead.' I looked back to Rezzitti. 'Help me?' I said. 'What has he done?'

'The drawing,' Rezzitti whispered.

'Of his mother?'

He nodded. 'He said there was only one thing in this stadium that could burn.' He lost his breath and looked at me.

'The stadium's made of concrete,' Harrison said.

I looked back at the TV as the camera moved across the rows of faces, all staring toward the Pope.

'Oh, Jesus,' I whispered.

'What?' Harris said.

'People. People will burn,' I said.

'Yes,' Rezzitti said weakly.

'There's a bomb inside,' I said.

Rezzitti nodded and passed out.

A cheer rose from the ground above us and I glanced at the TV as the camera panned over the ecstatic crowds.

'He couldn't have gotten a bomb in here. There were dogs at every entrance,' Harrison said.

I looked through the door toward the workbench. 'Maybe he didn't have to.'

'What do you mean?'

'Maybe he didn't bring it in, I think he made it here when he was working on the grounds crew.'

'How?'

'Look on the workbench. You're the bomb expert, you tell me.'

'The workbench?'

I nodded. 'There're empty fuel and chemicals jugs.'

Harrison rushed over to the workbench and began looking through the empty cans and jugs. I laid Rezzitti down and propped his hand against the wound in his chest, then eased myself to my feet and walked over to Harrison.

'Could he do it?' I asked.

Dylan looked at me and nodded. 'It's going to be just as the drawing you found at the nursing home said it would be.'

He reached down and picked up several empty gallon jugs from the floor.

'Benzene, gasoline and polystyrene foam used to insulate houses,' he said. 'He could have smuggled this in here weeks ago when he was working on the grounds crew.'

The crowd roared again and the stadium shook.

'And that makes what?' I asked.

'A crude form of napalm.'

'Santa Maria.'

Harrison nodded.

'How big an explosion could this make?'

359

'That would depend on the delivery system and the amount of explosives.'

I glanced back toward the elevator, and worked my way back in memory to the entrance of the tunnel where I had talked to the usher.

'How about something that could fit on a wheelchair, like a bottle of oxygen or maybe even more than one.'

Dylan nodded. 'Depending on the size and number of bottles, even a small charge would have a twenty-five-foot radius, but it could easily be double that, and the burning gel would go much farther in either case. You would have shrapnel from the canisters.'

'And what follows that is one hundred thousand people panicking to get out through the tunnels.'

'The nightmare that's always been talked about,' Harrison said.

I looked back at Goya, his blood spreading out in a wide circle around his head, the light of the TV reflecting on its surface.

'The birth of a new Church. He doesn't have to kill the Pope for that to happen,' I said. 'In his mind anyone who stepped in this stadium today is complicit.'

'With him dead, it means it's on a timer,' Harrison said. 'We'll be looking for a needle in a stack of needles.'

I shook my head.

'Chavez is in that wheelchair,' I said. 'Maria Perez is pushing him, dressed as a nun.' I looked back at Rezzitti. 'We have to get him help.'

Rezzitti shook his head and opened his eyes. 'No.'

I kneeled down and placed his hand against the wound in his chest.

'Leave me. Hurry,' he said. 'Twenty minutes into the Pope's homily . . .' He began to drift.

'What happens at twenty minutes?' I said.

He took a breath. 'A silent prayer.'

'For victims of priests. Did Goya know that?'

He nodded.

'We'll send someone back to help you. Keep your hand on the wound,' I said.

He took a weak breath. 'Go.'

We started running but the crack in my rib sent a jolt of pain through my chest and I doubled over.

'Can you do this?' Dylan asked and took my arm.

I nodded and then began to run again. We passed through the chain-link fence and then beyond the elevator toward the exit sign. Harrison hit the handle and the door flew open and we stepped out into the light of day as the crowd burst into applause.

I spun round to get my bearings and looked out at the massive crowd around us. We were standing at midfield.

'Was there a special section for handicapped and wheelchairs?'

Harrison shook his head. 'Not just one. They're spread around the entire stadium on the concourse and field level.'

'Get on the radio and tell them what we're looking for.'

'But where?' Dylan said.

'At that end,' I said, and turned toward the Pope. 'Where every eye in the stadium will be looking.'

# thirty-nine

We climbed the steps from the field up to the concourse where Chavez and Maria had entered the stadium. With every step I took the cracked rib pressed against my chest and I began to fall behind Harrison as we dashed toward the papal platform.

'Don't wait for me,' I said.

Harrison shook his head. 'You won't know how to defuse it.'

The Pope's voice echoed across the stadium as he spoke in his heavily accented English. 'We are all God's children . . . some priests have broken that most important trust.'

Harrison turned to me. 'It's starting.'

I glanced at my watch.

'We've got less than twenty minutes,' I said, the words taking the breath from me. 'We'll cover more ground separately. I can call you on your cell if I find him.'

Harrison hesitated, then turned and began running through the crowd and I quickly lost him.

'God's love . . .' the Pope said and the crowd began to cheer.

I passed one of the long narrow tunnels and glanced down its length. The concrete was polished smooth from eighty-five years of crowds shuffling their feet and pressing their shoulders against the walls as they entered and exited.

'God will punish those who have trespassed. But only he can forgive.'

I searched the crowd. Every face I passed was looking in his direction; some were clutching their rosaries to their chests. I ran past the next tunnel and then the next one.

'The Church must seek a new beginning . . .'

My phone rang and I picked up.

'I'm at the front. I haven't found him,' Harrison said.

'He's got to—'

I looked down the aisle as I spoke, and saw a group of disabled children sitting on the running track surrounding the grass.

'Wheelchairs,' I said.

'What?' Harrison asked.

'I'm going down to the field. You keep looking there,' I said. 'Keep the line open.'

'Ten minutes,' Harrison said.

'Trust in God's words to heal us,' said the Pope.

'Maybe less than that,' I said to Harrison, and I started running down the steps toward the children in the chairs.

I reached field level. An usher tried to stop me from entering.

'You can't come—'

I ignored him and he reached out to stop me, his hand pressing against my ribs. A jolt of pain went through me and my knees buckled.

'Police,' I managed to say. 'Have you seen a nun pushing a chair?'

He nodded as if I had said something incredibly stupid.

'Forty or fifty of them. They brought people from the hospit—'

'Where?'

He pointed forward, toward the Pope. 'Just up there, the entire section. Are you all right?'

'Show me.'

I pushed the gate open and stepped down onto the track and began working through the crowd with the usher in tow.

'How far?' I asked.

We pushed through a group of people until I had a clear view. The entire section in front of us was filled with nuns sitting next to someone in a wheelchair.

'Right here,' the usher said.

'I'm looking for a man in a chair – he has an oxygen mask on.'

The usher looked at me in surprise. 'He came by me earlier.'

'Where?'

He shook his head. 'Down here somewhere.'

I picked up the phone and started moving through the crowd of nuns and people in wheelchairs.

'What section?' I asked.

'Twenty-two or three, I don't know.'

'Dylan,' I said.

Harrison answered right away.

'He's down here,' I said.

'I'm on my way.'

'Twenty-two or three,' I said.

'Forgive us our trespasses . . .' said the Pope.

I stopped running and stared at the section full of the disabled. They were all children, every one of them; there wasn't a single adult occupying one of the wheelchairs. I spun around, searching for Chavez and had started running back toward the track on the edge of the field when I saw a nun stand up and hold her hands toward the sky.

'Santa Maria,' I whispered.

I pressed my way through the narrow rows of seating until I stepped up behind her and could look down at the figure slumped in the chair next to her.

'Maria?' I said.

She turned around and looked at me. The curves of her face were those of the girl I had seen in the old photograph, but time and madness had taken their toll. She looked at me and smiled. Several of her front teeth were missing.

'Yes, my child,' she said.

I stepped around to the front of the wheelchair and my heart sank. It was a young woman, her legs in braces, her eyes locked on me but giving no indication that I registered.

'Maria, where's the man you brought?'

She looked at me as if she didn't understand.

'The man your son sent with you in the wheelchair?'

Her face lit up. 'My son, yes.'

'Where's the man?'

Her eyes searched for an answer, but it was clear she had none.

'I'm going to be a saint,' she said.

I turned and searched the crowd. The usher was standing thirty yards away next to the running track waving his hands at me.

'In your heart, you must forgive, just as God will . . .'

I pressed my way back through the rows of wheelchairs until I reached the usher.

'Is that him?' he said, pointing into the crowd ahead.

Twenty feet in front of me a man wearing a blue baseball cap sat in a wheelchair. His head was tilted forward, his face hidden, but I could see enough.

'Yes,' I said, already moving.

I reached the chair and stepped around in front of him. Chavez's wrists were taped to the arms of the chair; his chin rested forward on the mask covering his mouth. I lifted the mask off his face and reached out and felt for a pulse. It was there. He appeared drawn and thin; whatever he had endured the last few days had been etched in the lines of his face, but he was alive.

'Albert?' I said, but he didn't respond.

I checked the pupils of his eyes. They were responsive, but the light that they had always held wasn't there. A blanket had been tucked around him, covering his chest. I pulled it back. A large cylindrical oxygen canister rested on his feet all the way up to chest level. Rolls of tape bound it to Chavez's legs and chest. Just below the top of the canister the detonating device had been encased in more tape.

'I found him,' I said into the phone. 'There's a four-foot cylinder, he's been bound to it. Near the top there's another shape that's been encased in more tape.'

'Any wires visible?' Harrison asked.

'No,' I said. 'How far are you?'

'I just reached the field at the south end.'

'What do I do?'

'You need to cut away the tape from the ignition source.'

I looked up at the usher. 'Do you have a knife?'

He nodded and reached into his pocket, producing a small jackknife with a tiny blade. I started to cut at the tape around the canister at Chavez's legs.

'Let us pray . . .' said the Pope.

There was layer after layer of tape; the knife could barely cut through it.

'I'm out of time,' I said.

The entire stadium began to recite the Lord's Prayer. 'Our Father . . .'

Something clicked inside the bulge at the tope of the cylinder.

'Something's happening,' I said.

'What?' Harrison said.

'Who art in heaven . . .'

I leaned in to the top of the cylinder.

'It's clicking. Tell me what to do.'

'You don't . . .'

367

'I don't what? What do I do?'

Harrison said nothing.

'Tell me what to do?'

'Thy kingdom come . . .'

Still silence.

'Dylan . . .'

'Thy will be done . . .'

I looked down at the screen on the phone. I had lost the signal. I glanced over beyond the running track and my eyes settled on a smaller tunnel leaving field level and a sign reading RESTROOMS.

'Help me get him over there,' I said to the usher.

He froze.

'What is that?' he asked.

'Help me,' I said.

He stared at the cylinder, shook his head and took off, running away through the crowd. I started pushing Chavez through the grass softened from the rain, the wheels of the chair sinking in. I reached the edge of the track and the chair stopped dead as it hit the track's edge. I stepped around to lift the front wheels as another hand reached down and lifted him up. It was a priest.

He looked into my face and began to smile, then his eyes moved to the cylinder. The smile vanished and he took a step back.

'Our daily bread . . .'

'Oh dear God,' the priest whispered.

I pushed the chair past him and rolled Chavez over to the entrance to the restrooms. The tunnel was maybe thirty feet long. I moved him into the far end where I thought the walls might contain the blast. Frantically I began cutting the tape around the detonator, peeling one layer away after the other, the clicking from inside becoming louder with each layer I took away.

The knife slipped through the final layers of tape and I cut

368

upward, slicing along the length of the device, then pulled the last of the tape off. I stared at the small device. A digital timer, counting down, twenty seconds, two wires, one black, one white, leading from the timer into the top of the cylinder.

'What do I do,' I whispered.

I placed the blade on one of the wires, and then moved it to the other.

'Which one?'

I heard footsteps walking up the tunnel and I looked up. A mother was standing several feet away holding her daughter.

'Get out of here,' I said.

She opened her mouth as if to say something, but didn't.

'Run,' I said. 'As fast as you can. Get out of here!'

She hesitated for a second then turned and began running back towards the field. I took both of the wires in my fingers. The blade of the knife began to tremble in my hand. I couldn't hold it still.

Fifteen seconds.

'Who trespass against us . . .'

I placed the blade on the black wire.

'Not into temptation . . .'

I began to mouth the words.

Ten seconds.

'But deliver us from evil . . .'

A hundred thousand people became dead silent.

'Let each of us pray,' said the Pope.

Five seconds.

I had begun to put pressure on the wire when a hand grabbed mine and pulled it away from the wire. I tried to regain control but he was too strong and pinned my arm to my side, and then I saw the knife blade in his other hand as it moved in past my neck and quickly sliced through the white wire, stopping the timer at two seconds.

He released my hand and I swung around and looked into Harrison's face.

We stared at each other for a moment. The silence inside the stadium began to break and turn to applause, just a few hands clapping at first, then building in one section and then another until the entire stadium had joined in.

Chavez raised his head at the sound and opened his eyes. The chief looked at me, his eyes holding the only question that could possibly matter. I leaned in and softly whispered the answer into his ear, then I took his hand in mine and looked back down the long dark tunnel into the light of day at the far end.

# Epilogue

I know precisely the number of homicides I've investigated. I know how many I've made arrests on. I know exactly the number of those that slipped through my fingers even though I had the answer. And I carry with me every day the ones in which I failed to find any truth at all. I've never told anyone any of those numbers. Not because they're failures, but rather because they're never entirely over. So I hold them as secrets deep inside where a casual conversation will never intrude.

In the days ahead I would sit in front of the board of inquiry that follows any officer-involved shooting. They asked for details and instead I gave them facts that they would understand – I talked about the light in the room, Rezzitti's physical condition, Goya's assault on me, our positions in the grounds keeper's office both before and during the escalation to the use of lethal force. The number of rounds I fired.

What I didn't tell them was that after I left Chavez and Rezzitti in the hospital where they would recover from their wounds, that night I returned to the Rose Bowl and walked out onto the empty field where it had all begun with the body of a young girl, her skin covered with delicate crystals of frost.

I didn't tell them about the silence an empty stadium holds and how deeply it can penetrate your heart, or the way swallows come out of their nests in the concrete nooks of the stadium and swoop down over the surface of the grass in a kind of dance. Or that the Pope was right, that taking a life, even one so twisted and broken as Goya's, is a sin that you will carry with you the rest of your days.

Outside the stadium runners were pounding out their circuits around the arroyo, one step at a time, pushing themselves forward, occasionally glancing back over their shoulders to see what was behind them, and for the first time in recent memory, I had no desire join them.

It took less than an hour for the board of inquiry to deem my killing of Goya a good shooting, consistent with all the regulations governing the use of deadly force by an officer.

Days later the burned body of the journalist Morrison was found on the rocks of Long Beach Harbor not far from where the retired ocean liner the Queen Mary is permanently docked. In time the coroners' office matched the severed hands found in St Gabriel's to the murdered priest, Father Monroe. But neither law enforcement nor forensic science could offer any solution to the one remaining mystery.

How Goya knew that I would be the one to finally take his tormented life remains a mystery. If thought out step by step from the first moment I walked on that field and found Keri's frozen body to the instant I fired the first shot and he spun from the impact, there is a kind of logic of progression. Perhaps it was the only outcome that was possible. Perhaps some things are written.

Except that nothing in life is ever quite so simple or easy to understand. As I relive that moment when I fired the first round and Goya's body reacted to the bullet tearing through his shoulder, I remember details that weren't present at the moment it happened. Most of them are little more than a quality of movement, or a sound – the kind of details that make up a memory but add little to its understanding. One is different, and now carried in that depository I keep locked and hidden away from all other eyes.

As the bullet struck him he turned and looked at me. And what I saw in his face was complete astonishment. In the myth he had created of his life he had imagined everything down to the smallest detail except for that instant, and in that moment of surprise it wasn't Goya's eyes I was looking at at all. It was a boy named Andrew, born of rape, who in his wildest dreams never imagined something so elusive as a future, or the cruelty that he would inflict.

I like to imagine I'm right about that, but I'll never really know. Truth is fragile that way, and in the end, perhaps just as much of a mystery as faith.